THE PIPING TRADITIONS
OF THE INNER ISLES

The Piping Traditions
of the Inner Isles

of the West Coast of Scotland

BRIDGET MACKENZIE

For Alex
a reminder of happy visits to the islands

First published in Great Britain in 2012 by
John Donald, an imprint of Birlinn Ltd
West Newington House
10 Newington Road
Edinburgh
EH9 1QS

www.birlinn.co.uk

ISBN: 978 1 906566 54 8

British Library Cataloguing-in-Publication Data
A catalogue record for this book is available
on request from the British Library

Music engraving by The Art of Music, Dunblane:
www.theartofmusic.com

Typeset by Carnegie Book Production, Lancaster
Printed and bound in Britain by Bell and Bain Ltd, Glasgow

Contents

Introduction

This volume, covering the Inner Isles, that is, the Western Isles of Scotland except for Skye and the Outer Isles, is the third volume of the *Piping Traditions* series, the first being *Piping Traditions of the North of Scotland* (1998), and the second *Piping Traditions of Argyll* (2004). The intention was to have all the Western Isles in one volume, but this grew much too large, and had to be divided. Then it was planned to include Skye with the rest of the Inner Isles, but the sheer amount of the material on Skye made that impossible. Skye and the Outer Isles will appear as two separate books, as the same thing has happened: there is too much material to fit into one volume. It is a constant surprise how much there is to be put on record.

Just as were its predecessors, this is an over-all look at the piping material, an attempt to bring the inherited traditions together before they are lost, and I hope it might be an easy reference source for pipers, whether teachers or pupils.

This is a book which has a little about a lot, rather than a lot about a little, that is, it is not a detailed analysis of a limited subject, and has no pretensions to being a scholarly work drawn from primary sources. The aim is to be readable and, if possible, interesting, and perhaps to give the piper a scrap of new information – or if not, at least to present a favourite well-worn item in its proper place.

Those of us who have made any sort of study of piping history tend to think that what is familiar to us is well-known to all, and of course this is not so. When speaking in public, I try to address the deaf old fellow on the back row, and similarly when recording piping traditions I bear in mind the lone piper in the outback of Australia or the beginner in some city in Wisconsin, who does not have access to back numbers of the *Piping Times* or to any elderly piping teacher who recalls John MacDonald, Inverness. This is probably naïve in the age of the Internet, when no piper need be out of touch – but, Internet notwithstanding, I find the young pipers of today still as ignorant as they were when there were only books to consult. Even now they come and ask who was Donald of Laggan, or how they should tackle *The King's Taxes*. They want to know, but they don't know where to look.

What pipers need is a collection of information in a friendly style, not cluttered with scholarly references and bristling with footnotes. It should have a clear, simple index, and a list of books consulted. Nothing will put them off more rapidly than a feeling that they are being blinded with science or getting lost in deepest academia. If we want our youngsters to know something of the background of their music, the information which was, in the old days, given to them by their teachers along with the music, we must have it in a form which is palatable to them. I hope that this series fits the bill.

As a general rule, I try to visit all the places mentioned in the text, and with the islands this is real pleasure. But as I work my way further and further west, the series becomes more difficult to compile, partly for geographical reasons and partly because it is not easy to collect oral tradition if you are not a Gaelic speaker. There may, of course, no longer be an oral tradition or Gaelic, if an island has been over-run by incomers. This means that, although I have had a lot of help from native-born islanders or their descendants, I have had to look to written sources as well, and they are less than satisfactory.

The Old Parish Registers for the islands mostly start late, and sometimes the state of the Census returns might suggest they had been left out in the Hebridean rain for a month or two. Books on the stories and legends of the islands are often written by incomers who have an approach different from that of a born islander – though there are some excellent works, such as the memories of Ulva published by Donald MacKenzie. Highly recommended as background reading are the works of Peter Youngson on Jura, John Love on Rum, Camille Dressler on Eigg, Jo Curry on Mull and Norma MacLeod on Raasay.

In islands where there are no pipers left, it is hard to find any information other than the written records. This did not prevent my husband and myself from enjoying wonderful visits to the different islands, and we found the people, both native and incomer, most welcoming and helpful.

It was a sadness to find no piping left in islands such as Coll and Colonsay (a ceilidh was held there during our visit, and when we asked if there would be piping, the answer was 'No, but we have an Egyptian belly-dancer' – and very good she was, too). There was no piobaireachd teaching available in Islay and Mull, where there is so much inborn talent crying out to be fed. Where teaching is provided, as it is in Skye, Tiree and Lewis, the pipers, young and not so young, have responded even more eagerly than was anticipated, and it is certain that the same would happen in Islay and Mull (where Arthur Gillies and Ronnie Lawrie made a start). We need piobaireachd players and more piobaireachd teaching, in all the islands from Gigha to Harris, and we cannot have too much of it. Lewis seems to be the only island where demand is being met, with excellent results. Robert Beck is fighting a one-man campaign in Tiree, and lucky they are there to have him. In the other islands, there is a huge reservoir of inherited talent which is largely being wasted.

I would have offered the usual warning in this book, that I do not discuss currently competing pipers here, for fear of jeopardising their chances before the bench, but, alas, there is no need: there are no currently competing senior pipers in any of the Inner Isles except Skye. Even Islay, so rich in piping in former years, has no solo competitors these days, though the band is flourishing.

The format of the book is much as before, working from south to north, dealing first with the islands south of Ardnamurchan, from Arran to Coll, then with the Small Isles to the north of Ardnamurchan, and ending with Raasay. Skye has had to be held over for a separate volume, as there is so much material. I like to make each section complete in itself, and this, as before, leads to some repetition, but I have tried to keep that to the minimum.

I would like to be informed of the inevitable mistakes I have made, and to be given any additional information. Please address correspondence to me c/o the publishers, by land-mail. All letters will be answered.

Everywhere that Alex and I have visited, the mention of piping has opened doors, and we have been made to feel welcome by all who share our interest. I would like to thank all who helped, and in particular those named here – but there were many more, and my debt to them is as great as ever.

My thanks to:

Annie Anderson, Bowmore, Islay
Robert Beck, Tiree
Catriona Bell, Bridgend, Islay
Neil Cameron, Strone, Jura
Alastair Campbell of Airds
Catherine Campbell, Fort William
Jeannie Campbell, Glasgow

Myles Campbell, Gairloch
Sheila and Ronnie Campbell, Uisken, Mull
Camille Dressler, Eigg
Duncan Ferguson, Eigg
David Garrett, Achiltibuie, Wester Ross

Margaret Gray, Port Ellen, Islay
Duncan Heads, Port Ellen, Islay
Ivar Ingram, Kilbrennan, Mull
Kate Johnston, Bruichladdich, Islay
Michael Lloyd, Lagg, Jura
Lindsay MacArthur, Bowmore, Islay
Lexie MacCallum, Ardfenaig, Mull
Donna MacCulloch, Eigg
Dr Angus and Emily MacDonald, Skye
William MacDonald ('Benbecula'), Inverness
Lily MacDougall, Caol Ila, Islay
Andrew MacEachern, Port Charlotte, Islay
Iain MacInnes, Lagg, Jura
Keith MacKellar, Craighouse, Jura

Donald MacKenzie, formerly of Ulva
John Don MacKenzie, Dornie
Winnie MacKinnon, Canna
Mrs MacLean-Bristol, Coll
Robert MacLellan, Ballygrant, Islay
Norma MacLeod, Portree
Robert MacLeod, Bunessan, Mull
Dugald MacNeill, Edinburgh
Flora MacNeill, Colonsay
Seumas MacNeill, Glasgow
Dr Lindsay Neill, Selkirk
Mr and Mrs Oliphant, Coll Hotel
David Robertson, Eigg
Magdalena Sagarzazu, Canna
Rob Wainwright, Coll
Robert Wallace, Glasgow
Roy Wentworth, Gairloch
Scott Williams, Nova Scotia
Peter Youngson, Kirriemuir

Inverness Central Library, Reference and Family History Section, and the Highland Archive, Inverness, with special thanks to Alistair MacLeod, Family Genealogist, Highland Council
Oban Central Library
The Museum of Islay Life, Port Charlotte, Islay

I owe all of the above an unpayable debt, and can offer only my gratitude.

Some of those listed have died since they gave me their help. I have kept their names among the acknowledgements, and I hope this does not give pain to their families.

Abbreviations

In the lists of tunes, the following abbreviations are used:

J	Jig, preceded by the time signature and followed by the number of parts
GA	Gaelic Air
H	Hornpipe, preceded by the time signature and followed by the number of parts
M	March, preceded by the time signature and followed by the number of parts
P	Piobaireachd (Ceol Mor), followed by the number of variations, including the Ground (Urlar)
QSt	Quick Step
R	Reel, followed by the number of parts
RM	Retreat March
S	Strathspey, followed by the number of parts
SA	Slow Air, followed by the number of parts
SM	Slow March

In the text, sources and bibliography, the following abbreviations are used:

MSR	Marches, Strathspeys and Reels
QOH	Queens Own Highlanders
SPA	Scottish Pipers Association
TGSI	*Transactions of the Gaelic Society of Inverness*

Where names only are given in the lists of Sources in the text, the source was a personal interview.

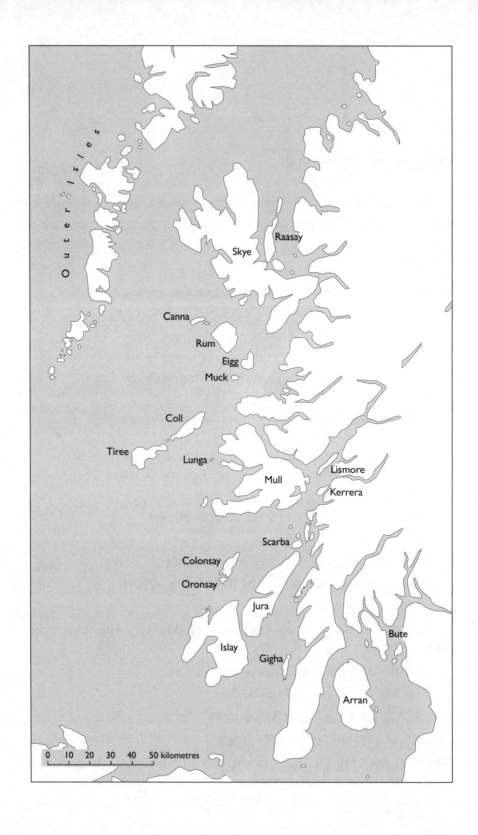

Outer Isles

Skye
Raasay
Canna
Rum
Eigg
Muck
Coll
Tiree
Lunga
Mull
Lismore
Kerrera
Scarba
Colonsay
Oronsay
Jura
Bute
Islay
Gigha
Arran

0 10 20 30 40 50 kilometres

Arran

Arran is reached by car-ferry from Ardrossan, on the Ayrshire coast. There is a train service from Glasgow. The crossing takes about fifty-five minutes. There is also a passenger ferry in summer between Claonaig in Kintyre to Lochranza in the north of Arran; the crossing takes thirty minutes.

Tunes associated with Arran include:

Jimmy Anderson's Welcome to Arran, by Duncan Johnstone 6/8 M 4
Mrs Mary Anderson of Lochranza, by Duncan Johnstone 2/4 M 4
The Day We Were At Arran, by Donald MacPhedran 2/4 M 2

Michael McCarfrae

The Duke of Hamilton, who owned Brodick Castle in the late 19th century, had MICHAEL MCCARFRAE as his piper. Michael, born in 1810 in Dailly, Ayrshire to Irish parents, won the Prize Pipe at Inverness in 1854. (He later docked ten years off his age, declaring in the 1871 Census that he was only fifty-one). He was a pupil of Angus MacKay, and was a Gaelic speaker. It is believed that he collaborated with Angus in transcribing written canntaireachd manuscripts into staff notation – though the tradition does not tell us which manuscripts these were. After Michael had won the Prize Pipe, he can have had no further tuition from Angus, as that was the year that Angus lost his sanity and had to be confined.

Five years later, Angus died, probably drowned in the river Nith while trying to escape from Crichton Royal mental hospital. His wife was left in poverty, and Michael bought Angus' collection of manuscript music from her.

Michael died in 1881, and bequeathed most of the collection to his employer, the Duke of Hamilton. The Duke must have done well by Michael, for in 1871 he described himself as Piper to the Duke of Hamilton, and was still living in Glensherrag, near Brodick in Arran, with a farm of 100 acres, of which 16 were arable. He employed a house-servant and two farm servants, so clearly was living comfortably. His wife Jane was from Girvan, and they had two children living at home in 1871. The enumerator was suspicious of the name MacCarfrae, and wrote 'Surname questionable' beside each family member listed.

After the Duke's death, the music was bound in rich leather with gold lettering, and kept in the Duke's library at Brodick Castle. Many years later a clearance was made of the older items in the library, which had been much neglected, and it is said that valuable books were thrown onto a bonfire. Angus' collection was spared, not because of its importance to piping but because of the sumptuous binding. Eventually, in 1926, the collection was acquired by the Piobaireachd Society, and the priceless manuscripts were deposited in the National Library of Scotland, in Edinburgh (MSS 3753–4).

Another manuscript, the MacArthur-MacGregor MS of 1820, had been borrowed by Angus MacKay from the Highland Society of London, who had commissioned it. Angus failed to return it, and on his death in 1859, his widow 'disposed of all his music to Michael Mac-Carfrae, a favourite pupil who was piper to the Duke of Hamilton, and MacCarfrae bequeathed most of it to the Duke'. But in 1904, Dr Charles Bannatyne bought two manuscripts from MacCarfrae's daughter, and these were the MacArthur manuscript and the John MacKay manuscript; they remained in Bannatyne's possession until 1926, when the Piobaireachd Society bought them both, for £20. They are now in the National Library of Scotland – the MacArthur manuscript catalogued as MS 1679, and the John MacKay as Acc. 9231.

Sources

John MacLellan, *Proceedings of the Piobaireachd Society
    Conferences*
Roderick Cannon, *The Highland Bagpipe*

Piping in Arran

The Arran High School Project, whose report was published in 2002, gives information about the history of the island. Chapter 4 ends with an account contributed in 1984 by James Gibson, who said that, during the Second World War, the 11th Scottish Commandos had their headquarters in the Whitehouse, beside the school. The Whitehouse was pulled down in the 1980s, but the Project book gives an earlier photograph of it. The soldiers and officers were billeted with families in the village, and one of the houses was 'a small cottage down at Cordon, and the officer staying there used to take the regimental pipe band there to practise marching. They did this because the house had very low beams in the ceiling which the bagpipes just fitted into. So they had to march between the beams and this kept them in a straight line'. It may come as a surprise to some to learn that the 11th Commandos had a pipe band.

It is clear that in the 20th century there was dance music played in Arran on the pipes, but no recorded tradition of piobaireachd on the island. However, Alister MacAlister said 'My father and my uncle were both pipers, and they learned from the Shiskine policeman who lived at the Road End'. Donald Ferguson, the blacksmith, also learned from this unnamed policeman. It is not clear whether any piobaireachd was taught.

The stories from the South End of Arran include one about the farm of Auchalettan, where the MacKinnons lived. A daughter of the house married a Mr Stewart from Kildonan. 'On the day of her wedding, she walked from Auchalettan with a piper marching and playing the pipes in front of her all the way along the four-mile track to Kilmory church.' It is not clear just when this was, possibly around 1900 or a little earlier.

The school logbook of the Primary School at Lamlash describes the Coronation celebrations in 1937. After a service from 10 a.m. to 11 a.m., the children assembled on the village green and marched, headed by pipers, to the recreation field at the public hall, for sports and a picnic. There was a bonfire later that night, at 10 p.m.

These glimpses of the past in Arran make it clear that piping was part of the social life of the island, but that there was no remembered tradition of piobaireachd.

The pipemaker HENRY MURDO runs a business, Dunfion Bagpipes, at Corriegills, Brodick. There, 'working in the traditional way' as a crafts-man, he produces a pipe 'of superb tonal quality, giving that excellent balanced sound everyone is looking for' (this is his advertisement in the *Piping Times*). His instruments are tested by Angus J. MacLellan, and may be ornamented by traditional combing on the drones, or a variety of designs on silver mounting. Dunfion Bagpipes also offer Scottish smallpipes, and electronic practice chanters.

Piper's Cave

At Dippen Head in Arran there is a cave that extends for fifty feet, with the usual story about the piper and his dog entering it, the piper being lost for ever, but the dog returning bald. According to local legend, muffled piobaireachd is still heard sometimes, usually at night, rising and falling with the wind. This seems to be the only surviving tradition of piobaireachd on Arran – and the word may well mean simply 'pipe music' here.

On Pipers' Caves in general, Tony Oldham quoted a General Mac-Bridge who was of the opinion that 'piper' in the names of caves is a corruption of a word 'pypar' meaning priests, as it is well known that monks, hermits and other holy men lived in caves, for the mortification of the flesh (a short cut to Heaven). There is such a cave on Holy Island, near Lamlash, where a hermit-saint of the Celtic church is known to have lived. The word *pypar*, however, must be in doubt: *papar* is the usual form, less likely to be corrupted to *piper*.

Tony Oldham felt that 'a piper must be extremely deaf to want to play the bagpipes in the narrow confines of a cave', but many of the stories make it clear that this was a safety-measure: if he could be heard from outside, he might be rescued – but in all the tales, the music ceases and the player is lost for ever.

Tony Oldham listed eight caves called the Piper's Cave, and eight more which do not have that name but are associated with the same story. He said it was well-known in caves in England as well as Scotland, but did not specify whether the English musicians were bagpipers.

Para Handy's Piper

In his book *The Vital Spark*, Neil Munro has a story, part of which is reproduced here:

Para Handy's Piper

I was standing one day on Brodick Quay with Para Handy when the place looked so vacant, and was so quiet, we unconsciously talked in whispers for fear of wakening somebody. The *Vital Spark* shared the peace of that benign hour; she nodded idly at the quay, her engineer half asleep with a penny novelette in his hands . . . If anybody had dropped a postage-stamp in Brodick that day, it would have sounded like a dynamite explosion. It was the breakfast hour.

Suddenly a thing happened that seemed to rend the very heavens: it was the unexpected outburst of a tinker piper, who came into sight round the corner of a house, with his instrument in the preliminary stages of the attack.

'My Chove!' said Para Handy, 'isn't that fine? Splendid aalthegether!'

'What's your favourite instrument?' I asked.

'When Dougie's in trum, it's the trump [Jew's harp] . . . but, man! for gaiety, the pipes. They're truly sublime! A trump's fine for small occasions, but for style you need the pipes. And good pipers iss difficult nooadays to get; there's not many in it. You'll maybe can get a kind of plain piper going aboot the streets of Gleska noo and then, but they're like the herrin', and the turnips, and rhubarb, and things like that – you don't get them fresh in Gleska; if you want them at their best, you have to go up to the right Hielands and pull them off the tree. You ken what I mean yoursel.'

And the Captain of the *Vital Spark* widely opened his mouth and inhaled the sound of the bagpipe with an air of great refreshment.

'That's "The Barren Rocks of Aden" he iss on now,' he informed me by and by. 'I can tell by the sound of it. Oh, music! music! it's me that's fond of it. It makes me feel that droll I could bound over the mountains, if you understand. Do you know that I wance had a piper of my own?'

'A piper of your own?'

'Ay, chust that, a piper of my own, the same ass if I wass the Marquis of Bute. You'll be thinkin' I couldna afford it,' Para Handy went on, smiling slyly, 'but a Macfarlane never wass bate. Aal the fine gentry hass their piper that plays to them in the mornin' to put them up, and goes playin' roond the table at dinner-time when there's any English visitors there, and let them chust take it! It serves them right; they should stay in their own country. My piper wass a Macdonald.'

'You mean one of the tinker pipers?' I said mischievously, for I knew a tribe of tinker pipers of that name.

Para Handy was a little annoyed. 'Well,' he said, 'I wouldna deny but that he wass a kind of a tinker, but he wass in the Militia when he wass workin', and looked quite smert when he wass sober.'

'How long did you keep the piper?' I asked, really curious about this unexpected incident in the Captain's career.

'Nearly a whole day,' he answered. 'Whiles I kept him and whiles he wass going ashore for a dram.

'To let you understand, it wass the time of the fine fushin's in Loch Fyne, and I had a cousin yonder that wass gettin' mairried at Kilfinan. The weddin' wass to be on a Friday, and I was passin' up the loch with a cargo of salt, when my cousin hailed me from the shore, and came oot in a smaal boat to speak to me.

'"Peter", he said to me, quite bashful, "they're sayin' I'm goin' to get mairried on Friday, and I'm lookin' for you to be at the thing."

'"You can depend on me bein' there, Dougald," I assured him. "It would be a poor thing if the Macfarlanes would not stick by wan another at a time of trial."

'"Chust that!" said my cousin; "there's to be sixteen hens on the table and plenty of refreshment. What's botherin' me iss that there's not a piper in Kilfinan. I wass thinkin' that maybe between this and Friday you would meet wan on your trevels, and take him back with you on your shup."

'"Mercy on us! You would think it was a parrot from foreign perts I wass to get for you," I said. "But I'll do my best," and off we went. I watched the hillsides aal the way up the loch to see if I could see a piper; but it wass the time of the year when there's lots of work at the hay, and the pipers wass keepin' oot of sight, till I came to Cairndow. Dougie and me wass ashore at Cairndow in the mornin', when we saw this Macdonald I'm telling you aboot standin' in front of the Inns with pipes under his oxter. He wass not playin' them at the time. I said to him, "There's a weddin' yonder at Kilfinan to-morrow, that they're wantin' a piper for. What would you take to come away doon on my vessel and play for them?"

'"Ten shillin's and my drink," he said, as quick as anything.

'"Say five and it's a bargain," I said; and he engaged himself on the spot. He wass a great big fellow with a tartan trooser and a cocketty bonnet, and oh, my goodness! but his hair wass rud! I couldna but offer him a dram before we left Cairndow, for we were startin' there and then, but he wouldna set foot in the Inns, and we went on board the *Vital Spark* withoot anything at all, and started doon the loch. I thought it wass a droll kind of a piper I had that would lose a chance.

'When we would be a mile or two on the passage, I said to him, "Macdonald, tune up your pipes and give us the Macfarlanes' Merch."

'He said he didna know the Macfarlanes had a Merch, but would do the best he could by the ear, and he began to screw the bits of his pipes together. It took him aboot an hour, and by that time we were off Strachur.

'"Stop you the boat," he said, "I'll need to get ashore a meenute to get something to soften the bag of this pipes; it's ass hard ass a bit of stick."

'"You can get oil from the enchineer," I said to him.

'"Oil!" said he; "do you think it's a clock I'm mendin'? No, no; there's nothing will put a pipe bag in trum but some treacle poured in by the stock."

'Well, we went ashore and up to the Inns, and he asked if they could give him treacle for his bagpipes. They said they had none. "Weel," said he, "next to that the best thing for it iss whusky – give me a gill of the best, and the Captain here will pay for it; I'm his piper." He got the gill, and what did he do but pour a small sensation of it into the inside of his pipes and drink the rest? "It comes to the same thing in the long-run," said he, and we got aboard again, and away we started.

'"There's another tune I am very fond of," I said to him, watchin' him workin' away puttin' his drones in order. "It's 'The 93rd's Farewell to Gibraltar'."

'"I ken it fine," he said, "but I don't ken the tune. Stop you, and I'll give you a trate if I could get this cursed pipe in order. What aboot the dinner?"

'The dinner wass nearly ready, so he put the pipes past till he was done eatin', and then he had a smoke, and by the time that wass done we were off Lochgair.

'"That puts me in mind," said he; "I wonder if I could get a chanter reed from Maclachlan the innkeeper? He plays the pipes himself. The chanter reed I have iss bad, and I would like to do the best I could at your cousin's weddin'."

'We stopped, and Dougie went ashore in the smaal boat with him, and when they came back in half-an-hour the piper said it wass a peety, but the innkeeper wasna a piper after aal, and didna have a reed, but maybe we would get wan in Ardrishaig.

'"We're no' goin' to Ardrishaig, we're goin' to Kilfinan," I told him. And he said he couldna help it, but we must make for Ardrishaig, right or wrong, for he couldna play the pipes right withoot a new reed. "When you hear me playing," he said, "you will be glad you took the trouble. There iss not my equal in the three parishes," and man, but his hair was rud, rud!

'We wouldna be half-an-oor oot from Lochgair when he asked if the tea would soon be ready. He wass that busy puttin' his pipes in order, he said, he wass quite fatigued. Pipers iss like canaries, you have to keep them going weel with meat and drink if you want music from them. We gave him his tea, and by the time it wass finished we were off Ardrishaig, and he made me put her in there to see if he could get a reed for his chanter. Him and Dougie went ashore in the smaal boat. Dougie came back in an oor wi' his hair awfu' tousy and nobody wi' him.

'"Where's my piper?" I said to him.

'"Man, it's terrible!" said Dougie; "the man's no' a piper at aal, and he's away on the road to Kilmertin. When he wass standin' at Cairndow Inns yonder, he wass chust holdin' the pipes for a man that wass inside for his mornin', and you and me 'll maybe get into trouble for helpin' him to steal a pair o' pipes."

'That wass the time I kept a piper of my own,' said Para Handy, in conclusion. 'And Dougie had to play the trump to the dancin' at my cousin's weddin'.'

This story was published first around 1901, in the Glasgow newspaper the *Evening News*. This was of course before there was any idea of political correctness, and terms such as tinker and Jew seemed to cause little offence.

Ailsa Craig

Known in Gaelic as Creag Ealasaid (Ailsa Craig is a corruption of this. In English it would be Elizabeth Rock), this rock in the Firth of Clyde is now uninhabited, but was formerly the home of lighthouse keepers. It is a familiar landmark to ships passing up or down the Clyde. In Gaelic poetry it was Ealasaid a'Chuain, Elizabeth of the Ocean.

It was also known as Paddy's Milestone as so many Irish boats passed it in the 19th century, bringing Irish immigrants to Glasgow. It was always a welcome sight after a rough crossing of the Irish Sea, and a sign that the vessel was now in the calmer waters of the Clyde estuary. G.L. Mullin, Aberdeen, made a 6/8 Jig in four parts called *Paddy's Milestone.*

Great Cumbrae and Little Cumbrae

Millport on the Great Cumbrae is no longer a calling port for the Arran ferry. Nowadays the Cumbrae car ferry runs from Cumbrae Slip, on the east side of the island, to Largs, on the Ayrshire coast. The crossing takes ten minutes.

I have been unable to find any piping tradition associated with the Great Cumbrae. This may be because, latterly, the islanders would call upon pipers from Largs, on the mainland, when they were required for functions such as weddings. In the 17th century the Cumbraes belonged to the Eglinton family, who had a strong piping tradition, but they were across on the mainland of Ayrshire and may not have influenced the islands.

I am sure there were pipers on Cumbrae, but all memory of them seems to have been lost. Reports of any surviving tradition about them would be welcomed.

Bute

Bute is reached by a short car-ferry trip to Rothesay from Wemyss Bay, which is connected to Glasgow by electric train. The ferry crossing takes thirty-five minutes.

Bute is Bod or Boid in Gaelic (with a long *o*); the meaning is unknown.

Tunes associated with Bute include:

> *Comunn Gaidhealach Bhoid (The Highland Society of Rothesay)*, by
> J.C. MacLean
> *Donald MacLellan of Rothesay*, by Donald MacLeod 2/4 M 4
> *George Bell's Farewell to Bute*, by Alexander Campbell 2/4 M 4
> *The Isle of Bute* J 4
> *The Kyles of Bute*, by Captain Charles Smith 2/4 M 4
> *Lord Bute's March*, by Roderick Campbell 2/4 M 4
> *The Maids of Bute*, by Archie Kenneth 3/4 M 4

See also the compositions of Willie Barrie, below.

Donald Boyd

DONALD BOYD, said by Colin Cameron to have composed the *Lament for the Union*, was piper to King James VI (James I of England), and his surname may indicate that he came from the island of Bute. This has led some people to assume that the unusual construction of the *Lament for the Union* is a 'Lowland' form of piobaireachd, now lost, but the so-called *Lament for King James VI* and *King James VI's Salute*, both nameless in the MacArthur-MacGregor manuscript, do not have that structure. If they were indeed composed to honour the king, they would presumably be the work of Donald Boyd, but they have little in common with the *Lament for the Union*.

Professor William Matheson said that there was a family called Boyd in North Uist, whose Gaelic name was Bodach, with a long *o*, so named because a man called Donald MacDonald had sent his son, also Donald, to be fostered in Bute, around 1600, shortly before King James came to the English throne. Could he have had a spell as the King's piper while in the south? The name Donald Boyd recurs in this family, and some of Donald's descendants lived in Uist and in Barra. Some of them adopted the alternative name of Johnson, for reasons unknown.

In North Uist, according to Professor Matheson, another source of the name Boyd as used by English speakers was the Gaelic form Mac Iain Buidhe ('son of yellow-haired John'), and branches of this MacDonald family are found in Benbecula. Many of them were also called Donald.

It seems clear that there were Boyd families in the Outer Isles, some with a link to Bute, and Donald the King's piper may have been one of these.

Local piper in Bute

The 1851 Census tells of a piper named John Campbell, a local man of fifty-five whose wife came from Sutherland. Their son Andrew, fifteen, was born in Inveraray, their daughter Isabella, six, in 'North Bute', and the youngest, Elizabeth, aged three, in Rothesay. Their address was 'Tree House', and the census enumerator added a note to each entry. 'Family slept in shed 30 Mar'. John was probably an itinerant piper making a living as best he could around the villages of Bute and Cowal. Most of the travelling pipers of this kind were Irish, but here we have a home-grown itinerant.

Angus MacRae

ANGUS MACRAE, from Ensay, was piper to Duncan MacRae of Kames, Isle of Bute, in the 1870s, his first position as a professional piper. He went on to win both Gold Medals and the Inverness Clasp in the 1880s.

William MacLellan Barrie (1910–2004)

The foremost piper to have come out of Bute was WILLIAM M. BARRIE. Born in Rothesay in 1910, he began to learn to play at eleven years old, after the family had moved to Glasgow. His obituary in the *Piping Times* says that he was the only pupil to have been taught from scratch by John MacDougall Gillies, who was a friend of his father. He agreed to give the boy three lessons, and if he showed no ability, that would be it. But Willie took to piping like a duckling plunging into a pond, and never looked back. After his teacher's death five years later, he was taken on by Robert Reid, so he was well steeped in the Cameron tradition of playing.

By 1925 he was competing among the top players of his day, and in 1930 won the cup for the best all-round player at Braemar, against formidable opposition. This was the last time he competed in Scotland. The titles of his compositions tell us of his travels after leaving Scotland: New Zealand, America and Canada all felt the benefit of his presence. He finally settled in the west of Canada.

At the age of about seventy-nine, he recorded some of the music he had learned as a young man, both singing and playing piobaireachd. In 1990, he and his son Jim published an audio cassette tape (*Ancient Piobaireachd*, Vol. I), which Willie introduced by playing on the pipe *The Mist Covered Mountains*, leading into his own composition

Andrew MacNeill of Colonsay, which he made in December 1989. This is followed by Willie singing *The Big Spree*, and the *Lament for the Earl of Antrim*, and, on the second side, the *Lament for Donald Duaghal MacKay*, *Black Donald's March*, *MacLeod of Raasay's Salute* and the *Lament for Mary MacLeod*.

These audio cassettes have since been transferred to CD and may be bought in either format.

This is an unusual achievement for a man of nearly eighty, but for some the presentation is spoiled by an accompaniment on keyboard, with full sound effects; this means that the works are sung in the even-tempered (piano) scale rather than the true pipe scale, and there is no denying that it makes them sound rather 'ordinary'. Those who enjoy singing piobaireachd, however, do seem to like the tape, and when it was played at a Conference of the Piobaireachd Society, the entire audience was singing along. It is also valuable as a record of the Cameron style as taught by John MacDougall Gillies and Robert Reid.

Volume II came out in 1993, when Willie was eighty-two. It opens with him playing his own composition, *Lament for Pipe Major Robert Reid*, his teacher, composed in 1966. This was one of the tunes set in 1993, when the Clasp was devoted to 20th-century works, and again in 2008. Willie then sings the *King's Taxes*, the *Lament for the Children*, the *Prince's Salute*, and another of his own works, *The Message from Dunvegan Castle*; on the second side we have the *Lament for MacSwan of Roaig*, the *Lament for Patrick Og MacCrimmon* and *MacCrimmon's Sweetheart*. Most of these works are not sung in their entirety, but enough is given to put over the flavour of the composition. The form of singing was described by Seumas MacNeill as 'a loose type of Canntaireachd, which has no pretensions to being a scientific system'.

Willie Barrie died in 2004, at his home in Canada.

Willie Barrie was a prolific composer of pipe music. His works include:

Andrew MacNeill of Colonsay P 7
Aukland March (for Sid Scott) 2/4 M 4
Aukland Police Pipe Band March 4/4 M 2
Avondale Races 6/8 M 4
Blockhouse Bay March 2/4 M 4
City of Hastings Highland Pipe Band March 4/4 M 3
The Glasgow March 2/4 M 4
The Heather Inn of Seattle's Strathspey S 4
Hornpipe for James Barrie 2/4 HP 4

The Isle of Butte (sic) 6/8 J 4
Jack Campbell's Jig 6/8 J 4
Lament for Pipe Major Robert Reid P 8
The Lark in the Morning 6/8 J 4
Madam Gayre of Gayre and Nigg's Strathspey S 4
March for Elaine Barrie 2/4 M 4
March for Jean Barrie 6/8 M 4
The Meeting of Barrie and Magee in New Zealand R 4
Message from Dunvegan Castle P 6
Neil Gow's Lamentations 2/4 SM 2
New Year's Eve 1973 R 4
A Night at the Opera 6/8 J 4
The Nova Scotian Fiddler R 2
Palmerston North March (or *Palmerston North Square*) 6/8 M 3
Pipe Major Jimmy Watt
The Piper's Prayer 6/8 SA 2
Reel for Pipe Major Robert Reid R 3
The Scottish Tavern, San Francisco HP 4
Slow March for June MacLean 4/4 M 1
Slow March for Mrs Barrie 6/8 SM 4
Slow March for Pipe Major Brian Jackson 6/8 SM 2
(arr.) *The Tenpenny Bit* 6/8 J 4
Vancouver (for Andy Kirk) 6/8 J 4
Vancouver March 2/4 M 4
Vancouver Police (for Pipe Major Alex Jackson) 6/8 J 4
Wee Piper 6/8 J 4 (the family pet was a budgie named Piper
    MacCrimmon, who could whistle pipe tunes)

Willie's son JAMES BARRIE has followed in his father's footsteps as piper and composer. Among his best known works is a hornpipe in four parts called *Donald MacLeod*. Jim and his father published a collection of their works, called *A Lifetime of Compositions*. He composes for both pipes and accordion, and plays other instruments as well.

Jim Barrie was born in Canada and learned all of his piping from his father, starting on the chanter at the age of four. He became a highly successful solo competitor in both Canada and New Zealand, before returning to Vancouver Island to make his home. He now judges both band and solo competitions.

Among the pupils of William Barrie was probably SANDY R. BOYD, born in Largs, Ayrshire, but later living in Nova Scotia. He emigrated there in the 1940s. One version of his piping pedigree lists Barrie, Willie

Ross and John MacColl as Boyd's teachers, but another says he was taught by Duncan Grant, John MacColl and Robert Reid. Barry Shears, in his book *Dance to the Piper* (2008), described him as an 'itinerant', able to read music and to play Ceol Mor. Of him, Barry Shears wrote:

> Sandy came from a piping family. Two of his uncles played, as did two of his brothers. He started learning to play the bagpipes with the Boys Brigade, and was an extremely talented piper in the 20th-century Scottish style. After he came to Canada in 1942, he joined the Pictou Highlanders in Halifax and was later appointed Pipe Major. After the war and a failed marriage, Sandy adopted the life of an itinerant musician. He moved around the countryside, staying with host families and performing in rural areas, towns and villages in Nova Scotia and other Canadian provinces. When in Ontario he was presented with a set of Henderson pipes, silver- and ivory-mounted, which he took wherever he travelled.

Sandy Boyd was also an accomplished fiddle-player, and his impact on Nova Scotian music was considerable, especially when he introduced pipe tunes into the fiddlers' repertoire.

He taught many pupils, as well as instructing and training pipe bands in many districts, and they handed on the knowledge. Barry Shears' book has a photograph of him with Seumas MacNeill.

In his *Collection of Pipe Music* (2000), Allan J. MacKenzie of Cape Breton, Nova Scotia, says that Sandy was distantly related to Willie Ross, Edinburgh Castle. His 6/8 March *Mrs Mildred Fraser's Welcome Home*, made in 1947, appears in Allan J. MacKenzie's Collection. Mrs Fraser was Allan's aunt.

Dan Rory MacDonald, also related to Allan, composed *Sandy Boyd's Reel*, another piece in the Collection.

John Balloch

In a BBC interview, William M. MacDonald referred to Pipe Major Balloch in Rothesay. This was JOHN BALLOCH who is listed in the Notices of Pipers. He joined the 57th Depot Brigade (42nd and 79th Highlanders) in 1878. He then went to the 79th (Cameron Highlanders), serving as a piper in the Egyptian Campaign of 1881–84, where he played the leading company of the 79th in the charge at Tel-el-Kebir. In 1886 he was transferred as Pipe Major to the 1st Battalion King's Own Scottish Borderers, and served in the expedition to Upper Burma.

Pipe Major Balloch went on pension in 1899, and became P/M of the 5th (Volunteer) Battalion Argyll and Sutherland Highlanders. In 1914, when in his fifties, he became P/M of the 8th Battalion of his old regiment, the King's Own Scottish Borderers, and served in France, until early in 1918 he was invalided home. He then was appointed P/M of the 9th Officers Cadet Battalion at Gailes.

He composed several good tunes, notably the *25th King's Own Borderers Slow March,* and the *25th King's Own Borderers Farewell to Meerut* (2/4 M 4). A tune of this latter name is said to have been the work of two cousins in Rogart, Sutherland, both called William MacDonald; one of the two served in the 25th, and it may be that John Balloch made over their tune later. Certainly William was in the 25th long before John Balloch, and William did serve in India, but John did not. It is usually attributed to John Balloch, in modern collections, but William's collection, made before 1873, gives his own name as composer. It would appear that John Balloch made over an older tune, as happened quite often, when the old 'two-steps' were converted into competition marches. It was regarded as bringing a piece up to date, rather than plagiarism.

ANGUS J. MACLELLAN from Glasgow, with roots in South Uist, lived in Rothesay in the 1940s, and had piping lessons there from ALEX MACINTYRE, believed to be related to WILLIE MACINTYRE from Port Bannatyne, near Rothesay, currently living in Edinburgh and competing in Highland Games. Willie is a pupil of Tom Speirs, and plays a fine set of Robertson pipes.

Another pupil of Alex MacIntyre was BRIAN MACRAE (1942–2000). Although born in Aberdeen of a family from Ross-shire, he was brought up in Rothesay. Started by Alex MacIntyre, he went on to Donald MacLeod and Bob Nicol, and eventually became Pipe Major in the Gordon Highlanders. This led to his appointment in 1980 as the Queen's Piper, a position from which he retired in 1995. He compiled the two volumes of the Gordon Highlanders Collection of Pipe Music. Brian died suddenly while on holiday in France, and left all his personal collection of piping books, music and tapes to the College of Piping in Glasgow.

Sources

William Matheson, 'Notes on North Uist Families' in *TGSI* LII 1982
William Barrie's tapes
William M. MacDonald
William Hugh MacDonald, Rogart
Eric Murray, Rogart
Notices of Pipers

Gigha

To reach Gigha, make your way to Tayinloan, on the west side of the Mull of Kintyre, some twenty miles from Tarbert, Loch Fyne. A small car ferry leaves for Gigha at regular intervals, every hour, during daylight hours. The crossing takes twenty minutes. Gigha is a small island, some six miles long by a mile wide, and was recently bought from the proprietors by its residents.

The Book of the Dean of Lismore

The Book of the Dean of Lismore is a collection of Scottish poems dating from between 1310 and 1520. In one of them, composed in the late 1400s, by a woman, Aiffric nic Coirceadail, we find the words: 'Sad is the state of Gigha of the smooth soil, I see Dun Suibhne without music, that green sward of a stronghold of generous men; the sorrow of the MacNeills is known to them' (translated by W.J. Watson from the original Gaelic). The kind of music is not specified, but at that time it would almost certainly have been harp music. The poet was a relation of Neil of Gigha, the son of Torquil MacNeill of Castle Sween, ancestors of Dugald MacNeill of the College of Piping.

Allan of Gigha

Ailean nan Sop, the father of the Hector MacLean named in the title *Hector MacLean's Warning*, was also known as Allan of Gigha. Some say he was the composer of the piobaireachd work *The MacLeans' March*. In 1539, Allan was granted the ownership of Gigha, which rightfully belonged to the MacNeills. The estate of Gigha also included lands in parts of Kintyre, Knapdale and Islay. The MacNeills had no male heir, and it was felt by the Scottish courts that the estate should go to an experienced warrior – which Allan certainly was. He had a long career of piracy, and accumulated much ill-gotten wealth. On his death, he was buried in Iona, among other Highland chieftains (see below, Mull).

After many lawsuits, his son Hector MacLean lost the island to the Campbells. They held it from the late 16th century until 1700, when the MacNeills gave up two farms they owned in Knapdale, Drumdrishaig and Crear, in exchange for the restoration of their right of ownership of Gigha and Colonsay.

There were two main families on Gigha of interest to pipers. The MacNeills, who were the ferrymen in the early 1800s, gave us Blind Archie MacNeill and his nephew Seumas MacNeill (who ran the College of Piping in Glasgow, founded and edited the *Piping Times*, and was Secretary of the Piobaireachd Society: see below). These Gigha MacNeills were presumably descended from the original MacNeills of Gigha, and so they were related distantly to the MacNeills of Taynish and the Captains of Castle Sween, the ancestors of Dugald MacNeill. They were also related to Lachlan MacNeill Campbell of Kintarbert, whose father was MacNeill of Drumdrishaig, and to the MacNeills of Colonsay, to whom Andrew MacNeill belonged (see below).

The other Gigha family with piping links were the MacQuilkans, and in recent times on Gigha, the sole remaining piper has been Hector MacQuilkan. Of his family, the Gigha minister wrote in the Register that they 'came from Ireland', probably in the late 18th century. There were many MacQuilkan families in Kintyre and Knapdale in the late 1700s and early 1800s. Many of them emigrated to Australia. The mother of the Gold Medallist Duncan MacGillivray, who lives at Calrossie, near Tain, Easter Ross, was Diana Killen before her marriage; she came from an Australian family of Killens who can trace their roots to Argyll, where they were MacQuilkans. Diana's piping genes have made her an excellent singer of piobaireachd, traditionally the women's role. Her husband was Donald MacGillivray, also a Gold Medallist, who died in 2011.

The name took many forms: it seems to be based on an Irish form of William or Wilkie, and over the years was modified and anglicised, so that we find MacQuilkan, Quilkan, Quillan, Killen, Williamson, Wilkison, Wilkinson, Wilkie and Wilkin, and sometimes the same person used the two forms interchangeably, both MacQuilkan and Wilkinson appearing in the same document.

The earliest MacQuilkans we know of in Gigha, in the 18th century, were brothers Archie and Swain, and probably Duncan and Malcolm were their brothers or cousins. As three of them gave their eldest sons the name John, it is likely that this was their father's name. But we do not know if they were the first generation of the family to live in Gigha, nor do we know if any of them were pipers.

It should be noted that Coll Ciotach, the father of Alasdair Mac-Colla MacDonald (who fought for Montrose in the mid-17th century) had a grandmother called Eveleen MacQuillan (= MacUilleim). The fact that her name is given in this form indicates that it was not merely a patronymic, which would begin with Nic 'daughter' rather than

Mac 'son'; so we may deduce that her family name was MacUilleim. Her husband was Colla nan Capull, brother of James (MacDonald) of Dunyveg, who died in 1565. Colla nan Capull was an uncle of the first Earl of Antrim, so it is clear that the MacQuilkans were well connected in Ireland. They had a name in Kintyre and Gigha for wildness, being drinking and fighting 'hellers', but along with that went artistic talent in both music and poetry.

The piping of Gigha was probably in MacQuilkan hands, as Blind Archie MacNeill said in his *Memoirs* that when he was a boy in Gigha, the only piper was a MacQuilkan who was a lobster fisherman. Archie wrote: 'He had a set of pipes that were at the Battle of Waterloo, but it was not the original chanter. When I went back (to Gigha) as a man, we used to play together for the people at the big house, and for a concert in the school hall for the people of the island'.

Archie had no knowledge of any piping among the MacNeills in Gigha before himself, but it must have been in the MacNeill genes, to judge by outbreaks of piping talent in the different branches of the family.

Local tradition says that pipers came over from the mainland in the 1920s and 1930s, especially from Inveraray, to play at games, weddings, etc. The *Piping Times* in 1991, in an article about the *Oban Times*' piping reports from 1938, mentions a picture of the Saskatoon Girls Pipe Band in Canada, 'comprising a group of High School girls trained by Pipe Major DUNCAN CAMPBELL, a native of the Island of Gigha, who seems to have made a success of life overseas'. The author of the article, Jeannie Campbell, adds her own comment: 'Perhaps there was little scope for Girls High School Pipe Bands in Gigha'.

The MacNeills

There were several MacNeill families in Gigha. The forebears of Blind Archie were the MacNeills who lived at Ardmeanish, Drumyonbeg and Culnacraig in the early 1800s, all farms on the east side of the island. The furthest back we can trace them with any certainty is to Archie MacNeill, born 1773, died probably in the 1850s. He lived at Drumyonbeg, just north of the present-day ferry slip in the middle of the east side, and he married Catherine MacNeill from Campbeltown, who may have been his cousin. The marriage was in Gigha in 1805.

Archie (I) and Catherine had six children. The eldest was Archie (II) who was the grandfather of Blind Archie and great-grandfather of Seumas MacNeill. The eldest son of each generation of the family was always called Archie. The birth or baptism of Archie (II) was not registered, possibly because he was born only a few months after his parents' marriage.

Archie (II) 1805, Malcolm 1806, Flora 1808 and Donald 1809 were all born at Drumyonbeg, before the family moved to Culnacraig, where Catherine was born in 1811, and Margaret in 1812.

Malcolm married Catherine MacTaggart, and had seven children; Flora died young, and so did Donald; Catherine and Margaret both became teachers and ran a small school of their own on the mainland. Both contracted tuberculosis, gave up teaching and returned to Gigha, where they died, Catherine in the 1840s, Margaret ten years later.

The MacNeills were hard hit by tuberculosis, which was rife in the Highlands all through the 19th century. In the generation of Seumas' grandfather, three of the family of five were struck down, coming home to Gigha to die.

Archie (II) married Margaret MacDonald who became a well-known figure in Gigha after her husband's death. She took over the Post Office, and was postmistress for many years before she died in 1903, at the age of ninety-one. She and Archie had five sons: Archie (III) 1841, John 1844, Malcolm 1848, Alexander 1850 and Donald 1851, who was Seumas' grandfather.

Archie (III) became a minister in Sleat, Skye, where he lived for ten years before he went to South Africa in an attempt to cure his TB. When this failed he returned to Gigha, where he died.

John was a seaman, who in 1870 married Susanne MacSporran from Tayinloan. They had several children, including Susannah, who died as a young child. The circumstances of her death must have been particularly harrowing, as the parents could not bear to stay in Gigha after that, and they emigrated to Canada. There tragedy struck again: John was shot dead by armed robbers while travelling on a train.

Malcolm died young, from TB, at his home in Gigha.

Alexander, like John, started as a seaman, but when offered a position in a bank in Melbourne, Australia, he went out there; but he too had TB, and came home to die.

Blind Archie MacNeill

Donald, father of Blind Archie, left Gigha for Glasgow, where he married Jessie Napier, from Kippen, Stirlingshire. Blind ARCHIE MACNEILL said there was music in Jessie's family, and her brother Sandy was a violinist. Donald had been living in Gowanlea Cottage Row, Dumbarton, but when he became the captain of an ocean-going vessel, his family moved back to Gigha for some years. Archie, born in Govan in 1879, had a happy boyhood on the island. The MacNeills were not well off, and the baby Archie slept in an orange-box for his cradle; but as a child he enjoyed the freedom of his island life. He was fully sighted throughout his boyhood.

Donald was the captain of a sailing ship which made long voyages. He broke the world record for the fastest passage between New Zealand and Britain, holding it for only five days before the next vessel in was even faster. He gave up long voyages when he was offered a position at Rhu, near Helensburgh, as skipper of the steam yacht *Nesta*. The family moved to Rhu when Archie was about eleven.

He was a clever boy who won scholarships to pay for his education, and his parents hoped he would enter the ministry, but he developed retinitis pigmentosa, which gradually destroyed his sight. At twenty-one he became totally blind. His *Memoirs* give a moving account of this time: it is clear that his strength of character and lack of self-pity helped him to make the best of his circumstances. He had already started playing the pipes, when working at Ardencaple Castle, near Helensburgh. The piper there was RODERICK FRASER, from Easter Ross, a pupil of John MacDonald, Inverness, and he gave the young Archie his first lessons, for about a year.

Archie's next teacher was JOHN MACGREGOR, from Loch Fyne, who let him play his pipe as well as giving him lessons. This lasted for another year before MacGregor left the district, and then MURDOCH MACDONALD from the Black Isle, in Easter Ross, came as piper to Ardencaple. When Murdoch went to fight in the South African War, he left his pipes with Archie, on loan until his return, so that Archie was able to practise on his own. He began to enter competitions at the Games, and to listen to piobaireachd played by professionals. He also talked to pipers whenever he could, and lost no opportunity to pick up information about piping.

When Murdoch returned, his employers bought him new Henderson pipes, so Archie was able to continue on the old ones. At this time, in his mid-teens, he caught scarlet fever, a serious disease in those days, and he spent ten weeks in hospital. On his recovery, he found he was owed ten weeks' wages, which enabled him to buy his own pipes, ebony with full ivory mounts, for £8. His former teacher, Roderick Fraser, came back to the district, and Archie resumed his lessons. He continued to attend all the Games he could, and to talk to knowledgeable pipers.

In 1900, he lost the last vestiges of his sight, and had to give up his job. He was too old at twenty-one to go for training as an organist, and his only option was to enter the Blind Asylum in Glasgow, to learn brush-making. He had tried to make a living from piping at functions, but there was not enough work available.

He worked for minimal wages at the Blind Asylum for seventeen years; in 1918 he and his fellow-workers came out on strike and gradually managed to improve conditions for blind employees. Throughout this time, Archie was playing, meeting other pipers and composing pipe music. He made a strathspey for his friend Neil Sutherland from Lairg. John MacDougall Gillies, then manager of Peter Henderson's shop, agreed to take Archie as a pupil, and to give him lessons in piobaireachd on Saturday afternoons. He learned about a dozen piobaireachd works from MacDougall Gillies, including the *Battle of Waternish* and *Scarce of Fishing*.

Archie was beginning to get engagements to play at gatherings in Glasgow, and he entered competitions, overcoming his diffidence that his blindness made it difficult for him to march in a straight line. He also learned to play the fiddle, and studied musical theory.

On one occasion he was to play in a piobaireachd competition, and his tune was *The Earl of Seaforth*. The judges told him that the Ground and one variation would be sufficient, but Archie took exception to this, understandably, and duly played the whole piece, from beginning to end. It must have been galling to be patronised like this, and he clearly resented it, however kindly it was meant.

In 1917 he embarked on a teaching career with the Boys' Brigade. He had married in 1903, and had two sons, Donald, born 1904, and Alexander, born 1906; when Archie began to teach, his boys joined the 139th Company Boys' Brigade band. He taught this band for seventeen years, and took them to success in many competitions. For many boys at that time, the Boys' Brigade was their only chance to learn to play the pipes. Among the many lads that Archie trained were his nephew Seumas MacNeill, and Tommy Pearston. These two went on to found the College of Piping in Glasgow, and both became leading players on the competition circuit.

Dugald MacNeill, in his account of the history of the College, given at the Piobaireachd Society Conference in 1993, paid tribute to Archie MacNeill:

> The progenitor of the College of Piping was undoubtedly Archie
> MacNeill. He had a life-long interest in piping and he had very
> considerable musical appreciation. He was a keen observer of all the

good pipers – and probably the not-so-good. This allowed him to determine what the best techniques were and in a long teaching career he introduced standards and teaching methods which subsequently, with some development, became those of the College. Archie taught the 139th Company of the Boys' Brigade which was in the Alexandra Park area of Glasgow. He taught them from 1917 to 1935 and in that company were John Allan MacGee, Seumas MacNeill, his brother David, Thomas Pearston and many other good players.

... Archie continued to teach and influence with his skill and enthusiasm many others after he stopped teaching the BB; there was, in fact, after the war, a MacNeill pipe band which was almost entirely Archie's pupils. The Pipe Major was Bobby Black.

Archie entered with gusto into the debate about the high G gracenote in front of the little finger doubling at the end of each measure, known as 'the G Gracenote on the Birl' debate. Players were being penalised by the judges at Oban for this, and angry correspondence in the *Oban Times* followed when in 1928 both George S. MacLennan and John MacDonald of the Glasgow Police were 'victimised', two of the finest Ceol Beag players of all time. Of the three judges, Somerled MacDonald said he was over-ruled by the other two, who maintained that G.S. was playing false notes, and gave no award to John MacDonald for the same reason.

In 1949, Archie MacNeill wrote to the *Piping Times* to say this 'petty dictatorship' was still going on, with the result that pipers were now missing out the G gracenote altogether, not only at the end of the march but in the first bar of tunes such as *Bonnie Anne* and *Glengarry's Gathering*, and in strathspeys and reels, too. Some did this only if certain judges were on the bench: others said it sounded like a Cockney dropping his h's.

Tommy Pearston published a technical article on this subject in the *Piping Times* (November 1967), and it was reprinted in January 1997. Archie MacNeill was always keenly interested in such matters and expressed his views with forthright clarity.

In the 1950s he dictated his *Memoirs* to his friend and neighbour Jimmy Taylor, but as they named a number of people still living at that time, he said that they should not be published before 1992. They appeared in the *Piping Times* between September 1992 and April 1993, a valuable record of the piping world, especially between the wars.

Archie had two piping sons, DONALD and ALEX MACNEILL. The latter served his time as a bagpipe maker with R.G. Lawrie Ltd in Glasgow, and also trained as a reed-maker, and learned piobaireachd from

John MacColl. In 1926 he emigrated to Canada, when he was invited out there to take over a pipe band. For the next fifty years he had a huge influence on Canadian piping. He died in 1992.

Blind Archie MacNeill died in Glasgow in 1962. Tommy Pearston played the Ground of *His Father's Lament for Donald MacKenzie* at the graveside in Riddrie Park Cemetery, Glasgow. His nephew and devoted pupil, Seumas, is buried beside him.

Archie MacNeill was a deeply respected piper, teacher and composer. Among his works are:

> *David Ross* 2/4 M 4
> *The Detroit Highlanders* 2/4 M 4
> *Donald MacLean's Farewell to Oban* 2/4 M 4
> *Duncan Angus MacPherson* 2/4 M 4
> *Gareloch* 3/4 Waltz 3
> *James MacMillan, B.C.*
> *Leaving Gigha* 2/4 M 4 (see below)
> *Neil Sutherland of Lairg* S 4
> *Rory MacNeill* 6/8 M 4
> *Verna Leith's Wedding March* 2/4 M 4.

He also made several arrangements of tunes:

> *The Banks of the Allan* 6/8 J 4
> (seconds to) *The Battle of the Somme* 9/8 RM 2
> *The Islay Ball* S 4.

Archie's son Alex composed:

> *Across from Rosneath* R 4
> *Elly MacNeill* 6/8 M 4
> *Isabella MacNeill* 2/4 M 4

and Angus J. MacDowell composed a 2/4 March in 4 parts called *Alex MacNeill.*

Seumas MacNeill

Blind Archie was the eldest of a family of six: himself, Margaret, James, Sandy, Donald and Jessie. His brother James was the father of Seumas MacNeill.

James MacNeill (1883–1953) married Christina Lumsden, who came from Fife. James had been brought up in Gigha and Rhu (see above), and served in the Royal Scots in the First World War. On his return

Leaving Gigha

March

Archie MacNeil

This setting of *Leaving Gigha* was given to Barry Shears, Nova Scotia, who has kindly given his permission for it to be used here. The tune was collected from Archie MacNeill, Glasgow, by Sandy MacBeth and the late Duncan MacIntyre, while serving with the North Nova Scotia Highlanders during the Second World War.

from the army, he had a hard time finding a job. He worked on the railways for a time, but his employment seems always to have been precarious, during the Depression years.

His son JAMES (SEUMAS) MACNEILL, who decided to use the Gaelic form of his name, Seumas, in the piping world, was born at 32 Dowanhill Street, Partick, Glasgow, in 1917, the second of James' three children. Although he became known as Seumas in the piping world, he remained James to many of his family – and his friends outside piping sometimes called him Jimmy. His wife Netta, however, called him Seumas.

He spent almost his entire life in Glasgow. He was educated at Hyndland School, and went on to the University of Glasgow, where he took an Honours degree in Mathematics and Natural Philosophy (Physics). He then attended Jordanhill Teacher Training College for a year, to give him a Scottish teaching qualification, before being offered an appointment to the Nat. Phil. department at Glasgow University. There he rose to become a Senior Lecturer, and he remained in the department for the rest of his working life. It seems likely that the uncertainties of his father's employment made him unadventurous in his own work. He appeared never tempted to move on or to further his academic career, and although a brilliant lecturer – one of his students rated him the best lecturer she ever heard in her life – he gave little time to research in Physics, preferring to put his energy into piping.

His heart was in piping from the days when he was taught by his uncle, Blind Archie MacNeill, and joined the Boys' Brigade band, along with his lifelong friend, Tommy Pearston. He and Tommy later set up the College of Piping, now at Otago Street, Glasgow, conveniently close to the university. Both of them were tutors, as well as Joint Principals. The College became a centre for the running of the Piobaireachd Society, the publication of the *Piping Times* and other works, and with its self-awarded title 'The Centre of the Piping World', it established itself within a world-wide network of pipers. Seumas' obituary in the *Guardian* newspaper said: 'He was at the heart of a series of bold initiatives each of which has survived and flourished down to the present day' (1996). His influence on piping will be felt for generations to come.

Seumas founded the *Piping Times* and edited it for forty-eight years. It was rightly described as 'always lively due to his forthright style and liking for a good argument'. He was outspoken in his views and often controversial, but being a noted piper himself – he won the Gold Medal at Oban in 1962 – he had a sound basis for his critical opinions. The historical material accumulated in the *Piping Times* makes it an essential work of reference.

The Summer Schools which the College set up for tuition outwith Glasgow began in tents in the Highlands, moved to Canada and America, and are now held annually in California. An American magazine commented: 'Of those who have given service to piping, McNeill stands head and shoulders above any other person in our time' (1995).

Succeeding John MacFadyen as Hon. Secretary to the Piobaireachd Society, Seumas had helped to initiate the Annual Conference, and was responsible for editing the *Proceedings*, another valuable source of information for posterity. He wrote scholarly Prefaces to the reprints of piobaireachd collections published by the society. He was also Secretary of the John MacFadyen Memorial Trust, and a founder-member of the Professional Pipers' Association. He was involved, too, in the starting of the Glenfiddich Championship and the Silver Chanter competition.

His work in radio and television enlarged the horizons of piping and probably did more than anything else to raise the profile of the music and have it accepted by other musicians. He was active in the campaign to have the Scottish Education Department admit the bagpipe as an optional instrument in the music curriculum of Scottish schools.

His own published works were not numerous, but have proved of lasting value. He and Tommy Pearston published three Tutors for the College; the first was the 'Green Tutor' (1953), which has sold more than 350,000 copies and is still selling, by far the best-selling book of any in piping. It has been translated into French, German and Norwegian, and has a good market in Japan. In 1990, Seumas added a Tutor for Piobaireachd, which was well received.

His booklet *Piobaireachd*, issued in 1968 by the BBC to accompany a series of radio talks and reprinted in 1976, has become a classic, as has the article by John Lenihan and Seumas MacNeill, 'An Acoustical Study of the Highland Bagpipe' (1954). Both of these became stepping-stones for further research, and are regarded as authoritative. In 1987, Seumas MacNeill and Frank Richardson published *Piobaireachd and its Interpretation*.

He published a few of his own compositions, though his output of music was not large, and as far as is known he did not attempt to compose any piobaireachd works. His light music included:

George Penny CBE 6/8 M 4
Glenfiddich 6/8 M 4
Hugh K. Clarkson 6/8 M 4 (Hugh is the printer of the *Piping Times*)
Ranald Beag 6/6 SA 2
Salute to Winston Churchill

Bobby MacLeod, the Mull bandleader, piper and accordionist, made a 6/8 March in four parts called *Seumas MacNeill*, and Captain John A. MacLellan composed a 6/8 Jig in four parts which he named *Mrs Seumas MacNeill*.

As a lecturer, Seumas was supreme. He had a witty turn of phrase and his enthusiasm held his audiences, even those who knew little of piping. In the 1970s, his seminal evening classes on piobaireachd opened many minds to the Great Music. He brought in a different top player every week, to play his illustrations, and the numbers attending remained steady throughout the term, most unusual for evening classes. His weekly 'Chanter' programmes on the radio (the wireless in those days) will also be long remembered for their rich variety of topic and wealth of authoritative information.

It was said in his lifetime that when he went it would take at least seven good men to replace him in the piping world. His tireless work for piping was not for monetary gain: he was not a wealthy man, and money meant little to him, other than as a means of furthering the cause of piping.

In the 1980s he was presented by the City of Glasgow with the Loving Cup awarded to a citizen deemed to have brought honour to the city. This gave him enormous pleasure. Presenting the award, the Lord Provost spoke of Seumas' achievements and all he had done for Glasgow.

In the same year, the Saltire Society presented Seumas with an illuminated scroll and plaque to mark the occasion of his becoming one of their Honorary Presidents, both for his services to piping and as a token of the Society's high regard for the Highland bagpipe. In his reply, Seumas said that the scroll would be hung in the College of Piping so that visitors could see that the bagpipe was appreciated in Scotland as well as overseas.

He was a familiar figure at piping occasions, a tallish, lean, neat man who wore light-rimmed glasses. His light brown hair receded in his later years. Though not a military man, he bore himself well and always gave an impression of smartness and attention to detail. He often wore a kilt and Lovat green tweed jacket, a reflection of his passionate loyalty to his country.

As a young man, he made frequent visits to the hills with a group of walking and camping friends, some of whom knew him as Jimmy MacNeill. In the late 1940s he was Secretary of the Scottish Youth Hostels Association, and he retained his interest in the outdoor life and the mountains of Scotland all his days.

As James MacNeill, he was a staunch member of the Church of Scotland, actively supporting the work of his local church. I remember, at his funeral, speaking to a cousin of his who was unaware that he was ever called Seumas, and knew nothing of his position in the piping world. She said she thought his main hobby was church activities.

It was hard to believe that anyone could keep his life so completely in sealed compartments.

In September 1948, Seumas married Janet Boyd, known as Netta. They had a son, Rory, and grandchildren Hayley, Kylie and Eve. Their first home was near the university, at 4 Lilybank Gardens, Hillhead, Glasgow. They lived there until 1957, when they moved out to 22 Mosshead Road, Bearsden.

By nature abstemious – though he enjoyed an occasional dram – Seumas mainly indulged himself in the exercise of his wit, often at the expense of others less able than himself. Although he inspired fierce loyalty in his friends, who were many, he also had a host of enemies, possibly more than anyone else in the piping world. He was fond of quoting F.D. Roosevelt's remark about hoping to be judged by the quality of his enemies, and took gleeful pleasure in stirring controversy. He seemed unable to resist the temptation to exercise his biting wit, and his rapier thrusts, though brilliantly amusing, did sometimes give pain to the victim, often unable to counter them.

He needed a foil, and John MacFadyen was the man, equally brilliant in his witty exchanges with Seumas. At the Piobaireachd Society conferences the confrontations between the two were a spectator sport enjoyed as much by the audience as by the protagonists. Less enjoyable to onlookers was the discomfiture of some of his victims – but as one of them cheerfully remarked, 'if you haven't been savaged by Seumas, you're a nobody in piping'. Others, hit hard in their vanity, were less forgiving; many bore a lifetime grudge, if not on their own behalf, then out of loyalty to their friends.

Yet Seumas was not an unkind man. He was capable of great patience and gentle charm, and his courtesy to foreigners was impeccable. What some saw as malice was often just the practice of wit, and the umbrage taken was sometimes merely misunderstanding of his motives. He thought he was only teasing, while the butt of his humour found it offensive.

As he grew older his wit became more acid, and his verbal attacks more savage. In his last year, clouded by painful illness, he was disappointed in his great aim, his dream of expanding the College in the converted church building in Cowcaddens (now the Piping Centre). A huge sum of money had been raised, much of it by his own efforts, but when it came to the bit he found himself unable to accept the changed terms under which he was to hand over the College. Dispute about his own status in the new Centre, and other points of disagreement with his fellow fund-raisers, led the college committee to withdraw the

College from the whole enterprise, and Seumas had to see most of the money he had raised go into the establishment of a rival Centre. As a sick man of nearly eighty years old, he was not able to fling himself into the fray as he might once have done. Many considered that he had been treated shabbily, but his College continues to flourish in its old home in Otago Street. In 2004 it was pulled down and a fine new College built on the site to replace it; it goes on expanding under its Chairman, Dugald MacNeill, and the new Principal, Robert Wallace.

Seumas died, a disappointed man, on 4 April 1995, at his home in Bearsden. He had been suffering from cancer of the colon. At his own request, he was buried at Riddrie Park Cemetery, Glasgow, beside his beloved piping teacher and mentor, his uncle, Blind Archie MacNeill. The piper at the funeral was his pupil, Dr John MacAskill.

Sources

W.J. Watson, *Scottish Verse*
Jeannie Campbell, *Highland Bagpipe Makers*
Piping Times September 1992 – April 1993: Memoirs of Archie MacNeill
Old Parish Register and Census for Gigha
Campbell papers
Obituary of Seumas MacNeill, *Guardian* 1995
Proceedings of the Piobaireachd Society Conferences
Piping Times, February 1962

Islay

To reach Islay and Jura, take the car-ferry from Kennacraig, on West Loch Tarbert, Kintyre, to Port Askaig on the east coast of Islay, or to Port Ellen in the south. The crossing takes just over two hours to Port Askaig, and an extra fifteen minutes to Port Ellen. From Port Askaig, a small car-ferry provides a link to Jura. It is also possible to fly to Islay from Glasgow.

Tunes Associated with Islay

Bowmore Fair R 2
The Bowmore Reel (also known as *Miss Girdle*) R 2. This was part of the Crimean Reveille
Charles D. MacTaggart, by Ian C. Cameron R 4

Islay

Charlie MacEachern of Conesby, by Donald MacLeod 2/4 M 4
Chief Inspector Angus MacDonald, by Ian C. Cameron 6/8 M 4
Dr Alexander Bisset of Islay, by Alexander M. MacIver 2/4 M 4
Dreaming of Islay, by James Haugh 9/8 M 4
Farewell to the Laird of Islay, by Angus MacKay P 7
The Islay Ball, arr. by Archie MacNeill S 4

The Islay Carol (=*Bunessan*, traditional) 9/8 SA 4
An Islay Jig 6/8 J 2
An Islay Reel R 2
Islay's Charms, by Ian C. Cameron 6/8 J 4
I Was Born In Islay R 2
John C. Johnston (Glasgow Police), by Peter MacLeod 2/4 M 4
John Wilson, by Ian C. Cameron 6/8 J 4
Lament for Charlie MacEachern of Islay, by Dugald C. MacLeod P 7
Lament for Donald MacPhee, by John MacColl P
Lament for Neil MacEachern of Conisby 1933, by John MacColl P
Lament for the Castle of Dunyveg P 7
Laphroaig, by Donald MacLeod 6/8 M 4
Leaving Port Askaig, by William Ross 6/8 M 4
Lochiel's Farewell to Isla(y) 2/4 M 2
Lochiel's Welcome to Islay 6/8 M 2
MacDonald of the Isles (March to Harlaw) 6/8 M 4
The MacIvers' March P (see below)
The Maid of Islay S 2
Major Kenneth Lumsden, by Ian C. Cameron R 4
Miss Sheelah J. Nicol of the Glasgow Islay Choir, by Donald
    MacArthur 6/8 M 2
Mrs MacWhirter of Coalhill, by John Gillespie 2/4 M 4
The Mull of Oa, by George M. MacIntyre 4/4 M 2
Neil MacEachern, by James Haugh 6/8 J 4
The Old Farm House, by Ian C. Cameron 6/8 J 4
Over to Islay, by Archie Kenneth 6/8 J 4
The Piper of Dunyveg, by G.S. MacLennan 3/4 RM 2
The Piper's Warning to his Master (Piobaireachd Dhunnaomhaig) P 7
Reel, by Donald Galbraith R 2
The Road to the Mull of Oa, by Hamilton Workman 6/8 J 4
Salute to Captain D.R. MacLennan, by Ian C. Cameron P 7
Traigh Ghruinneard 6/8 Quickstep 2 (see below)
W.A. MacPherson of St Thomas, by Ian C. Cameron 6/8 J 4

Traigh Ghruinneard, described as 'a very old Quickstep', seems to be
the tune known in Islay as *Batail Traigh Ghruineairt*, 'The Battle of the
Gruinard Shore', which was fought in 1592. In some parts of Islay, the
word *batail(t)* is used for 'battle', rather than *blar* or *latha*. Islay has
four different dialects of Gaelic, corresponding to the different types
of terrain, and this seems to belong to the Kilchoman district, which
includes Gruinard. (I am indebted to Bobby MacLellan of Ballygrant
for this information).

Margaret Stewart sings a song *'S Ann Aig Ceann Traigh Ghruin-neart (At the Head of Gruinard)* which she describes as 'a song generally accepted as being a piobaireachd song', i.e. a song sung to the tune of a piobaireachd work.

The Piper's Warning to his Master and the *Lament for the Castle of Dunyveg* are two piobaireachd works discussed by Professor Alec Haddow in his book *The History and Structure of Ceol Mor*. Both were part of the struggle for Islay in the 17th century, and were bound up with the Covenanting Wars.

Farewell to the Laird of Islay is thought to be the only piobaireachd composition made by Angus MacKay (see below). The Laird was Walter F. Campbell of Shawfield and Islay, and it seems certain that the work was composed in Islay, around 1840, when Angus was leaving for Glengarry.

The *Lament for Charlie MacEachern of Islay* was probably the work of Dugald C. MacLeod in Skye, though some say it was made by 'Wee Donald' MacLeod who was a close friend of Charlie's nephew, Neil MacEachern. Presumably it was composed when Charlie died, in 1975 (see below).

The Campbell Canntaireachd manuscript has a piobaireachd work entitled *The MacIvers' March*, which Willie Gray said was 'on much the same lines' as the work known as *The MacCrimmons' Lament*. Willie Gray added a note that MacIver, MacIvor and MacCaffer or MacAffer were all forms of the same name, common in Islay among the descendants of the Campbells of Cawdor (Calder). The implication seems to be that Willie Gray believed *The MacIvers' March* originated in Islay.

A 2/4 March in four parts, *The MacEacherns' March*, composed by Dan Hughie MacEachern, was made in Nova Scotia and is to be found in Allan J. MacKenzie's Collection of Pipe Tunes (2000). It does not appear to have any connection with the Islay MacEacherns – unless, of course, the Nova Scotian MacEacherns came from Islay.

How Islay gave Piping to Skye

Lord Archibald Campbell, brother of the Duke of Argyll, published in 1885 a collection of local stories and traditions, entitled *The Records of Argyll*.

One of the tales was about the MacDonald chief of the Isles, who at that time lived in the palace on Finlaggan Isle, in Islay, and he had a big ploughman. One day this ploughman was hungry when along came an old grey-haired man who offered him food. When he had eaten it, he was given a chanter to play, and at once stood up and began to play it. This was the Black Chanter, and when the Chief heard him playing he gave him a three-drone pipe, and he became the MacDonald chief's piper as long as he lived. The Black Chanter remained with the family in Islay, but a piping MacDonald then went to Skye, and from Skye he took a man called MacCrimmon, and sent him over to Islay, to learn from the Big Ploughman. MacCrimmon began courting the Big Ploughman's daughter, who gave him the Black Chanter on loan – but MacCrimmon took it and left her, and returned with it to Skye. And that was how the MacCrimmons learned their piping and took it home to Skye.

The three-drone pipe somewhat discredits this story.

Dunyveg and the Lords of the Isles

Clan Iain Mor, or Clan Donald South, took its name from Iain Mor MacDonald, killed in 1427. He was a younger brother of Donald, Lord of the Isles. Iain Mor's Scottish possessions centred on the Castle of Dunyveg, on the south coast of Islay. By marriage to an heiress, Marjorie Bissett, in 1399, he acquired land in the north and east of Antrim, Northern Ireland, the area known as The Glens, the part of Ireland that is closest geographically to Scotland. So the chiefs of the Clan Iain Mor are called either the MacDonalds of Dunyveg and the Glens, or the MacDonalds of Islay and Antrim.

Note that the MacDonalds in Skye are often called MacDonalds of the Isles, but were in fact MacDonalds of Sleat, a different branch of the clan from the Dunyveg Lords of the Isles.

When John, Lord of the Isles, died in 1380, he was able to pass on to his son Donald, elder brother of Iain Mor, the lands of Lochaber, Moidart, Arisaig, Morar, Knoydart, Morvern, Knapdale, Kintyre and Glencoe; and the islands of Islay, Gigha, Mull, Colonsay, Jura, Scarba, Tiree, Eigg, Rum, Lewis, Harris, the Uists, Benbecula and Barra. This was probably the highest point of the Lordship of the Isles.

On the fall of the Lordship in the 1490s, Iain Mor's son and his grandson were both executed, but the clan survived, and by the early 16th century they had become a powerful branch of the Clan Donald. Later in that century, their power dwindled, and a younger brother of James MacDonald of Dunyveg and the Glens, a man called Sorley Buidhe MacDonnell, seized the clan's lands in Antrim for his son Ranald (or Randal). This was in 1589. As a result, Sorley Buidhe's nephew Angus became 'of Dunyveg' only, and the Glens designation went to Ranald's line (later, they became the Earls of Antrim).

Ranald was made the first Earl of Antrim in 1620, and he died in 1636. He was probably the Earl commemorated in the piobaireachd lament of that name. He was the brother-in-law of one of the great Irish leaders, Hugh O'Neill of Tyrone, and there is a possibility that the *Lament for Hugh* was named for O'Neill. The work known today as *Stewart's White Banner* has a secondary, possibly older, title which appears in English as *Lament for Samuel,* in Gaelic as *Cumha Somhairle,* which is the same name as Sorley. Could this have been a lament for Sorley Buidhe, in Antrim, the father of Ranald? This title is given to the work by Donald MacDonald, and as a Hebridean MacDonald himself, he may have picked up an old Antrim tradition – but this is speculation.

The downfall of the Clan Iain Mor was a feud with the MacLeans of Duart over the ownership of the north-western part of Islay, the fertile lands known as the Rinns of Islay. Angus MacDonald of Dunyveg was the brother-in-law of the MacLean chief, Sir Lachlan Mor MacLean, but this did not prevent the disagreement from boiling over, and in 1598, in the Battle of the Rinns, or Traigh Gruineart, Sir Lachlan was killed.

In a reprisal raid, the MacLeans joined forces with the MacNeills of Barra, and invaded Islay. They swept through the island, destroying all the MacDonalds they could find, and ravaging the countryside yet again. Dunyveg Castle was surrendered, and the MacDonalds driven out of Islay. It is possible that the piobaireachd works, *The MacLeans' March* and *MacNeill of Barra's March,* were composed to commemorate this savage invasion, but 'March' may here be merely the old word for a piobaireachd composition, not referring to an invasive march at all. If they were commemorations of that campaign, that does not necessarily mean that these works were composed at that time: there are examples of piobaireachd works being given titles which look back to the heroic past of a clan, rather than being contemporary with the event. *The Unjust Incarceration* is one such.

The defeated James MacDonald married a Campbell, a sister of the Earl of Argyll, and this marriage gave the Campbells entry to Islay. During the 17th century they took over the island. Dunyveg continued to be a bone of contention, passing from legitimate MacDonald claimants to the Bishops of Argyll, then to an illegitimate upstart, Angus Og MacDonald, and then back to the Campbells. During this period, Coll Ciotach MacDonald and his son Alasdair MacColla were on the rise (see below, Colonsay), and the Civil Wars of the 17th century were starting. Works such as the *Lament for MacDonald of Sanda*, *The Rout of the MacPhees*, *The Piper's Warning to his Master* and all of the Duntrune/Dunyveg piobaireachd compositions belong to this time.

The piobaireachd works associated with Dunyveg in Islay have become inextricably confused with the traditions of Duntrune, near Crinan. Professor Alec Haddow's essay on *The Piper's Warning to his Master* discusses its relation to the *Lament for the Castle of Dunyveg* and *The Sound of the Waves Against Duntrune Castle*. He concludes that the historical events which gave rise to the naming of the music took place at Duntrune, near Crinan, but were later associated with two other castles, Dunyveg in Islay and Dunaverty in Kintyre, possibly varying according to the audience listening to the story.

In 2009, however, Keith Sanger published his interesting find of a report in a newspaper dated 30 September 1647 (issue 133 of the *Moderate Intelligenser* (London)), which casts new light on the so-called Piper's Warning.

It had previously been thought that the piper was a captive of the Campbells in Duntrune Castle, and that he played the tune we know as *The Piper's Warning to his Master* in a truncated form, to warn his chief, Alasdair MacColla, that he was sailing into a trap – and a mutilated skeleton found buried in the castle was assumed to be that of the piper, punished by having his hand cut off. Different attempts have been made to represent the alleged form of the warning, by, for example, both the Piobaireachd Society (Book 12) and Simon Fraser.

Keith Sanger's find indicates that the chief concerned was Coll Ciotach, the father of Alasdair MacColla, and that the incident was at Dunyveg, rather than Duntrune. The report on the capture and execution of Coll Ciotach refers back to the time in 1615, when Coll's enemies had him holed up in Dunyveg, 'and had ships and force enough to have battered the place and have taken him'. But Coll had two or three boats hidden beneath the castle, and in the dark of night, he slipped into one of them, 'and set a Bag-piper in the other, who playing, All the ship boats followed the sound of the Bag-piper, while in the mean time, Cole-Ketogh in the other boat escaped away'.

As Keith Sanger points out, this use of the piper to divert the enemy's attention means that it was the fact that the piper was playing and not what he was playing that mattered, and the tune does not need to be mutilated at all. The warning to his master was presumably an instruction to the piper to strike up if his diversionary boat encountered any of the hostile vessels, to warn Coll's men to take a different course.

The end of the report remarks on the depopulation of that part of Argyll, mentioning that 'both man, woman and childe (of those that were in the Rebellion) went to pot, being throwen down the Rocks'. This must be a reference to the siege of Dunaverty, in the south of Kintyre, when hundreds were massacred and thrown over an eighty-foot cliff. Its apparent irrelevance to the capture and death of Coll seems to reflect the traditional association of the three castles, Duntrune, Dunyveg and Dunaverty. But who introduced the tradition of the mutilation of both piper and music?

At this time in the history of Islay (17th century), when the Campbells, especially the Campbells of Cawdor, were taking over and the MacDonalds driven out, there are stories of Janet Campbell, 'the Black Bitch of Dunstaffnage', who was married to one of the Cawdor family, Sir George Campbell of Airds, owner of much of Islay. It seems she had a burning hatred of the Islay MacDonalds, and she pursued a personal vendetta against them. If she managed to capture any of the followers of the MacDonald chief, she would have them tied up and marooned on a rock at low tide, so that they would drown as the water rose. Some were rescued by a passing boat, which took them to safety in Antrim, but she continued with her murderous vindictiveness, and was hated in Islay.

Another of her acts of cruelty was to cut off the fingers of a piper, who was almost certainly one of the pipers kept by the MacDonalds of the Isles, possibly a MacArthur from Proaig. This is recorded in a manuscript history of the Campbells of Craignish, written in the early 18th century. It says that the story came from the victim's children, between 1696 and 1704. Could this story have been transferred to that of Coll Ciotach's escape from Dunyveg, giving rise to the mutilation theory reflected in some versions of *The Piper's Warning to his Master?*

Sources

David Stevenson, *Highland Warrior*
The two Rev. A.J. MacDonalds (MacDonald Clan History)
J. Michael Hill, *Fire and Sword*
Alec Haddow, *Ceol Mor*
Clifford Jupp, *History of Islay*
MS History of the Campbells of Craignish
Keith Sanger, *Piping Times*

Cnoc Na Piobaireachd

Just to the north of Bunnahabhain, a few miles north of Port Askaig, on the east coast of Islay, there is a ridge of hillside called CNOC NA PIOBAIREACHD, Hill of the Pipe Music, or Hill of the Piping. Today the name is still recognised, but nobody seems to know its origin. The hill is a ridge, about half a mile in length, sloping diagonally across the southern side of a bigger hill, Shun Bheinn. It is not associated with any famous centre of Islay piping such as Conisby or Proaig, and it looks an unlikely place for pipers to play. Nearby, however, are a number of old shieling sites, where cattle were taken for summer grazing, and it may be that the herdsmen associated with the shielings used the ridge for playing their pipes on a summer's evening. Maybe the ridge caught a sea breeze off the Sound of Islay which kept the midges off.

But why is it called Cnoc na Piobaireachd, rather than Cnoc Nam Piobairean, Hill of the Pipers? This is the only instance on record of the word Piobaireachd being used in a placename, and it may be a corrupt spelling. The name is puzzling, not least because there is no longer a local tradition associated with it, and we have no idea how old the name might be.

There are some other strange placenames in the area, difficult to interpret: a nearby slope is called Bachlaig, which seems to refer to something curled or bent, and it is separated from Cnoc na Piobaireachd by a dip called Glac Gille gun Cheann, the Hollow of the Lad with No Head (presumably not a piper). It is evident that we have lost a rich vein of local tradition.

Piper's Caves

In 1772, Thomas Pennant paid a short visit to Islay, and he recorded how he and his party explored the complex of caves and natural underground passages at Sanegmore (Sannaig Mor), in the parish of Kilchoman. He found the place 'passable but with difficulty, a perfect subterraneous labyrinth'. He went on: 'A bagpiper preceded: at times the whole space was filled with the sound, which died away by degrees to a mere murmur, and soon after again astonished us with the bellowing, according as the meanders conducted him to, or from, our singular stations.'

It would be too much to expect Pennant to name the piper, if indeed he knew the name. It may have been one of the MacEacherns, who were numerous in that area (see below). At least Pennant spared us the story of the hairless dog, sometimes associated with this cave, as with so many others.

David Caldwell has recorded another, near Bolsta, in the north-east headland of Islay (OS map reference NR 398 783). This was a cave called Uamh Mhor, Big Cave, and the piper's hairless dog emerged, after a suitable interval, several miles away at Duisker. That part of the coast is riddled with caves, a different cave-system from that visited by Pennant's party. Uamh Mhor is only one of several Piper's Caves in the islands and on the mainland which all have the same story of a piper, playing a lament, entering the cave with his dog. The piper always vanishes for ever, but the miserable dog emerges several miles away, and is always hairless (see also Arran, Mull, Tiree, Colonsay, etc).

A Macdonald Piper

In 1793, the list of men serving in Grant's Strathspey or 1st Highland Fencible Regiment, in Cromdale Parish on Speyside, included a young piper, aged nineteen, called ARCHIBALD MACDONALD, whose birthplace is given as Kilchoman, in Islay. Nothing more is known of him – but that Fencible Regiment had another piper, DONALD MACDONALD, twenty-three, from Glenurquhart, and they may have been related. It is unusual for an island piper to appear in a Grant regiment unless there was some link through other mainland MacDonalds, and it is known that the Grants had close connections with the MacDonald pipers in Glenurquhart.

There is a tradition, mentioned in his *Memoirs* by William Collie, the grandfather of William Ross of Edinburgh Castle, that some of the MacDonalds who escaped from the massacre at Glencoe in 1692 made their way to Islay, where they settled among their MacDonald kin in the island. For safety, since by this time Islay was in Campbell hands, these MacDonalds changed their name to MacPhail (son of Paul, a MacDonald name), but some of them in later generations reverted to MacDonald. It must be at least possible that this piper from Kilchoman, Archibald MacDonald, born in 1774, was one of them, and the link with Glenurquhart might support this, as some of the Glencoe MacDonald refugees are known to have settled there.

Colin Mor Campbell

No account of the piping traditions of Islay can omit a mention of COLIN MOR CAMPBELL, the piper who in the 1790s wrote out the Campbell

Canntaireachd manuscript (now in the National Library of Scotland, NLS MSS 3714–5), recording in written form the piobaireachd tunes of his time, probably works he had learned from his father, Donald. He used a written form of Canntaireachd, a system of vocables evolved for the singing of piobaireachd music, and this may have been the first time it was written down – though there is reason to believe that William MacMurchy in Kintyre might have done it in the 1760s. William's manuscript has been lost, but we know that he wrote down the music of both harp and bagpipe, and it is thought that he may have used a written form of Canntaireachd. He died around 1770.

Meanwhile, the young Joseph MacDonald had written his *Compleat Theory* in 1762, although it was not published until 1805. He used staff notation, as did his elder brother, the Rev. Patrick MacDonald, in his *Highland Vocal Airs*, published in 1784. It is not clear whether Colin Campbell knew this book.

Colin was sometimes referred to as being 'from Islay', but it is difficult to find evidence for this. His father Donald lived in Nether Lorne, but John Gibson thinks the family may have originated in Keppoch. They are believed to have been hereditary pipers to the Campbells of Breadalbane, but later family tradition says that Donald was with MacDonald of Glenaladale until Glenaladale emigrated to Canada around 1773, and it was not until then that Donald went to the Campbells. If Colin Mor was indeed in Islay, his laird would have been Walter Campbell of Shawfield and Islay, the father of Walter F. Campbell, the laird who later encouraged Angus MacKay to write his manuscript of piobaireachd (see below).

Keith Sanger has shown (*Piping Times*, vol. 58, no. 1, October 2005) that Colin was living on his croft at Ardrioch in Ardmaddy in June 1798, having previously served with the Argyle Fencible Regiment until he was discharged in 1781, when he was unwell. He must have been one of the two pipers mentioned in the Duty Book of the regiment in 1778 (see below, Canna). In 1795, half of his croft had been taken from him as he refused to be recruited into the 3rd Battalion of the Breadalbane Fencibles, raised by his landlord, Campbell of Lochend. He was petitioning the Earl of Breadalbane, whose father had employed Colin's father Donald as piper, to have his full croft restored. It is clear from this and from a later petition by his daughter-in-law in Ardrioch that the family remained there for many years; there seems to be little justification for giving Colin the designation 'of Islay'.

Colin Mor wrote out his father's tunes in or around 1791, and the volumes of manuscript passed to his son JOHN CAMPBELL (1795–1831), who was born in Nether Lorne, probably at Ardrioch. John was for ten years piper to Walter F. Campbell, living in Islay and acting as 'piper-nurse' to the laird's son, John Francis Campbell, later known as Iain Ileach 'John the Islayman'. It seems likely that Colin Mor was called 'of Islay' through confusion with his son, but we cannot be sure of this.

Islay House, island home of the Campbells of Shawfield and Islay, was built as an L-plan dwelling in 1677, for Sir Hugh Campbell of Cawdor (father of Young George, for whom *Young George's Salute* was made). The Campbells of Shawfield and Islay were related to him, and later inherited the house. They remodelled and extended it during the 18th century, but in 1827 Joseph Mitchell described it as 'a large uncouth structure with no external architectural ornament', though he thought the interior handsome and the gardens tasteful. The south-east wing was re-designed in the early 20th century, to make it harmonise with the rest of the building.

In Angus MacKay's time there, it must have been much the same size as it is now – a huge house, believed to have 365 windows, one for each day of the year (but this is a local tradition attached to several other large Scottish mansions). It was here that Angus MacKay is said to have compiled his manuscript, some of it published as a book in 1838.

Joseph Mitchell described his visit to Islay House in 1827, in a party with Lord Colchester, in whose honour their host, Walter F. Campbell, held a number of banquets: 'There were two or three days of feasting, a party of some forty ladies and gentlemen sitting down each day to dinner. The procession from the drawing-room to the dining-room must have been striking to a stranger. Many of the native guests were in Highland costume. The servants, in Highland dress, stood arrayed in two rows, from the foot of the staircase to the dining-room door, and a piper behind on each side in grand costume discoursed spirited if not sweet music' (Joseph was not a fan of piping).

One of these two pipers would have been John Campbell from Nether Lorne, but who was the other? Possibly a local player brought in for the occasion.

After the death of John Campbell at the early age of thirty-six in 1831, Walter F. Campbell had other pipers whose names we do not know. In 1837 or thereabouts, Angus MacKay, who had been one of several pipers employed at Drummond Castle and then at Tulloch Castle, near Dingwall, became piper to Walter F., and moved to Islay. He was there for a few years, during which he is believed to have compiled his manuscript collection of pipe music, writing out in staff notation the tunes taught to him by his father, John MacKay, Raasay.

He prepared his book for publication, and its impact on the piping world is still felt, to this day.

Although there is no documentary evidence, it is widely held that the laird took him to Islay to further his work, to give him not only the necessary encouragement but also peace and quiet, and plenty of time, in which to tackle the mammoth task. It seems he remained with Campbell only until 1840, when he went to Glengarry as piper to Baron Ward of Birmingham (later the Earl of Dudley), an English peer who had bought the bankrupt Glengarry estates; and finally, on 25 July 1843, Angus was appointed as first piper to Queen Victoria (see below).

Although it is thought that he compiled his collection while living in Islay as Campbell's piper, he may have done some of the preliminary work while he was at Drummond and Tulloch. There had been announcements of its impending publication as early as 1835, when on 8 August a forthcoming 'publication by subscription of his collection of Ancient Piobaireachds or Pipe Tunes, planned to appear on 1st February 1836' was announced, over his name and address, 'Angus MacKay, Drummond Castle'. When the book did appear, two years later, it contained an apology for the delay. The bulk of the work was undoubtedly done in Islay, but he must have been planning it for years before that. Was the wording of that announcement his own? It may have been the work of someone in the Highland Society of London, and it seems unlikely that Angus, a Gaelic speaker, would have used the word 'Piobaireachds' (see also Captain John A. MacLellan, *Piping Times*, March 1966).

Walter F. Campbell went bankrupt in 1847 and was forced to sell his Islay estates, including Islay House, to a London linen draper called Morrison, a man who came from very humble origins but was worth £4,000,000 when he died. Joseph Mitchell said he 'worshipped money', but for two years before he died, he became senile and was convinced that he was going to end in the workhouse. His attendants used to pay him twelve shillings a week, of his own money, to allay his fears. His heirs had the title of Lord Margadale.

Willie Ross held his summer schools in Islay House, giving tuition to Islay pipers, between the wars. Latterly the numbers grew so that other classes were held, organised by the Islay Piping Society in conjunction with the Piobaireachd Society (who paid at least half of his fee, including his travelling expenses). The classes were at Bridgend, Ballygrant, Bowmore and Port Charlotte. When Willie gave up the classes in 1925, his pupils and the Piping Society held a ceremony at which they presented him with 'a well-filled wallet of Treasury notes'. His wife preserved a newspaper cutting at the time, recording the event.

Sources

Notices of Pipers
J.F. Campbell, *Canntaireachd* 1880
William Donaldson, *The Highland Pipe*
Census Records
Clifford Jupp, *History of Islay*
Keith Sanger, *Piping Times*
Joseph Mitchell, *Reminiscences*

Donald MacPhee

DONALD MACPHEE was born in Bothwell in 1842, but his parents were both from Islay. He was a pupil of William Gunn, in Glasgow, and later went also to Alexander Cameron in Greenock (brother of Donald Cameron). He became the teacher of many pipers, the best known being John MacColl, and opened a shop called the Bagpipe Emporium, in the Royal Arcade, Glasgow. He played piobaireachd at many of the Games in the 1870s, and was also an accomplished Highland dancer.

In 1876 he published a collection of about 150 light music tunes, and four years later a collection of piobaireachd works which pipers use today because they like his settings. Not long after its publication, Donald developed an increasingly severe nervous disease, possibly caused by syphilis, as in the case of Angus MacKay; it destroyed first his eyesight and then his memory. Rapidly he became completely insane, so that he had to be confined in Woodielee Asylum. He died there in December 1880, leaving a wife and young family. He was a good piper, pipe-maker, teacher and dancer. In memory of his teacher, John Mac-Coll is known to have composed a piobaireachd work, the *Lament for Donald MacPhee*, but the manuscript seems to have gone missing.

Jeannie Campbell has pointed out that in the 1871 Census, the MacPhee family, living in Thistle Street, Glasgow, had relatives from Islay staying with them, and also neighbours who were joiners and woodworkers from Islay, Neil MacLellan, Donald MacIndeor, Colin Carmichael and Alexander Currie – all names found in Islay piping families, although we have no way of knowing if any of these were pipers. It is clear that Donald MacPhee kept up his Islay connections, and in 1873 he competed as 'Donald MacPhee, Islay'.

Pipe Major William Gray said that DONALD MACPHEE and DONALD

GALBRAITH were two well-known Islay pipers who had been pupils of Angus MacKay, implying that this had been when Angus was living in Islay, between 1837 and 1840. As the well-known Donald MacPhee who published the two collections was born in 1842, he cannot be the same Donald who went to Angus MacKay.

It seems, however, that Donald MacPhee, Glasgow, was taught by Donald Galbraith, in the days when MacPhee was living in Coatbridge, and that Donald Galbraith had indeed been taught by Angus Mac-Kay in Islay. Galbraith was 'a frequent prize winner' during the years between 1850 and 1875. Another of his pupils was William Sutherland of Airdrie.

Lily MacDougall of Caol Ila (see below) was taught by a piper called DONALD MACPHEE living in Islay in the 1920s and 1930s; he may have been descended from the Donald MacPhee mentioned by Willie Gray, but this is not certain.

The MacEachern Family

The family of the piping MacEacherns seems to have dominated the piping scene in Islay in the early 20th century. The line is said to have been introduced into Islay by the MacDonald Lords of the Isles, who brought MacEacherns from Kintyre in the 14th century, as armourers and blacksmiths.

Once established on the island, they became hereditary swordsmiths, makers of the famous six-foot blades with the distinctive Islay hilt. They had a hidden forge behind the rock of Creag Uinsinn, about three-quarters of a mile from Kilchoman Church, among the crags which rise so dramatically as a backdrop to the church. Traces of their forge may still be seen. David Caldwell gives the OS map reference as NR 220 633, and says the site overlooks Gleann na Ceardaich, Glen of the Smiddy. It was in 'a cave in the side of a crag with good views, and a stream running down the adjacent cliff. The cave itself is dry, 7.0m deep by 3.5m wide, with a height of 3.2m it would have made a convenient dwelling place'.

Throughout the centuries, there are records of MacEachern men who were blacksmiths and taught apprentice smiths their trade. Calum MacAffer, from Bowmore, a stalwart of Islay piping in the 20th century, has a big MacDonald sword made by the MacEacherns in the old days, and his family tradition is that it was forged in Kintyre. The MacEachern smiths themselves originated there, presumably bringing their designs with them.

MacEacherns were widely distributed over the island, but there were concentrations of them in the north-west of Kilchoman parish, around Kilchoman church. There is no way of knowing which, if any, of these were pipers. A descendant, Greg MacEchron, now living in Florida, writes that his MacEachern ancestor left Islay as early as 1638, and he has records of the family living at Smaull, north of Kilchoman, long before MacEacherns were recorded at Gearach.

The centre of the piping MacEacherns was Conisby, near Bruichladdich; they are known to have been there in the 19th century, and probably back into the 18th but appear to have moved there gradually, from Kilchoman district.

In 1741, Conisby, then spelled Konigsbay, was held by eight tenants, but none of them was a MacEachern. At Gerrich (now spelled Gearach), a few miles from Conisby, on the hill road between Port Charlotte and Kilchiaran, we find in 1741 six tenants, one of whom was Neil MacEachern. He may well have been a forebear of the Conisby MacEacherns and a descendant of the Kilchoman swordsmiths, a link between them and the Conisby pipers.

The Old Parish Register for Kilchoman starts late, in 1821, and the Census returns give us additional information. In 1841, three families of MacEacherns are listed, out of a total of thirty-five families at Conesby (at that time, Conesby was a district, not just the cluster of houses it is now). One of the families was Peter MacEachern, farmer, born in 1781, and his wife was Catherine Currie. They had at least four sons, Archie, James, John and Niel. Peter and Catherine were the great-grandparents of the piping MacEachern brothers, and John, married to Betty MacAulay, was their grandfather.

In 1851, John was farming sixteen acres and employed a labourer. He and Betty had six children, including Neil, born in 1843, who was the father of the piping brothers. They had MacIntyre neighbours who were the forebears of Duncan MacIntyre, the piper killed in North Africa in 1942.

John's wife Betty died in 1857, giving birth to twin girls, neither of whom survived. John remained in Conisby, with his six children. By 1871, two families of Johnstons had come to live there, too, and they were the forebears of John C. Johnston. Two of them married into the MacEacherns. And a couple called MacIndeor, also of a piping family, were neighbours of the MacEacherns; they had connections in Jura. It is clear that Conisby had become a 'nest' of piping families.

The 1851 Census records a Duncan McCalman, aged sixty-eight and described as a Piper, born locally. His wife Rachel, also sixty-eight, was a MacEachern, and they were visited on Census day by Effie MacEachern, sixty-four, presumably Rachel's sister. We assume that Rachel and Effie were sisters of John.

Duncan and Rachel had two daughters present, Mary twenty-six and Peggy twenty-two, both described as House Servants, and in the household was an eight-year-old, Mary Johnston, described oddly as Dlaw, which normally means daughter-in-law, but here must be a mistake for grand-daughter. There were also two grandsons, Duncan McCalman four and John Barclay six months. This notice is interesting in that it names female family members, and also demonstrates that there were other pipers in the township – Duncan McCalman gave Piper as his occupation. And here we have an early link between the MacEacherns and the Johnstons.

Neil MacEachern married Catherine MacKelvie from Campbeltown in 1874. The wedding was in Islay, which suggests she had been working there. By 1881, they were farming thirty-five acres, quite a large holding. They had ten children, whom they brought up with strict principles and strong religious beliefs.

The family were JOHN 1876, Annie 1878, PETER 1885, ROBERT 1888, JAMES 1890, CHARLES 1892 and CATHERINE 1895. These all appear in the 1901 Census, and there were three other girls, Agnes, Bessie and Jessie. All were Gaelic speakers, all born at Conisby, and all five boys became pipers, and good pipers, too.

Their youngest sister KATIE (Catherine) defied the men of the family by learning to play as well. It is said of her that if she was in the next room and someone she could not see began to play, she could say which brother it was, so intimately did she know their individual styles. She learned to play by picking up the knowledge of her brothers and listening carefully while she watched their fingers. She became a good player, to the disapproval of her menfolk. She was not allowed to compete or to play in public, partly because in those days men could not thole being beaten by a lassie, and partly because it meant wearing Highland dress, which entailed girls showing their legs, even their *knees*, in public (times have certainly changed). Katie married David MacLellan of Mulindry, near Ballygrant, and had three children, including the piper, Robert MacLellan, known as Bobby (see below).

Of the other sisters, Agnes married a MacDiarmaid, but died of measles soon after her marriage; Bessie married Donald Morrison and had three children, but died giving birth to the fourth. Jessie married Lachlan MacLachlan of Bruichladdich and they had seven children.

Of the five brothers, the youngest, Charlie, was probably the best known. He was in the Glasgow City Police pipe band in the time of Pipe Major William Gray, when they were winning many prizes. It may have been Charlie who taught John C. Johnston, who was also recruited into the Police band (see below).

Both JOHN and CHARLIE MACEACHERN were in the City of Glasgow Police pipe band, and Charlie stayed on the mainland when John returned to Islay. JAMES and ROBERT were also much away from the island, and it was PETER who remained at home to work the family croft at Conisby and look after his elderly parents. Neil died in 1933, when he was over eighty, and Catherine about fifteen years later. In memory of Neil, John MacColl composed a piobaireachd work, the *Lament for Neil MacEachern (1933)*; the manuscript is in the College of Piping in Glasgow.

Who taught the five brothers? Was it their father, Neil? Family tradition says he was not keen for his sons to become pipers, because it meant they would be asked to play at weddings, ceilidhs, and so on, where they would be pressed to take strong drink. He need not have worried: while none of them was teetotal, they all avoided letting drink become a serious problem.

Their main advanced tuition in Islay came from Pipe Major Willie Ross, who held summer schools in Islay and always stayed with the MacEacherns at Conisby. He taught classes in Islay House. This was when he composed his famous 6/8 march *Leaving Port Askaig*. All the brothers were excellent piobaireachd players, except for Peter, and he excelled as a player for dancing.

John married a girl from Portnahaven, Margaret Curry, and they settled at a farm called Carrabus, not far from Bridgend. They had three children, Jeanie, Mary and Neil. John was piper to the laird, Lord Margadale, formerly Morrison of Islay House, who allowed the house to be used for the classes held in the summer by Willie Ross. John was a solo competitor who won many prizes, especially at Cowal.

When Willie Ross stopped coming to teach in Islay, his place was taken by John MacEachern, who taught in the barn – at Carrabus or Conisby? If any of his pupils made a mistake in his playing, a sheaf of corn would fly through the air and hit him on the back of the neck.

The second brother, Peter, stayed at Conisby, never married, and did not compete as a piper; his services were much in demand to play for dancing at weddings and ceilidhs all over the island.

Robert, the third brother, served his time on Islay as a carpenter/ cabinetmaker, before he went to sea as a ship's carpenter on merchant ships. He went round the world more than once, and during this time he tried always to time his shore-leave in Scotland to coincide with the summer Games, wanting most of all to attend Cowal Games. One year he won the Cowal Cup and the Ibrox Cup, but was due to rejoin his ship immediately after the Games. Not knowing what to do with the cups, but unwilling to take them abroad, he sent them to the Bank Manager in Bridgend, who must have been quite surprised.

In 1930, when he was forty-three, Robert met Lilian Victoria Davies, twenty years his junior, and on their marriage he gave up the sea and took the tenancy of the farm of Corrary, on the road between Bowmore and Port Ellen. Their children were Catherine, Lily, Annie, Robert, Neil and James.

Robert taught several Islay pipers, including his nephew, Neil MacEachern at Ardnave, James' son, who later won the Gold Medal at Oban. Another of Robert's pupils, Angus Currie, Bowmore, was for a long time a leading light in Islay piping. Robert's own son, also called Robert, was another pupil.

James, known as Jimmy, went out to South Africa where he met and married a girl, Winifred MacDonald, whose family came from Skye. Two of their sons were later working in the gold mines of Rhodesia, where they both bought farms. James and Winifred returned to Islay, to farm at Ardnave, beside Loch Gruinart. Their children were Neil, Catherine, Hector, Robert, Charles and Gracie. It was Hector and Robert who were in Rhodesia, and Neil who won the Gold Medal at Oban.

James was a competing piper, and won the Cowal Cup. Cowal Games seem to have been the highlight of the year for many Islay pipers. According to family tradition, James won a Veterans' Competition in the 1960s, at the Northern Meeting in Inverness. He was then in his seventies.

Charlie MacEachern, on retirement from the police, became a railwayman, and was the relief-stationmaster at Perth, Wemyss Bay, Wick, Thurso and other Highland stations. He is remembered as a jolly man and a fine piper, full of fun. He was said to have fewer piobaireachd than three of his brothers, possibly because he excelled at the light music, played more in bands, and so played piobaireachd less often. His by-name in the family was 'The World Champion', presumably because he was with the City of Glasgow Police pipe band when they took the World Championship – and perhaps he was fond of mentioning this. It seems to have made more impact than the Gold Medal at Oban, won by his nephew Neil. There are accounts of Charlie winning the MSR at Oban, but the date is uncertain.

William M. MacDonald, born and brought up in Kingussie,

remembered Charlie in the 1930s, when he was working as a stand-in stationmaster, replacing the regulars when they were away on holiday or sick-leave. When he came to Kingussie station, he was boarding with the MacDonalds (Willie's father was an engine-driver). Willie was then in his teens. His parents were not pipers, though keen on pipe music, and probably did not realise what they had let themselves in for. Charlie, when asked if he played, said 'Aye, a bittie', but 'the bittie turned out to be a big one', as Willie put it. He and Charlie sat up every night, playing practice chanters and full pipes until two or three in the morning, and the parents were not delighted. Perhaps it was as well that the appointment as stationmaster was temporary. Willie said that as a young piper he benefited hugely from this visit, which influenced his playing of light music. Willie went on to become a pupil of John MacDonald, and won both Gold Medals in 1955, and the Clasp the following year. He was also an outstanding player of light music.

Charlie married when he was at Thurso. His two daughters, Barbara and Catherine, and his son Iain, were all born in Thurso. Barbara married a Thurso man, Catherine married an American who was working at Dounreay, but Iain remained a bachelor.

Charlie died on 5 January 1975, in his eighty-third year. Donald MacLeod commemorated him with two tunes, one a 2/4 march called *Charlie MacEachern of Conesby*, presumably made during his lifetime, and the other a piobaireachd work, the *Lament for Charlie MacEachern of Islay* – unless the latter was composed by Dugald C. MacLeod, of Skye.

James' eldest son was NEIL MACEACHERN who won the Gold Medal at Oban in 1965, playing *The Bicker*. He appeared frequently in the prize-lists in the early 1960s, as 'Neil MacEachern, Stromness': he was a bank employee in Orkney at that time. He had been taught by both his father and his uncle Robert, and was a fine piobaireachd player. He married a girl from Elgin, became a banker, and inherited his father's silver-mounted Henderson pipes.

When Neil was working in a bank at Shotts, near Glasgow, he played in the famous Shotts and Dykehead pipe band. In the 1950s he played with the 8th Argylls (Territorial Army) band, beside John M. MacKenzie and the cousins Ronald and Angus Lawrie.

After his return to Islay, Neil was offered promotion to manager of the Bridgend bank (now the Royal Bank of Scotland, formerly the Royal Commercial), but he declined as he preferred to give more time to the croft at Conisby, and to teaching his elder son James to play the pipes.

Young James was a good junior player, who won prizes at Cowal; he had learned by ear from his father. When Neil had a series of strokes before he died in 1982, aged fifty-eight, James was unable to read pipe music off the book. His brother Andrew had been too young to learn from his father, so, of necessity when his father became ill, Andrew learned from the book, and is today a good player, able to read music without difficulty. The piper who played at the graveside at their father's funeral was the Islay player Dougie Ferguson.

A jig called *Neil MacEachern* was composed by Jimmy Haugh of the Red Hackle pipe band in Glasgow, a band which had many pipers from Islay. It was played by Iain MacFadyen on his audiotape, issued by Lismor in 1989 as Volume Seven of the series *The World's Greatest Pipers*.

ANDREW MACEACHERN is a stalwart of Islay piping. His occupation as a fisherman means his time ashore is often unpredictable, but he plays in the band when he can. He has one piobaireachd, the *Wee Spree*, a rarity now in Islay, since the emphasis is on the band, as is the modern trend. Youngsters learn from practising with the pipe band, taking tuition from whoever the current pipe major might be. At one time there were four different pipe majors in four years.

Two promising girl players, NICOLA HAMMOND and LINDSAY MAC-ARTHUR, were sent for a week's tuition at the Piping Centre in Glasgow, generously sponsored by local estate owners, and they had great benefit from it. Both girls are now members of the Islay band.

Nowadays Islay has the necessary piping instruction, at least in the light music, and the growing success of the band reflects this. The pipe band is taking on beginners, and all credit to men like ALAN BROWN, JAMES CARMICHAEL and DUNCAN HEADS, former pipe majors, and to the 2003 pipe major, KAREN ROBERTSON, all of whom kept the Islay tradition going. Piping in Islay has had a renaissance, supported by sponsorship from local companies: the band has gone from strength to strength, competing on the mainland under their Pipe Major NIGEL MORRIS (see below). There seems, however, to be no longer a tradition of playing piobaireachd in Islay.

In the 1920s, Willie Ross used to come to Islay in the summertime, to give lessons to classes of local pipers. These were held in different venues throughout the island, as well as in Islay House, and players came from all over Islay and Jura. These lessons were sponsored by the Piobaireachd Society, who paid the instructor's salary and expenses.

One departure from tradition, introduced by Willie Ross, was that girls were taught on an equal footing with the boys, and Willie Ross

Neil MacEachern

Jig

James Haugh

Music for the jig *Neil MacEachern*
kindly lent by Andrew MacEachern

would permit no discrimination against them. After all, he was taught by his mother. He would have been pleased by the appointment of Karen Robertson as Pipe Major.

ROBERT MACLELLAN, known as Bobby, living at Woodend Cottages, Ballygrant, was a son of Katie MacEachern, herself a good piper, married to David MacLellan of Mulindry. Bobby was a staunch supporter of the Islay Pipe Band. He and Neil MacEachern, Calum MacAffer and Johnny MacIntyre founded the Islay Piping Society, which lasted about ten years.

Before that, in the 1950s, there had been the Islay Pipers, who had a pipe band. The name seems to be an echo of the Islay Pipers who played in Glasgow in the period after the First World War. Bobby had played with the band as a boy in the 1950s, before he went into the army. He said they were a band of exceptionally good players, but they did not take on many engagements. They wore Royal Stewart tartan, with blue battle-dress uniform jackets. In the end the band 'fell apart' when most of the players left the island, either for mainland jobs or going into the forces. Bobby did his National Service in a non-piping regiment, but of course he took his pipes with him. He had happy memories of playing at weddings in Poland.

The Islay Piping Society was vigorous and had a varied programme. They held a number of Balls throughout the year: the Tartan Ball, the Islay Ball, the Pipers' Ball, the TA Ball, and others, all memorable. And they had recitals from noted mainland players, mostly those with a West Highland background, such as Ronnie Lawrie and Arthur Gillies.

The Conisby Cup was a trophy in a competition held in Bowmore Hall, and mainland players were invited to compete for it, along with Islay pipers. Arthur Gillies, Colin Drummond and Dougie Ferguson were among the players who came.

As is inevitable in remote communities, the band has had its ups and downs. After a lapse in the 1980s, it was revived in 1992, with plenty of keen beginners joining the older stalwarts. In 1995 the band competed at Cowal, and by 2011 it had risen through the ranks to Grade 3A, when it won the Grade 3 Championship. Under Pipe Major Nigel Morris, the band is achieving great things, known for its passionate dedication to the cause, but still beset by the former problems: players leaving the islands to find work, not to mention the vast expense of travelling to compete on the mainland.

Latterly, Bobby MacLellan played only on the chanter, because of his health, but his playing of the Islay tune *Am Batailt Traigh Gruineart* (The Battle of the Gruineart Shore, a tune which commemorates the death of Lachlan Mor MacLean in 1598), showed that he had lost nothing of the crispness and clean fingering that he must have had as a band player in his time, when he was pipe major of the Islay band. He loved piobaireachd, but was never taught to play it – he sang it, and could pick it out on his chanter. He had a fine reputation as a setter-up of pipes for the band, and understood, as few do, the intricacies of reeding and matching chanters. Bobby preferred cane reeds, but for band playing he used synthetic – although often there was a cane reed for the bass drone.

Bobby said that there is a loch beside the road between Bowmore and Port Ellen, named in the OS map as Loch Airigh Dhaibhaidh (the Loch of Davey's Shieling). Here there is a thick bed of reeds, now growing on both sides of the road. Bobby said that in the old days pipers came from all over the island for these reeds, and even from other islands such as Colonsay and Gigha. In those days pipers had to make their own reeds, which often did not last long, so that suitable reed-beds were much prized. There are a few other reed-beds in Islay, but the quality of the reeds at Loch Airigh Dhaibhaidh made them specially suitable for the pipes. A similar bed grows below Talisker House, in west Skye, where Iain Dall MacKay was often a visitor in the early 18th century.

Bobby had a reed which, unusually, had a broad rubber-band instead of a cane or plastic tongue – and it worked.

Duncan Heads

DUNCAN HEADS came from a piping family, and the Museum of Islay Life, in Port Charlotte, has pipes which belonged to Duncan's great-grandfather, donated by Duncan to the Museum. They are ivory-mounted, possibly with walrus ivory, as were many pipes in the old days. Fishing boats landing their catches in east-coast ports such as Anstruther would sell walrus ivory to pipemakers.

Duncan was a founder member of the Govan Police Pipe Band, with John MacLellan (Dunoon), and Willie Gray. This band later became the renowned City of Glasgow Police pipe band. Duncan was a respected authority on piping in present-day Islay (2003).

The Tartan Parade

A highlight for the modern Islay Pipe Band in the spring of 2002 was a trip to New York, to take part in the Tartan Parade. Fifteen of the island's pipers, generously sponsored by estate-owners in Islay, travelled with their families, and were among the 8,700 pipers who took part in the parade, an experience that none of them will ever forget.

Sources

Census and OPR records for Islay
Greg McEachron, Florida (private correspondence)
William M. MacDonald
Catherine Campbell, Fort William

Andrew MacEachern, Port Charlotte
Robert MacLellan, Ballygrant
Annie Anderson, Bowmore
Margaret Gray, Port Ellen

The MacArthurs

The MACARTHUR pipers of Skye, Ulva and Edinburgh are said, in persistent oral traditions in Mull, Skye and Islay, to have originated at Proaig, on the east coast of Islay, near to the headland known as Mac-Arthur's Head, to the south of Port Askaig.

It is not known exactly when MacArthur pipers, or perhaps a piper, left Proaig to settle in Skye, where they became hereditary pipers to MacDonald of Sleat. It was probably in the late 1690s or around 1700. They were given a holding of land at Hunglader, Kilmuir, in Trotternish. Around the same time, a MacArthur piper from Proaig is said to have settled in the island of Ulva, on the west side of Mull.

Keith Sanger thinks the MacArthurs were connected with the Campbells, and Frans Buisman said 'their spread over Islay and Mull seems to have occurred in the wake of the Campbell take-over of these islands', that is, during and after the 17th century. There is no certain evidence to support this view, other than the use of the Campbell name Archibald among later MacArthurs, and this is offset by the more frequent use of the MacDonald name Charles in MacArthur families. In Ulva, the name Archibald was probably introduced after marriages into the Lamonts: Archibald was a Lamont name. Writers such as Fionn (Henry Whyte) and one of the compilers of the Notices of Pipers were emphatic that the island MacArthurs had been hereditary pipers to the MacDonald Lords of the Isles, based at Dunyveg. Oral tradition in both Islay and Mull supports this.

Recent work on the DNA of Highland clans has shown that the MacArthurs of Lochaweside were indeed related to the Argyll Campbells, but that MacArthurs at Ardencaple, on the Gareloch, were not. This suggests that the MacArthur pipers of Islay, Skye and Ulva may not have been of Campbell descent. This is not conclusive, however, and a case could be made for either of the theories.

David Caldwell has drawn attention to a reference in the Exchequer Rolls of Scotland (xvii, 611–20) which indicates that MacDonalds who were MacIains from Ardnamurchan were in Islay in the 16th century. One of them, Allestar McKane, appears in the royal rental of 1541, as holding Proaig and Baleachdrach.

There are no records of Archibald used as a MacArthur name in Islay within the Proaig family: Charles, Neil, Alexander, John, yes, but no Archibald. Certainly the pattern makes more sense if the Mac-Arthur pipers in Islay were related to the MacDonalds, and it might explain why they went to Skye and Ulva, both MacDonald possessions, when they left Islay. The departure of two brothers (or cousins) from Proaig in the late 1690s might have been caused partly by trouble with Campbell landlords – but this is, of course, conjecture.

The earliest of the piping MacArthurs on record in Skye was Angus, said in the Notices of Pipers to have been known as Angus Dubh (Black-haired Angus). He is believed to have accompanied his MacDonald chief to the Battle of Sheriffmuir in 1715. His son was Charles, probably born around 1710, who became well known as a piobaireachd composer in the 18th century, and went with his chief to St Andrews and Edinburgh. This led to most of the family establishing itself in Edinburgh rather than Skye, though his son Donald remained at Hunglader. Charles died around 1780, and is buried in the graveyard at Peingowan, Kilmuir, Trotternish, close to Hunglader. When Charles was away in Edinburgh, Donald took over as the piping teacher in northern Skye, as we know from the Seafield (Grant) papers.

The earliest recorded MacArthur in Ulva, to the west of Mull, belongs to about the same time as Angus MacArthur, around 1700 or a little earlier, and it is possible that he and Angus were brothers who left home, seeking a better life in other islands. Both North Skye and Ulva seem to have been relatively prosperous at that time, both held by island MacDonalds, as Proaig had been, earlier in the 17th century.

There is a tradition that the piping MacArthurs in Ulva were descended from the Skye family; there is even an idea that the Ulva pipers moved from there to Skye – but this can easily be shown to be mistaken. Local tradition in Ulva and Mull rejects both of these theories, maintaining that the Ulva pipers came originally direct from Proaig in Islay (see below, Mull).

Keith Sanger, however, has shown that John MacArthur, known as 'the Professor', a nephew of the Skye Charles MacArthur and living in Edinburgh, had four sons, of whom two were Archibald, born 1779, and John, born 1785. These two seem to have been pipers to Mac-Donald of Staffa, and lived in Ulva. Though not conclusive proof, this suggests that the tradition of the Ulva MacArthurs being of the same family as those from Skye is correct – but there were undoubtedly Mac-Arthurs living in Ulva long before these two arrived, as we know from the Old Parish Registers (see below, Mull and Ulva).

Proaig is named in some of the charters of Dunyveg in the time of the MacDonalds. The name Proaig appears often enough between 1509 and 1614 to make it clear that the place did then belong to the MacDonalds, but apart from Allestar McKane (MacIain) in 1541 (see above), no tenants are named. In 1614 the name Proaig is found also in a charter of the Campbells of Cawdor, who were much involved in the struggle for the ownership of Islay.

The *Book of Islay* records a Charles MacArthur who in 1686 was granted the tenancy of Proaig, Paroch of Kildaltane, paying 'of silver rent and tynd silver jc pundis' (£90 Scots), and no rent in kind. We have no way of knowing if this was a renewal, or a new tenancy. This Charles was probably the same man whose gravestone is in Kildalton Church, decorated with a carving which appears to show his long gun, powder horn and hunting dog – but since the engraving is almost oblit-erated now, we have to rely on a drawing made in the late 19th century, and it may be that the drawer of the sketch was interpreting what he saw. Who knows, others might have seen a single-drone bagpipe. We have to accept, however, that this Charles MacArthur was probably a huntsman rather than a piper. He died in 1696. Was he the father of the two who left for Skye and Ulva? The fact that Angus named his eldest son Charles, and that the Ulva MacArthurs used the name Charles in the 18th century, suggests that he might have been.

Perhaps we may assume that Angus and his brother, possibly himself called Charles, left home when their father died. Did they leave because of their father's death? Perhaps there was trouble over the inheritance of the tenancy, leading to the departure of younger brothers from the family home – but this is guesswork. It was a common enough pattern elsewhere. The change of regime from MacDonald landlords to Camp-bell during the course of the 17th century may have been a factor in their decision to leave.

In 1722, a Rental for Kildalton Parish lists Proaig as being 'a town [farm] very beneficiall for pasturage, good for fatning and nurishing cattle'. No tenant is named. In the 18th century there was a drove road through the hills from Ballygrant to Proaig, where cattle were fattened before being shipped out to market on the mainland.

This estate Rental of 1722 does not name a tenant for Proaig, but has a note about deductions in the parish for Ministers' and Bishops' sala-ries, officers' and surgeons' fees, and 'to the pipers pention, £40'. Was this one piper, or more? And where? And, more to the point, who? The fact that the estate paid his pension (or their pensions) suggests that the laird had official pipers, or had had at least one.

The next Rentals, from 1733 and 1741, give the name of the Proaig tenant as Charles MacAlister of Tarbert. Which Tarbert was this? Kintyre, Jura, Gigha, Harris, Canna? The name MacAlister suggests he might have been a grazier from Kintyre, and he probably did not himself live at Proaig but sub-let it. There were still MacArthurs in Proaig at this time, possibly employed by Charles MacAlister.

The Rental of 1733 mentions deductions from the estate's income in either Jura or Kildalton, or both, for the salaries paid out to the schoolmaster, surgeon, piper and officers (estate or church?), totalling £22 for the year among the lot of them. It is interesting to find the piper listed among the professional men, and not ranked as a servant as he would have been in Victorian times – but, alas, he is not named. Note that there was only the one piper then.

There were MacArthurs at Proaig until the middle of the 18th century, but it is not known if any of them were pipers. The last of them on record in the Old Parish Register for Kildalton Parish was Neil MacArthur in Proaig who had a child baptised in 1761, but the child's name was lost when that page of the register was torn. After this, there were no entries written in the register until 1789. When registration was resumed, the MacArthurs had gone from Proaig, and the few Proaig entries are for births to other families. It seems that the house was used by estate shepherds, possibly seasonally. There is evidence that some families were there for at least part of the year, until around the 1930s. Today the place is deserted.

The Old Parish Register for Kildalton started in 1721, after the two pipers had departed for Skye and Ulva. It is quite badly damaged by corrosion and tearing, so that many of the names of children baptised have been lost. John MacArthur and his wife Margaret MacAlister had a child at Proaig in 1721 – was this John perhaps a nephew of Angus in Skye? The following year, Neil MacArthur, Proake (another brother?), had a daughter, Kirsten. In 1727, Alexander MacArthur and Kate Gillis in Proag had a son Patrick, and in 1728, a MacArthur whose first name has gone had a daughter Janet. John, Neil and Alexander are all names which appear in the family line of the Skye MacArthurs. Neil had a son John in 1730, and there were other families at Proaig, as Niel MacQuilkan had a son Neil there in 1737, and the wife of John Annis, a shepherd, had twin girls at Proaig in 1740.

Two other births were recorded at Proaig in 1796 and 1801, so there seems to have been continuous habitation there, at least in summer, even though the MacArthurs had gone. There were many other MacArthur families elsewhere in Kildalton and in all the other parishes in Islay. Whether the Proaig MacArthurs were still on the island or whether they had emigrated, we have no way of knowing, nor do we know if any pipers were among them. Angus Dubh in Skye is the first named MacArthur piper from Proaig, and we assume he was already a trained player when he left home. This suggests that the family he left behind had some pipers of reasonable standard, but this is all conjectural, from lack of evidence.

Access to Proaig today is by a rough track along the coast, and it cannot be reached by car. Vehicles designed for rough terrain are necessary, otherwise it must be approached on foot, or by boat. The track is indistinct in places, very rough and wet, even after a dry spell. Walkers should wear very strong footwear and be prepared to battle through deep bog and scrub. The approach is also infested with ticks, which eagerly welcome new blood as a change from sheep.

David Caldwell describes Proaig as 'a mid-19th-century shepherd's house and sheepfold, the single-storey cottage now abandoned and its roof collapsed. The complex stands on a platform adjacent to a shelving shingle beach, with the possible remains of an earlier house projecting at the back of the present one'. He gives a sketch of the ruined buildings.

It seems clear that the family of the piping MacArthurs remained at Proaig when Angus and his brother left around 1700, after the death of their father in 1696. Whether any of those still in Proaig at that time were pipers, we do not know, but Islay tradition associates the name MacArthur with piping, to this day.

Donald MacArthur

A 20th-century descendant of MacArthur pipers in Islay was DONALD MACARTHUR. He was born in Glasgow in 1919, but both of his parents were from Islay. He retained a strong loyalty to the island all his life, and counted himself an Islayman. It may be partly his reputation as a piper which leads islanders to think of the MacArthurs as a piping family, but there must have been others – and today Lindsay MacArthur has picked up the baton.

As a young child, Donald MacArthur moved with his family to Southbar, in Renfrewshire, and he attended Inchinnan Primary and Renfrew High School, later being employed by Renfrew County Council. In later life he was Establishment Officer with Strathclyde Region.

A photograph of his wedding to Marjorie Wishart, Paisley, with piper J.C. Weatherston in attendance, appeared in the *Oban Times* in 1946.

His first piping teacher was an Islayman, JOHN WOODROW, and then JOHN MACDONALD, also from Islay. When the cairn commemorating the Skye MacArthurs was unveiled at Duntulm Castle in Trotternish, Donald was invited to play at the ceremony.

He joined the Army in 1939 and saw active service in Europe. He seized the chance of tuition from Willie Ross in Edinburgh Castle, and as a result became Pipe Major in the Royal Scots Fusiliers.

Seumas MacNeill wrote: 'Although not a regular competitor, Donald was a splendid piper and was heavily involved in the piping societies in the West of Scotland. He was appointed Pipe Major to the Glasgow Islay Association and played at fifty-six of their annual gatherings. He was a highly respected member of the Glasgow Highland Club and each Friday afternoon in recent years he was to be found at the meetings of the Veteran Pipers Society which he enjoyed immensely.'

In July 1990, he had undertaken an engagement to play his pipes on the four mornings of the British Open Golf championship at St Andrews, but tragically he was involved in a car accident on his way there, in which he lost his life.

Sources

OS Map
Census records
Old Parish Registers Islay, Ulva, Mull
Notices of Pipers
Norman Newton, *Islay*
David H. Caldwell, *Islay, Jura and Colonsay*
David H. Caldwell, *Islay: The Land of the Lordship*
Gregory Smith, *The Book of Islay*
Jean MacDougall, *Highland Postbag*

Angus MacKay

Angus MacKay, Raasay, was one of the pipers to Duncan Davidson of Tulloch, near Dingwall, Ross-shire, from about 1831 to 1837. In 1835 he (or the Highland Society of London) announced in a prospectus that he was about to bring out his own collection of pipe music, scheduled for February 1836. It did not appear until two years later, the reason for the delay not being clear. Some accounts say he went from Drummond Castle, where his father had left him as piper in 1830, to go to Islay, but this overlooks Angus' time at Tulloch. It is not clear exactly when he left Drummond for Tulloch, but it must have been early in the 1830s.

There are discrepancies in the dates which seem to suggest that he was piper at both Drummond and Tulloch simultaneously. His link with Tulloch may have been on paper only, i.e. he may not have been there in person but may have been paid a retainer by Davidson of Tulloch, buying the prestige of having Angus on his books. There is, however, no precedent for this.

In 1837 Angus went to Islay as piper to Walter F. Campbell of Shawfield and Islay, and it was during his stay in Islay that he compiled his manuscript of pipe music, both piobaireachd and light music, the work which made such an impact on the piping world. It must have been written at Islay House, Bridgend (see above). It is now in the National Library of Scotland in Edinburgh, catalogued as NLS MSS 3753-4.

It is not known how much, if any, was committed to paper before he left Tulloch, but in view of the 1835 announcement, it seems likely that some of the work had been started, possibly only in outline. Angus had learned to write pipe music in staff notation when still a boy, probably taught how to do it by Eliza Ross at Raasay House, and he seems to have had access to the MacArthur-MacGregor manuscript when he was working on his own. He borrowed the Highland Society's copy, and failed to return it, so that it was among his papers, most of which were acquired after his death by his pupil, Michael MacCarfrae.

Nobody knows for certain how much encouragement Angus had from his laird in Islay, but tradition says Walter F. Campbell took him to Islay House in order to give him peace and quiet to complete the work. A later suggestion was made that it was chagrin at the many errors in the printing of his book which later drove Angus out of his mind, but Alistair Campsie has shown that his madness was the result of disease, syphilis affecting his brain.

In 1838, the Highland Society published a selection of the piobaireachd works he had learned from his father, entitled *A Collection of Ancient Piobaireachd* (possibly not his own choice of title), with a Preface now thought to have been written by James Logan. The influence of this book, and its successor, a collection of light music, is still felt today.

Angus was in Islay until 1840, and seems to have taught a number of local pupils, including Hugh Lindsay, Donald Galbraith, and possibly Donald MacIndeor. It is assumed that 1840 was the year that he composed his only piobaireachd work, *Farewell to the Laird of Islay*, the laird being Walter Frederick Campbell, father of J.F. Campbell, the folklorist who wrote a (very poor) booklet about Canntaireachd. Walter F. had employed John Campbell of Nether Lorne as his piper before Angus; among John's duties had been the role of 'piper-nurse' to the laird's son. He succeeded in steeping the boy in Gaelic cultural tradition, so that when he was sent to Eton he was a fluent Gaelic speaker and well versed in Celtic poetry, story, music and dance.

Angus MacKay left the service of Walter F. to go to Glengarry as piper to Lord Ward, an Englishman who had just bought the bankrupt Glengarry estates. This appointment did not last long, nor was Lord Ward long at Glengarry. By 1843, Angus' brother John had replaced him there as piper, but to yet another proprietor, and Angus took up an appointment as first piper to Queen Victoria. He moved south to live in Windsor, but in 1854 he succumbed to mental illness and had to be confined. He died in 1859.

Islay Pipers

ROBERT GALBRAITH was born in Falkirk, but came of an Islay family, and is believed to have been related to Donald Galbraith, pupil of Angus MacKay. Robert was a piper in the Black Watch who enlisted in 1853, one of five pipers in the regiment who came from Falkirk. He retired in 1876, after service in the Crimea, the Indian Mutiny and the Ashanti Wars of 1874–75.

DONALD MACINDEOR was one of a well-known piping family of the MacIndeors of Islay and Jura. In the Notices of Pipers he is called Dougald MacIndeor, but this is probably a misreading of the name Donald: in the 1841 Census an entry for Donald MacIndeor in Kilchoman is written above a name which has a big upward loop in the writing, and at first glance it looks as if that is the downward loop of a g in Dougald. Closer examination shows this to be mistaken. The name there is definitely Donald. Dougald is a name never recorded in the MacIndeor family records in Islay, but there are many of the name of Donald, and it is likely that Notices of Pipers had it wrong.

The Notices say that in 1847 Donald (Dougald) crossed with many from Islay to go to Inveraray for the visit of Queen Victoria. He seems to have been one of the 'tail' of J.F. Campbell of Islay, who, as a cousin of the Duke of Argyll, provided the Queen's bodyguard during the visit. Campbell's 'tail' was made up largely of men from Islay and Jura, dressed in pseudo-mediaeval uniforms and armed with halberds. Among them were, it is thought, the pipers Donald MacIndeor from Islay and Hugh Lindsay from Jura. Donald was given a new pipe for the occasion. The MacIndeors had an old pipe (with three drones, so not all that old); it was exhibited in the Inverness Exhibition in 1934.

Donald was a dancer as well as a piper – as were many pipers in those days – and the Notices say he both played and danced for the Queen. It is not entirely clear where he did this, but it may have been beside the Crinan Canal, in the pouring rain, on her way back from her holiday, in September. She had complained of the tedium of the locks on the canal, and pipers were brought in to entertain her at each lock.

There is evidence that some at least of the MacIndeor families in Islay had come there from Jura. There were not many of them and it is likely that they were all related. Some Islay people believe that they came from Kintyre, where there are still MacIndeor families (of various spellings), and we know that some were fine musicians. It seems likely that they came to Kintyre from Ireland, way back.

Keith Sanger and Alison Kinnaird in their book *Tree of Strings, Crann nan Teud* (1992) have an interesting discussion of the Dewar (MacIndeor) family. They quote a bond of man-rent dated 1561, signed by 'Donald Pypar McYndoir Pypar', at Strathfillan; he was agreeing to take Colin Campbell of Glenorchy as his adopted son, presumably a form of fosterage. The form of Donald's designation shows that he was a piper and also the son of a piper, and that this position was important enough to be mentioned in the document.

Keith Sanger goes on: 'Under Campbell patronage these MacIndeors appear to have spread west along Loch Aweside into Glassary' – and presumably they reached Kintyre, Islay and Jura. There was a family called Deoir who were the hereditary custodians of the bell-shrines in 6th-century chapels, including one at Kilmichael Glassary, but Keith Sanger thinks this may have been a different line of Deoirs, separate from those who came west from Loch Awe. Wherever the MacIndeors turn up, they seem to be associated with music, whether pipes, harp or bells.

The *Book of Islay* records a payment of £10 to Donald MacIndeor in 1649, for his expenses in travelling from Islay to Edinburgh and back, to fetch the laird's trunks. No other detail is given, and we are left wondering.

There are MacIndeors recorded in the oldest of the Islay registers, that of Kildalton and Oa, and we find them from 1726 until the present day – but they were never numerous. Alexander MacIndeor, born in 1795, and his wife Margaret, somewhat younger, were living in Conisby in 1871, among the piping MacEachern, Johnston and Mac-Intyre families. Alexander was previously living in Port Charlotte, and it may have been one of his (great?)grandchildren who married a piper in Jura, Neil Lindsay, the nephew of Hugh Lindsay from Lagg. Neil had returned to Jura after losing his livelihood in the San Francisco earthquake, and was living at Caigenhouse in Jura at the time of his marriage, probably around 1910 (see below, Jura).

The name MacIndeor appears with many spellings, from MacIndore to Dewar. The form MacInjore, used in 1804, is probably an approximation of the way it was pronounced.

Names which recur in the families are Duncan, Donald, Neil, James, Ronald, John and Angus – what we might think of as MacDonald names. The girls were Mary, Catherine, Ann, Isabel and Marion. There are no Margarets among the MacIndeors, and no Dougalds.

We have no way of knowing which of the MacIndeors recorded in Islay were pipers, apart from Donald in the middle of the 19th century, but island tradition insists that this was an old piping family.

Annie MacDiarmaid

Kildalton Parish was the birthplace of ANNIE MACDIARMAID who married Calum Piobaire MacPherson, from Skye and Laggan. She was probably born at Lagavullin.

Among the travelling folk of Scotland there is a story about Calum Piobaire, who was then living in Greenock. He visited a travellers' encampment somewhere in Renfrewshire, to join their pipers for a ceilidh, and there, they say, he saw a lovely young red-haired lassie, and was instantly desperate to marry her. He asked her family for her, and they stipulated that it must be a 'tinker' wedding, with the young couple leaping over the fire, hand in hand. This may be a bowdlerised version of the tradition: it has also been said that the ceremony involved both parties urinating into the same bucket, as a symbol of their union. This was a very old tradition among the travelling people, going back centuries.

In the Renfrewshire records there is a marriage, dated 3 October 1856, of Malcolm (Calum) MacPherson, whose age is given as twenty-one, and Ann McDiarmid, aged nineteen, who were married according to the forms of the Established Church of Scotland, in the Gaelic Church in Greenock. Ann's parents were John McDiarmid and his wife Marion Keith, Malcolm's were Angus MacPherson, Piper, and Euphemia MacLeod. Malcolm gave his occupation as Labourer. Soon after this, he was the piper on a Fisheries cutter, patrolling the west coast. He and his young family lived for a short time in Stornoway.

This official marriage does not necessarily mean that the story of the 'tinker' wedding is untrue. Both ceremonies could have taken place, the church wedding to validate or legalise the campfire marriage. The old Scots form of marriage by declaration before witnesses had been declared illegal in 1855.

Annie is sometimes described as being 'of Islay', but if she was indeed of the travelling folk, she cannot strictly speaking be counted as an Islay woman, even though she was born there: the travellers belonged to no single place but were constantly moving on.

One Islay tradition says that Calum Piobaire met his wife in Islay, when she was living at Lagavullin, in the south of the island, and that he had come over to see his dear friend Angus MacKay, then piper at Islay House. This does not seem likely as Calum was born in 1833 and Angus came to Islay House only four years later, and was gone by 1840. This same tradition says Calum's wife was called Bessie and belonged to an established Islay family, but this conflicts with the MacPherson versions and with that of the official records. Perhaps there has been a merging of traditions about another MacPherson piper and another girl.

Calum's son, Angus MacPherson of Inveran, said his father was taken to Islay by his piping teacher, Archibald Munro, and there he met Angus MacKay, but if so Calum must have been very young.

Annie MacDiarmaid was related to Elizabeth Stewart, the mother of G.S. MacLennan (the S. stands for Stewart). Both women had the reputation of being very musical themselves, both of them fine Gaelic singers, as are so many of that family. Calum's granddaughter, Phosa MacPherson, said that when Calum Piobaire was suffering from breathing difficulties – the result of a long-standing heart condition – he found it hard to blow while reaching up to his drones, and it was Annie who tuned his drones for him: she stood behind him while he blew, and she adjusted his tuning. She had an acute ear for the harmonics.

Annie is buried beside her husband in the churchyard at Laggan, near Newtonmore, Inverness-shire.

The Stewarts were well known as pipers. Pipe Major John Stewart of the Black Watch (Elizabeth's brother) was one of them, and George Stewart, the East Sutherland schools instructor, based in Golspie, is a descendant, as is James Stewart, from Banff, a Silver Medallist. There were several Stewart winners in the Prize Pipe competitions in Edinburgh, in the 19th century, all from this same Stewart family.

Sources

Census records
William Donaldson, *The Highland Pipe*

Alasdair MacLean
Jeannie Campbell, *Highland Bagpipe Makers*
George Stewart
Phosa MacPherson

John C. Johnston

There are records of Johnsons, Johnstons, Johnstones, Jonsons and
Jonstons, from the earliest Islay registers, going back to 1720. The
registrars made no distinction between the different spellings, and
the same man might be Johnson in one entry, Johnstone in the next.
The differences have no significance whatsoever, and were at the whim
of the person recording the event. The varying spellings could be the
result of the clerk's old age, or how drunk, deaf or tired he was, or
whether he was in a hurry to get to his dinner.

Names which recur through the generations of Johnstons were
John, Angus and Donald, with, later, Archie, Alexander and Malcolm. Ronald or Ranald was introduced in the 1790s. The Johnstons
were numerous, and spread all over the island, with concentrations
especially in Bowmore parish.

John C. Johnston of the City of Glasgow Police pipe band was born
in Islay, and was taught his piping there by one or more of the Mac-
Eachern brothers. The Johnstons were living in Conisby from 1871
on, alongside the MacEacherns, and the two families were linked
by marriage as early as 1843 – a child, Mary Johnston, was eight by
1851. It is likely that one of John C.'s grandmothers was a MacEachern of Conisby. He was also a cousin of Duncan MacIntyre, player of
exceptionally good light music in the 1930s, killed at El Alamein in the
Second World War. As far as is known, these Islay Johnstons were not
related to the piping Johnstones of Barra and Uist.

John C. Johnston's line can be traced back to 1791, in the Kilchoman
parish of Islay. They were shop-keepers and dyke-builders, but seem to
have been less deeply rooted in Kilchoman than were the MacEacherns,
leaving from time to time to take work on the mainland, but always
returning. John C.'s piping roots were certainly embedded in the Islay
tradition, and he was already a fine player when in his teens.

According to an account by Johnny Roidean (John MacDonald,
South Uist), John C. Johnston went over to Cowal Games as a teenaged
lad, and his playing was heard by Willie Gray, then Pipe Major of the
Police pipe band. Willie would not allow him to return to 'obscurity'
in Islay, but insisted on taking him to Glasgow, where he was enrolled

in the City of Glasgow Police, even though he was below the required age (and height).

This must have been in the late 1920s. The band included not only Willie Gray but the next Pipe Major, Johnnie Roidean himself, and other famous names such as Johnnie's brother Roddy Roidean, Charlie Scott, Philip Melville, Archie MacNab, Charlie MacEachern and John Garroway. Seumas MacNeill's tribute to John C., published in the *Piping Times* on his death in 1990, mentions that the talk at band practices was as much of piobaireachd as of band music. Willie Gray gave many of the band-players instruction in piobaireachd playing, including John Johnston, who proved to have a natural talent for the song in the tune, and 'first class fingers which produced one of the best Crunluaths heard this century'.

Johnnie Johnston's favourite piobaireachd work was *Mary's Praise*, which won him many prizes. So keen was he to play it that, so they say, he used to submit it in his list of tunes three times, under different titles: as the *MacLachlans' March*, its title in the Campbell Canntaireachd manuscript; as *Moladh Mairi*, the Gaelic name for it; and as *Mary's Praise for her Gift*, one of its English names. Whether the judges were deceived, knowing his sense of humour, is not on record. They would perhaps not understand Gaelic – but that is not beyond the bounds of possibility.

The *Piping Times* obituary tells how John Johnston would always spend his holidays in Islay, and on one occasion, when it was time to go back to Glasgow, he was piped down to the boat, with one of the island dignitaries carrying his cases. 'Brigadier Dudgeon, who was Inspector of Police for Scotland at the time, was on board, and he inquired of another passenger who this very important person might be. The passenger, an Islayman, was astounded to learn that somebody had never heard of John C. Johnston of Islay and the Glasgow Police, and proceeded to give John a major build-up. Once the boat left Port Askaig, Brigadier Dudgeon (in his own words) scraped up an acquaintance with this famous man, and they spent a large part of the journey in the bar, singing Gaelic songs and having the odd dram.

'At the next, and all subsequent inspections of the Glasgow Police, Brigadier Dudgeon insisted on going along the ranks of the band until he renewed acquaintance with Johnnie, which caused his schedule to be considerably put out of kilter.'

John Johnston taught at the College of Piping in Glasgow for thirty-five years without payment. One of his many pupils was Robert Richardson, who later became Pipe Major of the British Caledonian band. Robert came to the College as a somewhat badly taught player, and a year later, to his dismay, Johnnie entered him for an amateur competition, playing against a number of well known, accomplished youngsters. 'Don't worry', said Johnnie. 'You've got something they haven't. You've got me.'

John Johnston lost a foot in a car accident in 1973, but surmounted this disability without complaint. He died in July 1990.

Peter MacLeod composed a 2/4 March in four parts called *John C. Johnston (Glasgow Police)*.

See also DONALD U. JOHNSON, below

Dr J.C. Caird

Dr Colin Caird, born in Islay, was at the time of his death in 1990 the Honorary Vice President of the Piobaireachd Society, and was described as 'a distinguished player, an acknowledged authority on Ceol Mor, and a respected and popular judge'. Of him, the Notices of Pipers said: 'He was Pipe Major of the Royal Scottish Pipers' Society, 1922–25, and in his youth was a most talented player, quite on a level with the best competing professionals of his time'.

Dr Caird was one of a group of amateur pipers who were stalwarts of the Royal Scottish Pipers' Society, comprising himself, Charles MacTaggart, Ian C. Cameron and Frank Richardson. Colin's younger brother, Francis Caird, was almost his equal as a player, 'with the same wonderful fingers'.

As a young medic in Edinburgh, Colin was playing beautiful piobaireachd. He always regretted that he never had a course of lessons from John MacDonald, Inverness, but he had many meetings with him over the years, and John was 'always prepared to give me an hour or three of his time. He always treated me as if I were his equal, which was very flattering but quite misinformed.'

Colin Caird was taught by James Sutherland, Willie Ross and John MacDougall Gillies, so he had a solid grounding. His mother was musical, and his uncle was a singer. He followed his father, a surgeon, into the medical profession, but became a physician.

He was awarded the OBE for wartime services in the Royal Army Medical Corps as a lieutenant colonel. Of him, Frank Richardson wrote: 'I can imagine no one whom I would rather have as my doctor. He was most kindly and generous-hearted, and I cannot imagine him having an enemy. On the bench his views were balanced, fair and soundly based in deep knowledge. He won all the coveted prizes open to amateurs, and I have always considered him the leading amateur player of the 1920s and 1930s.'

Ian C. Cameron

The *Piping Times* for January 1991 published this account of Ian C. Cameron:

> The passing of Ian Cameron brought a sense of loss to his many friends throughout the piping world. His friendly rubicund features and his jolly manner made him a welcome presence at all our functions.
>
> Although a Gaelic-speaking Islay man, Ian was quite proud of the fact that he was born in Partick, once a village of its own but later absorbed into Glasgow. He was soon taken to Islay where he grew up, but his jig *The Partick Pipers* showed that he never forgot his birthplace.
>
> Ian's first feeling for the great music came when Willie Ross visited the island on one of his teaching missions for the Piobaireachd Society. With this inspiration he began competing, with at first moderate success, but later his inborn talent took him into the highest ranks.
>
> He left Islay and in due course graduated as a lawyer, which restricted his competing career a bit. During the war he served in the Argyll and Sutherland Highlanders and was wounded in action. For a long time thereafter he did not compete, but then he decided to have another shot at it and became one of the serious contenders once again. He never quite managed to win the coveted Gold Medal, but he came very close on many occasions. His excellent bagpipe, his feeling for the great music and his fine fingering were a delight to hear.
>
> He was a very fine composer and delighted in the production of eminently playable jigs particularly [see the list of tunes with Islay associations, above]. As a member of the General Committee of the Piobaireachd Society he gave ungrudging service and as a senior judge he was welcomed both at home and overseas for his clear decisions and kindly criticisms.

To this obituary, Frank Richardson added:

> I must be one of the few who can remember Ian Cameron as an upstanding young competitor, particularly successful in jig playing, with a crest of unruly red hair on which a Glengarry bonnet was perched. Perhaps Army service in the Argylls led him to the Balmoral bonnet which he more recently wore. As Intelligence Officer to the redoubtable Brigadier Lorne Campbell V.C., he was naturally much exposed to enemy fire, and carried a bullet or two in a wounded leg to the end of his life. He wrote the history of the 7th Argylls in the Second World War.

Ian and I were often passengers in one another's cars; and on the way to Falkirk in 1981, where we were to hear the results of a composing competition, I said I had been intrigued by one entry, evidently based on the *Laird of Anapool's Lament*. Much later, he told me that he himself had composed it.

While judging at Lochearnhead Games last summer (1990), Ian suffered a heart attack from which he did not manage to recover, passing away peacefully at a hospital in Edinburgh on 7 November. John D. Burgess, a close friend from boyhood, played at the committal.

Ian Cameron gave a talk entitled *Reminiscences* at the conference of the Piobaireachd Society in 1989. The following extracts are taken from that talk:

My piping goes back to 1919 when I was 9 years of age. I remember my beginnings very well. It so happened that my father and I were passing through the village of Bowmore in Islay one lovely summer evening when we heard the sound of bagpipes coming from a nearby house. My father then asked me if I wanted to learn the piano, the violin or the pipes, and as the setting was idyllic, I immediately said, the pipes. There and then we called at the house and I had my first lesson.

My teacher was a piper of the 8th Argylls called Nicol MacKay who had been taught by John MacDonald, Inverness. He was a very good all-round player and an excellent teacher. I still remember the first tunes he taught me, the slow march *Lord Lovat's Lament, The 92nd Gordon Highlanders March* and *Lord Panmure's March*. He also taught me my first piobaireachd – *The Lament for the Only Son* – a favourite of his. Around that time he also taught Charles D. MacTaggart.

Nicol MacKay died in 1922, and Willie Ross, who had come to teach in Islay in 1921 and 1922, was at the funeral.

Of course we were all looking forward to hearing the great Willie Ross. His method of teaching was unique. First, he wouldn't allow one to look at the book. He would play a tune on the chanter and one had to follow it as best one could. I must say, I found no difficulty in this method, for I had a good basic training from my previous teacher and also I was on fire to learn in these days. Of course, when I got home I referred to the book to see if I was playing it correctly. I think this is a very good method for it helps one to learn the tune quicker and also it makes one try to emulate one's teacher.

I learned far more from listening to Willie Ross playing than in any other way. The first piobaireachd he taught me was *Too Long In This Condition*, but when he left Islay, I wasn't satisfied with one or two piobaireachds, so I used to write to him for copies of other tunes, and by return would come *Corrienessan's Salute, The Blue Ribbon* and others. I admired him for this, for it seemed that nothing was too much trouble for him to help someone who was really interested.

I shall never forget listening to Willie Ross playing many strathspeys and reels without stopping. He was at the peak of his form in those early days and I would go so far as to say he was the best all-round player I have ever heard. His fingering was immaculate and his doublings were crystal clear and completely controlled. When he came on the platform, the pipes and he were one and in perfect unison.

Great as he was, however, he could develop faults like other humans. I remember he once devloped a skirl on low A when he performed the birl which he found difficult to rectify, just like a golfer who develops a slice or hook . . .

On one occasion when Willie was playing his strathspey and reel he turned his back on the judge, who happened to be Sheriff Grant of Rothiemurchus. The Sheriff wasn't going to be outdone, however, for he got up off his seat and went round to the other side of the platform to face Willie, to make sure that he didn't miss anything.

In the early 1920s it wasn't easy to get from Islay to, for example, the Northern Meeting because of the long and awkward journey, and I only managed it twice in these days. Pipers then were the poor relations of the present day affluent competing pipers. However, in 1922, when I was thirteen years of age and very keen, I managed my first visit. Piping was in the open, then. There was a March, Strathspey and Reel competition for boys under 18 which I was fortunate to win. Three years later in 1925 when I was about 16 years of age I managed to get to Inverness for the second time, and this time I got second in the Marches.

In 1926 I came to Edinburgh and went to the Castle for lessons every Thursday. On these occasions I met Willie Ross's mother who was very spruce and alert although she was well over 80 years of age at the time. Willie Ross had a flat in Crown Square at the Castle and my lessons took place in the attic above the main rooms. I remember his mother telling Willie Ross to bring me downstairs as she wanted to listen. I always remember Willie Ross's pipes were lower pitched than those of today and produced a beautiful mellow tone and were always perfectly in tune. He was such a great player when he was at his peak that I feel it is a pity he made records later on in life when he was long past his best and played far too fast, and, therefore, gives a wrong impression to posterity'. [Often in those days, recordings on 78 discs had to be speeded up in order to fit the tunes onto the record. Sometimes the player was asked to play faster, but sometimes playing at a normal tempo was re-recorded at greater speed, which gave a false impression of the pitch of the pipe. The quality of a pipe should not be judged by an early recording.]

I used to visit him in his latter days when he was in the Earl Haig Home in Edinburgh. I tried to dig up some information about his early contemporaries, but he became very emotional when all the memories came flooding back.

In 1927, Willie was away somewhere when I wanted some tuition in the Gold Medal tunes for that year, so John Wilson put me onto Roddy Campbell who lived at 42 Grove Street, off Fountainbridge, Edinburgh, at that time. Roddy used to come to my digs and I found him an excellent teacher. He was also a very good all-round player and an excellent composer, some of his tunes being *The Royal Scottish Pipers' Society, Loch Loskin* and *Cecily Ross*, just to mention only a few of his compositions.

Roddy Campbell was a pupil of Sandy Cameron [son of Donald] and he also had some lessons from Colin Cameron [Sandy's brother] who differed in some respects. So far as I can gather, Willie Ross was nearer to the Cameron style than the MacPherson style. Perhaps he took what he considered the best of both styles; whatever style it was, it served him well for he won eight clasps with it.

In *MacSwan of Roaig*, Roddy Campbell taught me to play the short Bs not only in the quick run-down in the second bar but also in the first. Of course, Brown and Nicol frowned on the short Bs, and I presume that John MacDonald, Inverness, did the same.

In *Mary MacLeod*, Roddy taught me to play exactly as per the Piobaireachd Society which was the way Sandy Cameron played it. However, Roddy Campbell preferred to play the high A instead of G in the second last bar in the third line of Var 1 Doubling. Sandy Cameron said either was permissible.

Roddy Campbell won the Oban Gold Medal in 1908 and the Oban Open in 1910. He was in delicate health for a number of years and in poor circumstances, and it appears he lost the will to live. He died in 1934 and is buried in Liberton Cemetery . . .

It has been said that nowadays there are far more good pipers, but fewer stars than there were in the 1920s. Pipers today play so much more slowly that it is well-nigh impossible to compare. Also, there is the thought that there is often a halo round the heads of some pipers who have long since passed away.

Pipes today are, of course, much higher pitched than in the 1920s and 1930s. I hope they won't go any higher. But there appears to be better maintenance today, for the reeds are better. It was quite something to get through a piobaireachd in the old days without the drones going off, but this is not so today. And there was no taping of the chanter before the war, and if F was sharp all one could do was lift the reed a bit and hope that the other notes didn't become flat in the process. It is seldom that one hears a bad pipe now, in a top class professional competition.

In the 1920s and 1930s I don't remember ever hearing anyone play
the ground after the end of a piobaireachd, but it is common practice
today [it was introduced by Mickey MacKay in 1946] . . .

Although I seldom went to Inverness before the war, I went more
often to Oban, which was nearer. I used to catch the 4.20 p.m. train at
the old Caley station in Edinburgh and when we got to Callander, the
Glasgow pipers joined us. From there on there was nothing but playing
pipes until we arrived in Oban shortly before 10 p.m. I particularly
remember John MacDonald of the Glasgow Police playing dozens of
hornpipes and jigs. The South Uist pipers were famous for jig playing in
these days and it was a jolt to listen to John MacDonald for he was then
at the peak of his form.

In 1933 I moved away from Edinburgh and it wasn't until after
the war that I returned. In the early 1950s I went to work and live in
Liverpool until 1963, when I returned to Scotland for good and started
to compete again, so you see I missed over 20 years when I didn't
compete at all.

Ian Cameron then spoke of memorable pipers and performances he
recalled:

Calum MacPherson [Calum Piobaire's grandson, Malcolm R.
MacPherson] playing *MacDougall's Gathering* to win the Gold Medal
at Oban in 1933. Calum was an excellent piobaireachd player, but not
so good in the light music.

. . . I remember Duncan MacIntyre playing *Delvinside* and *Charlie's
Welcome* at Oban before the war. It was an outstanding performance
and, of course, he won the Strathspeys and Reels that day. I knew
him well. He belonged to Islay, although he lived in Glasgow at that
time. On the outbreak of war he joined the 5/7th Gordons and Jimmie
MacGregor became his pipe major. Sadly, Duncan was killed at Alamein
in October 1942.

Robert Reid's playing of *In Praise of Morag*, or *Marion's Wailing* as
he always called it, impressed me. I heard him playing it at Cowal in
1925 for the first time. He had excellent fingers and his playing of the
Highland Wedding was also first class. His Strathspey and Reel playing
left much to be desired, however, for his timing of *The Ewie with the
Crooked Horn* was peculiarly irregular.

Archie MacNab was another first-class all-round player, his playing
of marches being particularly impressive.

Another well-known personality before the war was Peter MacLeod
junior, Partick. Peter used to come and stay with me in my digs in
Edinburgh for weekend piping sessions, and it was then that he and I
composed some of the tunes in the late John Wilson's Book 1.
Peter was a very fine player and his dexterity in fingering enabled

him to play almost anything. Both father and son were great
composers . . .

The talk then listed other personalities remembered by Ian Cameron:

J.D. MacDonald, Scots Guards, who came from Melness, in the north
   of Sutherland
Peter Bain, Scots Guards, from Portree
Sandy Thomson, the Camerons
Willie Barrie from Bute, who went to Vancouver
Owen MacNiven from Islay, later a headmaster in Nottingham
David Ross, originally from Rosehall, Sutherland, and later of
   Manchester and London [this may be the wrong way round: David
   Ross was brought up in London and married a Rosehall girl]
John and Roddy MacDonald, Glasgow Police
Dr Donald F. Ross, who returned from Ecuador and Liberia to
   become a doctor in England. He was killed in a road accident, and
   was buried in his native Lochgilphead

Ian heard John MacDonald, Inverness, only twice, and thought his
playing superb. Bob Brown and Bob Nicol were Ian's contemporaries,
and he thought them both very good players; in his view, Nicol was the
better of the two.

He heard G.S. MacLennan two or three times and was impressed by
his clear crisp fingering; but he was less impressed by his pipe, as his
drones sometimes went off during his playing of piobaireachd. 'Willie
Gray, Glasgow Police, was a well-known personality and a highly intelligent man who would talk for hours on the redundant A if you gave
him a chance.'

Other memories included the two Taylors, James and Willie,
J.B. Robertson of the Scots Guards, Hugh Kennedy from Tiree who
became a schoolmaster in Glasgow, Donald MacLean of the Seaforths
(Big Donald, from Lewis), and Donald MacLean from Oban (Wee
Donald) who also came to Glasgow, G.S. Allan who loved to tease
G.S. MacLennan, and Jimmie Sutherland in Edinburgh.

In the ranks of amateur piping, Ian recalled Dr Colin Caird, Gen-
eral Frank Richardson, Sir Douglas Ramsay, Dr J.C. Simpson, Neil
Ramsay, Charles D. MacTaggart, Rev. Dr Neil Ross, Col Jock Mac-
Donald from Skye, Archibald Campbell of Kilberry, Sheriff Grant of
Rothiemurchus, Major Bob Slater of the Argylls, Euan MacDiarmaid,
L. Balfour Paul, Innes Stuart and John Burgess senior.

The talk ended with two stories of himself on the bench. At one
of the Scottish Pipers' Society competitions, John Burgess senior was

playing, and Ian placed him third. His son, John D. Burgess, then aged eleven, was not pleased. On meeting Mrs Cameron next day, he said 'All the Argylls should have been shot.' Mrs Cameron replied 'A lot of them were, you know', to which John retorted 'But not the right ones.'

When the Highland Division was in Algeria in 1943, a composing competition was held, and Ian was one of the two judges. He gave first place to a march by Piper A. Williams of the Gordons – but it had no title. The other judge suggested *Mussolini's Downfall*, but the Divisional Commander did not like that. He sent for Piper Williams and asked him if he had been in Cairo, and he said he had. The General asked if he had also been in Tunis, and he had. 'Right', said the General, 'the title is *Cairo to Tunis*'. And that is its name to this day. Some think it should be the other way round.

Ian's brother DUNCAN CAMERON was also a piper.

In the discussion which followed the talk, a question was asked about teaching methods. Ian said Roddy Campbell taught him partly by singing, partly by playing the chanter, and he would also use the written music, but Willie Ross expected his pupils to pick up the tunes off his fingers – but that was the light music.

A 6/8 Jig, *Ian C. Cameron*, was composed by John Wilson.

Sources

Piping Times
Proceedings of the Piobaireachd Society Conference

Other Pipers Associated with Islay

DONALD MACDOUGALL from Islay was Pipe Major of the Lanark Rifles, and later of the 8th Battalion Scottish Rifles, piping instructor to the O.T.C. band of Kelvinside Academy in Glasgow. He was a pupil of John MacColl, and for twenty-six years was the manager of the pipes department of R.G. Lawrie Ltd. An article about him, and a photograph, appeared in the *Oban Times* in June 1938.

JAMES MACKILLOP (1874–1946) though not born in Islay made it his home for many years when he was Factor to Morrison of Islay (later Lord Margadale). MacKillop was described by Seton Gordon as 'a skilled piper'; Seton Gordon used to stay with the MacKillops when he was in Islay, after James had written to him about the Piob Bhreac (Speckled Pipe) at Dunvegan.

The Notices of Pipers describe MacKillop as 'one of the most distinguished amateur pipers of his time', a pupil of John MacDougall Gillies and a friend of General Thomason.

He became the Hon. Pipe Major of the Scottish Pipers' Society from 1900 to 1911, and was the first Hon. Secretary of the Piobaireachd Society, being a founder member in 1903.

He used to play piobaireachd on the organ, and was a good musician, and according to the Notices was much in demand as a judge before 1914. After holding a commission in the Scottish Horse for some time, he retired to Islay after the First World War. He died in Edinburgh in 1946.

c.d. (CHARLIE) MACTAGGART was an Islay man, who had been taught there by Nicol MacKay. When he died in 1990, his friend Frank Richardson wrote in the *Piping Times*:

> I met Charlie when we were members of our respective schools' pipe bands; but first got to know him at the Scottish Pipers' Society in the 1920s. I knew he was a native of Islay, but did not then realise what a pull that gave to a budding champion piper; and in due course he won all the major prizes open to amateurs, many times. For many years he willingly served as a judge at games both great and small. No wonder so many pipers attended his funeral, where the piper was the great – the very great – Donald MacPherson.
>
> When the Army posted me to Perth, I shared digs twice with Charlie. In our early days he sometimes seemed to enjoy playing the part of the simple man of Islay, quizzically observing the ways of mainland folk, both Highland and Lowland; but he was, of course, an astute observer of the social scene and a very shrewd man of affairs. Visiting New York for the first time his unmistakable Scottish appearance – bristling moustache, crotal overcoat and all – caught the eye of the guide at the top of the Empire State Building, to whose question, broadcast on the radio, Charlie gave his name as Mister MacTavish. Asked what brought him to the United States, he said that he had come to introduce them to Scotland's finest product, the Famous Grouse whisky, of Matthew Gloag, in Perth. Before they could pull the plug, he had scored thousands of dollars worth of free advertising. To crown the story, his boss, old Matthew Gloag, was far from delighted by such sharp practice – not quite the thing for Perth gentlemen of business.
>
> A groggy knee, legacy of schoolboy stardom in Rugby football, kept him off that field of sporting activity (and I think bothered him during his wartime service with the R.A.F.) but he enjoyed, and did well in, others, including golf, shooting and fishing. These pursuits and his business interests made him a well-known figure in the county and city where he had made his home. Perth has lost a useful and popular citizen.

Another Islay Man, Ian C. Cameron, composed a four-part reel for his friend, entitled *Charles D. MacTaggart*.

In Islay I was told of a tune made by Captain Alexander MacTaggart, called *The 8th Argylls' Farewell to Charlie MacTaggart*, but I think this was a different man of the same name.

DONALD U. JOHNSTON was described in the *Piping Times* in 1997 as 'a true Gael, proud of his Islay background and heritage, yet modest about his remarkable talents and immeasurable contribution to the language and music of Gaeldom'.

The tribute continues: 'At the request of the Govan Gaelic Choir, Angus Lawrie composed a slow air *Donald U. Johnston* in affectionate memory of its longest serving member. He was a founder member of the choir in 1929, active as a leading chorister until his death in 1988.' This slow air was published in the *Piping Times* in May 1997.

'Donald also had a great love of piping and of fiddle music. He was a member of the Bearsden Fiddlers Association and served as piper for Govan Choir and the Glasgow Islay Association. He was also deeply involved in the Glasgow Gaelic Drama Association both as a prolific playwright and as a producer. A man of many talents.'

In the First World War an Islay piper called PETER MACNIVEN was killed fighting in the Dardanelles, 'in a gallant attack on the Turkish forts'. He was described in the *Oban Times* as being 'as modest, intelligent, kindly and gentle a lad as ever left Islay'. It is thought that he was an uncle, or possibly the father, of Owen MacNiven. He belonged to Conisby.

PIPE MAJOR WILLIAM GRAY of the Govan and later the Glasgow Police Pipe Bands was married to an Islay girl called MacTaggart, and for some years they had a house in Charlotte Street, Port Ellen, which they visited regularly in the summer months. They had to give it up when Mrs Gray's mother became ill, and they moved to Cardross, near Dumbarton. This was Willie Gray's first wife. His daughter-in-law, Mrs Margaret Gray, widow of his son Alasdair, is a native of Islay, and when in her eighties was living in Port Ellen (2003).

MALCOLM MACLEAN CURRIE from Islay lived for many years in Glasgow where he was one of the officials running the Scottish Pipers Asociation (SPA) competitions in the 1930s. Andrew MacNeill of Oransay remembered him as being 'short and stout with a large moustache', and that he kept calling Andrew 'Mr Magneill'. Bob MacFie also recalled him at SPA functions, when Bob was a boy who held him in considerable awe; Bob said 'the club secretary, Malcolm Currie, and our pipey, Archie MacPhedran, would have frightened the devil himself'.

In 1995, a letter to the *Piping Times* from Bill Jones, Placentia, California, said:

> As a boy I recall hearing about a wonderful tool invented and patented by the late Malcolm Currie for the purpose of reaming a pipe chanter inside and outside simultaneously, so that both diameters were absolutely concentric with each other. I had not seen a product of this tool until coming to Los Angeles prior to the Second World War. It was there that I met an old ex-Cameron piper of Boer War vintage, and a fine player, who had a pipe chanter done on Malcolm Currie's reamer. This chanter was slightly sharper than the prevailing key of A Major pitch of other makers of that time. In addition to the accuracy of its scale the tone quality was excellent. Every note was resonant with the drones in that way we all dream of accomplishing with our own instruments.
>
> A question now arises: does this special tool of Currie's still exist, and if so, is it on public display? Perhaps this might stir up a little interest among some of the old timers who might recall something of this invention and what became of it.

It is not clear if this Malcolm Currie was the same as the one who ran the SPA in the 1930s, but it seems likely that it was. Bill Jones' appeal for information was not successful, as nobody seems to have heard of the Currie reamer. If its design was indeed patented, surely it could be traced?

Duncan MacIntyre

DUNCAN MACINTYRE was born in Islay but went to live in Glasgow. He was a cousin of John C. Johnston (see above). His father was a keen piper who brought up his seven children to be players and made their Partick home a centre for gatherings of pipers. The MacIntyres belonged to Port Ellen, where Iain MacIntyre is continuing the family piping tradition, but there was also a branch of the family at Conisby. Three MacEacherns in the generation of the grandfather of the five piping brothers were married to MacIntyres.

Duncan was a close friend of 'Wee Donald' MacLean from Oban. They had first met in 1931, and were 'almost like brothers' until the outbreak of war in 1939. During the 1930s they both served as stewards and pipers on board Atlantic liners of the Donaldson line, sailing between Glasgow and Montreal; from 1935, Duncan, Wee Donald and Peter MacLeod junior were all on the *Athenia*, playing in a small pipe band run by the company on board the ship, and enjoying 'some grand piping nights together after work was over'. Peter MacLeod commemorated these with two compositions, both four-part reels, *Duncan MacIntyre* (RMS *Athenia*) and *Donald MacLean* (RMS *Athenia*).

Duncan was an excellent player of light music, impressing John MacColl and other eminent judges. He won the Strathspey and Reel at Inverness in 1937, and 'his performances at the Scottish Pipers' competitions in Glasgow used to bring him a standing ovation'.

When Duncan went to Archie MacNeill for lessons, Archie had to turn him away, saying he could see no way of improving his playing.

Shortly before the outbreak of war he joined the Glasgow Transport Pipe Band, but was not long with them before he enlisted in the Black Watch (Ian C. Cameron gave his regiment as the 5th/7th Gordons; see above) and he was sent overseas with the Highland Division. His obituary in the *Piping Times* says he was a small man, about five foot six in height, and as a piper was 'practically a non-combatant'. He did not accept this, and at the battle of El Alamein in North Africa, he led his battalion into the fray, playing his pipes all the way. He was hit several times, and in the end he was killed, 'but not before he had inspired all within earshot with the sound of his pipes. In the morning he was found dead, lying in the sand with his pipes still under his arm. He was twenty-eight years of age'.

He was recommended for the Victoria Cross, though the award of the medal was never made. His heroism was long remembered, and after the war the pipe band of Glasgow Transport presented the SPA with the Monteith Rose Bowl in Duncan's memory. It is a trophy awarded for the Strathspey and Reel competition, and 'those who compete for it should appreciate that they are helping to commemorate one of the greatest light music players of all time' (*Piping Times* 1992, on the fiftieth anniversary of the Battle of Alamein).

A piper who taught many youngsters to play in the 1940s was ALASDAIR LOGAN. He gave weekly lessons at the Lagavullin Distillery. Among his pupils was JAMES MATHESON, whose father was working in Islay for a short time. On leaving the island, the boy eventually gave up piping, and became well-known as a Gaelic singer, living in Newtonmore. His son is the piper NIALL MATHESON, holder of both the Gold Medals.

NEIL MACAFFUR aged seventy-five is named in the 1841 Census, where he is described as a Piper, the only one who claimed it as his occupation in a large family of MacAffurs. Ten years later, however, DUNCAN MACAFFUR, a widower of eighty, is described as a Piper; possibly he was Neil's brother.

ANGUS MACAFFER from Port Ellen was a piper in a family of MacAffer players long established in Islay. Angus was taught by Jimmy Center and by Duncan MacLennan in this country, before he emigrated to Australia. There he became a piping teacher of high reputation, as well as a respected judge, and he was a close friend of Hugh Fraser, son of Simon Fraser. He and Hugh used to drive to the Games 'singing piobaireachd and talking piobaireachd' as they went.

Angus' son is ALASDAIR MACAFFER, who returned to this country from Australia, and became the schools piping instructor in Inverness. His three daughters are good players, trained by their father and winning prizes in both junior and senior competitions. The Inverness Schools Pipe Band had many successes under Alasdair's leadership.

CALUM MACAFFER was well known as Pipe Major of the Islay Pipe Band in the 1950s. He had a large and ancient sword, made by the MacEachern swordsmiths, possibly back in Kintyre.

Another Islayman who had to leave home to make his living was NEIL WOODROW, a fine piper who lived in Lochgilphead, and worked in the County Buildings there. He was in great demand to play at dances in Argyll, and one of his favourite tunes was *Mrs MacDonald of Dunach*, which he played as a polka, for the Canadian Barn Dance. He was related to JOHN WOODROW, who taught Donald MacArthur (see above).

DONALD CURRIE: in 1914 a photograph was taken of the Pipes and Drums of the 3rd/6th Argylls, on the platform of one of the railway stations in Paisley, which was decorated with flags and bunting for the occasion. It is not clear what the occasion was, possibly the battalion's departure to the First World War. The Pipe Major was Donald Currie from Islay.

LILY MACDOUGALL, living in a house beside the water at Caol Ila, just north of Port Askaig, was a MacEachern by birth, but said she was not related to the Conisby family of MacEacherns. She was born at Finlaggan in 1916, and as a girl was determined to learn to play the pipes. Being a female was a considerable handicap in those days: Katie MacEachern in Conisby had similar problems, but she had the advantage of daily contact with piping, and was able to learn from her father and brothers, whether they liked it or not.

Lily's family were not pipers, and she had to find a teacher. A local player, DONALD MACPHEE, agreed to take her as a pupil, but he suffered from tuberculosis, so badly that after several courses of treatment on the mainland, he was told he was incurable, and sent home to Islay to die. He had no intention of dying, however, and sought his own remedy by consulting a herbalist. This improved his health, but he was warned that he must not let himself become chilled through, or soaked with cold water.

One day, he was walking home from Ballygrant, through woods and fields, when he was caught in a sudden downpour. Cold and wet, he struggled on in the wind and rain, but finally fell, exhausted. When he did not return home, his family went looking for him, and noticed a herd of cows standing round something. On investigation, this turned out to be Donald, lying on the ground. The doctor said it was the warm breath and body heat of the cows that had saved his life. He lived to a ripe old age, incurable or not, and he taught Lily her piping.

She also went to Willie Ross in Islay House, and thoroughly enjoyed the lessons, though she found him a hard task-master. She was grateful to him for stopping the boys from bullying her when they tried to oust her, as a mere girl, from the piping. She competed at Cowal and Oban, which must have taken some courage for an island lassie in those days – but she said some of the male players were kind and encouraging, though others gave her the cold shoulder. She named Angus J. MacLellan in particular as being good to her.

As she grew up, she found herself in demand as a piper at weddings, and on ceremonial occasions. This caused some acrimony from male pipers who felt they had been pushed aside.

Lily had three sets of pipes, including one procured for her by Willie Ross from Robert Reid. She kept a letter from Willie, about this transaction, dated 1939. Her pipes had Henderson drones and a Hardy chanter; they were silver-mounted, with a thistle design on the mounts. Having three pipes, she felt guilty when she read of an appeal by a young piper who had none, so she gave away the pipe she had obtained through Willie Ross.

A woman of boundless creative energy, Lily, in 2003 nearly ninety, no longer played the full pipe, but she felt she needed an outlet, so she taught herself to paint, in both oils and watercolour. Self-taught ('it's just a matter of commonsense, really'), she produces landscapes and still-life paintings, including beautiful flower pictures. She has the work in hand set up on an easel in her bedroom, where she can see it as she lies in bed; she studies it, noting the faults and working out how she might rectify them. Her paintings sell well, for prices which surprise her.

This was not enough artistic output for Lily. She also writes poems and songs, and composes music, including pipe tunes – and just to fill any gaps in her day, she was writing her life-story. Lily is an amazing woman, friendly and enthusiastic, with the energy of a person half her age. Rumour has it that, in her nineties, she was picked up for speeding.

She was delighted when one of her line married a descendant of Willie Ross, her former teacher. Willie's grand-daughter Lesley Alexander was equally pleased to have fresh piping genes brought into the family.

OWEN MACNIVEN, who came from Islay and never forgot his roots, became a teacher in England and was a headmaster in Nottingham. He was an important influence on piping in England.

A man of forthright views who did not hesitate to state his opinions, he was a devoted pupil of Robert Reid and an adherent to the style of John MacDougall Gillies and the Camerons. He felt particularly strongly about a setting of *The Earl of Seaforth's Salute* as taught by John MacDonald, Inverness, which was timed quite differently and was described by Owen MacNiven as 'a monstrosity'. John MacDonald was teaching the Piobaireachd Society settings to pupils about to enter competitions, and many regarded these with disapproval. Certainly the setting of the *Earl of Seaforth* played by Owen MacNiven seems to make more sense, with lovely patterns which have been lost in the modern approach. It is thought that John MacDonald taught the setting he thought the Piobaireachd Society judges wanted to hear, rather than his own preference.

DOUGIE FERGUSON was born in Islay, and is sometimes referred to as being 'from Islay and Kirkintilloch'. In 2003 he was living in Lochgilphead, where he was a leading figure on the piping scene. When at Kirkintilloch he worked in Glasgow, in Grainger and Campbell's pipe-making shop, and was known as 'a great character'. He was a pupil of Donald MacLeod, who taught him the art of circular breathing. Dougie passed this on to Blind Archie MacNeill.

Dougie himself taught a number of distiguished pupils, including Jim Motherwell, the Queen's piper, and John Patrick. It was Dougie who played the lament at the funeral of Neil MacEachern in 1982.

In Lochgilphead in 2003 he would not speak of his piping days, as it roused too many memories. He is remembered in Islay with particular affection, especially by the Highland dancers for whom he played exceptionally well. He is esteemed also by the Islay folk as a 'character', a worthy who enriched their lives and brought colour to the humdrum business of ordinary life. He would have been surprised by the warmth with which he is recalled in his native island.

Marching in Islay

In 1994 Seumas MacNeill reported that he was once discussing the problems of teaching young boys to march while playing. He happened to mention to Robert Reid a particularly good march player called Carmichael, a young lad who just could not put his feet down on the strong beat while he was playing. Seumas asked Robert Reid for his advice. Reid looked at him and said 'Does he come from Islay?' Seumas said both his parents were from Islay. 'Ah well then,' said Robert Reid, 'that explains it. It's a lost cause. Nobody from Islay can march properly.'

[Before the hate-mail pours in from the west, note that it was Robert Reid who said this, not myself.]

Tuition in Islay

In 2011, the *Piping Times* reported that the Argyll Piping Trust has handed over twelve sets of McCallum bagpipes to promising young players in the county. They were paid for by a £10,000 grant from the Awards for All scheme. Four of the pipes went to Islay youngsters, pupils of the new tutor, JAMES CARRUTHERS.

I am conscious of the richness of piping tradition in Islay, and I know that I must have left out important figures in this account. I would be grateful for any information and corrections which should be addressed to me, by post, please, c/o the publishers.

Sources

Piping Times
Notices of Pipers
Oban Times
Bob MacFie
Niall Matheson
James Jackson
Dr Barrie Orme
Lily MacDougall
John Don Mackenzie

A Code of Conduct for Stewards at the Games

[Some time ago the *Piping Times* published a Code of Practice for Judges, issued by the Joint Committee on judging, advising them on conduct recommended. It seemed a little unrealistic to many of us: if we never allow them to sit in judgement on their own pupils or relatives, there will be no piping at the Games, as we will have no judges left, especially in the north where everyone is related to everyone else and is only teaching young Jimmy to oblige his grandad, a cousin of the judge . . . The following Code of Conduct for Stewards aims to be more down-to-earth.]

Try to arrive first at the piping platform, looking eager, in order to encourage the rest. You may find a whey-faced piper who has been there since 5.30, having slept overnight in his car. Give him the freedom of your coffee flask and tell him where he can have a wash, a shave and some breakfast. This is all the encouragement he needs, as he must be pretty keen already.

If you find the judges' shelter completely unfurnished, do not ask if there are any tables left in the store-shed; if there are, they will have only two-and-a-half legs. The steward should find a strong helper and liberate a clean solid table and comfortable chairs from the V.I.P.s' tent. It is advisable to despatch a junior with a complicated query for the Games Secretary during this operation.

When starting the list of competitors, be prepared for latecomers. Fit them in unobtrusively – the easiest way is to list only those who have arrived, regardless of who phoned at a quarter past twelve last night to ask you to put their name down as they were *definitely* coming at ten-thirty; then have the draw, and slot any latecomers in so that each will appear just before a friendly and agreeable player who won't make a fuss. You may want to consult the known trouble-makers on your list before doing this – the CPA rules say you have to have the consent of a majority of the players present, so ask their advice. It is essential to keep it all good-natured; if necessary give the impression that the latecomers had to play in the band-parade through the town, even if they did not (no need to lie, just say 'We have to allow for the band-players, you know').

As you take the names, make a mental note of which player

(a) is married to the sister of the divorced wife of a cousin of one of the judges;

(b) is a pupil of one of the judges, stayed at his house overnight and drove him to the Games;

(c) once played alongside one of the judges in the Glasgow Police Pipe Band;

(d) used to be a pupil of one of the judges, but changed teachers without explanation;

(e) was sold a duff pipe by one of the judges six years ago, but never mentioned it to him;

(f) is the grandson of a piper that beat one of the judges at Oban in 1954.

One of the steward's duties is to intimate gently to the bench that any or all of the above are common knowledge, and to allude, but only obliquely, to the stramash which ensued when a newspaper reporter took up the matter of judicial bias. A casual mention of the *West Highland Free Press* may be helpful. Worth a try, anyway.

When writing out the Order of Play for public display, it is customary to give army pipers their rank; give the title of Dr to medical doctors – you never know when you might need one – but not to mere PhDs. Any other titles may be ignored, whether Sir, Mrs, or the Rev. Places of domicile should be added. The steward obviously prefers those who come from Moy or Luss to those from Wester Achiltibuie, especially when the weather is cold and fingers numb. Note that 'USA' is permissible for someone who lives in Boston, Massachusetts or Pittsburgh, Pennsylvania. If a player has been unpleasant or uncooperative, just spell his name wrong.

It is not advisable to allow anyone to sit with the judges, as it unnerves the players (mutters of 'Whoozzat boogger? Whassee there for?'). Especially avoid letting players' teachers, friends, agents or (above all) fathers sit in or beside the shelter and attempt to influence the judgments. Not for nothing the Gaelic saying 'fussy as a dancer's mother, aggrieved as a piper's father'. Note that there is always an inverse ratio between the extent of a father's knowledge of the music and the intensity of his rage. Judges should be shielded from paternal onslaught.

On no account should a foreign visitor be allowed to join the bench, even if she is French and pouts prettily, weeshing only to lairn of ze muzeek. What she really wants is a wee flirt with the judges and shelter from the cold wind, but she interferes seriously with the judges' concentration. This may seem a severe attitude, but they are not there to enjoy themselves.

A steward cannot be expected to prevent spectators from standing beside the platform eating hot chips, even though it makes the pipers drool; after all, most of them have a water trap. Just be thankful if Chippie Man throws his Jack Russell a morsel when it is howling along with *Donald of Laggan*. Every endeavour should be made, however, to stop photographers from pointing a camera into the player's face (or up his kilt) and releasing a huge flash. It makes the pipers think they have been struck by lightning.

Do not let Belgian film-makers climb on the platform to interview a piper already grappling with *Donald Duaghal*; nor should well-meaning ladies be allowed to sell the judges raffle tickets in the middle of *MacCrimmon's Sweetheart*. Family picnics are not permitted on the platform while the piper is walking on it, even if the grass is wet.

A steward should discourage a Gaelic-speaking piper from addressing the judges and presenting his tunes in that language. If they understand him, his fellow pipers will accuse him (rightly) of trying to curry favour; if they don't, all parties look foolish. Things may become complicated if only one of the judges is a Gaelic speaker. Better to avoid the tangle altogether.

In case the judges accept the drams pressed on them by the Chieftain of the Games, the steward should have a half-full bottle of Irn Bru to hand, to put on the table so that passers-by will think they are sampling Scotland's other drink. This protects their good name from attacks by the CPA.

If the judges are really well up in years and/or alcohol, the steward should be ready to keep them on the right lines, indicating tactfully that *Glengarry's March* is the same as *Cill Chriosd*, and that three pipers in succession have already played *MacFarlane's Gathering*. If there are more than four MacKays playing that day, use your discretion about pointing out that one of them is a lassie. There are some judges who have never been known to give a prize to a girl: the difference should then not be stressed and it is to be hoped they did not notice. If a judge says 'Are you a lesbian?' to a female competitor, pretend you didn't hear (if she has plenty of spirit, she will reply 'Oh, I thought it was yourself that was gay' – but if she complains to you, refer her to the Games Secretary).

No direct comment should be made if the steward hears a judge tell a player that he might have been in the list if his D hadn't been so sharp, when both player and steward know there was no D in his tune; if the player doesn't mention it, neither should the steward, but a remark within earshot of the other judge, later that afternoon, may be allowed. Don't go in with both feet, saying loudly 'Surely even he knows there's no D in that tune', but approach with subtlety, sowing doubt. Try a comment such as 'His pipe *seemed* OK – difficult to tell, in that tune', so that the judges begin to wonder what you mean and have to look it up.

The steward should keep an eye open for the approach of a breathless committee member dashing across the field to silence the performing piper when the Chieftain is beginning his speech. Everyone else knows that the performer must never be stopped in full flow unless the platform is on fire, but committee members always have their priorities wrong. Wrestle him to the ground if necessary, or threaten him with the local press, but do not let him pass.

The march-past of the local pipe band should be regarded as a natural hazard of the Games. It is not easy to play the *Bealach nam Brog* when a band of seven pipers, more or less together, is wandering by, telling everyone that *The Battle Is O'er,* but it can be done, by an experienced player. *Mary MacLeod* sounds quite good accompanied by *Farewell to the Creeks*; it is almost like seconds, especially if they all start at the same time. But with a nervous youngster it is advisable to warn him while still tuning that the band will be approaching, and he had better wait. It will then be held up for twenty minutes, during which the poor boy goes to pieces and his pipe goes irreparably out.

If on a stormy day the shelter is blown over with the judges inside, there is an established procedure. If they are roaring in the wreckage, assume they are unharmed and rescue their piping books first; if they are silent but moving, begin to pick debris from around them, and send for hot sweet tea; if they are prone and silent, send an urgent message to the Secretary and put the responsibility on him. There will be no shortage of helpers, but try to restrain the over-enthusiastic, as judges are scarce. Do not administer alcohol, not to the victims, anyway. Most judges survive this experience, shaken but unscathed. It does not usually affect their judgement, as far as one can tell.

Overseas players should always be given special treatment, and care devoted to making sure they are supplied with local knowledge such as the whereabouts of the Gents, what the player before them on the list looks like, and who is likely to break down early. They will find their own way to the Beer Tent.

In the event of any racist or xenophobic remarks from the bench, it is the steward's duty to make sure the foreign player is well out of earshot. If by unavoidable mischance a judge addresses an insulting remark directly to an overseas player, the steward should stand by with consolation for the innocent German lad, who will be quite upset, or with soothing words for the raging New Zealander – and how they do rage. (Funny how these foreign types have no sense of humour; surely they should laugh happily when addressed as arrogant Krauts or ignorant colonials, and told they are not welcome.)

In mid-afternoon the steward should offer to fetch the judges tea and hot doughnuts, or cold drinks and ice cream, depending on the weather, usually the former. This is not for their gratification but to keep their minds on the job and prevent their attention wandering to the caber-tossers in the ring. It also stops them singing along with the piper, slightly off-key, making him think his drones are going out. Accept that nothing, not even a doughnut, will deter them from telling each other jokes during the *Lament for the Children*. The steward should not feel this as failure.

A steward should never give in to the temptation to award the prizes, however much the judges may beg. Strict impartiality must be observed – unless they are proposing to give second place to the one who broke down in the Taorluath Singling. In that case, ask gently which of the two MacKenzies was that . . .? Pretend that it is yourself who is confused, and ask for clarification, so that no feelings are hurt.

When the judges have written out the results list, the steward should not take it to the Secretary's tent until the remaining three pipers have played. It does tend to vex a fellow if, in full flow with the *Earl of Antrim,* he hears the tannoy loudly announcing who has won. So hang on to the list until all have duly played.

On reading through the list the steward should make no verbal comment, but a faint smile or a raised eyebrow is permissible, or (in extreme cases only) a look of blank astonishment. It is not a good idea to exclaim 'Jesus *Christ*!!!' on seeing who has come first. The pipers will do that for you.

The main duty of a steward is to whizz them through. A rate of four-and-a-half piobaireachd to the hour is the ideal, if the list is long; the secret is to know that the next man is tuning behind the ladies' toilets, and to set off during the Crunluath Doubling to find him, and have him ready to step forward as the Urlar Repeat peters out. When the list is very short, however, the aim is to spin out the piping, and you have to allow extra-long intervals between tunes: encourage the judges to visit the Gents, preferably at a distance across the field. Obviously this will not fill all the intervals, so be ready to ask intelligent questions about the last tune played, or unleash a spate of reminiscence by enquiring about their memories of previous Games on this ground. This will make the piping last indefinitely.

The MSR is obviously over more briskly, seven or eight p.h. is the norm, allowing for the odd break-down, and as for Jigs, seventeen of them should take seventeen minutes, if you are a good runner. Keep it all moving, or you'll be there until midnight, with the floodlights on (if you are in luck), and the music echoing eerily across the empty ground . . .

[The above may perhaps seem unkind to judges, and will give offence to those who regard all judges as sacred, worrying about the dignity of the bench. It is, however, based entirely on actual happenings, spread over some twenty years. It is not directed at the majority of judges, who are respected and kindly, full of integrity, wisdom and boundless knowledge. They tell you interesting things about the music, and it is a pleasure and privilege for a steward to serve them, to be allowed to cover their books with plastic sheets against the rain, to put warm rugs round their knees, or to supply them with sun-block. I salute them, and thank them for treating their steward with consideration, making the day an enjoyable experience.]

Jura

Jura is a long, narrow, mountainous island lying to the north-east of Islay, separated from it by a narrow channel, the Sound of Islay. Jura is reached by a short car-ferry trip from Port Askaig, in Islay, which takes about five minutes.

Tunes Associated with Jura

The Bens of Jura, otherwise known as *The Road to the Isles*, by John MacLellan, Dunoon 2/4 M 2. It has other names, given to it by different regiments in the army: *The Highland Brigade's March to Heilbron, The 71st's Farewell to Dover, The Burning Sands of Egypt* and *The Sands of Cairo*. The title given by the composer was *The Bens of Jura*.

The Bonnie Isle of Jura, by M. Darroch/J. MacFadyen 6/8 SA 2

Corrievrechan (sic) *Lullaby*, by Donald MacLeod P 5. Strictly speaking, the name of the whirlpool ot the north end of Jura is Corrievreckan (Coire-Bhreacain), the Cauldron of Breacan, an Irish prince. The word Lullaby translates the Gaelic word Cronan (see below).

Glen Feulen, by R.D. Adams 6/8 M 4
The Maid of Glengarrisdale 6/8 M 2
The Maids of Jura, by John MacLellan, Dunoon 6/8 SA 2
Mary Darroch, by John MacLellan, Dunoon 12/8 Waltz 2 (Mary was John's mother)
The Old Woman's Lullaby P 3

The Old Woman's Lullaby is a piobaireachd work sometimes associated with Jura. Some say it was the tune known in former times as *The Widow's Grief*, and was often played at funerals in the 19th century; it may have been the work played at Donald Cameron's funeral in Inverness in 1868. There is some argument about the name *The Widow's Grief*, as others say this was one of the several names of the work now known as *MacCrimmon's Sweetheart (Maol Donn* in Gaelic).

The word Lullaby is a poor translation of the Gaelic word Cronan (from which our modern word 'croon' is derived). Cronan means a type of song sung by women, especially to children, but not always so, and not necessarily to send them to sleep. It was a type of simple verse, lacking the intricate internal rhyme-schemes of bardic poetry. We have no exact equivalent in English. It was considered proper for women to sing or compose a cronan, but not to attempt any bardic involvement. Mary MacLeod fell foul of this unwritten rule when she composed her fine bardic poetry at Dunvegan, and was eventually expelled, possibly for continuing to do so, in spite of warnings. The tradition is that the official (male) bards resented her intrusion into their preserves, and worked on their chief to send her away. Another theory, however, maintains that she had composed a poem in praise of her MacLeod chief on Bernera, Sir Norman, to the detriment of the chief at Dunvegan, who was offended enough to send her out of his household. This (alleged) poem has not survived, nor is there any evidence that it ever existed.

A Gaelic legend from Jura may be behind the title of the piobaireachd. The Old Woman was a hag who lived in the Paps of Jura, the striking mountain peaks which form the backbone of the island. There she used to sit, spinning a magic thread – and this is a parody of the womanly convention of spinning as a respectable feminine occupation. When a vessel sailed up the Sound of Jura, she would throw out her thread to lasso it and draw it in, complete with its crew, who then, poor souls, met with what used to be called a fate worse than death. Her reign of terror ended when she captured MacPhee of Colonsay, and he managed to cut the thread with his magic axe. This would put the legend back before 1623, when the last MacPhee chief in Colonsay, Malcolm, was killed by the MacDonalds (see Colonsay, below).

Peter Youngson's excellent book, *Jura: Island of Deer*, gives us slightly different versions which he gathered from local people and from Donald Budge's book. One story is called *The Witch of the Paps of Jura*, and it goes like this:

> Cailleach a'Bheinn Mhoir, the Witch (or Old Woman) of Ben More, lived at Largiebreac. She had a ball of thread by which she could draw towards her any person or thing if she could throw the ball beyond them. She got MacPhie of Colonsay into her coils and would not allow him to depart. Every time he attempted to leave her, she used to intercept him, and even after he had got into his birlinn (boat) and got off from the shore, she would get him ashore again by throwing the ball into his boat. At last he pretended that he was perfectly content in his bondage, and managed to get the secret from her that she had a hatchet which would cut the thread. He watched his opportunity and stole the hatchet, having previously ordered his boat to be waiting at Knockbreac at the foot of Beinn a'Chaluim [this is Beinn a'Chaolais on the map]. He set out at dawn of day and was seated in his boat before the Cailleach got to the top of the hill, which she climbed with speed as soon as she missed him. When she saw him in the boat, she called out piteously to him:

> > *A Mhic-a-Phi, a ghaoil mo chridhe,*
> > *An d'fhag thu air a'chladach mi?*

> > Oh, MacPhie, my heart's treasure,
> > Hast thou left me on the shore?

> This she oft repeated, throwing at the same time the magic ball into the boat and drawing it in to the shore. But when she saw the thread cut and saw the boat sailing beyond her reach, she tried desperately to follow it and slid down from the top of the Ben, leaving a mark from the top to the foot. This is called to this day 'The Old Woman's Furrow' (Sgriob na Caillich).
>
>   As she descended she was crying out:

> > *A Mhic-a-Phi, charraich ghrannda,*
> > *An d'fhag thu air a'chladach mi?*

> > Oh, MacPhie, rough-skinned and ugly,
> > Hast thou left me on the shore?

> But MacPhie made good his escape and returned safely to Colonsay.

In these modern times of psychological awareness, it has been suggested that this story is a personification of a common dilemma, of a man tied by marriage to an aging wife and trying desperately to escape from his situation. This seems more American than Highland – but anyone may read any symbolism into a legend.

Mr Youngson has collected many stories about the Cailleach in Jura – and, of course, there are many more about Old Hags in other parts of the country, usually associated with mountains. In Jura there were two separate strands of tradition, one about the old witch on the Paps of Jura, the other concerning a historical figure, a sort of highwaywoman who terrified travellers on the island. The two sets of stories began to overlap, and now it is difficult to keep them entirely separate.

In the Oban area, there is a tradition in the family of the MacDougall chiefs of Dunollie that the *Old Woman's Lullaby* was composed by one of their MacDougall pipers at Moleigh. This may indicate that there was a song underlying the piobaireachd composition, and that more than one composer took it up – just as the *Lament for Iain Ciar* developed a song theme also used in *The Glen Is Mine*.

Archie Buie

ARCHIBALD BUIE, known as Archie the Piper, is named by Peter Youngson as one of a group of Jura people, including Archie's brother John, who emigrated to America before 1755. Their names appear on a list made in North Carolina in 1755, when Archie bought ninety-one acres of land on the north-eastern side of the north-west branch of the Cape Fear river, in Cumberland County. Ninety-one acres of land must have seemed a huge holding, after his life in Jura, where he would have had no chance of becoming a land-owner.

Later, Archie moved to the Barbeque district. He died in 1806, unmarried, and left all he had to the children of his brother John; they moved to Georgia in the early 1800s. Not much is known of the family, and nothing of their time in Jura. They were among the earliest settlers in the New World.

One tradition says that Archie the Piper was blind. He is said to have been irreligious, never a church-goer, and his piping was frowned upon when the local churches were affected by the strict revivalist movement at the end of the 18th century; but he died before the pressure became too great. Other pipers and dancers were forced to give up, or move away. Pipers in North Carolina in the late 18th century included Malcolm MacRummen from Skye, possibly a grandson or nephew of Patrick Og.

Peter Youngson has most kindly sent me an extract from an American publication, *They Passed This Way: A Personal Narrative of Harnett*

County History, written by Malcolm Fowler, and published in 1955 by Harnett County Centennial, Inc. This has an interesting chapter on 'The Legion of Restless Men', whom the author describes as settlers in North Carolina 'obsessed with unquenchable desire to see what might lie around the curve of the river, might hide behind the brow of the hill. These were the trail blazers, the ones who explored the wilderness, tamed the Indians and made the valley safe for the permanent settlers who were to follow hard on their heels'.

These men were mainly of British descent, many of them Scots, and the author names a few, including 'bow-legged little Archie Buie, whose pipes droned and wailed away many a lonely hour in the far stretching vistas of the wilderness trails'.

The most colourful of the Restless Men was a Highlander (or Islander?) called Neill MacNeill, a big man, formerly a sailor, whose red hair and beard gave him the name An Ruadh Mor, the Big Red One, also known as Niall Ruadh, Red-haired Neill. He had arrived in Carolina in 1739, just as the Scots were beginning to claim land there, and he seems to have bought and sold tracts of land for some years, too restless himself to settle for long. He is said to have invented the barbecue: he used to kill cattle by stunning them with his fist, and having cut their throats, would cook the carcases on an open fire, inviting all his friends to join him. He would have a thirty-gallon keg of apple brandy laid on to go with the meat. Archie Buie the bow-legged piper was one of the friends who attended the barbecues, 'and his pipes would moan and drone the wild melodies of the Highland hills', and there was great telling of stories and singing of songs.

This way of life continued until 1759 when a contagious fever struck the area. Red Neill, who had intended moving on, stayed to help his friends, and was joined by little Archie Buie, who remained with Neill, assisting him with the grave-digging and playing laments at the burials. It seems that Neill knew his own time was near, and he got Archie to cut a huge log from a gum tree, ten feet long, and then to split it lengthwise. Red used to sit gouging out a hollow in it with a hammer and chisel, while Archie 'played doleful laments on his pipes'.

This log was to be Red Neill's coffin. He steadfastly refused all spiritual help from the local preacher – he and Archie were in agreement on this – and just before his death, he made Archie promise to bury him, inside the log, at a special place across the river. He then died, and wee Archie duly coffined him, but the river was in spate, too high to be crossed, so there was no choice but to bury him in the wrong place. 'And when Archie had finished heaping up the mound of dirt, he stood at its head and his pipes wailed the doleful notes of the MacNeill lament.'

By the time the river was passable again, Archie Buie had moved on – he seems to have been immune to the fever. Local people expected him to come back to move his friend to the promised spot, and when he did not arrive, stories of sightings of Red Neill's ghost began to circulate. It would stand on a rock by the river, pointing across to the spot where Archie had promised to bury him.

Archie never came back, and in 1865, the river flooded and burst its banks. After the waters went down, an old log was found, split open on the bank, and inside was a huge red-haired skeleton. Luckily someone remembered the story of the bow-legged piper, the red-headed giant and the unfulfilled burial promise. So the local people re-buried him where he had wanted to lie, and his ghost troubled them no more.

But, Malcolm Fowler adds, 'sometimes there are nights when the North Wind blows down from the flatwoods, over the up-jutting rocks of the falls, through the whispering reeds of Smilie's Island, and then listeners can hear faint queer sounds. And they know they are listening to the ghostly pipes of bow-legged little Archie Buie moaning and droning mournful laments to the other ghosts of the Legion of Restless Men . . .'

It is pretty clear that the writer was not a piper; moaning, droning and wailing are not terms we use of the noble instrument. And if there is anything in these Carolina stories, as there certainly must be, it is evident that Archie the Piper was not blind – unless, of course, he lost his sight in old age.

The Buie family back in Jura, who spread also into Islay, continued to be pipers. Some of them were living at Conisby, alongside the piping MacEacherns, in the late 19th century.

See also above, Islay, Donald MacIndeor

Mary Darroch

Mary Darroch was the mother of John MacLellan, Dunoon, well known piper and composer, and member of the Glasgow Police pipe band. Mary came from the village of Keills in Jura, and is thought to have returned to her family there when she was widowed at the age of about forty, being left with six children to bring up. She went back to Dunoon after a few years, but it is thought that the young John may have had piping lessons in Jura, possibly from Neil Lindsay. Mary was related to the Lindsay family.

John later composed a two-part waltz which he named *Mary Darroch.*

Hugh Lindsay

HUGH LINDSAY was born in Lagg, on the island of Jura, and was baptised on 27 November 1820, the son of John Lindsay and Elizabeth MacColl. There were several Lindsay families in Jura, spread across the island, and they were presumably related.

Although the Lindsays had been in Jura for several generations, the name is not Highland or Gaelic but belongs to the Borders. Many Border names came north when shepherds were brought in by the big land-owners in the early 19th century, but the Lindsays go back much earlier in Jura. Donald Budge said that the first of them came to Jura to work on the ferry at Lagg (linking Jura to the mainland), but no date for this is given. The ferry was closely bound up with the postal service, at which the family made its living in later generations.

There is a family tradition that the original family name was MacLeaosachd, and that they were affiliated to the MacDonalds in the late 17th century, the time when the Campbells were taking over in Islay. The family took the Borders name of Lindsay, for security in their dealings with the invading Campbells. A Hugh Lindsay in Jura in 1677 was the first Lindsay recorded in the whole of Argyll, let alone Jura.

A descendant of Archie, a brother of the later Hugh Lindsay (the piper), is Dr Lindsay Neil, who has traced his forebears in Jura back to the first Hugh Lindsay of 1677. This Hugh married Darty MacPhaetras (Dorothy MacPhedran) from Islay, in 1703, and they had six children, including John, born at Lagg in 1709.

This John Lindsay married Mary MacMillan in 1739, and their four children were all born in Lagg, of whom Archibald 1741 was the grandfather of Hugh Lindsay the piper. Archie married Effie McPhail in 1780, and John, Hugh's father, was born two years later. Two other siblings emigrated to America.

John Lindsay married Elizabeth MacColl in 1816, and had nine children, of whom Hugh was the third, born in 1820, at Lagg.

Lagg is in the middle of the east coast of Jura, and well placed for a short sail across sheltered waters to the mainland. At one time cattle were brought over from Colonsay, as well as from Islay, to be shipped from Lagg over to Keills, in Knapdale. This made Lagg an important centre in the island, and explains why the post office was established there, as well as an inn.

The Lindsays at Lagg ran the postal system, being responsible for both taking the mail to and from the post office at Port Askaig, as well as the mainland, and for delivering it to houses in Jura. This work seems to have been in the hands of the Lindsays at Lagg for several generations, covering some 150 years, John being followed as postmaster by his son Archie (Hugh's elder brother), and Archie in turn by his own son Alexander, and grandsons.

Hugh appears to have remained in Jura and Islay for most of his life. He is listed in the Census of 1841 as Hugh, eighteen, son of John Lindsay, foot post, but no occupation is given for Hugh or for his brother Archie. They probably helped their father in the postal business.

It is said that Hugh learned his piping – or perhaps had a polish put on it – when he was in his teens. Angus MacKay was then in Islay, close to Jura, coming to Bridgend when Hugh was seventeen. It is thought that Hugh may have had tuition from him, at a critical point in his piping development.

Hugh competed in Edinburgh and Inverness as 'Hugh Lindsay from Jura'. The Notices of Pipers give us a glimpse of his competing career: in 1841, when he was twenty-one, he came fourth in the Piobaireachd at Edinburgh, and 'his performance was greatly appreciated', which presumably means he was given prolonged applause. In 1844, however – the Edinburgh competitions were by this time held only once every three years – he failed to get beyond the heats for the short leet, but that same year he competed also at Inverness, and gained 3rd place, beaten only by John MacBeath, piper to the Duke of Sutherland, and by John MacAlister, the Cromarty piper.

1845 was the year of Hugh's glory. Competing at the Northern Meeting, he won the Prize Pipe, beating Alexander Cameron (brother of Donald) into second place, and Duncan MacKay, Kintail, into third. Donald Cameron himself was not in this competition as he had already won the Prize Pipe, two years earlier, but Hugh beat John Ban MacKenzie and other great players of the time. And in 'the Strathspeys and Marches' Hugh was first again, beating both of the Camerons, into second and third place. Clearly this was no mean piper.

The report of that year's Northern Meeting in the *Inverness Courier* says that the weather when Hugh was playing was 'bitter cold' (the Meetings were held in October then, and out of doors. This one was in Farraline Park, now the Inverness bus station). A large crowd had gathered around the platform to listen to the piping, and 'the pipers one by one poured forth their soul-stirring pibrochs and were loudly cheered at the conclusion of the wild laments and martial airs. It was obvious, however, that these displays were prolonged to an extent which made the attention flag', so that people began to warm themselves up by running impromptu races beside the platform, which must have been distracting for the pipers.

After the piping, the dancing was on the same platform; the crowd returned, invigorated, but now the heavens opened and icy cold torrential rain drenched the whole event. What with the cold and the unruly audience, Hugh Lindsay had more than his fellow competitors to overcome. All the more credit to an island boy, not accustomed to large noisy crowds.

Two years later, Queen Victoria made her tour of the West Highlands, and the tradition is that Hugh Lindsay 'both piped and danced before her, at either Ardrishaig or Crinan', according to the Notices of Pipers. Many islanders, especially those from Islay and Jura, crossed over to the mainland on that occasion, to see the Queen, at Crinan, Ardrishaig or Inveraray. It is likely that both Hugh Lindsay and Donald MacIndeor were at Inveraray, brought over by J.F. Campbell as part of his 'tail' of Highlanders, a sort of mediaeval bodyguard in ancient dress, carrying halberds. They were on duty in Inveraray Castle, lining the dining room while the Queen took her lunch, but it was probably on her return journey in September that Hugh Lindsay piped and danced for her entertainment, as her barge was slowly making its way along the Crinan Canal. Press reports spoke of pipers being stationed at each lock as she passed through, and as the canal links Crinan and Ardrishaig, that might account for the wording of the Notices.

Hugh never married, and it is not known exactly when or where he died. The Notices say vaguely that he died young, and certainly he is not listed in the 1851 Census for Jura (but that might mean merely that he was away somewhere). His death is not recorded in Scotland, however, which suggests that possibly he died before 1855, the year when registration became compulsory – or that he went abroad. If his grave is in Jura, it is not marked, and there is no tradition of where it might be. Family tradition says he died a few years after his triumph at Inverness.

He left his Prize Pipe, won in 1845, to his nephew Neil, tenth child of his brother Archie. Neil was born in the early 1860s, so would not have been playing the pipes until the 1870s. If Hugh had died some ten years before Neil's birth, we must assume that his pipes were kept in the family and later given to young Neil when he showed promise as a player – rather than Hugh having bequeathed them directly to Neil. It would still have been said that Neil inherited them, even if their lives did not overlap. But we cannot be certain that Hugh was dead, and it is possible that he taught not only the young Neil but also John MacLellan, in Jura after his father's death in Dunoon in 1882.

Dr Lindsay Neil says that Hugh Lindsay's pipe is still in the family, although the inscribed silver plate which used to be on it has been lost. This is said to be the Prize Pipe he won at Inverness; if so, what happened to the pipe he was playing when he won that day? It must have been a pipe good enough to hold its own with those of the giants of piping. What did he do with it?

The pipe still in the family is not silver-mounted, but it has ivory mounts. It passed from Neil Lindsay to his daughter Effie MacDougall, and then to her son Lindsay MacDougall in Greenock.

Hugh Lindsay was an example of a gifted island piper who benefited from a brief spell of expert tuition to bring his natural talents into full flower. We do not know who his first teacher was, but it seems that Angus MacKay brought him on, in his late teens, and his double achievement at the Northern Meeting in 1845 proved his worth. For an island boy to beat the giants of piping without the benefit of patronage from an employer or the army was indeed a feat. We might perhaps wonder to what extent he had the support of J.F. Campbell.

There is no longer a post office at Lagg, nor are any of the Lindsays of Lagg living on the island, but their descendant, Dr Lindsay Neil, has a holiday home at Knockrome, a few miles to the south of Lagg, and he maintains his Jura connections.

Neil Lindsay

Peter Youngson gives an interesting account of Hugh Lindsay's nephew, NEIL LINDSAY, son of Hugh's elder brother Archie and his wife Effie McGilp (she came from the island of Danna, in Knapdale, just across the Sound of Jura from Lagg).

Neil became a fine piper, possibly taught by his uncle (see above) and certainly playing his uncle's pipe. If his teacher was not his uncle, we do not know who it might have been. There is a possibility that Neil himself taught the young John MacLellan from Dunoon, in the early 1880s; John came to Jura in 1882 when his father died in Dunoon, and was there for a few years. Neil followed the family tradition by becoming a postman in Jura, before, at some point in his twenties, that is in the 1880s, he left Jura and emigrated to America. He had inherited his uncle's pipe, and took it with him.

Peter Youngson tells us that Neil went to San Francisco, 'where he became a significant member of the Scottish community'. He kept a scrap-book from about 1890, putting together cuttings, photographs and items of interest about his life in California. It makes an interesting record. He had met a fellow-Scot, Iain S.R. Tevendale, 'reputedly the finest piper in the United States'. Tevendale had a 'drinking establishment', presumably a bar or saloon, at 536 Sacramento Street, and he took Neil on as a barman. In the 1890s, a contemporary newspaper account said the place had been remodelled and refurnished, and Neil Lindsay, 'so widely known to the customers of the house', had purchased an interest in the business. 'This makes a hot combination, for Tevendale and Lindsay are the two most famous pipers in the Scotch colony.'

The name of the business was changed from Tevendale's to Tevendale & Lindsay's, and we have to wonder where Neil found the money to buy a partnership – not in Jura, I would think. 'Those who enjoy a delicious mixed drink should drop in and get a pleasant surprise. All that is necessary is to call for a "Neil's Patent", and the man in the Scotch cap will do the rest. You can't find out how it is made, but that makes it all the more attractive. Try one'.

Another cutting in the scrap-book says: 'The well known bagpiper, Neil Lindsay, cut a wide swathe at the Sacramento Scotch games last week. Neil, being a boy of "buirdly" build, wore the philabeg to such perfection, dirk, sporran, plaid and all, that he got away with the first prize for "the best dressed Hielandman". Some say that his "cairngorm" dazzled the eyes of the judges.'

This begins to make us squirm slightly, but worse is to come. Another cutting is headed 'the True Scotsman', and goes on:

> among the Highland Pipers, who led the Jubilee procession at the
> chutes, the most conspicuous for elegance of attire, martial bearing and
> skill in piping [skill being well down the list] was Neil Lindsay who
> otherwise bears an illustrious record. Born in the Isle of Jura about
> thirty years ago, Mr Lindsay for some time carried Her Majesty's
> mail in the Highlands of Scotland. He is now Pipe Major of both the
> Caledonia and Thistle Clubs of this city, and has been offered the same
> position in a Scottish regiment, now stationed in Aberdeen. [Would this
> have been the Gordons?] For several years he has carried off first prize
> for 'best dressed Highlander', also in many competitions for piping.

Perhaps this is not so bad, but in the next cutting the journalist lets him(her?)self go:

Kissing goes by favour in California, and that is the reason why Neil Lindsay was not awarded the first prize as the best dressed Highlander on the ground at the picnic of the Caledonia Club at Shell Mound last Thursday. It is well known to all true sons of Scotia that his real Lindsay tartan, his solid silver ornaments set off with cairngorms of the first water, his sporran, hose, shoes and Glengarry all mounted with heather, thoroughly corresponded, and formed, all together, the handsomest costume in California. These are the facts, in spite of the judge's decision, and Lindsay, if he did not get the prize, gets the credit for having been the best full-dressed Highlander on the picnic.

Sporran, hose and shoes mounted with heather? And was the winner not full-dressed? And who won the actual competition as the best player?

The piece concludes: 'The shrill music of Neil Lindsay's Scotch bag-pipes, attuned to "Cameronians South", was heard at Shell Mound Park, calling the lads and lasses to their national games and dances.' This was the 32nd Annual Gathering of the Caledonia Club. I wonder what *Cameronians South* was.

On 19 April 1906, this pleasant American life came to an abrupt end. The whole of Sacramento Street, including Tevendale & Lindsay's, was destroyed in the San Francisco earthquake. Neil was clearly ruined by this catastrophe, as he could not insure against an Act of God. He left America and returned to Jura, where he was taken in and given a home by an elderly crofter near Craighouse, named Sandy Lindsay. Sandy lived in the most southerly of a row of houses at Caigenhouse (pronounced 'Cahgain-house'), just north of the village of Craighouse. He worked his own croft, which went with the house. He and Neil believed they must be related, but were not sure how. It was probably not easy to work out the connection, as family relationships were complex: Neil's sister-in-law Effie Lindsay, nee McGilp, for example, had a brother Neil whose daughter Effie married Alexander Lindsay, her first cousin, son of Archie and Effie, causing confusion even within the immediate family.

Old Sandy Lindsay was another Alexander. His parents were Neil Lindsay and Mary Campbell, and he was brought up at Crakaig, where he was born in 1839, one of a family of five. It is not possible to trace the father's roots as the register for Jura before 1810 has huge gaps, and the first Lindsay now recorded in it is in the year 1813. It is possible that he was a brother of John Lindsay at Lagg, and so he would have been Hugh Lindsay's first cousin and Neil junior's second cousin – but if the relationship was as straightforward as that, the two of them at

Caigenhouse would have had no difficulty in working it out. It is more likely that Neil senior and John at Lagg were distant cousins, so that relations in the third generation would be intricate.

Sandy never married. He lived with his family at Crakaig until his parents both died in the 1860s, and presumably the tenancy of Crakaig died with his father. By 1871 he was on the small croft at Caigenhouse, living with his younger brother and sister, but ten years later he was on his own, with a lodger for company. In 1891, his nephew Neil Campbell was with him, but by the time Neil Lindsay appeared from America, Sandy was alone again, and probably not just lonely but needing a hand with the croft.

Neil and Sandy seem to have got on well together, and when Sandy died, he left both house and croft to Neil, who settled there. He had the house rebuilt, larger and more imposing, giving it the name Frisco, which it still bears today. He married Mary MacIndeor from Kilchoman, in Islay, a family known for its pipers and musical ability. Mary was born in 1897 in Port Charlotte, daughter of Donald MacIndeor, farmer, living at 3 Blackbrae Street with his wife Catherine. She was the sixth of their seven children; they were related to a family of MacIndeors living at Conisby.

Neil and Mary Lindsay had a daughter Effie, who married Dan Mac-Dougall and became a notable personality in Jura, in the 20th century. Effie lived to a good age, and died in the 1990s. She inherited Hugh Lindsay's pipe from her father.

Neil Lindsay died at Caigenhouse in 1945, said to be eighty, but this does not quite tally with his birthdate of 1862. He was reported in 1937 to be still playing his uncle Hugh's pipe.

The house called Frisco, at the end of the row of cottages called Caigenhouse, remained in the Lindsay family. It is now a holiday home belonging to Lindsay MacDougall, son of the last Lindsay to live there – she was a grandaughter of Neil Lindsay of San Francisco.

Gilbert Gillies

Gilbert Gillies, brother of John Gillies of the Scots Guards (who went to Vancouver), was a pupil of his distant cousin, John MacDougall Gillies. On his teacher's advice he took a post as piper to Campbell of Jura, and married a Jura girl. She died, however, after about two years of marriage, and Gilbert then left the island. He went to Tayside.

Donald MacDougall

Donald MacDougall from Jura is named by Archie MacNeill in his *Memoirs*. He was a piper employed at Ardencaple Castle, Rhu, on the Clyde estuary, late in the 19th century. Archie said that Donald had a set of reel-sized pipes made by Fraser of Greenock. He told Archie that Fraser had made forty sets, all the same, fully mounted with ivory, and sold them at £4 per set to sailors who came into Greenock. Archie described the pipes as 'quite modern' in appearance (see Jeannie Campbell, *Highland Pipe Makers* (2011) under *Duncan Fraser*, pp. 84–87). This Donald MacDougall was probably related to the Lindsays.

Today there is little piping in Jura, although the pipe band from Islay sometimes goes over to play there. NEIL CAMERON, whose work brought him to live in Jura in 1999, is a piper, living at Strone, not far from Craighouse. In 2003, Neil was instructing two local boys, hoping to revive piping among the youngsters of Jura. He and his pupils would like to join the Islay Pipe Band, but it is impossible for them to attend the practices, as the ferry stops running at sunset, which in mid-winter is around four o'clock, and band practices are on Monday nights, usually in Port Ellen, difficult to reach from Jura. Neil and his pupils accept that they are up against it. What the islands desperately need are good qualified instructors, and then the piping there would really take off. Meanwhile, Neil Cameron in Jura and the pipe majors in Islay are doing a great job, holding it all together, but you cannot help feeling that too much potential talent is being lost.

Sources

Notices of Pipers
Census Records, Jura
Piping Times
Donald Budge, *Jura*
Peter Youngson, *Jura, Island of Deer*
Malcolm Fowler, *They Passed this Way*
Douglas F. Kelly and Caroline Switzen Kelly, *Carolina Scots*
Keith MacKellar, Craighouse

Scarba

Scarba is a small island to the north of Jura, separated from it by the Corrievreckan whirlpool. To visit Scarba, private arrangements have to be made for a boat trip from Luing or Seil Island. Speedboat trips for holiday-makers are run from Easdale, passing through the Corrievreckan, going close to Scarba, but no landing is made there.

Scarba is said to be the island to which Mary MacLeod was banished after she was sent away from Dunvegan. Whatever her offence, she was forbidden to return to Skye, and went first to relatives in Mull. This was, however, not far enough away, and her verses were still reaching Dunvegan, so she was then sent further afield. One of her poems describes how she sat in Scarba looking out towards Islay and resenting that she was cut off from what she regarded as civilisation in Skye. Tradition in Harris, however, says she was not in Scarba but in Pabay, to the west of Harris, a small island where her brother lived, next to the isle of Scarp. It may be that there has been confusion between Scarba and Scarp, but this is not certain.

Cronan Corrievrecan, The Corrievreccan Lullaby, is a 20th-century piobaireachd made by Donald MacLeod. In his collection of his own piobaireachd works, the name is spelled both Corrievreccan and Corrievrechan, thus managing to irritate both schools of thought. The Corrievreckan is a whirlpool or maelstrom, dangerous at certain states of the tide. George Orwell, when living in Jura, came to grief in it while out in a small boat, but managed to scramble ashore. The Cronan or song of the whirlpool is the roaring noise it makes as the tides races through the narrow channel: it can be heard from several miles away, and is a warning to small craft to give it a wide berth, or they may be sucked into it. Sometimes the tide creates a 'step' of water, one or two feet in height, dangerous to a small vessel and disconcerting for an unwary skipper.

A resemblance has been detected between Donald MacLeod's work and Iain Dall MacKay's composition, *The Munros' Salute*, though the timing is different. It has been described unkindly as '*Munros' Salute* jazzed up', but the resemblance is possibly because both works were based on the same old song.

Donald MacLeod also made 'this old Gaelic air' into a Slow Air in two parts, with the same title – so perhaps we have three works all based on the one song.

Lunga

Lunga lies to the north of Scarba, the most northerly of the chain of islands on the south-west side of the entrance to the Firth of Lorne. Lunga was the title or designation of a branch of the MacDougalls who lived near Ardfern, in Craignish, on the mainland. They named their big house and estate Lunga, but did not live on the island. They were well known as patrons of piping, and employed a number of famous players as their personal pipers, including Ronald MacKenzie and William Lawrie. To reach the island, private arrangements would have to be made.

Fionn (Henry Whyte), whose family belonged to Easdale so that he had a lot of local knowledge, wrote in his Historical Notes to Glen's *Collection of Ancient Piobaireachd* that there was a work 'said to have been composed by Ranald MacDougall, piper to MacDougall of Lunga'. It was *The Waking of the Bridegroom*, and the tradition was that when a good wedding lasted several days, the piper played outside the bridal couple's house each morning, to rouse them for further festivities. No honeymooning in the Seychelles in those days.

Leaving Lunga is a 2/4 march in four parts composed by John Gordon, who was butler and piper to MacDougall of Lunga.

Seil, Luing and Easdale

Seil Island is reached by road, across the 'Bridge over the Atlantic', from the Oban–Lochgilphead road. Luing lies to the south of Seil, accessible by a small car ferry across the Cuan Sound, a crossing which takes a few minutes. Easdale Island is reached by a small passenger ferry from Easdale village (Ellenabeich), a few minutes away.

The father of John MacKenzie, famed as the Loch Fyne piper, was John MacArthur from Balvicar, on Seil Island. The child was born out of wedlock in 1807, at Ardmaddy, just across Seil Sound. His mother was Christy MacKenzie, an aunt of John Ban MacKenzie, one of the giants of 19th-century piping. Nothing more is known of John MacArthur, but it is thought that he probably belonged to the Argyll branch of the MacArthurs, clustered around Loch Awe. Some of these MacArthurs are known to have been pipers, and a John MacArthur from Cladich (on Loch Awe) was piper to Barbreck, but the dates are uncertain; late 18th century is most likely, so the two men called John MacArthur may have been one and the same.

In her book about Easdale, Mary Withall tells how, when Queen Victoria was visiting Taymouth Castle in 1842, her host, the Marquess of Breadalbane, sent for the most expert boatmen on his estates, the men of Easdale. Twenty quarrymen of the local Volunteer regiment, wearing full Highland dress in Campbell of Breadalbane tartan, and led by their senior NCO, John MacPherson (described as the Right Hand Man), made the three-day march to Aberfeldy to attend their Queen.

They rowed her up Loch Tay, while John Ban MacKenzie and John MacGregor from Glenlyon played for her in the bows of the boat; she later wrote in her diary that the Easdale men sang two Gaelic boat-songs for her, 'very wild and singular'. One, she said, was *Tuireach bean Mhic-an-t-Saoir*, which begins 'A nighean ud thall Tug O' – or so the Queen has it. This was a version of what we now call the *Loch Tay Boat Song*, which seems to have formed the basis for John Ban's piobaireachd composition in memory of his son, *His Father's Lament for Donald MacKenzie* (1863). The *Loch Tay Boat Song* was also made into a Slow March with one part, published in the Scots Guards Standard Settings, volume II, and attributed to 'R. MacLeod/A. MacDonald'.

John Gibson (2002) mentions that in 1834 a piping grandson of Donald Campbell of Nether Lorne was living in Luing, and he gave information about his grandfather, who was the father of Colin Mor Campbell, writer of the Campbell Canntaireachd manuscript in the 1790s.

HENRY WHYTE, whose pen-name was Fionn (the Gaelic for White), was a journalist and piping enthusiast who came from Easdale. His family had Mull connections, it is said. His father was John Whyte, engineer and overseer of the Easdale Slate Quarrying Company. The family lived on Easdale Island at Ivy Cottage (and Robert Wallace had a cottage close by, at one time). Henry was born there in 1862, one of the younger sons in a family of seven or eight children. In 1870 his elder brother, Angus Whyte, who succeeded his father as overseer of the quarries, built the big house which is now the Inshaig Park Hotel. Henry went to Glasgow to work as a journalist, but returned to live in Easdale after his retirement. (I am indebted to Mary Withall, Easdale Museum, for information about Henry Whyte.)

During the late 19th and early 20th centuries, many letters signed 'Fionn' appeared in the *Oban Times*, contributing to debate on a variety of piping topics. It was the fashion in those days to conduct these discussions, often fiery, even abusive, under pen-names. Pipe Major Willie Gray was another participant, as were Dr Charles Bannatyne and Lt John MacLennan.

In 1904, Henry won an essay competition with an account of the Rankin pipers in Mull, a work which is now in the museum in Tobermory.

Henry Whyte is credited with being the composer of the melody of the Gaelic song *Suas leis a'Ghaidhlig! (Up with Gaelic!)*, the rallying chorus of the Gael, sung with fervour at every National Mod. The words were written by Duncan Reid, Glasgow. Fionn took a great interest in Gaelic song, and arranged the harmonies of several old songs for use by Gaelic choirs, as well as translating some of them into English. He also put Gaelic words to the songs *An Ribhinn Donn (The Brown-haired Maiden)* and *Mo Ghille Dubh (My Dark-haired Laddie)*, as well as to *Fuadach nan Gaidheal (The Dispersal of the Highlanders)*, which is sung to the tune of *Lord Lovat's Lament*. These were published in 1921, in *Choisir-chiuil, The St Columba Collection of Gaelic Songs*. This book, compiled for use by Gaelic choirs, has settings of several of the poems of Duncan Ban MacIntyre.

Edward Dwelly, in his *Illustrated Gaelic-English Dictionary*, a marvel of detailed erudition, published first in the decade 1901–11, listed all who had helped him, and included Henry Whyte among those who had kept him right with detail of dialect vocabulary. He singled out two men, Henry Whyte and the Rev. C.M. Robertson, both of whom, he said, had assisted him considerably with Proper Names and Technical Terms. Henry not only had a sound knowledge of Gaelic, but was also fully literate in the language, by no means a common accomplishment. It is thought he was behind Dwelly's detailed diagram and list of the many parts of a bagpipe, with their Gaelic names.

Mary Withall reports that the piping tradition is still alive in Easdale, where three players, STEPHEN MCNALLY, COLIN BLAKEY and IAN HILL, are keeping it going.

Colonsay and Oronsay

To reach Colonsay, take a car ferry from Oban. The voyage takes about two and a quarter hours, and the scenery is outstanding. Oronsay is a small tidal island at the southern tip of Colonsay, reached on foot, or in a robust vehicle, at low tide only.

Tunes associated with the two islands include:

Andrew MacNeill, by Donald MacLeod 6/8 J 4
Andrew MacNeill (Colonsay), by William M. MacDonald 2/4 M 4
Andrew MacNeill of Oransay, by John M. MacKenzie
A.S. MacNeill of Oransay's Salute, by Donald MacLeod P 5
Flora MacNeill of Oronsay, by Robert G. Hardie 6/8 M 4
Kiloran Bay, by Archibald MacMillan 6/8 M 4
The Rout of the MacPhees P 8 (see below)

There is a remote possibility that the piobaireachd work *The Young Laird of Dungallon's Salute* might be associated with the ancient fort of Dungalan in Colonsay, but it is more likely to refer to a different Dungalan, in Loch Sunart, Ardnamurchan. If a link with Colonsay is suggested, the Young Laird would have been Coll Ciotach MacDonald or his son Alasdair, and the work would then be bound up with the history of *The Rout of the MacPhees*. The Young Laird in Ardnamurchan was a Cameron, and the evidence for the composition being made for him is more convincing.

The two main families in Colonsay who may be associated with piping are the MacPhies and the MacNeills.

The MacPhies of Colonsay

The oldest known chiefs in Colonsay were the MacPhies. The name may be spelled MacPhie, MacPhee, MacFee, MacFie, MacDuffie or Duffie. They were traditionally the keepers of the records and charters of the Lords of the Isles, the MacDonalds of Dunyveg and the Glens (see above, Islay). Some say they were established in Colonsay as vassals of the Norwegian king Magnus in the 13th century, and that they were themselves of Norse descent, but the name suggests Irish roots.

The MacPhies or MacDuffies were for generations buried in the Priory on Oronsay, and in 1549, Sir Donald MacDuffie was the Prior there. The rod of office of the MacDuffies was kept at the Priory long after the last of the clan had been driven off Colonsay.

The Rout of the MacPhees

With the rise to power of Coll Ciotach MacDonald, known later as Colkitto, the MacPhees were in trouble. Coll wanted Colonsay, and laid his plans. Although the MacPhees were affiliated to the MacDonalds in Islay, Coll disregarded this, and in 1623 he made his move. It was February, and the Prior of Oronsay, Donald MacPhee lay dying. His kinsman, Malcolm MacPhee, the island's chief, planned to go to see him, and Coll Ciotach heard of the proposed visit. He laid an ambush of about two dozen armed men, hidden on Oronsay, beside the track to the Priory.

Malcolm sent two men ahead of him to announce his arrival, and they were both shot dead. The noise of gunfire warned Malcolm, who had already crossed the Strand and could not return to Colonsay because of the rising tide. He fled to the southernmost point of Oronsay. David Stephenson describes the scene:

> Cornered there, he scrambled over the rocks and swam out to low rocky Eilean nan Ron, the Isle of the Seals. There the last chief of the MacPhees of Colonsay spent his last night, alone and without food or shelter, in wet clothes in mid-winter. The following morning, Coll and his men came out by boat and, according to tradition, after a long search found Malcolm hiding under seaweed on the shore. He fled, but his enemies caught up with him after he had been hit twice by musket balls, and finished him off with swords and dirks. The thrifty murderers then carefully dug the musket balls out of the corpse: lead was scarce. Another leading MacPhee, Dougal, had surrendered on Oransay on promise of his life; but after twenty days of captivity on Colonsay he too was murdered.

The killers were later outlawed for these deeds, but the sentence, passed in their absence, meant little, and they went unpunished.

A somewhat different version of the killing is given by Kevin Byrne, who, living in Colonsay, has extensive local knowledge. He describes how the feud between MacPhee and Coll Ciotach intensified after Malcolm returned from Edinburgh to find Coll in possession of the island. Eventually Malcolm became a fugitive in Colonsay, and

> according to the story, he was hunted the length and breadth of the island, and many of his refuges are remembered. These hiding-places

are called Leab' Fhalaich Mhic a'Phi ('MacDuffie's Hiding Bed') and they are all quite small, nearly always one within sight of another, and they overlook the pathways that existed at that time between the various clachans. One can imagine that the fugitive will have watched to see signals or where supplies might be stashed by any who dared to help him. The chance of escape was slight – there were few boats and they would have been carefully secured.

The sites that are still remembered can be listed, starting from the most northerly, the Leab' on the southern slope of Beinn Bheag. This is a natural cave, a kind of gully in the tumbled rocks, reasonably sheltered. Another is said to have been on the northern slope of Dubh Charn at Kilchattan, but it is hard to identify the exact spot now . . . There is another nearby, near the top of a low cliff behind Druim Haugh . . . This provides little shelter from the elements but can conceal a prostrate figure.

The next one is close to the golf-course, the Crannaig or Pulpit at Maola-Chlibhi. . . . it is a little deeper than it looks and provides reasonable shelter and concealment. A very similar cave is on the north side of the promontory of Dun Gallain: and near the summit of Carn Spiris is a hollow covered by a massive rock which might have been a useful lair. MacDuffie is said to have been hunted from place to place 'as if he had been a wild beast' . . . and finally, in February 1623, he was hounded from all his hiding-places, and fled across to Oronsay. Then at low tide, in the darkness of early morning, he swam out to Eilean nan Ron, and tradition says he swam with his boots on.

When his pursuers came after him by boat, he concealed himself under a pile of seaweed, but was betrayed by a squawking gull that he had disturbed. His enemies dragged him out, and according to Colonsay tradition they brought him back to Colonsay where they stood him up against the standing stone at Pairc na h-Eaglais, Church Meadow, and shot him. This stone is now known as Carragh Mhic a'Phi (MacPhee's Standing Stone). Malcolm was buried close by, in the small graveyard of the ancient chapel there. The stone and chapel ruins are at Balarumonmore, a couple of miles south of Scalasaig.

Some years after MacPhee was shot, but still in the 17th century, a much hated Factor known as Domhnall Breac was taken by the Colonsay tenants, after he had pushed them too far – he was free with their women, as his factorial right – and they shot him, too, at Carragh Mhic a'Phi.

Some years ago, a dog in Colonsay was caught killing sheep. As this was its third offence, the owner agreed that it would have to be shot. It was taken to Carragh Mhic a'Phi for the execution, and it never seemed to occur to anyone that the deed could be done anywhere else.

After the murders Coll Ciotach was busy killing or driving out the rest of the MacPhees, who were now leaderless. This time, around 1623–24, must have been when *The Rout of the MacPhees* was composed. Alex Haddow, following Skene, says that only a very few MacPhees survived in Colonsay; many went to Loch Arkaig and became associated with the Camerons – who held the other ancient stronghold called Dungalan. Many of the dispossessed MacPhees took to the road, as landless folk often had to, in those days. It has been said that the alternative title to one of the two tunes known as *The Bicker, The Extirpation of the Tinkers*, may be a paraphrase of the title *The Rout of the MacPhees*.

Peter Youngson, in his book on Jura, gives some stories about these times, including several about a man called Darroch and his struggles with a man called Buie (both are common surnames in Jura). This version covers the time after the killing of the chief:

> Darroch was engaged by Argyll to take possession of Colonsay and exterminate the MacPhee family who held the island at that time. [Note that the villain is now a Campbell rather than a MacDonald. Storytellers adjusted the cast of characters to suit their audiences.]
>
> As Darroch was getting his followers together, Buie came up to him and asked him for a passage in his war galley . . . When they reached Colonsay, Darroch and his men set off for MacPhee's house to carry out their mission. Buie followed at a safe distance. He saw a girl carrying something in her arms, and asked what it was.
>
> 'It's nothing of any value' she replied.
>
> 'Don't be afraid' said Buie, 'although I am here along with these men, I don't belong to their company, and I mean you no harm.'
>
> The girl showed him a baby boy, and said 'That is the only one now alive of the family of MacPhee'.
>
> Buie took the infant and concealed him against his own breast underneath his plaid. When Darroch's company had finished their work of killing the MacPhees, he joined them on the return journey. Buie wanted Darroch to make straight for Jura and set him off at the nearest point, but Darroch chose to make for the Sound of Islay, the way he had come. Buie was doing his share of the rowing, and trying hard to keep the head of the boat towards Jura, he broke his oar. His hands flew back and struck his chest, or rather, struck the baby on his chest. The child gave a cry.
>
> Darroch exclaimed 'There's a stowaway in the boat!', but Buie said 'It's only the creaking of the oar'.

They gave him another oar, but he broke it as well. 'You'll have to give me a stronger oar', said Buie. There was a great heavy oar the galley carried to use for steering [when under sail], so they gave him that. So well did he wield his oar that he brought the boat to land in Jura, just north of the opening of the Sound of Islay. When they were near enough, Buie used his oar as a vaulting pole, and before the others were aware of what was happening, he was ashore and facing them with his drawn sword in his hand.

'You'll need all your sprightliness now, Buie', said Darroch. Buie replied 'Land if you like, for I'm ready for you'.

'I don't think so' said Darroch, declining the invitation.

Buie held the baby aloft in his arms and called out 'This is the heir of the MacPhees, and there are as many arrows in the quiver as you have men, and not one of you will pass'.

'Buie was afraid to take the child to his own house, lest his enemies might come while he was away from home, so he took the boy to a remote cave on the side of Beinn an Oir, the highest of the Paps of Jura, and hid him there. He went regularly with food to the child, and would leave a piece of meat, tied to the child's toe with a piece of cord of such a length that if the meat were to go into the child's throat so that he was on the point of choking, the sudden straightening of his body would automatically pull the meat out of his throat. [Don't try this at home.]

In due course the boy grew up, and with Buie's help he was able to win back his inheritance in Colonsay, although it is said that he lost it again later. . .

Donald Budge had another, slightly different version, called *Yellow-haired John of the Deer*. He said that MacPhie of Colonsay left a son who was a child when his father perished. It was known that Colkitto [we are now back with the MacDonalds as the enemy] was anxious to get hold of the child to destroy him, lest he should later avenge the death of his father, killed by Colkitto. In Jura there was a forester of the MacDonalds who had a great regard for the MacPhees of Colonsay, and so it was planned to send the boy to Jura to be cared for by this forester, whose name was Yellow-haired John (Iain Buie) of the Deer ['forester' here means 'keeper of the deer forest', nothing to do with trees]. The child was hidden first in Colonsay by a man called Currie, who then brought him to Jura, where the forester agreed to take charge of him. He brought him up in a cave on Beinn an Oir, where he put up a bed and slept at nights with the child held to his breast. The boy was afterwards removed to Kintyre, where he was brought up. This version is less entertaining, but possibly more authentic. There is no tale, at least no surviving tale, of MacPhee's son returning to avenge his father.

Willie (Benbecula) MacDonald says that a work called *Cumha Mhic a'Phi, Lament for MacPhee*, now called the *Rout of the MacPhees*, was originally known as *Cu dubh Mhic a'Phi (Black dog of the MacPhees)*. His story goes that MacPhee lived on a shieling, with his two sons, their cattle and a black dog, and they were there during the summer months. This black dog never did a hand's turn in its life, was totally disobedient, never did what was required of it, never did anything. It was seven years old. One day MacPhee was sitting by the fire and his two sons had gone out for a stroll, and after a while they came back with two beautiful ladies and disappeared into the sleeping room. MacPhee and the dog went on sitting by the fire, and then MacPhee noticed blood coming out from under the bedroom door, so he got up to see what it was. Before he reached the door, it opened and the two girls ran away into the night, and his two big sons were lying there with their throats cut. He said to the dog 'Come on, Black Dog, get after them! Though you've never done a hand's turn in your life before, do something tonight', and the dog went off after the two women.

There are two variations on what happened next. One is that the dog came back without a hair on its body and MacPhee took down a huge big basin and filled it with milk, put it down for the dog, and the dog drinks it all and drops down dead. The other is that the dog didn't come back, and in the morning he found it dead beside the stream without a hair on its body and just along from it were two haggard old women torn to pieces by the dog. The two lovely girls had been witches in disguise.

A hairless dog appears in stories attached to most of the Piper's Caves in Scotland. The implication is that the fires of hell had singed the fur off, i.e. there is a link with the supernatural and the devil.

Piper's Cave

On the west coast of Colonsay, between Kilchattan and Kiloran Bay, there are several caves in the sea-cliffs, and one of them is Uamh Phiobaire, the Piper's Cave. The accompanying story, all too familiar, is told by W.H. Murray: 'The legend is that an exploratory piper playing *MacCrimmon's Lament* led his dog into the cave in the hope of discovering hell. That was the last ever heard of the piper, but his dog emerged from a cave on Beinn Eibhne, four miles away at the south end of Colonsay, with its coat singed off.'

MacCrimmon's Lament was probably *Cha Till MacCrimmein*, which was formerly *Cha Till Mi Tuille, I Shall Return No More*, a suitably prophetic tune. The association with MacCrimmon would date from 1745. In most versions of this story, which seems to have attached itself to scores of caves in the Highlands and Islands, the piper is playing either *Cha Till* or a tune called *Da Laimh 'sa Piob, Laimh 'sa Chlaidheamh, Two Hands on the Pipe, and a Hand on the Sword*. The former tune represents the piper's despair or depression, the second his alertness to danger.

In John MacPhee's book, the piper is playing the *Lament for Donald Ban MacCrimmon*, but this would be a bit on the late side, since the legend goes back earlier than 1746. It has been suggested that the name Piper's Cave is a corruption of an old word *papar*, meaning hermit monks of the Celtic church who often lived in caves in order to mortify the flesh and thus increase their chances of going to heaven. Certainly there is more evidence of these ascetics living in caves than there is of pipers and their dogs.

It is strange how the dog usually seems to cover the same distance, averaging four miles, before it emerges, bald – except in Tiree, where it came out of the same cave that it had entered, since there is no complex of caves there.

Sources

David Stevenson, *Highland Warrior*
Ronald Williams, *The Lord of the Isles*
Kevin Byrne, *Colkitto!*
Peter Youngson, *Jura*
Donald Budge, *Jura*
William MacDonald ('Benbecula')
W.H. Murray, *The Hebrides*
Tony Oldham, *The Caves of Scotland*

The MacNeills of Colonsay and Oronsay

In the Civil Wars of the mid-17th century, the MacNeills supported Montrose, and this must have made relations with the Earl of Argyll uneasy. Some fifty years later, Donald MacNeill was in possession of two farms in Knapdale which Argyll wanted, Drumdrishaig and Crear (on the west coast of Knapdale, north of Kilberry). Around 1700, a legal agreement was drawn up, and MacNeill gave up his ownership of the farms, but retained the tenancies for his family, and in return, Argyll restored to him the proprietorship of the islands of Colonsay and Gigha. From these MacNeills was descended Lachlan MacNeill Campbell of Kintarbert.

From the Colonsay MacNeills we have Andrew MacNeill of Oronsay, and his forebear Colonel Malcolm MacNeill of Colonsay. Malcolm was appointed to the Argyll and Sutherland Highlanders in 1885, and commanded the 11th Battalion during the First World War. Himself a piper of ability, according to the Notices of Pipers, he did the piping world a favour by giving orders that regimental pipers were not to be assigned to dangerous tasks like shifting ammunition, as too many of them were being killed in action. The colonel, who is reputed to have said 'I'd rather be Pipe Major than Colonel', was a lifelong piping enthusiast, as was his descendant, Andrew.

Andrew MacNeill

ANDREW MACNEILL was a stalwart of piping who managed to convey his enthusiasm to the world even from his farm on Oronsay. He was far from being the bucolic character he sometimes liked to impersonate. Born in 1916, in Helensburgh, on the Clyde, where he was brought up, Andrew Somerville MacNeill served in the 2nd Battalion The Glasgow Highlanders throughout the Second World War.

Donald MacLeod composed *MacNeill of Oransay's Salute*, a piobaireachd work with five variations, and published with it a note: 'Andrew MacNeill, who during the Second World War served in the Glasgow Highlanders, lives on the island of Oronsay. A pupil, one could almost say a disciple, of the late Pipe Major Robert Reid, he is both a serious student and a fine player of Ceol Mor.'

When Andrew died on 26 September 1997, at the age of eighty-one, his friend Sandy MacPherson wrote this obituary for the *Piping Times*:

> Andrew Oransay, as he was known to his huge circle of friends, was a multi-faceted man of many interests. By profession a farmer on the Hebridean island of Oransay, tidally connected to Colonsay, his skill with sheep and sheepdog training and handling was a byword. He retired to Colonsay some time ago, but never allowed his Hebridean remoteness to interfere in the slightest with his maintenance and fostering of friendships all over the world. He had a very special gift for encompassing and enduring friendships. A telephone call from him invariably brightened a day; a letter, idiosyncratically typed, was a

joy of pithy observation and anecdote. His network of news-gathering would put MI5 to shame.

His passion was the music of the great Highland bagpipe, and especially its classical music – piobaireachd. He learned to play at an early age, and was a masterly exponent, albeit diffident of public performance. His mentor for many years was Pipe Major Robert Reid from Slamannan, who had in turn been taught by J. MacDougall Gillies. Andrew was fiercely loyal to their style of phrasing a tune as passed to him, but as a distinguished judge of piping competitions at the highest level, he accepted and appreciated fine playing from other schools. His facility in expressing his love for a beautiful and melodic line made it contagious. He was bitingly critical of careless execution. His knowledge of piobaireachd was encyclopaedic, and was unstintingly shared by tape or in engrossing conversations, by reference to his Master's style, but also, scrupulously, to other turns of phrasing. For many years he enjoyed in particular such exchanges with James Campbell of Kilberry . . .

Andrew was raised in Helensburgh, where he acquired a keen eye for fine china [his brother had a china shop in Helensburgh]. He left his individual mark on the 2nd Battalion The Glasgow Highlanders, with whom he served throughout the war.

Andrew had the liveliest and most enquiring of minds. Widely read, with informed and thoughtful views on many subjects, he constantly astonished the writer with another hitherto unsuspected field of erudition. And he had the gift of words, with a mischievous sense of humour. He was capable of lobbing a verbal grenade into any conversation and enjoying the fallout with a chuckle. An inveterate and inventive practical joker, the latest butt could do no other than join in the laughter – eventually.

He was one of the prime movers in the establishment of the purpose-built Piping Centre at McPhater Street, Glasgow [in fact, it was a converted building]. The world of piping has its share of characters. Andrew took his place unselfconsciously as one of its most colourful.

To the end – just eight days before the golden wedding celebrations with his beloved wife Flora – he was vital, engaging, and a fount of fun . . .

His grave is in the burial ground at Kilchattan, in Colonsay.

In the same issue of the *Piping Times* there appeared this letter from Jay T. Close, of Williamsburg, Virginia, with another sincere tribute:

On behalf of myself and the other organisers of the 'Williamsburg Ceol Mor Weekend' I would like to make this statement of gratitude for Andrew MacNeill's support and our sorrow in his passing.

Andrew had slight interest in academic theories or speculation about piobaireachd; he had, after all, learned the living music from Robert Reid, one of its great modern masters. Andrew once wrote 'Personally I was just a parrot and tried to copy Robert – my only piobaireachd teacher – minutely, and anything I've heard since has never caused me to try to deviate'.

The Second World War and its aftermath denied Andrew a professional piping career. Tapes of his playing in later years convince me he would have risen to the heights of that profession. Instead, living the crofter's life, Andrew worked behind the scenes, corresponding voluminously the world over with those interested in the old piping styles.

To my loss, I never met the man personally, but a binder of letters filled with good humoured commentary on piping matters is a treasured legacy of a too brief four year association carried out via the U.S. and U.K. postal systems. Trips to the mail box will certainly be less eventful.

Pipers everywhere have lost a friend; I feel I've lost a mentor; and the Great Music has lost a champion.

In November 1997, the *Piper Press* added its tribute:

Andrew was always willing to impart his knowledge to young pipers. Tapes of tunes would be dispatched with alacrity to anyone seeking advice.

He was a frequent attendant at Piobaireachd Society conferences, where his forthright views and sense of humour enlivened many a heavy debate on the intricacies of the art.

He gave a talk in 1987 to the conference, entitled 'Some Piobaireachd Thoughts of Robert Reid'. While most of the talk was a recorded tape of Robert Reid's own words, especially on the 'Donald Mor run-down', the subsequent discussion revealed the depth and scope of Andrew MacNeill's knowledge and understanding of piobaireachd.

In a book entitled *The Crofter and the Laird*, an American descendant of the Colonsay MacPhees, John MacPhee, wrote of the five years he and his family spent in Colonsay in the 1960s. He met Andrew and Flora MacNeill, and the book gives a good idea of how well integrated the MacNeills were into island life. They had married in 1947, Flora being an island girl who was born on Oronsay, and for five years they had the shop in Scalasaig – the only shop in Colonsay – before they took the tenancy of the farm of Oronsay, with 1,400 acres of land. There, in the 1960s, they had 630 sheep, 30 cows and a bull. This was not, by any stretch of the imagination, a croft, nor could the impressive Oronsay House be described as a crofthouse.

Flora's brother, DONALD MACNEILL, was well known as a piper in Colonsay. Although he did not compete, he was much in demand for weddings and ceilidhs, and is remembered as a good player.

The MacNeill hospitality at Oronsay House was famous. It was said that pipers would arrive with pipe cases and small weekend bags, prepared for a stay of perhaps two nights, but a fortnight later would still be there, looked after by Flora, and talking piping and playing pipes into the nights.

John MacPhee recalls his first meeting with Andrew: 'He was a short man with a round weather-reddened face. He looked youthful although his hair was gray. He had a mustache. His eyes were blue and quick and bright, but they turned aside at times in shyness . . . he spoke in an extraordinarily soft voice.'

John visited Oronsay where he was greeted with great hospitality and talk of piping, before Andrew played for him – not Ceol Mor, but a few pieces of light music. Then Andrew spoke with passion of his love for piobaireachd, which evidently made an impression on John MacPhee, although he himself was unable to enjoy pipe music. Andrew explained about the structure of Ceol Mor, 'to which individuals attach their own variations', wrote John (and we feel that he did not understand what he was being told). 'Young pipers often exasperated Andrew because they leave out fundamental elements.' This has a more authentic Andrew MacNeill ring.

The writer goes on: 'He hummed some of the tunes, and the tunes he was humming were so sad, beautiful, lilting and melodic that I found myself wondering if, when these themes emerged from the great Highland bagpipes, Andrew could hear something I could not,' which seems undeniable. John MacPhee found the strange titles of the tunes more absorbing than the music, and was faintly puzzled by Andrew's passion for piobaireachd – and a little envious.

The book tells of a running feud, perhaps more a friendly rivalry, between Andrew and the laird's factor, Tommy Findlay, whom he considered dilatory in seeing to the repair of the roof of Oronsay House, which was the responsibility of the Colonsay estate. When Andrew's roof was still not mended, he invited the factor to dinner at Oronsay, and deliberately failed to remind him of the incoming tide: he could not cross over the strand to return to Colonsay once the tide had reached a certain height. So the factor, as Andrew had intended, was obliged to stay overnight, and he was given the bedroom with the leaking roof. In the morning, his clothes and bedding were wet, but still he did not get round to the mending.

Andrew's chance came the next time they were racing their dinghies. The factor made an error and capsized his boat, throwing both his crewman and himself into deep water. Andrew, of course, abandoned the race and went to the rescue. He pulled the dripping crewman on board, and then reached for the factor. 'Haul me up, I'm drowning', cried the factor, but Andrew held him by the belt and ducked him under the surface. As he came up, spluttering, Andrew said 'Are you going to mend my roof?' 'Yes, yes, I'll mend your roof !' Another ducking. '*When* will you mend my roof?' 'Oh, soon, soon – haul me up!' Another ducking. 'What day precisely will you mend my roof?' 'Oh, whenever you like – next Wednesday.' Andrew said 'There's witnesses to that promise', and hauled him on board. And so the roof at Oronsay was mended.

It was said in Colonsay that Andrew MacNeill had been the piper when the liner *Queen Elizabeth* was launched at Clydebank, and that the Queen (before she became the Queen Mother) had sought him out afterwards to congratulate him. This was in 1938, when Andrew was still living on the Clyde.

Another flavour of Andrew MacNeill may be had from two items in the *Piping Times*: in January 1996 there is a notice about a tape recording donated by him to the College of Piping in Glasgow, of 'parts of piobaireachds played by John MacDonald of Inverness and Donald MacLeod, a donation gratefully accepted.' And in December 1994, he wrote a letter from Oronsay:

Dear Seumas,
The Duncan MacInnes whom Peter MacLeod made the march for was an American or Canadian, and much was made of him when he was over here in the 1930s by Mr McMurchie and Hugh Kennedy, at that time president and secretary respectively of the Scottish Pipers' Association.

MacInnes was chief of some big Highland Society out there and he chaired a lot of the Scottish Pipers' social events. I cannot remember the name of the Highland Society but do remember it amused me quite a bit.

I have not heard of the Currie reamer, but I remember well Malcolm Currie from Islay, short and stout with a large moustache. He used to call me Mr MagNeill when I attended the SP meetings on a Saturday night.

The meetings were held in the room at the right hand side ground floor of the old Highlanders' Institute and this was usually packed every Saturday night. Many attended at that time – the Peters MacLeod,

Wee Donald MacLeod, Wee Donald MacLean, Pook MacKenzie (from Portree) and others – between drinks.
    Slainte,
        Andrew MacNeill

This seems to be a typical communication: gossipy, reminiscent, interesting and above all generous with his information. He was a sharer, of what he knew and of the enjoyment it gave him.

In 1992, in recognition of his work on behalf of the then-planned new College of Piping, Andrew MacNeill was awarded the Balvenie Medal for outstanding services to piping. The award was accompanied by these words from Seumas MacNeill:

> Andrew has been involved in piping all his days, being a pupil of the late Robert Reid and having competed as a boy against Bob Hardie, Donald Ramsay, Thomas Pearston and Seumas MacNeill, among others. During the war he served in the 91st HLI and had a course with Willie Ross at Edinburgh Castle.
>
> For most of his life he farmed at Oronsay, and kept open house for top pipers, and it was there that he earned the description by General Frank Richardson of being 'the root and most of the branches of the piping grapevine'.
>
> Andrew has been a serious student of piobaireachd all his life. He has an outstanding collection of tape recordings of various masters, principally his own teacher, Robert Reid. Copies of these he has supplied to competitors and students of piobaireachd, and in the further encouragement of piping he has given away at least four sets of pipes.
>
> At the Ardvasar seminars organised by the John MacFadyen Trust he has been a great source of information and encouragement. His effervescent sense of humour and his ready wit made these and other gatherings a great pleasure to all who attend.

Seumas added: 'The medal was handed over by the Duke of Atholl. The reception given by the audience was eloquent testimony of the popularity of the choice.'

Sources

Piping Times
Piper Press
John MacPhee, *The Crofter and the Land*

Kerrera

Kerrera is a small island close to Oban, reached by a passenger ferry every half-hour (in summer) from the Gallanach road (near to Kilbowie Cottage). The crossing takes five minutes. Although not much in the way of piping tradition is associated with the island, most of its history being bound up with that of Oban, it used to be part of the lands of the MacDougalls of Dunollie, and so it was used as a place of refuge for the wife of Iain Ciar, Mary MacDonald, when her husband was a fugitive after the 1715 Rising. Iain was commemorated in the *Lament for Iain Ciar* composed in 1737 by his piper, Ronald Ban MacDougall of Moleigh.

After the '15 Rising, Iain Ciar was in hiding from government forces, and his wife and family had been forced out of Dunollie Castle. Taking her two youngest children, and lodging the rest of them with loyal clansmen, Mary went to live in a hut at Gylen, in the south of Kerrera. There she lived in conditions of abject poverty, supported by gifts of food from local people. For part of the time her husband was in concealment close by, across the Sound of Kerrera, on the mainland, and she managed to visit him, under cover of darkness, with the result that she found she was expecting another child. She could not explain this for fear of betraying his safety, and she suffered greatly from the gossip which was aroused. She wrote that if any man called at her hut, he was assumed to be her lover, and she hotly resented this. Poor Mary then found a lump in her breast, and assumed the worst, expecting to die within the year. Her husband's letters to her in Kerrera show that he recognised that she was deeply depressed. Kerrera cannot have been a happy memory for either of them.

As it turned out, the child was born safely and thrived, and the lump must have been benign, as Mary outlived her husband by many years.

The MacDougall pipers to the Dunollie chiefs had a croft at Moleigh, a few miles to the south of Oban, and they held it for about 150 years. They appear to have been related to many MacDougall families in Kerrera, and the last MacDougall piper, Ranald Mor, married a girl called Elizabeth MacDougall, who came from Kerrera. Their elder son was born in 1796.

Lismore

Lismore is an island in the Firth of Lorne, not far from Oban. It can be reached by car ferry from both Oban and Appin. The crossing from Oban takes about fifty minutes, from Appin about ten.

Mention Lismore to a piper, and he will probably at once start to hum *Leaving Lismore*, a tune composed by Mrs Martin Hardie (for the piano) and later adapted for the pipe as a 6/8 Slow Air with two parts. It is a great favourite, not only with pipers but with all players of Scottish traditional music.

Another possible link of Lismore with piping is that the famous Rankin pipers who had their piping school at Kilbrennan, in the west of Mull, in the late 17th and early 18th centuries, were said to be descended from an early Abbot of Lismore. His name was Cu-duilig, giving us the form Conduiligh or Condullie, by which the Rankin family was also known. He seems to have come over from Ireland, perhaps in the 12th century. He was said to be the son or grandson of Raincge, who gave the Rankins their other name. The clergy of the Irish church were allowed to marry and have families (see below, the Rankins).

This was the tradition preserved in the MacLean family, but it has recently been suggested that the Lismore where Conduiligh was born was Lismore in County Waterford, in Ireland, where there was also an abbey. It is thought that Ceallach, Conduiligh's father, was abbot there, and there is a possibility that he had previously been abbot of Iona. His three sons were Cu Catha ('dog of war'), Cu Sidhe ('dog of peace') and Cu Duiligh ('steadfast dog'), and they crossed over to Scotland. Their names, with the prefix Cu, originated in Ireland's pre-Christian past (see Nicholas MacLean-Bristol, 1995). Ceallach's grandfather, known as Old Dubhghall (Dougal), was at the abbey at Scone around 1100. Clearly there had been exchanges between the religious establishments of the Celtic churches of Ireland and Scotland over a considerable period of time.

James Robertson, a lawyer in Tobermory in the mid-1840s, kept a diary in which he recorded that, when on a professional visit to Oban, he went for a sail in a boat which was taking crew out to the lighthouse on Lismore: 'Off with Duncan MacLachlan and John Dallas at 9. Wind moderate but ahead. Tacked to Lismore, landed Light House people. MacInnes Piper. Went through Needle's eye. Landed at Achnacroish at 4.' His laconic style conceals as much as it reveals. Who was MacInnes Piper?

Mull, Iona, Staffa and Ulva

Mull is reached by car ferry from Oban to Craignure, which takes about forty-five minutes. There is also a small car-ferry from Lochaline to Fishnish, near Salen, a crossing of fifteen minutes. A car-ferry crossing between Tobermory and Kilchoan in Ardnamurchan takes thirty-five minutes. There is a small air-strip near Salen, but no public service to Mull by air.

Iona is accessible by passenger ferry from Fionnphort in the west of Mull (5 minutes), and Staffa from Iona itself, by private arrangement, if the weather is favourable. To reach Ulva, a small passenger ferry leaves from the west side of Mull, for the short crossing, a matter of minutes. In recent years a car ferry has run to Iona from Oban.

Piobaireachd Works Associated with Mull, Iona, Staffa and Ulva

Piobaireachd works associated with Mull, Iona, Staffa and Ulva include the MacLean works:

1. *(Lament for) Red Hector of the Battles* P 2
2. *Hector MacLean's Warning* P 7
3. *The MacLeans' March* P 11
4. *MacLaine of Lochbuie's Lament* P 5
5. *John Garve MacLean of Coll's Lament* P 9
6. *John Garve MacLean of Coll's Claymore* P 7
7. *The Battle of the Pass of Crieff (MacLean of Coll's Barge)* P 13

as well as:

8. *Alasdair Mor MacDonald of Boisdale's Salute* P
9. *MacDonald of Staffa's Salute* P 11

and possibly there are Mull connections with:

10. *The Finger Lock* P 8
11. *Lament for the Bishop of Argyll* P 4
12. *The Blue Ribbon* P 14
13. *Weighing from Land* P 8

More recently we have:

14. *Salute to the Isle of Iona*, a 20th-century work by John Good-enow P 8

15. *The Clan MacLean's Salute*, a late-19th/early-20th-century
    piobaireachd by Hector MacLean P 8
16. *Lament for Duncan MacFadyen*, a 20th-century composition by
    Donald MacLeod P 5

Several MacKinnon piobaireachd works, including *MacKinnon's
Lament* and *MacKinnon's Salute*, may belong to Mull where the
MacKinnons appear to have originated; but later they moved to Skye,
and are generally held to be a Skye clan, so these works are not included
here.

Dugald MacNeill adds that there is a tradition that *MacIntosh's
Lament* was composed originally for a MacLean of Mull who was exe-
cuted in Spain. The name, he says, was mistranslated from the Gaelic.
This possible origin for the tune might be disputed.

Notes on the above compositions:

1. *Red Hector of the Battles*, sometimes known as the *Lament for Red
Hector of the Battles* (see also the section on the Rankins, below). Red
Hector, Eachainn Ruadh, was the 6th Chief of the MacLeans of Duart.
Born in 1367, he fought at the Battle of Harlaw in 1411, where he was
killed at the age of forty-four. Alec Haddow tells how he died 'after a
tremendous single combat with Sir Alexander Irvine of Drum, in which
both were mortally wounded. The respect in which Red Hector was
held is shown by the fact that his body was carried from the field by the
MacInnes and Morison clans (both are Mull names), and was buried
in Iona. This was a famous incident, and as Harlaw is always depicted
as an entirely savage battle, it is of interest to recall that for years afterwards the MacLeans of Duart and the Irvines of Drum exchanged a
sword on the anniversary of the battle, in memory of a gallant enemy
... It seems quite unlikely that a piobaireachd commemorating such a
renowned chief as Red Hector was not written [sic] at the time of his
death in 1411 or shortly after, in which case it is the oldest piobaireachd we know of. There was, however, a later MacLean chief called
Red Hector, who also fell in battle, at Inverkeithing in 1651', fighting
for Montrose.

There may have been confusion between the two Red Hectors, or the
piobaireachd work may have been composed in the 17th century and
given this title as a compliment to the later Hector, at the same time
recalling his illustrious ancestor. This seems more likely than a date as
early as 1411.

2. *Hector MacLean's Warning.* Hector was one of the two illegitimate

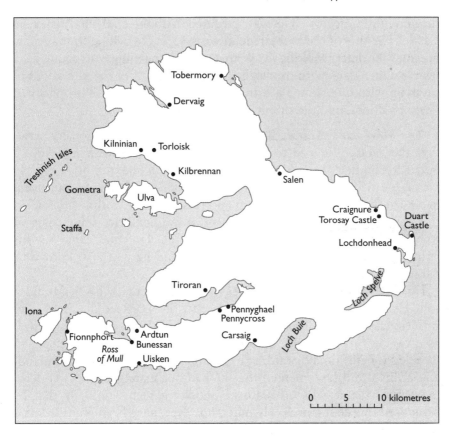

Mull and adjacent islands

sons of Allan nan Sop (of Gigha), a notorious pirate and predator on the west coast. He had his boys declared legitimate in 1547, and Hector inherited his father's possessions, both legal and ill-gotten.

Hector married a daughter of the Earl of Argyll, and was constantly plotting to overthrow and murder his cousin, Lachlan Mor, the chief of the Clan MacLean, and to instal himself as chief. He first tried to have Lachlan excluded from the succession on the grounds that he was too effeminate to be a leader – as Alec Haddow put it, 'a most serious misjudgement of character' (Lachlan Mor had his faults, but effeminate he was not). After many plots and counter-plots, Hector over-reached himself, was seized by Lachlan and imprisoned in Duart Castle, with his son, Allan Og.

In 1578, Hector was removed from Duart and taken to Coll, where Lachlan Mor 'maist cruelie and unnaturallie causit streik the heid fra the umquhile Hector'. He was executed without trial, at Breacacha Castle. The title of the piobaireachd work seems to belong to that time, but may be later, looking back to earlier happenings. It could have been a name given with hindsight, warning Hector of the fate about to catch up with him. There is a tradition of an old woman's prophecy of Hector's doom, and the title may refer to that.

3. *The MacLeans' March.* Book 10 of the Piobaireachd Society series says this March 'is said to be the composition of Ailean nan Sop, a noted freebooter of the 16th century'. The by-name *nan Sop* possibly means 'of the Straw', an implication that Allan was born, or conceived, in a barn, i.e. was baseborn. Born and raised in the Treshnish Isles, off the west coast of Mull, probably in primitive conditions, he was said to be a bastard son of MacLean of Duart, the clan chief. Some say his name means Allan of the Burning Torch, and he was also known as Allan of Gigha.

He died in or around 1551, leaving all he had to his legitimised son, Hector MacLean. Allan was a man of exceptional cruelty and ruthlessness, who murdered and plundered his own clansmen as well as ravaging further afield, up and down the west coast. He is said to have led nineteen major raiding expeditions, including two in Ireland, and at his death he lamented that he had not managed the twentieth. In view of his attacks on his own people, it seems unlikely that he composed this clan march. He must, however, have been regarded as a suitably warlike leader, because on his death he was given the honour of burial in Iona, with an elaborately carved gravestone, among the clan chieftains.

It is not clear whether the term March (Gaelic *spaidseareachd*) is here used in the way that Joseph MacDonald used it, to mean simply what we now call a piobaireachd work, or whether it commemorates a punitive march into Islay by the MacLeans, avenging the death of Lachlan Mor in 1598. If the latter, clearly it was not the work of Allan nan Sop; the former is perhaps more likely.

4. *MacLaine of Lochbuie's Lament.* The main source for this work is Duncan Campbell's manuscript. Little is known of the origins of the tune, but the clan history says that John MacLaine, XVII of Lochbuie [this branch of the family always spelled the name MacLaine] 'had his piper and was, perhaps, the last of the Lochbuies who particularly favoured this art'. John MacLean, on the garrison staff of Fort William, Bengal, wrote on 29 January 1799 that 'thirty years before, Hector MacLaine was piper to John MacLaine of Lochbooy and was

allowed [considered] to be the first [best] in Scotland'. What this judgement is worth is open to debate. It seems likely that Hector composed this lament for his laird, who died in 1785.

This laird, John MacLaine, XVII of Lochbuie, was a vigorous and aggressive man who was visited in 1773 by Dr Johnson and his friend Boswell. Dr Johnson described Lochbuie as 'a true Highland laird, rough and haughty and tenacious of his dignity', adding that he was 'a very powerful laird', while Boswell's verdict was: 'a bluff, comely, noisy old gentleman, proud of his hereditary consequence, and a very hearty and hospitable landlord [host]'. He was also a keen golfer, and is believed to have introduced the game to Mull.

5. and 6. *John Garve MacLean of Coll's Lament* and *John Garve MacLean of Coll's Claymore*. It is not certain which John Garve of Coll is named here, as there were three of them in the line of the MacLeans of Coll, and these could be any of them. Nor is it certain that both titles refer to the same man. Although they were the MacLeans of Coll, they were of the family of the MacLeans of Duart, who lost their castle and much of their lands in Mull to the Campbells in 1692.

The first MacLean of Coll, the first John Garve (Iain Garbh), was a grandson of Red Hector of the Battles. He married a daughter of Fraser of Lovat, and obtained from the Lord of the Isles a charter for the lands of Coll and, by sharp practice, also the island of Rum. This was around 1430. He was a ruthless and ambitious man.

In contrast, the seventh Laird of Coll was quiet, pious and scholarly, also known as Iain Garbh, though it is not clear why. Garbh may refer to his complexion. He was an excellent harp player, and taught others, as well as encouraging harpers to visit him in Coll. He was so passionate about the harp that it seems unlikely that a pipe lament would be made for him, unless, of course, there is a harp composition underlying it. There are examples of piobaireachd works being developed from harp music, such as *Corrienessan's Salute*, and possibly *The Groat*.

The ninth Laird was another John Garve, and he met a sudden and violent end on the streets of Edinburgh, at the age of only eighteen. He was a student at Edinburgh University, and was walking through the town, minding his own business, when a street riot broke out. Someone threw a primitive grenade, and young Coll was killed by a fragment of metal. He had taken no part in the riot. It may be that grief and shock at the news of his death gave rise to the *Lament for John Garve MacLean of Coll*. Again, we do not know why he was called Garbh.

Without further evidence, we cannot tell which John Garve is commemorated in either of these works.

7. *The Battle of the Pass of Crieff.* This work has the alternative titles *Bhratich Bhan 'White Banner'* (in the Campbell Canntaireachd manuscript), *The Laird of Coll's Barge* (in John MacKay's manuscript, where his brother Angus pencilled in the titles), and *MacLean of Coll's* (in the Peter Reid collection).

The Pass of Crieff links it to a skirmish in Perthshire in 1730, between redcoats and smugglers, but the Coll names may suggest that it is an iorram or rowing tune. Alec Haddow considered 'barge' an unfortunate translation, when the vessel was probably a war-galley or birlinn; in the 18th century, a barge was any open vessel propelled by sails or sets of oars. It is impossible to date this work, or to identify the Laird of the title.

8. *Alasdair Mor MacDonald of Boisdale's Salute.* In 1743, Ranald, 17th Chief of Clanranald, granted a tack (long lease) of all his lands in South Uist to his half-brother, Alasdair Mor of Boisdale, a man of great influence and forceful character. Alasdair had already inherited, in 1730, the designation 'of Boisdale', as his share of his father's patrimony.

It was Alasdair who introduced the kelp industry to the islands from Ireland; kelp was burned for potash, which commanded high prices when war on the continent made it unavailable from abroad. Among other uses, potash was important in the making and colouring of cloth. Gathering kelp gave many islanders a measure of prosperity as long as the British market had the monopoly, but the peace which followed Napoleon's downfall saw the bottom fall out of the island kelp industry, leading to extensive emigration. Alasdair had urged those on his estates to put large rocks on their sandy beaches, to encourage the growth of kelp. He seems to have had the welfare of his tenants at heart, and was a popular laird. He married three times and had nineteen children, of whom ten died in infancy and two were killed in the American Wars.

Alasdair was the grandfather of Ranald MacDonald who became Laird of Staffa and Ulva (see below). Alasdair Mor seems to have died around 1750, but the exact date is not known. This lament for him may have been made by one of the Ulva MacArthurs, or by one of the MacIntyre pipers to Clanranald. There is a tradition that the Boisdale MacDonalds had the Ulva MacArthurs as their pipers, and that they would have nothing to do with the Rankins because of enmity between the MacDonalds and the MacLeans in Mull.

9. *MacDonald of Staffa's Salute.* This work is found in the Peter Reid manuscript of 1826. There was only one MacDonald of Staffa. He was

Ranald MacDonald, sixth child of Colin MacDonald II of Boisdale. Ranald's mother was Colin's second wife, Isabella Campbell, sister of the Earl of Breadalbane, and she seems to have brought up her eldest son with a good conceit of himself and his social position.

As his share of his father's lands Ranald inherited the estates of Staffa and Ulva, two islands off the west coast of Mull, as well as land on Mull itself. As proprietor of two remote small islands he embraced the role of Highland laird with boyish enthusiasm. He became one of the 'tartan chiefs' who created the romantic Highland image later taken up by Walter Scott and Queen Victoria – but when Scott visited him in Ulva, even he had his doubts about the young Laird of Staffa (see below).

In 1812, Ranald married Elizabeth Stewart, only child and heiress of Sir Henry Stewart, Bart, of Allanton, in Lanarkshire. Ranald took his wife's surname, changed in spelling to Steuart (more mediaeval? or more French?), and he abandoned his first name Ranald in favour of a more Norman spelling, Reginald. When his wife inherited the estates of Touch Seton in Stirlingshire from her maternal uncle in 1835, she added Seton, or sometimes Touch Seton, to her name. Ranald had, by some means or other, assumed her father's baronetcy – money talked, then as now – and so he became Sir Reginald Touch-Seton-Steuart, sometimes with MacDonald tucked in somewhere, more often not. He was appointed Sheriff Depute for the County of Stirling, a role which he tackled with horrible enthusiasm. He seems to have enjoyed imposing the death sentence and then watching the subsequent executions in person, with relish.

Sir Reginald, Laird of Staffa, died in 1838. Sir J.C. Dalyell in his book *Musical Memoirs of Scotland* (1849) said that just a few months after his death, a *Lament for Sir Reginald MacDonald* was played at the Highland Society of London competition in 1838. No trace of this work is known, and it is thought to have been the *Salute*, played as a tribute to the dead man. Pipers sometimes say it feels more like a lament to them than a salute.

It is not known when the *Salute to MacDonald of Staffa* was made, but since the title uses his older designation, and if it was indeed a salute, it may have been composed while he was still in Ulva, probably before his marriage in 1812. The composer is not known, but his piper was Archibald MacArthur of Ormaig, Isle of Ulva, a pupil of Donald Ruadh MacCrimmon, and it may have been Archibald who made the salute. He outlived his laird, who had replaced him as his piper in the lowlands, so if it was a lament composed in 1838, it was perhaps not made by Archibald. Possibly, however, the Ulva folk continued to call Ranald the Laird of Staffa regardless of his elevation in the social life of the south. Archibald did not accompany him to his home in Stirling-shire, although he was part of Sir Reginald's 'tail' for the Royal Visit to Edinburgh in 1822.

10. *The Finger Lock.* This is generally accepted as being the work of Ronald MacDonald of Morar, one of three attributed to him, the others being *The Red Speckled Bull* and *The Vaunting*. There is, however, a tradition in Mull that *The Finger Lock* (*A'Ghlas Mheur* in Gaelic) was the name of a 'secret' tune of the Rankin pipers at Kilbrennan (see below, Rankins). As a composition of Ronald of Morar it would be dated around 1700; as a Rankin tune it would be earlier, probably early in the 1600s. There is no certainty, however, that these were the same tune.

Although *A'Ghlas Mheur* appears to mean 'the lock of the finger', some say *Glas* or *Gleus* was an old word for an exercise, so that the title would really mean 'the Finger Exercise'. The Gaelic word *glas* 'lock' which has the genitive form *glaise*, seems to have been confused with *gleus* 'exercise', of similar pronunciation in some Gaelic dialects, and there is evidence that in Sutherland *gleus* meant a type of local mini-piobaireachd composed to honour people within a township – not a full-blown classical piobaireachd composition, but a miniature version of it. A title such as *The Finger Exercise* could have been used for any number of compositions, just as *Etude* is used for many piano pieces.

11. *The Lament for the Bishop of Argyll.* In the Dow manuscript and the MacFarlane manuscript (around 1742), there is a harp or fiddle tune of this title. It has been described at a 'proto-piobaireachd', i.e. a very early stage in the development of this form of music, which 'seems to possess the character, though not the typical structure, of piobair-eachd' (editors' note, Book 15 of the Piobaireachd Society series). The MacFarlane manuscript does not give the grace-notes, and the editors of Book 15 published it in both forms, first as in the manuscript and then with the grace-noting added.

The editors add: 'A curious feature of this score (in the manuscript) is the fact that there are repeat dots at the end of each movement.' They omitted these on the grounds that they thought that 'each movement has an internal build-up and climax, the impact of which is likely to be dulled by repetition'.

It is not certain which Bishop of Argyll this was, but there are four possibilities:

(a) Robert Montgomery, son of the Earl of Eglinton, died around 1558;

(b) Neil Campbell, resigned 1608;

(c) Andrew Boyd, illegitimate son of Thomas, Lord Boyd (an Ulster family), died 1636;

(d) Hector MacLean, who supported Montrose and Charles I, and became Bishop of Argyll in 1680, died 1687.

Of these, Hector seems the most likely subject of the lament. He married Jean Boyd, a granddaughter of Andrew (c) above; they had sixteen daughters and several sons, one of whom was Anndra mac an Easbuig (Andrew the Bishop's son), well known as a MacLean poet. He is mentioned as 'the harper's son in Mull' in an account of the depredations committed on the Clan Campbell; and he fought alongside Dundee at the Battle of Killiecrankie.

12. *The Blue Ribbon* (or *Riband*). There are two traditions about the wearing of the blue ribbon: some say it was the badge of the Covenanters' army in the Civil Wars of the mid-17th century, others believe it was the emblem of the followers of Montrose, who was latterly a bitter enemy of the Covenanters. This confusion probably arose because Montrose had been a leader of the Covenanting forces earlier in his career (1638–44), and the wearing of the blue ribbon dates from that period.

The biographer of Montrose, C.V. Wedgwood, wrote (1952): 'Montrose's army marched on Aberdeen. At their head floated his banner of blue silk on which were painted in letters of gold 'For God, Covenant and Country'. He provided every man in his forces with a length of bright blue silk ribbon. The infantry twisted them into cockades and stuck them in their bonnets; the cavalry wore them slung from shoulder to hip as scarves. The more solemn ministers referred sourly to this frivolous ornament as 'Montrose's Whimsy', but the gay ribbons served a useful purpose, in a time when uniforms were unknown, in marking out the troops of the Covenant'.

The blue ribbon seems to have remained as the emblem of the Covenanters, even when fighting against Montrose.

Writing in the 1820s, Donald MacDonald said there were four Ribbon works, one from Mull, one from Skye, one from the MacGregor Clan and one from Clan Grant. He seems to have meant they were all different tunes, and he gave two in his collection. Of the Mull *Ribbon*, he said that in Mull, the MacNiels, MacLeans and MacQuarries all claimed it, but 'be it as it may, it is a bond, the signal of which is the wearing of the Ribbon in the button-hole of the waistcoat'.

13. *Weighing from Land.* Alec Haddow quoted General Thomason's notes to his book *Ceol Mor*, in which he says: 'Pipe Major [Allan] Patterson hears from his father in South Uist that this work was composed by a piper of Mull on the occasion of an emigrant ship *Dubh Gleannich* [sic] leaving the island for Charleston, U.S.A.' (unpublished notes, National Library of Scotland).

Donald Archie MacDonald found an account of a ship, the *Dubh Ghleannach*, which belonged to MacDonald of Glenaladale. She plied among the Inner Hebrides, and sank in Pollnampartan, Eigg, in 1817. There is a Gaelic song about her, but Alec Haddow thought the words did not seem to go with the piobaireachd *Weighing from Land,* which he considered to be either an iorram (rowing tune) or a sail-hoisting shanty. As the *Dubh Ghleannach* was not herself an emigrant ship, she was presumably shipping would-be emigrants on the first leg of their journey to the New World, to meet an ocean-going vessel at a bigger port. To those left behind, the effect would be the same.

14. *Salute to the Isle of Iona.* This is the work for which the American piper and composer, John Goodenow, is best known. It was placed second in a prestigious composing competition in this country. The work is pleasantly atmospheric, and as someone remarked on hearing it played, 'You can hear the seagulls talking.' It was a tune prescribed for the Clasp at the Northern Meeting in 2008, one of the years when they were all 20th-century works. John Goodenow was from Detroit, USA, and was described as 'an enthusiastic player of Ceol Mor'. He held the Piobaireachd Society's Gold Medal, won in Ottawa, Canada. He died in 2000.

15. *The Clan MacLean's Salute.* This is the work of Hector MacLean, who was the piper to the Clan MacLean. He belonged to Oban, but was of Mull descent, with a long line of pipers behind him, back into the 18th century. He had a strong influence on piping in Glasgow and the West Highlands, and was piper to Sir Charles MacLean of Duart and Morvern.

In 1895 Hector was presented with a magnificent plaid brooch, a gift from the Clan MacLean as a 'token of their respect and esteem'. The wording suggests that he was not a young man in 1895. The brooch is now in the possession of Hector's grandson, Keith MacKellar, who lives in Craighouse, on the island of Jura. Keith says that his grandfather was one of the original members of the Govan Police pipe band (which later became the City of Glasgow Police pipe band). It had many members who came from Argyll, and especially from Islay and Jura.

Hector died in 1925. One of his grandchildren, Janet Faulds, was married to Duncan MacFadyen junior (see below).

16. *Lament for Duncan MacFadyen*, by Donald MacLeod. This lament was made for Duncan MacFadyen senior, who died in 1930. He was the father of the three piping MacFadyen brothers, John, Duncan and Iain, and their sister Freena. Five of the family of ten were pipers, taught by their father. Duncan senior came of a Tiree family, one of whom had settled in the Ross of Mull.

Donald MacLeod's note in the published collection of his piobaireachd works says: 'Duncan MacFadyen was brought up on the Island of Mull. His father was from Tiree and his mother was a direct relative of the MacKays of Gairloch. He took an interest in piping as a boy, on the Island of Mull, and this interest was maintained until his death. His early working years were spent at sea, then he became harbour master at Glasgow. A keen student of his native Gaelic language, he was greatly interested in all forms of Gaelic music and song. For many years he was secretary of the Scottish Pipers Association, giving great service to the cause of piping. He encouraged his sons to study the music of the bagpipe, which they did to such an extent that the names of John, Duncan and Iain have become household names in the world of piping' (see also below, MacFadyens).

Duncan's sons knew nothing of the alleged link with the Gairloch MacKays, most of whom had emigrated to Nova Scotia.

Other Works, not Piobaireachd, Associated with Mull, Iona, Staffa and Ulva

Allan Beaton (Tobermory), by Peter MacLeod senior M
Angus Fraser MacLean of Tobermory, by Iain MacCrimmon 3/4 M 2
Brigadier Alastair MacLean CBE, by William Ross 6/8 M 4
Brigadier General Ronald Cheape of Tiroran, by William Ross 2/4 M 4
Bunessan, by Mairi MacDonald. Hymn tune, set for the pipes
Duart Castle, by Donald MacLean 6/8 J 4
Duncan Lamont, by Donald MacLeod R 4 or S 4
Fingal's Cave, (arr.) by Jacques Pincet 2/4 M 4
The Firth of Lorn, by Donald MacLeod S 4
The Iona Boat Song, traditional 6/8 SA 2
I See Mull, by D. MacLellan 3/4 RM 2
Kenneth J. MacLean, by Iain MacPherson 2/4 M 4
The Lads of Mull R 2 (with parts 3 & 4 added by L. MacCormick)

MacFail from Bunessan, by Freeland Barbour 4/4 M 4

MacLaine of Lochbuie's Reel R 2

MacLean of Pennycross, by A. Ferguson 2/4 M 4

MacLean of Pennycross's Welcome to the 93rd, by A. Ferguson 2/4 M 4

The MacLean's Welcome to Duart, by Hector MacLean 6/8 M 4

MacLeod of Mull, by D. MacLeod 6/8 M 4

Miss J. MacLean of Pennycross, by D. MacPhail

Mull of the Cool High Bens 6/8 SM 1

Mull of the Mountains 6/8 SM 2

Nellie Stewart's Farewell to Dervaig Post Office, by Allan C. Beaton 6/8 M 4

Pipe Major Hector MacLean, by Peter MacLeod S 4

Seumas MacNeill, by Bobby MacLeod 6/8 M 4

The Sweet Maid of Mull, by Allan C. Beaton 6/8 M 4

The Torloisk Song: My Faithful Fair One, by Colonel Allan MacLean 9/8 SM 2. This was a song composed by Colonel MacLean when he was in America serving with the 84th (Royal Highland Emigrant) Regiment, in the 18th century. He was a friend of Allan Cameron of Erracht, who raised the 79th Regiment. The tune may be played as a Retreat in 3/4 time, or as a Slow March.

Torosay Castle, by Jack Lawrie 3/4 RM 4

See also the list of MacFadyen tunes below.

Note that *Ronald MacDonald's Farewell to Ulva* does not refer to the island of Ulva on the west coast of Mull, but to Ulva near the island of Danna, in Knapdale, Argyll.

Sources

Notices of Pipers
Piping Times
William MacRobbie, Achgarve
William Matheson, *TGSI* XLI
Duncan MacLean, Ardrishaig
Keith Sanger and Alison Kinnaird
Eric Murray, Rogart
Alec Haddow, *History and Structure of Ceol Mor*
Donald Archie MacDonald, *Tocher* 15 (1974)
John Kay, *A Series of Original Portraits*
Sir John C. Dalyell
J.P. MacLean, *History of the Clan MacLean*

Piper's Cave

On 19 October 1773, Dr Johnson and Boswell were travelling by boat along the west coast of Mull, and at Gribun they visited MacKinnon's Cave. Boswell described it as 'very lofty', and estimated its extent underground as 'by our measurement, no less than four hundred and eighty-five feet'. He added: 'Tradition says, that a piper and twelve men once advanced into this cave, nobody can tell how far; and never returned.' This is a variation of the usual tale: no hairless dog, but a substantial loss of human life. Dr Johnson said it was the greatest natural curiosity he had ever seen, but they did not penetrate far because they had only one candle to tell them if the air was growing foul, and were afraid that if it went out, they might find themselves in danger.

The Rankins

There were two schools of piping in Mull, and they are sometimes confused or merged together, when in fact they were completely separate, in both time and place. One was that of the RANKINS at Kilbrennan, on the west coast of Mull, who were pipers to the MacLeans of Duart; the other was the MACARTHUR school on the island of Ulva, off western Mull. Only a few miles separated them, but they were not connected.

The older school was that run by the Rankin pipers at Kilbrennan, certainly in the first half of the 18th century and probably much earlier than that, as well. The MacArthur 'college' was at Ormaig, on the south side of Ulva, and it seems to have flourished, if at all, in the early years of the 19th century. Note that a Mull Rental of 1679, which lists all the tenants in Mull and Ulva, includes several pipers associated with the MacLeans in the south of Mull, but does not name any pipers in Ulva or Kilbrennan at that time.

The MacArthurs were pipers to the Ulva/Staffa branch of the Clanranald MacDonalds who had long been hostile to the MacLeans of Duart, and there seems to have been little contact between the two families of pipers. They were also separated in time, the MacArthurs having their heyday some time after the Rankins had given up their school. They may have overlapped during the late 18th century, but even that is doubtful.

There is some doubt about the very existence of this MacArthur school, as the main evidence comes from a book by John MacCormick, published in 1923 but written in the late 19th century. He claimed to have known a piper who had been a pupil of the MacArthur piping school in Ulva, but as much of his account of the Ulva pipers is wildly inaccurate and fanciful, it is difficult to give his claim much credence. There seems to be no independent evidence, either earlier or contemporary. Neil Rankin Morrison, who lived in the west of Mull in the early 20th century and was steeped in local traditions, said he knew nothing of a MacArthur piping school until he read MacCormick's book. He did not say he thought it a fabrication, but there is a delicate hint that he had his doubts.

MacCormick's claim is not helped by his trotting out the familiar description of a piping 'college', a building with rooms dedicated to piping lessons and practice, as well as the usual accommodation for the teacher's family; this can be shown to have originated in Skye, where Thomas Pennant's account of the typical late 18th-century tacksman's house at Hunglader, inhabited by the MacArthur pipers, was inflated into a description of a piping college by the Rev. Dr Norman MacLeod in the early 19th century. The description, patently false, became a literary convention used by writers when a piping college is mentioned: it has been used of the MacArthurs in Skye, the MacCrimmons in Skye, the MacDonalds in Morar, the MacDougalls in Kilbride and doubtless others, too. It is a figment of the Rev. Doctor's imagination, and there is no trace of any such building on Ulva.

It seems likely that the MacArthur 'school' amounted only to the Ulva MacArthurs taking one or two pupils, and MacCormick's romanticism, fed by story-tellers' tradition, exaggerated this. Or, perhaps, a school was imagined in Ulva because there was the MacArthur school in Skye. Even that amounted to no more than the MacArthur pipers taking pupils, or apprentices, in their home.

Henry Whyte (later known by his pen-name 'Fionn') wrote a prize essay in 1904 about the Rankin pipers, giving some interesting detail, but today the main source of information about the Rankins is Neil Rankin Morrison, who was a descendant of that family. In 1934, he presented a seminal paper to the Gaelic Society of Inverness, in which he brought together the published information about the family, sorting the nuggets from the dross. He then told a number of interesting old legends and stories about the Rankins, some of them clearly of great age, stories which were current in Mull during his boyhood there, in the 19th century.

This excellent paper has the title 'Clann Duiligh: Piobairean Chloinn Ghill-Eathain' (Clan Dullie, Pipers to the Clan MacLean), and it was published in the *Transactions of the Gaelic Society of Inverness*, vol. 37, 1934–36, pp. 59–79. It is in Gaelic.

Neil Morrison's account of the Rankins differs slightly from that given in the preface to Angus MacKay's collection (1838), and both of these differ from the version in the Notices of Pipers. Neil Morrison's word seems more acceptable than that of either of the other two sources, which were probably the work of James Logan and Lt John MacLennan respectively, neither of whom had close connections with Mull. William Matheson also gave an account of the Rankin line which does not always agree with that of Neil Morrison. Some details of the discrepancies are given below.

Kilbrennan

The Rankins' home, Kilbrennan, is on the west side of Mull, looking out over the sea loch, Loch Tuath, towards the island of Ulva. Kilbrennan is in a most beautiful setting, with the Mull hills to east of the house and spectacular views of sea, mountains, cliffs and islands to the south and west.

The present house, probably built in the late 18th century, is a stone house with a slate roof, and faces south, with a lower building on its east side. This has been converted into an extension of the house, but was probably once part of an older dwelling, possibly the steading or byre of a long-house. The old Hebridean long-houses were thatched, and had several rooms opening out of each other, housing the family, servants and cattle (but did not have music rooms).

Beside the house, to the south-east, is a rocky, flat-topped knoll, the Cnoc nam Piobairean, Hill of the Pipers, to which some of the stories refer. Here, according to tradition, the Rankin pipers and their pupils practised on calm summer evenings. Perhaps the rock caught a little of any breeze, to keep the midges off.

Between the house and the coastal road is a large field of short-cropped turf in which may be seen the remains of several circular structures and standing stones. These have almost disappeared into the ground, but are still discernible as shapes on the surface. This must be the *cill* which gave Kilbrennan its name, an early Christian holy site, a chapel, with hermit-cells and burial ground dedicated to St Brendan, a saint of the early Irish church, contemporary with St Columba. (Professor W.J. Watson said there were no fewer than seventeen saints called Brendan in Ireland and Scotland in the 6th century; one of them was Brendan the Voyager who is believed to have reached North America in his coracle. It is not certain which of the seventeen is commemorated at Kilbrennan, nor is it clear whether a St Brendan lived there himself.)

It is possible that this was already a sacred site before the monks arrived, as prehistoric remains abound in the area. Two Iron Age forts (Dun nan Gall – which probably means Fort of the Foreigners or Norsemen – and a broch) lie half a mile to the north-west of Kilbrennan, and another fort, Dun Choinichean or Chuagain – meaning unknown – is above Kilbrennan, on the same burn that flows past the house. These forts play a part in the tales of the Rankin pipers, which are closely tied in with the local terrain. There may have been a prehistoric stone circle at Kilbrennan at one time.

Although there are what appear to be old gravestones at Kilbrennan, they probably belong to an age earlier than that of the Rankins, and there is no tradition of their having been buried there. On the contrary, they are said to have been buried in the graveyard at Kilninian, further up the coast of western Mull, to the north-west of Kilbrennan. Here there are three stone slabs, one smooth and without inscription or carving, one ornamented with patterns of entwined foliage, and the third depicting a fully armed warrior, with his hound at his feet. Ann Mac-Kenzie says in her book that these stones are traditionally associated with the Rankins, and the third stone is identical in style with stones in Iona, dating from the beginning of the 15th century. Does this mean the Rankins were at Kilbrennan as early as 1400, or were old stones re-used for later graves? The depiction on the third stone suggests that it was the grave of a high-born warrior, and this ties in with the tradition of the Rankin descent from the MacLeans of Duart. If the Rankin of about 1400 was a warrior-chief, perhaps the fame of the Rankins as pipers belongs to a later age – but we cannot be sure.

About half a mile to the south-east of Kilbrennan, the coast road passes above a waterfall, known as Easa Fors (*easa* is the Gaelic word for a waterfall, *fors* is the Norse, with the same meaning). Here a burn flows down from the hill and as it reaches the steep cliffs of the coast it makes three great leaps into space. This beautiful (and potentially dangerous) tourist attraction is closely bound up with Rankin traditions. The Rankin pipers are said to have had a secret cave behind one of the three falls, probably the lowest of the three; there they could play unseen and unheard, when practising compositions which they did not want to reveal to their pupils.

It is now not entirely certain where this cave was. Neil Morrison said the roof of it had fallen in only a short time before he delivered his paper, that is, probably in the 1920s. It was said to be behind a curtain of falling water, and large enough for a piper to stand in, and walk about, while playing (surely the damp would affect his reeds?).

Ivar Ingram, living at Kilbrennan in 2004, said there were still caves in the cliff at sea level, where the longest and lowest of the three falls drops to the rocks of the shore. It is possible still, he said, to scramble through a hole into a hollow chamber in the cliff, but he did not think this was the pipers' practice room, as there is not enough headroom for a player to stand up, and it is not behind the fall itself. Presumably there was once a similar, but bigger, chamber behind the main fall, and that was where the Rankin pipers played.

The whole site should be approached and explored with caution, especially in wet weather when the paths are slippery. In any weather, the access is exposed, the paths being unfenced, with the risk of falling some distance onto jagged rocks below. Children and dogs should be restrained.

Rankin Descent

We cannot be sure when the Rankins came to Kilbrennan, or how long they had been pipers there. They were of the same family as their chiefs, the MacLeans of Duart, and they supplied the chief with a piper, said by Keith Sanger to have lived about five miles from Duart Castle.

In the (admittedly vague) early genealogy of the family, the second name in the line of ancestors is that of Raincge, from whom the name Rankin is derived. He was the son of Dugald (Dubhghall) of Scone, and Raincge's son, Cu-duilig, is said to have come out of Ireland, and to have been the first piper in Mull. It is not clear what is the authority for these beliefs. Other sources say that Cu-duilig was the son of Ceallach, abbot of Lismore, but which Lismore? In Lorne or in Ireland? (see above, Island of Lismore). It is unfortunate that the records of the abbots in Lorne are missing for the years between 753 and 1256. It has been established that Cu-duilig's grandfather was at Scone in 1100, and he probably came over to Scotland in the 11th century.

Neil Morrison said local tradition had it that Cu-duilig had been teaching music in Ireland before he came over with Lachlan Lubanach and Eachann Reanganach (this seems to imply that Eachann may have been Cu-duilig's brother or uncle, and Lachlan appears in the MacLean family tree). Legend associates these three with a prince of Norway, and this might mean a date around the 11th or 12th century. It is not easy to piece the picture together, but possibly Cu-duilig was a musician and churchman who came to Scotland from the Irish Lismore, and was joined by the other two, probably his relations. All three, it is said, held land in Mull – but who granted it to them? Mull at that time belonged to the MacDougalls.

From Cu-duilig the Rankins got their other designation, Clan Duiligh (Dullie or Dooley), and maybe it was at this stage that the Rankins became a line separate from that of the MacLean chiefs, presumably descending from a younger son of Cu-duilig. The clan historians suggest that the Rankins became subordinate to the MacLeans because the chiefs by necessity had to concentrate their skills on warlike activities, which required pipers in support, and the Rankins went for music and poetry, depending on their MacLean kin for protection. This may have been true enough, but the original divergence was probably simply the result of birth, the younger son's line naturally subordinate to that of the heir to the chieftainship. As the MacLean chiefs made Duart Castle their stronghold (after 1390), a Rankin piper would be based there as a member of the household, apparently having his home nearby, but the rest of the Rankins were at Kilbrennan, and probably started their piping school quite early, perhaps as early as the 16th century – but there is no proof of this.

The clergy of the Irish church were allowed to marry and have families, and Cu-duilig's descendants developed in the two lines, the chiefs and their pipers, until in 1692, the chiefs were put out of Duart by the Argyll Campbells and had to make their home elsewhere. The last Duart chief died in France and the succession moved to the Brolass branch, in the Ross of Mull, while another branch became the lairds of the island of Coll. Later, in the second half of the 18th century, these Coll lairds had Rankin pipers. Dr Johnson in 1773 was partly mistaken when he said the MacLeans of Coll had had Rankin pipers from time immemorial, but partly right in that the Rankins had served the lairds' forefathers when they were still in Duart.

A Rental, dated 1679, lists 'at Duart', under the name Feirgeyll, which is thought to have been near the castle: 'Pat. MacDonald piper hes this room (holding). Swey with ane pressant £33.6.8.' The last phrase means 'The same with a rent of £33.6.8.' This is quite a high rent for that time, indicating a decent-sized holding of land.

In this Rental, the Lands of Torissay include Gualchelis (on the north side of the entrance to Loch Spelve). The rent for this holding was £80, with the two tenants obliged to supply the landlord annually with 'of Cheese 4 stone, of Butter 4 quarts, of Sheep 4; the one half possest by John McEan vic Ewn vic Allan, Brolos Pypar', i.e. a joint tenant of Gualachaolish was John son of John son of John son of Allan, and he was piper to MacLean of Brolass, the line which later took over the chieftainship of the Clan MacLean when the Duart line died out.

It is notable that in this Rental of 1679, some estate employees, such as factors and ground officers, held their land 'rent-free for service', but the pipers did not. This was unusual for large estates at this time, but it is possible that they were paid a salary that is not mentioned in the Rental. Normally if the salary was the same as the annual rent, the accounts would omit mention of the piper's holding altogether. The fact that the pipers are named along with the value of their lands suggests that they had to pay up like everyone else. They may have received payment for individual performances.

The Rankin School at Kilbrennan

From the loss of Duart in 1692 until a date given variously as 1757 and 1763, more probably the former, the Rankins seem to have supported themselves at Kilbrennan by teaching pupils. Before 1692 they had the backing of their MacLean chief in this enterprise, but after the Campbells took over, the Rankins were struggling. A poem by John MacCodrum, made around 1760, speaks of the Campbells depriving the Rankins of their rights by violent means, but is annoyingly short of detail. He may have been referring to the Campbells seizing Duart, thus depriving the Rankins of their living.

Joseph MacDonald, writing about piping in 1761, twice mentioned 'the first masters of the instrument' being in Skye and Mull, implying that these were two centres of equal importance. In oral tradition it was said that Rankin pupils came to Kilbrennan from all over Scotland, and stories mention Ireland and Northumberland as the homes of some of them. It is impossible now to assess the size of the school, the number of pupils at any one time, or indeed over the period of a year, but Dr Johnson made an interesting comment, that the college had to close when the pupil numbers fell to seventeen. Obviously this implies that previously there were far more – but how many more? Was this seventeen per year, an annual total of seventeen in groups of two or three, or seventeen in a class together? How many instructors were there? Did they take beginners? Where did they all live? How long did the pupils stay? How did they get there? Who paid the fees? What were the fees? Almost the whole enterprise is shrouded in mist, and most of the glimpses we get are in the stories of later generations, and in the odd comment from outsiders. We do know that the Rankin school made enough to keep the Kilbrennan family for some generations, but we do not really know how.

Keith Sanger has drawn our attention to an item in the accounts of the Earl of Breadalbane (formerly Campbell of Glenorchy). Signed by the Earl at Taymouth on 22 April 1697, it says: 'Item payed to quantiliane McCraingie McLeans pyper for one complete year as prentyce fie for the Litle pyper before he was sent to McCrooman, the soume of £160.'

'The Litle pyper' was one of the MacIntyres. It seems a curious way to describe the apprentice, who may have been a son of Donald MacIntyre. 'Litle' may a translation of Gaelic beag or og, used to distinguish the lad from his uncle or grandfather of the same name, John MacIntyre. Or it may be that the term 'Litle' here meant Junior, the younger and less important of two household pipers. It could even mean he was a little fellow, small in stature.

Note the date of this entry, five years after the loss of Duart to the Campbells. Quintilian (= Condullie) Rankin is still described as 'MacLeans pyper', even by a Campbell. In the absurd 'civilising' of Gaelic names in official records, the Rankin name Condullie appears Latinised as Quintilian, here spelled Quantiliane, but McCraingie is closer to the Gaelic Mac Raincge than the modern Rankin. Condullie Rankin is known to have been living at Kilbrennan in 1716.

The sum of £160, which would be pounds Scots, seems enormous for one year in 1696–97. The pound Scots was worth about one twelfth of the pound sterling, so this was between £13 and £14. It is twice the amount paid to Donald MacArthur in Skye in the 1770s, for a year's tuition and board.

The entry above this in Breadalbane's accounts says: 'Item sent with John Macintyre the pyper at your Lordships desyre to be given McCrooman pyper in the Isles, £40' – but no period of time is mentioned. £40 Scots was just over £3 sterling. Keith Sanger thinks that John was with the MacCrimmons in the first half of 1697, but we have no idea for how long. Was this the follow-up on his year in Mull? In 1705, John went to Nether Lorne as piper at Ardmaddy, then owned by Breadalbane's son Colin. John was held in reserve there, to be sent for if Breadalbane needed him. Does this imply anything about John's piping abilities, notwithstanding his excellent tuition?

So far this reference to the young MacIntyre is the only documentary evidence to back up Dr Johnson's comment on the Rankin school – apart from a mention by the Frenchman, Faujas de Saint Fond, in 1784. We know that the school closed in the mid-18th century, probably in

1757, and that the foremost of the Rankin pipers at that time, Neil Rankin, went to Coll as piper to the MacLean laird there (see below, Coll).

John MacCodrum

The Gaelic poet John MacCodrum, who was bard to Sir James MacDonald of Sleat, in Skye, made a poem in around 1760, called *Diomoladh Pioba Dhomhuill Bhain (Dispraise of Donald Ban's Pipe)*. In it he is reproaching a fellow-bard for being too enthusiastic about a local piper called Donald Ban (not Donald Ban MacCrimmon, the subject of the piobaireachd lament of 1746).

He says that the poet had 'left aside MacCrimmon, Condullie and Charles', in order to drag wee Donald Ban to the fore. This reference (see Matheson, lines 887–9) tells us that Patrick (Og?) MacCrimmon, Condullie Rankin and Charles MacArthur were regarded as the three giants of piping, looking back some fifty years to the earlier part of the century. William Matheson, in his edition of MacCodrum's poems, was of the opinion that the MacCrimmon mentioned here was probably Patrick Mor, who is thought to have died around 1670; but Patrick Og, his son, seems more likely in this context, as a contemporary of both Condullie Rankin and Charles MacArthur. Admittedly John MacCodrum names Patrick Mor's pipe, known as The Idiot (An t-Oinseach) – but his son would have inherited it, anyway, and it was regarded as a MacCrimmon pipe, not belonging to any particular member of the family.

In the next two verses of his poem, John MacCodrum praises MacCrimmon for the beautiful quality of his pipe and for the inspiring nature of his playing, and turning to Charles MacArthur, is equally fulsome. Then, in lines 919–32, he goes on:

Nan cluinnt' ann an Muile	If it were heard in Mull
Mar dh'fhag thu Con-duiligh,	How you passed over Condullie,
Cha b'fhuilear leo t'fhuil	They would think your blood
Bhith air mullach do chinn;	Should be on your head;
'S i bu ghreadanta dealchainn	His pipe was the most vehemently keen
Air deas laimh na h-armachd,	on the right flank of the battle front,
A'breabadh nan garbhphort	beating out the wild tunes
Bu shearbh a'dol sios.	Vengeful in the charge.
Creach nach gann	It is a great loss that
Sibh gun cheann	you have no leader
Fo bhruid theann Sheorais;	under George's rule;

Luchd nam beul fiara	the folk with the wry mouth
	(Campbells)
'G ur pianadh 's 'g ur fogradh,	tormenting you and driving you out,
Rinn iad le foirneart	did by violence
Bhir coir a bhuin dibh.	deprive you of your rights.

Do these last lines refer to the Rankins specifically, or to their clan, the MacLeans? It does sound as if the poet was blaming the Campbells for forcing the Rankins to give up their school at Kilbrennan, although there were still Rankins living there at least until 1804. Certainly it was the Campbell invasion which made the school no longer viable; presumably pupils stopped, or were prevented from, coming.

The Rankins had closed the school only a few years before the poem was composed, but MacCodrum says only that Condullie was a good piper in battle. He was presumably referring to the battle of Sheriffmuir (1715), in which Condullie took part – but Gaelic story and song has a different version from this one: in the traditions handed down, Condullie did charge into the fray playing his pipes, but when the battle was at its height, he handed his pipe to his gillie and drawing his sword rushed into the thick of it, to fight (and the gillie fled with his pipe).

Condullie had accompanied his chief, Sir John MacLean, to Sheriffmuir, and the incident of the gillie and the pipe was immortalised in a song made by Lachlan MacLean, a Coll bard. It is quoted in William Matheson's book about John MacCodrum.

In contrast, a contemporary song in Scots English described the battle, probably quite realistically, although it is not clear which side the poet was on:

> There's some say that we wan,
> And some say that they wan,
> And some say that nane wan at a', man,
> But one thing is sure
> That at Sheriffmuir
> A battle was there that I saw, man,
> And we ran and they ran
> And they ran and we ran
> And we ran and they ran awa', man.

Later Descent of the Rankins

The line of the Rankin family has become confused, and the account of Neil Morrison, followed by William Matheson in the main but not entirely in the detail, conflicts with that given in the Notices of Pipers, compiled by Lt John MacLennan and drawing partly on the preface to Angus MacKay's collection. As the Notices were later revised and supplemented by various hands, those of Major Ian MacKay-Scobie, Archibald Campbell of Kilberry, Captain D.R. MacLennan and others, it is difficult to be sure whose opinion any comment might represent.

Neil Morrison said that the Condullie Rankin who fought at Sheriffmuir had a son Hector, and this Hector had a son Ewen who lived at Kilbrennan. Ewen became an Elder of the Church, and Treasurer to the Kirk Session in 1780, and he was the last teacher in the Kilbrennan school of piping, which closed in 1757. Ewen died in 1783.

Ewen had two sons, Hector and Niall. Hector like his father became an Elder, and remained in Kilninian Parish in Mull (the parish to which Kilbrennan belongs) until 1804, when he left Mull, to live with his sister in Greenock. He was the last Rankin piper in Mull. His brother Niall, son of Ewen, went to the island of Coll in 1773, and lived at Cliad, on the west side of the island. He was piper to MacLean of Coll, but when Dr Johnson was in Coll, Niall had only just become the laird's piper. In 1766 he had married Catherine MacLean, in Mull (she was a great-granddaughter of the 12th Laird of Coll).

Their children were Hector, Catherine, Ewen, Condullie and Janet. The eldest, Hector, was born in Kilbrennan, Mull, in 1767, but the next three children do not appear to have been baptised and therefore are not registered. The first Rankin entries in the Coll register are dated 1776 (see below), so it is possible that Catherine, Ewen and Condullie were born in Coll before the register was begun.

In the Coll register there is on record a couple, Niall Rankin and Catherine MacLean, whose children were Janet 1776, Mary 1779, and another Janet 1782. One, two or all of these may have died young. We do not know exactly when Niall and Catherine went to live at Cliad: Niall as piper to the laird until about 1806 was probably expected to live at least part of the year at the laird's residence at Breacacha, but his family may have been already at Cliad, and we know there were other Rankins there from at least 1802. We have to assume that Niall retired there in 1806. He died there in 1819, and was buried at Cill Lunaig, in Coll, in an unmarked grave.

John Johnston from Coll (quoted by Henry Whyte) said that Niall was not very tall, but well-built, and even in old age looked exceedingly handsome. When younger he had been considered the most handsome piper of his time. Tastes change, of course, and looks regarded as handsome in 1800 might have little appeal two hundred years later. No picture of him is known to have survived.

It was Niall Rankin, newly arrived from Mull in 1773, who played in Coll for Dr Johnson and his friend Boswell, earning himself the well-known comment: 'The bagpiper played regularly when dinner was served, whose person and dress made a good appearance; and he brought no disgrace upon the family of Rankin, which has long supplied the Lairds of Coll with hereditary musick.'

We might ask ourselves what did *he* know – and he was mistaken, anyway, in that Niall's family had supplied the related Chiefs of MacLean with music, but not the Lairds of Coll, until that year. Earlier that week, when stormbound in Skye, Dr Johnson had mused on the nature of the islanders, not just in Coll but in the Hebrides in general. He wrote:

> The solace which the bagpipe can give, they have long enjoyed; but among other changes which the last Revolution introduced [does he mean the '45?] the use of the bagpipe begins to be forgotten. Some of the chief families still entertain a piper, whose office was anciently hereditary. MacCrimmon was piper to MacLeod, and Rankin to MacLean of Col. The tunes of the bagpipe are traditional. There has been in Skye, beyond all time of memory, a college of pipers, under the direction of MacCrimmon, which is not quite extinct. There was another in Mull, superintended by Rankin, which expired about sixteen years ago. To these colleges, while the pipe retained its honour, the students of musick repaired for education. I have had my dinner exhilarated by the bagpipe at Armidale, at Dunvegan and in Col.

Not for the good doctor the usual English titter: he was prepared to listen intelligently to the music provided by his hosts. His remarks appear in the section on Ostig, in Skye, but were presumably written later, probably on his return home. Poor man, he did his best to understand what he was seeing and hearing, and what he was being told; we owe him a debt for giving us a contemporary glimpse of the islands in 1773. Boswell said that the doctor, who was a little deaf, liked to put his ear close to the big drone while listening to the pipes. We have to take this as a good sign.

Bartholemy Faujas de Saint Fond, touring Mull in 1784, wrote that he had been told about a college or society of bagpipers in Mull 'which was not even entirely extinguished after the death of the famous Rankine, who had the direction of it about thirty years ago'. Though vague, this is evidence of the existence of the Rankin school, and the dating tallies with Dr Johnson's account. Saint Fond was not a lover of the pipes, and in Oban he paid a piper to go away, admitting that he could not tell one tune from another.

Niall Rankin's third son, Condullie, succeeded him as piper to Coll. He appears in the register as 'Quintilian' or 'Quin', and his wife Finguala is registered as Flora Morrison. He married her in 1804, when he was living at Cliad, in Coll. Their son was born there in 1806, and, according to the register, baptised by the name George. It is hard to believe that Condullie Rankin would give his eldest son a Hanoverian name, and we have to wonder what Gaelic name has been forced into this English mould – Goiridh, perhaps? Certainly this name George is nowhere else mentioned in accounts of the family. He may have died young.

Condullie was a piper and teacher of piping. In the early 19th century he was in line to follow his father as piper to MacLean of Coll, but the position of piper seemed to enjoy less and less prestige. One day he was practising on his chanter at Breacacha when the factor came by. 'Put that away,' he said to Condullie, 'when the rest of them are hobnobbing with the gentry, you'll be out among the dogs.' An interesting comment on the changing status of pipers.

So Condullie went to the army, and accompanied his laird to the American War of 1812–14, where he distinguished himself so well that he was made a Captain. His wife died in 1817, and he returned home, to either Coll or Mull. The following year he married Margaret MacLean, daughter of the tacksman of Kengharar, in western Mull. The Kilninian register lists him as 'Captain Rankin from Coll', and this has led to some confusion as to whether this was Niall (the father) or Condullie (the son). It must have been Condullie, and Neil Rankin Morrison supported this.

The year after Condullie's second marriage, his father Niall died; and the year after that, 1820, both Condullie and his elder brother Hector left Coll and emigrated to Prince Edward Island, in Canada. There Condullie was an officer in the regiment of Highlanders raised for the defence of the island, and he became a Major. On the departure of the two brothers and their families from Coll, there were no Rankins left there. This is confirmed by the register, where the last Rankin entry was a baptism in 1819.

The Rankin pipers, as noted above, were remarkable for their good looks, and Condullie's brother Hector seems to have kept the minister busy writing entries in the register. Hector was evidently a bit of a lad, who made his presence felt in Coll. His departure for Canada must have come as a relief to many husbands and fathers on the island. It is not always easy to distinguish one Hector Rankin from another, but Hector in Cliad is given as the father of Kate MacLean's natural son Alexander, born in 1794, 'begotten in fornication'.

Another of Hector's peccadilloes seems to have gone unrecorded, the child presumably not baptised, as the next Rankin entry is that of Hector in Cliad and Anne MacPhaden, Grissapol (the farm next to Cliad); they had their natural son Archibald baptised in 1798, and the minister added a laconic note: 'Third ante-nuptial child for Hector, second for Anne'.

In 1802, Hector from Cliad married Anne MacLean from Ensay in Mull – not far from Kilbrennan, where the wedding was held. Their children were Quintilian (= Condullie) 1803, John 1805, Hugh 1809, all born at Cliad, and there is another entry for a lawful son Niel, born at Cliad in 1806, to Hector Rankin and Mary MacLean – should this be Anne, or was this a different Hector?

Anne MacLean seems to have died around 1810, and Hector began to stray again. In 1811, a daughter Flora, 'begotten in fornication', was born to him and Anne Stewart. It looks as if he was not an unfaithful husband so long as his wife was living, but looked further afield when he was single again. But in 1815, he married Susan(na) MacDonald, and their children were Lauchlan 1816, Niel 1817 and Catherine 1818, all born at Cliad. The baptism of Catherine in 1819 is the last Rankin entry in the Coll register. We assume that the whole Rankin family moved to Prince Edward Island in 1820.

The son of Major Condullie Rankin, born in Canada, was Niall, who became the Mayor of Charlottetown in Prince Edward Island. Niall's son Condullie, who died in Prince Edward Island in the 1920s, was the last of the line of the Rankin pipers.

William Matheson, who drew on a Canadian account of the family by the Rev. A. MacLean Sinclair, followed Neil Morrison's account quite closely, but said that Ewen Rankin the Church Elder who died in 1783 had a son Hector who went to Greenock in 1804, and that it was Hector's son Niall (not his brother) who went to Coll and married Catherine MacLean. He also added that it was Niall who went with his laird in the Earl of Breadalbane's regiment, to Grenada, in 1806, and not Condullie.

The dates in this version differed slightly: the school at Kilbrennan was said to have closed in 1760, rather than 1757, but these dates are only approximate anyway, and the school probably just dwindled to a stop.

The Notices of Pipers, probably written in the early 20th century, have more discrepancies. Unfortunately it is the Notices which are most generally accepted, probably because the Mull account was published in Gaelic, and in a relatively obscure journal, while William Matheson's is in a scholarly work not likely to be current among pipers. The short mention in the Preface to Angus MacKay's collection has also had an influence. Although it now seems that the Preface was written by James Logan, it was for so long accepted as the work of Angus himself, and therefore straight from the horse's mouth, that it has had a disproportionate influence. Both the Preface and the Notices have perpetuated what must be serious errors.

The Notices, for example, said that the Rankins founded their piping college on the island of Ulva, which is not so. The Ulva college was later, and was run by the MacArthurs, not the Rankins.

The Notices gave the year 1758 for the closure of the Rankin school, and said that Niall Rankin was Condullie senior's grandson, where other sources had him as a great-grandson. Niall's death was given in 1809, where 1819 is correct. The Notices also confused Niall with the second Condullie, saying it was Niall who went to the army, became an officer and died in Prince Edward Island in 1856. This was Condullie junior, and we know that Niall died and was buried in Coll.

Both Neil Morrison and the Notices mentioned a marriage of one of the Rankin pipers to a MacCrimmon girl in Skye, but again there are discrepancies. Mr Morrison told us that Duncan Rankin was 'one of a family who were the last of the pipers', i.e. presumably a brother of Hector and Niall, all sons of Ewen, living in the late 18th century.

Duncan and his brother Niall were both sent to Skye, to study piping in the MacCrimmon school at Boreraig ('to complete their tuition', as Neil Morrison put it).

It seems that MacCrimmon (unspecified) had a beautiful daughter named Janet (Seonaid), and both Duncan Rankin and a young man called MacDonald, from the mainland, were courting her. She preferred Rankin, but her father favoured MacDonald. Both the young men, said Neil Morrison's story, completed their course and returned to their homes. Later 'the MacDonald one' arrived with a boat and crew, to ask formally for the girl's hand in marriage. She greeted him kindly, and he thought he had won her. She told him her father set great store by pipe music, and she went out to arrange for her father to play them a tune. The music, played from the next room, was a piece called *The Old Man From The Mainland Is In A Hurry (To Leave)*. The suitor took this as a hint from her father and departed, not realising that it had been the girl herself playing. Soon after this she married Duncan Rankin, who was at that time piper to the laird of Muck (one of the MacLeans of Coll).

The Notices said that Duncan was Condullie senior's grandson, rather than great-grandson, and that he died in 1807, at the age of eighty-five. Piper to the laird of Muck, he married Bess MacCrimmon, the daughter of Donald Donn MacCrimmon of Lowergill, Skye. Donald Donn was the seventh, and youngest, son of Patrick Og MacCrimmon. Bess herself was an accomplished player. She died at Grissipol, Coll, in 1790, and was buried at Cill Lunaig, in Coll (see also below, Muck).

Rankin Stories

Neil Rankin collected a number of interesting tales about the Rankin pipers. The story of how the Rankins acquired their piping skill is familiar in many guises. There was a fairy hill or sithean near Laggan Ulva, a mile or so to the south-east of Kilbrennan, on the west side of Mull; one night, Rankin, 'a man of Clan Duiligh', was passing it when he saw a light, as they always do, shining from an open door in the side of the hill. Inside were the Wee Folk, or fairy beings, and they were dancing. He greeted them and went in. Before he left, they gave him the Fairy Chanter of Clan Duiligh, and taught him a tune, which turned out to be *The Finger Lock* (see above). In those days it was customary for a piper to have one tune which he did not pass on to anyone else, and Rankin kept this one as his own, his secret tune, known in Gaelic as his *port-falaich*.

What is unusual about this tale is that Rankin suffered no disadvantage from his contact with the sithean, but took only benefit from it. Often in later versions of stories like this, retribution of some kind follows: there has to be a down-side to the exchange, as the story-teller pays homage to decent Christian belief, which in Protestant times frowned on the supernatural. Does Rankin's acceptance of this gift unpunished suggest that it is a very old, pre-Reformation form of the story?

Rankin had one of those daughters often found in folk-tales, who cannot resist putting an oar in. She was a keen player herself, on the chanter. Her father usually played his secret tune in the hidden chamber behind the waterfall at Easa Fors, but sometimes he practised it at home. Having heard her father play it, she learned it, without telling him. Inevitably, she took a fancy to one of her father's pupils, and passed the tune on to him. When his course was finished and he was about to leave, his teacher asked him to play through all the piobaireachd works he had learned at Kilbrennan. He played the ones that Rankin had taught him, and was warmly praised. Then the boy said 'I have another yet', and he began to play *The Finger Lock*. Rankin listened to the end, then leapt suddenly for his sword, and drove the boy out of the house.

Another version of this tale tells how the Campbell Laird of Muckairn (near Loch Awe) took two men over from Ireland. One was a harper, called David, the other a smith and armourer, Robert by name (see below). Robert had a son, Calum, whom he sent to the Rankins to learn to play the pipes. But Calum was lazy, and not too attentive to the teaching he was given, and although he had a good ear, his fingering was nothing great.

One day, Calum was with Rankin at a wedding, and he took a drop too much. This did not improve his playing. His teacher was affronted, and put him out of the wedding house in the middle of the night. Wandering along in the darkness, his pipe on his shoulder, he saw a light some distance away, and made his way to it. When he reached it, he saw an old man sitting by the fire in a small house, and the old man greeted him and invited him in.

As they talked, the old man told him that Rankin was composing a tune, and it was complete except for one variation. And the old man sang the tune, and completed it to the very last variation. He then taught the whole thing to Calum, and said to him 'Go back, and when you are near the wedding-house, put your pipe on your shoulder and play the tune I have taught you.'

Calum did as he was told. And when Rankin heard the music, he recognised Calum's finger on the chanter, playing the tune just right, exactly as he himself played it, and adding the last variation. In this version, Rankin was delighted. After that, Calum paid better attention to his lessons, and was soon an expert player. And Rankin said there had earlier been a lock on Calum's fingers, so he called the tune *The Finger Lock* (a clear case of folk-etymology).

There is yet another form of this story, almost certainly a re-telling later in the 18th century. Rankin was going out one day to cut kelp, a mainstay and source of income in the islands at that time (see above). He took with him the leading pupil of his school.

Leading the way, with the boy following close behind him, Rankin was carrying his sickle over his shoulder, and holding it in place with his hands behind his back, on the handle. As they walked, the boy observed Rankin fingering a tune on the handle, and paid close attention, realising it was a tune he had not been taught. When the kelp was cut and they returned home, the boy began on his chanter, and tried out the tune. When he had it perfect, he saw Rankin and played for him the usual tunes he had been taught, and finished with the secret tune. Rankin in a great rage drew his sword and said to the boy 'Now you have a choice, either you promise faithfully not to teach that tune to anyone else, or I cut off your fingers.' As Neil Morrison put it, it is not told which choice the boy made.

Nowadays it is generally accepted that the tune we know as *The Finger Lock* was one of the piobaireachd works made by Ronald Mac-Donald of Morar, probably towards the end of the 17th century; but we do not know if this was the same *Finger Lock* which was Rankin's secret tune. It may have been a title used for more than one tune (see above).

There is a very old song, quoted by Neil Morrison, about Calum the son of Robert the Armourer. It is sometimes called the Torloisg Song, after a place not far from Kilbrennan, but it is not the song of that name composed by Colonel Allan MacLean in America (see above). The language of this old song is so archaic that it is almost a halfway stage between Scottish and Irish Gaelic, and this makes it difficult to translate with accuracy. It goes like this:

Song Sung in the Torloisg District

Thug mi cion gu de 'm fath –	I gave love for whatever reason –
(Ho ro ho hug o)	(Ho ro ho hug o)
Tomhais thusa co dha –	You guess to whom –
(Ho hao riri hoireann	(Ho hao riri hoireann
Ho ro ho hug o)	Ho ro ho hug o)
Do mac Roibeirt an ceard,	To the son of Robert the metal-smith,
Chan e ceard a ni spain	Not a tinker who would make a spoon
No a dh'fhiaclaicheas card	Or would put teeth in a carding comb
Ach an gobhainn ni 'n t-arm,	But a smith who would make weapons,
Claidheamh geur is sgiath dhearg	A sharp sword and a red shield,
Leis an cinneadh an t-sealg	For the progeny of the hunt,
Oileach dubh is boc earb.	Blackcock and roe deer.
Thug mi gaol, cuim' an ceileam,	I gave love, why should I hide it,
Do namhaid na h-eilid	To the enemy of the hinds
'S roin mhaoil o thaobh sgeire	And the bare seals on the rocks,
'Nuair a dhireadh tu 'n stuc	When you'd climb the hill
Le d'ghille le d'chu	With your gillie and your dog
Le d'chuilbheir caol ur	With your new narrow-bore gun,

'Nuair a lubadh tu ghlun	When you would bend your knee
'S a chaogadh tu 'n t-suil	And you would squint your eye
Bhiodh an eilid gun luth	The hind would be without strength
Call fal' air an driuchd.	Losing her blood on the dew.
Thug mi cion cuim' an ceileam,	I gave love, why should I hide it,
Do mhac mnath a tir eile.	To the son of a woman from another land.
C'aite am bheil e 's a'chruinne,	Where in the world is he
Aon mhac mnatha thug ort urram,	Who would put any man before you
Ann am boidhchead 's an gilead	For the beauty and clarity (of your music)
Ann an uaisle 's an grinnead –	For its dignity and its fineness –
Mach o phearsa Chloinn Duiligh	Apart from Clan Dullie (the Rankins)
'S Phara MacCruimein.	And Paddy MacCrimmon.

The meaning is not entirely clear in some parts of this song, and the last lines in particular are disputed. It seems to mean that nobody would put any mother's son before Calum for the greatness of his piping, apart from the acknowledged masters, the Rankins and Patrick MacCrimmon. This suggests that the qualities of beauty, dignity and fineness refer to Calum's piping rather than his looks. Gilead, which means literally 'whiteness', can also mean 'clarity'.

As did John MacCodrum, this poet regards the Rankins and MacCrimmons as the supreme pipers of the time. MacCodrum also included Charles MacArthur, and his omission here might suggest that this poem is older than MacCodrum's, and refers to older Rankins and to Patrick Og as a younger man, in the late 17th century – or Phara MacCruimein may possibly mean Patrick Mor. Note also the mention that Calum's mother was not a Scot, possible confirmation of his Irish origins.

This boy Calum Robertson (i.e. the patronymic, son of Robert) turned up later in Skye, where he was remembered as Malcolm Mac-Robert, a different form of the same name. He was a metal worker, as we might expect, his father being an armourer, and he made his living by fashioning household utensils in metal and wood. He was known as an excellent piper *who had not been trained by the MacCrimmons*, and this was always stressed when he was mentioned in stories in Skye. He had friends who maintained, as friends will, that their man was as good as MacCrimmon; this was probably Patrick Og, as we may date Malcolm roughly in the early 18th century, from other details associated with him.

A contest was arranged, and it was to be held on a little green flat piece of land beside the burn, just below the Fairy Bridge, at a point where the three estates meet, Dunvegan, Waternish and Greshornish. There is a natural amphitheatre there, with the banks curving steeply up on both sides. The green flat is known for its excellent naturally good acoustics, and was often used by open-air preachers in the old days. Here the followers of the two pipers met, armed to the teeth, and settled facing each other on the slopes.

Patrick played first, and Malcolm equalled him in merit, and all agreed that there was nothing between them (it is not told what tunes they played). So there was a re-match, and Malcolm played first, but this time it was agreed that Patrick had the edge, by a very small margin. Malcolm conceded defeat, and it all ended amicably. The place can be seen today from the Fairy Bridge, looking downstream.

According to Willie MacLean, Malcolm MacRobert was not only a fine player but also a composer, and in Skye they say that he composed two works, *Catherine's Lament* and *Catherine's Salute*, in that order, oddly enough. What happened was that Malcolm kept cattle which were dear to his heart, and none more so than a pretty cow he had raised from a calf, and he called her Catriona (Catherine). He doted on this animal, but times grew hard, and one by one he had to sell his beasts. When only Catriona was left, he knew he had to part with her. He sold her off, and was so unhappy to see her go that he composed *Catherine's Lament* in her honour. He moped and pined for several weeks, until one day his wife said 'What's that mooing I hear?' On going outside they found Catriona, who had made her way home from whoever had bought her. Evidently she missed Malcolm as much as he did her. He was so pleased that he vowed he would never let her go again, and he made *Catherine's Salute* in celebration.

Catherine's Lament is still played, but has anyone heard *Catherine's Salute*? Is it perhaps the same work, played more cheerfully?

Another story concerns a piper who is described not merely as an Englishman but as a Northumbrian. It is not related if he played a Northumbrian pipe, but it seems likely. He was a good player, and arrived in Mull to challenge Rankin. The newcomer climbed onto the walls of an old dun or Iron Age fort, said to have been Dun Chuagain, above Kilbrennan, and played from there. Rankin played on Cnoc nam Piobairean, at the end of his own house. (Was this Northumbrian staying at Kilbrennan? These things are never made clear.)

Rankin won the first contest. We can only wish we knew how these contests were judged, and by whom. Was it a matter of a judge's opinion, or was it an endurance feat, to see who could keep going the longest and had the biggest repertoire? And was this piper playing Ceol Mor or Northumbrian music?

After the contest, the Englishman left, but he returned the next year, much improved, and this time he beat Rankin. For three years he came, at great expense to himself each time, and after a keen struggle, eventually Rankin won the third and decisive round. He feared another contest, as he was getting old and the Northumbrian was still young and vigorous.

Rankin decided he must find another way of getting the better of the Englishman, so challenged him to a duel with swords, to take place near Aros, not far from Salen, on the east side of Mull (why there?). A duel with swords suggests a date before the middle of the 17th century, when guns became the weapons of choice. Rankin was handy with a sword, and in this duel he killed the Northumbrian and buried him near the mouth of the Aros river, with a cairn of stones over the grave. There are the usual tales of this site being disturbed when the modern road was under construction: it was reported that a human skeleton had been found, not far from the river.

The next Rankin tales move the scene to Duart Castle, commanding the southern end of the Sound of Mull. Rankin was there as piper to the chief of MacLean, which must have been before 1692. It is told that a high-born Irishman, the Lord of Connaught, used to come to Duart every autumn for the hunting, bringing with him no-one except his piper. It was arranged that the two pipers would compete, by themselves, in the same room. The Irishman was very good, and played tune after tune against Rankin (this does suggest that it was a contest of quantity as well as quality). Rankin would play, and the Irishman would start up again, and he moved his fingers with miraculous speed. He could play, it is said, with either hand on top and change them round in mid-tune – and Rankin could not do this. He had a problem with his little finger which was not working right that day. The Irishman won the contest, and this was such a blow to Rankin that in a rage he cut off his own finger.

The Irish lord and his piper used to discuss the day's events in the evening, and when he heard what had happened, the lord was very upset, and told the piper that when the Lord of Duart heard of it, he would kill them both. So, when the rest of the house was asleep, the two of them crept out and fled.

Next morning the Lord of Duart asked where his guests were. Full of suspicion he went after them. They had reached Tobermory and set sail for Ardnamurchan. Duart pursued them, caught them at Kilchoan, killed them both and buried them there. In their memory, and perhaps troubled by his conscience, Rankin composed a beautiful work, the *Lament for the Lord of Connaught*. Or so they say – surely the Lord of Duart would not look on this with favour, in the circumstances?

The title of this work is sometimes given as *Cumha Moraire Coinneimh, Lament for the Lord of the Meeting* or *Contest*, but this may be a corruption of the original title, when Scottish Gaelic speakers did not understand the Irish word for Connaught. Or, of course, it might be the other way round: the entire connection with Connaught and with Ireland may be a fiction based on the corruption to Connaught of the word for a meeting or contest. John Johnston from Coll said he heard the *Lament for the Lord of Connaught* played by his uncle in Canada in the 1860s (see below, Coll). Has this work survived into modern times?

Piping Contests – A Digression

The idea of a piping contest has been carried over into modern times, not only as a competition in front of judges but as an informal flyting. We do not hear many of them nowadays, but who can forget the flyting which arose spontaneously one night in the early 1980s, after the Glenurquhart Games? In the Legion Hall in Drumnadrochit, where a crowd had gone for a drink, the youthful Alasdair Gillies was playing jigs and hornpipes, and for each one he played, his father Norman would cap it, going one better, a longer jig, or a faster, or a trickier, to rapturous applause from the onlookers. This seems to have been the type of contest in the old days. I suppose the SPA Knock-Out contest is the nearest thing to it nowadays, though that is far from spontaneous.

In vocal form, a flyting is usually two people, or individual members of two teams, singing, in turn, impromptu verses to a tune previously decided, often a pipe tune, each verse a form of insult or satire on his or her opponent, loaded with references to local people and local happenings, to the great delight of the listeners. I have heard this done in both Gaelic and English, and it is always entertaining. The winner is the one whose invention lasts the longer.

A Highland New Year, or a wedding, may be the scene of such a contest, but it always appears unplanned and arises spontaneously when the participants feel like it, at a certain stage in the evening, with the tide of drams at half-flood. Naturally certain local characters become known for their skills, and are pressed into service; they will be ones who are well accustomed to performing in public, and to acting as local bards, so they will have stored up incidents and jokes throughout the year, and probably honed them into poetic form well in advance; so the verses in a flyting are about as spontaneous as the Ground of *I Got A Kiss of the King's Hand*, drawing on a store of material ready made in the composer's mind. In a society unaccustomed to writing down its work, the convention of spontaneous composition is maintained as a compliment to the poet or composer.

A piping flyting is probably an extension of the older vocal form, and doubtless there were flytings among the harpers, and the fiddlers.

I recall a good flyting in Gaelic one New Year, when the odd verse in English was inserted, for the sake of a few non-Gaelic speakers in our midst. A crofter called Donnie was contending with Farquhar, the lighthouse keeper (an endangered species, probably extinct by now). Among Donnie's verses I remember one near the beginning when he stood up and sang, to the tune of *Bonnie Dundee*:

> The lighthouse keeper has ten of a family,
> Nobody understands how,
> As seven of them has the tail of a haddie –
> Let's hear what you can do now

(or words to that effect). To this, Farquhar answered:

> When Donnie went courting the bailie's daughter
> He thought he would give her a wow,
> But her daddy was throwing him into the water –
> Let's hear what you can do now

Then they reverted to Gaelic, for some seventeen verses until one of them gave up. Most flytings in the west are (or used to be) in Gaelic, unless the majority of those present speak only English. If there are women and children in the company, the words are reasonably decent, relying heavily on innuendo, but I believe that in the old days they could become obscene and truly insulting, leading to fights and even killings. The modern flyting, where it survives at all, is a pale imitation, purely for entertainment rather than a form of guerilla warfare.

More Tales of the Rankins

Another story based on a poem or song tells how Rankin was practising one day when he was alone in the house at Kilbrennan, and a man came to the door, asking for food. Rankin put down his pipe and gave him a piece of dry bread. This set off the words of a song, the same one as quoted by Peter MacKintosh in Kintyre about the poet/piper William MacMurchie. Clearly these stories, songs and poems were current all over the Gaelic-speaking world, often carried from district to district by travelling pedlars, and they would attach themselves to suitable subjects. Story-telling was a profession for which people trained, assuming certain mannerisms, phrases and gestures, sometimes a special story-telling voice. John MacKenzie, piper and fisherman at Kenmore on Loch Fyne in the 19th century, was one such narrator. A modern-day professional story-teller is George MacPherson, from Glendale, Skye, who comes from a family well-known for its pipers.

There was a tradition about Condullie Rankin junior, son of Niall, the Coll piper. Soon after he joined the army (around 1803), he left Coll to accompany the laird's son-in-law, Lord Hobart, who had been appointed Governor of Grenada, in the West Indies. A number of local men went out as soldiers, including Condullie, their piper. Within six weeks of their arrival in Grenada, Lord Hobart died from fever.

The rest of his Highlanders were sent to join other regiments in different parts of the West Indies, but Lady Hobart, who was expecting a child, had to go home. As she was the daughter of the laird of Coll and Condullie was a distant relative, he was chosen to accompany her. It was a prolonged and rough passage, and the baby was born prematurely, at sea. The mother was weak and developed pneumonia. Nothing could be done for her, and she died just as the ship put in at Bristol. Condullie faced a long and difficult journey from Bristol to Coll with a weak new-born child, and he had to tend this premature baby himself. He was, however, a family man, and he managed so successfully that he brought her home to Coll in excellent health – to the great amusement of his kin who made rude jokes about wet-nurses. He later proved his masculinity by fighting bravely in the American Wars of 1812–14.

After he and his brother emigrated to Canada in 1820, Condullie showed his qualities again. Trouble arose over legal claim to settlers' land, and the British Government's demands for taxes. When the settlers refused to pay rents or taxes, Condullie led their revolt, and was elected their representative. He was the last of the Rankins to make his living from piping. As Neil Morrison put it, the Rankin piping had begun with a Conduiligh (probably in the the 12th century) and ended with a Conduiligh (in Canada in the 19th century).

See also Coll, below.

Sources

Henry Whyte (Fionn): Prize Essay
Neil Rankin Morrison, *TGSI* XXXVII 1934
Skene's *History of the MacLeans*
Tobermory Museum
Ivar Ingram, Kilbrennan
William Watson, *History of the Celtic Place-names of Scotland*
Census, Coll and Mull
Old Parish Registers, Coll and Mull
William Matheson, *Songs of John MacCodrum*
Ann MacKenzie, *Island Voices*
Keith Sanger, *Piping Times*

The MacArthurs

There are some doubts about the MacArthur pipers in Ulva, mainly
concerning their origins, but also about the MacArthur piping school
on the island (see above, the MacArthurs in Islay; also the Rankins).

The Notices of Pipers tell us of a piper named Angus Dubh (Black
Angus) MacArthur who lived in Islay in the late 17th century. The
family, say the Notices, had been in Islay 'for many generations', and
had 'furnished pipers and armourers to the MacDonalds of Islay' (the
Lords of the Isles). Angus Dubh is said to have been 'a gifted performer', but then, almost everyone in the Notices is that. The story is
told that Angus Dubh so pleased his chief that he was offered 'a large
reward in the shape of a bonnetful of silver and gold' if he would
change his name to MacDonald. These MacArthurs, however, were
of long lineage and a proud race, like all of that name; and the piper's
reply was characteristic. 'No', said he, 'I am always ready to follow
your banner, wear your badge and play your music, but my name must
be MacArthur'.

Of course this must be only a tale, and probably a Victorian tale
at that. There was no longer a MacDonald chief in Islay in Angus'
day – but maybe the reference is to MacDonald of Sleat, his chief in
Skye. Angus is said to have played at the Battle of Sheriffmuir in 1715,
and is the first known MacArthur of the Skye piping family. He was
presumably born in the late 1600s. He may have been a son of Charles
MacArthur in Proaig, a supposition borne out by his naming his own
eldest son Charles (see above, Islay).

The MacArthurs as a clan in mainland Argyll originated in the area of Loch Awe, and if the piping MacArthurs were of that line, related to the Inveraray Campbells, it is curious that some of them took service with MacDonald lairds, in Skye and Ulva. Oral tradition says that in Islay the MacArthurs had been pipers to the MacDonald Lords of the Isles, based at Dunyveg, and that they held the farm of Proaig by virtue of that position, granted to them by the MacDonalds. Recent theory, however, assumes that they were the same MacArthurs as the Campbell-affiliated Argyll clan, and therefore that they came into Islay after the Campbells had taken over, and were given the tenancy of Proaig by the Campbells in the 17th century. This would mean they had been in Proaig only for one or two generations at the most, before Angus left for Skye.

Recent research on the DNA of Highland families indicates that the Argyll-rooted Campbells were not of the same origin as a line of MacArthurs at Ardencaple, on the Gareloch. While not conclusive, this result suggests that oral tradition about the roots of the MacArthurs in the islands may be correct, and that they might indeed have been pipers to the MacDonalds in Islay.

The patterns make more sense that way: the movement of one or two pipers to Skye and Ulva, to take service with MacDonald lairds, and possibly also the reason for the migration of the pipers in the first place. As MacDonald-affiliated tenants in a Campbell-dominated island, their position was bound to be uncomfortable. Unfortunately there is not enough information from the earlier age of the MacDonalds in Islay to prove whether or not there were MacArthurs at Proaig, as tradition maintains. We know there were tenants there, and one of them in the mid-16th century was a MacDonald (a MacIan from Ardnamurchan), and we know the estate maintained at least one piper, but we do not have the proof that the Proaig tenants were pipers, let alone MacArthurs.

Angus settled in Skye as piper to MacDonald of Sleat, whose seat at that time was Duntulm Castle, in Trotternish. Angus was given the heritable tenancy of the lands of Hunglader, not far from Duntulm, and he had three sons, Charles, Niall and Iain Ban. Charles succeeded his father as MacDonald's piper, and travelled widely with his laird, starting by attending him when he was sent as a student to St Andrews. They were frequently in Edinburgh, and gradually Charles came to make his home there. He had started the piping school at Hunglader, and tradition has it that there was an exchange of students with the MacCrimmon college at Boreraig or Galtrigill. The MacCrimmons sent pupils to learn MacArthur's 'particular graces', which certainly suggests that this style of playing was not universal. Charles was an excellent composer of piobaireachd. Born about 1710, he died in or around 1780.

Charles' sons were Alexander and Donald, both probably born around 1750. It should be noted that neither was called Angus, as would be expected – was there perhaps an Angus who died young?

In 1800, Alexander applied for the position of piper to MacDonald, and in his letter of application he said that there were no MacArthur pipers left in Skye at all, and that he himself had 'a natural genius for the Bag Pipe Music'. When he was turned down, he emigrated to America. It is not known if he had any family.

His younger brother Donald had taken over as instructor at the Hunglader piping school when his father was away. In the 1770s one of his pupils was John Cumming, piper to Grant of Grant. It was Donald who commissioned a mason to carve an inscription on his father's gravestone, but Donald drowned while ferrying cattle from Uist to Skye, possibly before the inscription was finished. This must have been in or around 1781. Again, it is not known if he had sons.

The second son of old Angus was Niall, who became a soldier. Posted to the West Indies, he died there in 1762, leaving a son, John (and probably other children).

This John, known as 'the Professor', lived in Edinburgh, where he died in 1791. He was well known as a piper, teacher and authority on piping, and was much involved with the Highland Society of Edinburgh right up to the time of his death.

Old Angus' third son, Iain Ban (fair-haired John) married Marion MacLean, and died in 1779. One of his sons was Charles (known later as Charles II to distiguish him from his illustrious uncle, Charles I), who became piper to the Earl of Eglinton and competed at Falkirk in 1781, winning second prize. Willie Gray said he had previously been piper to Lady MacDonald in Skye, then to Murray of Abercairney, near Crieff, before going to Eglinton, in Ayrshire. The Earl of Eglinton's sister was married to Lord MacDonald.

Charles II's brother Angus followed his uncle Charles I as piper to Lord MacDonald, and lived in Edinburgh and London. Angus died around 1822. It is not known what children Charles II and Angus had.

Not long before Angus died, he helped in the compilation and writing down of the MacArthur-MacGregor manuscript of piobaireachd works, around 1820.

In an unpublished handwritten note, and in audio tape recordings made for the School of Scottish Studies, Pipe Major William Gray said:

> A nephew of Charles MacArthur, John, was taught by his uncle.
> He, this John, settled in Edinburgh and was appointed Piper to
> the Highland Society of Scotland. He was also styled 'Professor'
> MacArthur.
>   Two of Charles MacArthur's nephews who were in Edinburgh then
> settled in Ulva, Mull, and were pipers to Boisdale and Staffa. These
> two MacArthurs held small farms in Ulva where they kept a school of
> instruction in piping. Both are buried in Salen, Mull . . .

On his tape he confirmed that he meant that the two on Ulva were nephews of Charles from Skye, piper to MacDonald, but it can be shown that an Archibald MacArthur, possibly the Ulva piper, was born on the island in 1773, and was of Ulva parents and grandparents. He could have gone to Edinburgh with his brother, but might have been there only a few years.

Boisdale must mean Colin of Boisdale who died in 1818, and is known to have had an Ulva piper in his service, said to be a Mac-Arthur; Staffa was his son by a second marriage, to whom he made over the islands of Staffa and Ulva around 1800 – and Staffa's piper was Archibald MacArthur from Ulva. Willie Gray said the two Mac-Arthurs were brothers, who had come to Ulva from Edinburgh, and certainly in 1801 Archibald married a Janet Weir, who seems to have been an Edinburgh girl.

This was the situation before Keith Sanger published his article in the *Piping Times* in March 2007 (vol. 49/6). A Canadian descendant of John 'the Professor' had given him a list of John's children: Archibald, born 1779, Neil (1782), Donald (1784) John (1785), Anne (1787) and Dianna (1789). All were born in Edinburgh, and it was Dianna whose descendants are in Canada. Willie Gray said that there were four brothers, all pipers. This seems to indicate that the two pipers in Ulva were Archibald and John, sons of John the Professor.

Keith Sanger explains the confusion about these two pipers in the records of the Highland Society: in the competition of 1804, according to the Preface to Angus MacKay's book, John MacArthur, piper to MacDonald of Staffa, won third prize in Edinburgh, and two years later he was placed second but declined the award, saying he should have been first. The account of the 1804 third place is corroborated by the newspaper report at the time (*Edinburgh Evening Courant*), but that for the later competition, in 1806, shows that there was an error, and the second place was offered to Archibald rather than John. Archibald, too, was described as piper to Ranald MacDonald Esq. of Staffa. As that paragraph in the Preface to Angus MacKay's book has other errors (e.g. it refers to Joseph MacDonald as 'John'), it seems safe to assume that the newspaper report was correct, and the piper who refused second place was Archibald.

The identification of these two players as the sons of John 'the Professor' MacArthur is not conclusively proven, and all the sources are confused – Angus MacKay (or his publisher), Willie Gray, John MacArthur in Ayr (another descendant, who said he was a great-grandson of 'Professor Archibald MacArthur, piper to the Highland Society of Edinburgh') all have discrepancies in their accounts, but it does seem most likely that these two brothers were born in Edinburgh and were taken to Ulva by the laird, around 1800. Were they related to the Archibald MacArthur born in Ulva in 1773, to an Ulva father named John (see below)?

Willie Gray knew a member of the family (whom he names elsewhere as Jessie MacKinnon); she was related to Willie's mother, who came from Uisken, in the Ross of Mull. Willie wrote:

> The last descendant of these MacArthurs residing in Mull is an elderly maiden lady to whom I am related and upon whom I called when last in Mull. While conversing with her about the MacArthurs and their music, she sang to me one or two fine piobaireachds including *The Piper's Warning to His Master (Colle mo runn, sech-ainn an dun).* I have never heard, vocally, anything sweeter since. She had several brothers, all pipers, and who emigrated to Australia. She informed me that the family used to sing the words while some of her brothers played the piobaireachd on the pipes. I enquired where her brothers got their pipes, and she told me that they made them themselves. Her father, John MacArthur, whom I remember quite well, was an excellent tradesman, Joiner and Boatbuilder. He died well over 90 years of age.

This family belonged to Uisken, Mull, and may have been related to the mother of Simon Fraser, Australia. So far no link between them and the Ulva or Skye pipers has been established – and not for the want of trying.

There is conflict here, but if we turn to the Old Parish Register for Kilninian and Kilmore (which included the Quoad Sacra parish of Ulva), we find at least some evidence. There we read that Archibald MacArthur, 'Piper in Ulva', married Janet Weir on 2 December 1801. There is no indication of Janet's origin, but there are no other Weirs in the Kilninian register. The marriage took place in Ulva.

Whatever his background, Archibald was in Ulva by 1801, established as a piper by profession, and married. He and Janet had a family, and the register tells us whereabouts in Ulva each was born, so we know where they were living. Those whose baptisms were registered were:

> Robert, born 1802 at Cave (Uamh), on the south coast of Ulva, to the
>   west of Ormaig. It was an exposed and primitive place, without
>   much good land. (The family of David Livingstone originated here.)
> Catherine, born 1803, also at Cave.
> Ranald, born 1809 at Ardcalawig, Ulva – a holding much nearer to
>   Ulva House, on more fertile land. Ranald was named after the laird.
> Margaret, born 1814, at Ardelum, another reasonably good holding.

The Census gives us another son, John, born 1812. He died of smallpox in Glasgow, but was living in Ormaig, Ulva, with his parents in 1841. He may be the John MacArthur named by John Johnston of Coll as the last of the MacArthur pipers in Ulva.

John MacArthur, Ayr, seems to have been confused about the Edinburgh connection, since the by-name 'Professor' was that of John, nephew of the great Charles, not Archibald, and John was piper to the Highland Society of Scotland, not of Edinburgh – but Archibald, son of John the Professor, may have been given the same by-name as his father, almost as a patronymic, to show who his father was, and he may have been piper to the Edinburgh Highland Society, before going to Ulva.

The 'sort of large croft' granted to Archibald is elsewhere mentioned as being a substantial holding of land near Salen, in east Mull. It was not a family croft, but was said to have been given to him for his lifetime, as a form of pension, in exchange for his services as piper. John MacArthur in Ayr said Archibald held it until his death, but there is evidence (see below) that it was sold off when Ulva changed hands. Neither the Parish Register nor the Census has any reference to this croft, and in 1841, Archibald and his family were living at Ormaig, in Ulva, when Archibald was sixty-eight.

Facts we know for certain are that Archibald MacArthur was piper to the laird of Staffa from at least as far back as 1801, and we know who the laird was (see above). We know that Archibald married Janet Weir and settled in Ulva where he had his family. We know more of him from a number of references to him in contemporary sources, and also to his laird, Ranald MacDonald of Staffa, who turned himself into Sir Reginald Touch-Seton-(MacDonald)-Steuart.

Sir Reginald became a stalwart of the Highland Society of London, who ran the Edinburgh competitions. In 1838, after the three candidates for the Gold Medal (for former winners of the Prize Pipe) had performed in succession, 'the Committee of Judges retired to determine the merits of the whole competitors. On their return, Mr Farquharson of Invercauld, the preses (president), in a spirit of reserve which demands great approbation, requested Mr MacDonald of Staffa, as more familiar with the subject, to explain to the audience and to the candidates the objects of the institution and the resolutions of the Committee, after which the names of the successful candidates were announced' – and John Ban MacKenzie had won the Gold for former winners, with Angus MacKay taking the Prize Pipe. Note that the Highland Society still called Ranald by his former name, MacDonald of Staffa, and Mr rather than Sir. Presumably he was a member of the Committee of Judges, some 15–20 worthies; these included Lachlan MacNeill Campbell of Kintarbert, who had just qualified for inclusion by inheriting his grandfather's estates and designation.

Walter Scott in Ulva

Sir Reginald, in spite of his advantageous marriage, his title and his wealth, seems to have had more fun as plain Ranald MacDonald of Staffa. The smaller islands to the west of Mull were his: Staffa, Gometra, Ulva, Inchkenneth, Little Colonsay and the Treshnish Isles, but not Iona, which belonged to the Duke of Argyll. The laird of Staffa embraced his role with gusto, becoming one of the 'tartan chiefs' who figured prominently in the Royal Visit to Edinburgh in 1822. Before that, however, Ranald had established himself in Ulva House, where Walter Scott visited him in 1810, the year that Ranald came of age.

Scott wrote to Lady Abercorn on 29 June 1810: 'I intend to go for a fortnight to the Hebrides . . . my friend Ronald (sic) MacDonald of Staffa promises me a good barge, six rowers, a piper and his own company for pilot, which is a strong temptation . . .'

In a letter to Joanna Baillie from Ulva House, 19 July 1810, Scott wrote:

> We landed late, wet and cold, on the island of Mull, near a castle
> called Aros (near Salen) . . . Mr MacDonald of Staffa, my kind friend
> and guide, had sent his piper (a constant attendant – mark that !) to
> rouse a Highland gentleman's family in the neighbourhood where we
> were received with a profusion of kindness and hospitality . . . Next
> day we rode across the isle [of Mull] on Highland ponies attended by

a numerous retinue of gillies and arrived at the head of the salt water loch called Loch an Gaiol [Loch na Keal, Thomas Campbell's Loch Gyle on his poem *Lord Ullin's Daughter*] where Staffa's boats awaited us with colours flying and pipes playing. We proceeded in state to the lovely isle [Ulva] where our honoured landlord has a very comfortable residence . . . Yesterday we visited Staffa and Iona . . . I had become a sort of favourite with the Hebridean boatmen, I suppose from my anxiety about their old customs . . . so they took the whim of solemnly christening a great stone seat at the mouth of the cavern (Fingal's Cave), the Clachan-an-Bairdh, or the Poet's Stone [Scott was not a Gaelic speaker and evidently was of the school that believes in adding an *h* to make it look authentic]. It was consecrated with a pibroch which the echoes rendered tremendous, and the glass of whisky not poured forth in the ancient mode of libation, but turned over the throats of the Assistants . . .

He does not name either the pibroch or the piper, but we assume it was Archibald MacArthur.

Scott goes on:

Our return hither was less comfortable; we had to row twenty miles against an Atlantic tide . . . The ladies were sick, and none of the gentlemen escaped except Staffa and myself. The men, however, cheered by the pipes and by their own interesting boat songs which are immensely wild and beautiful, one man leading and the others answering in chorus, kept pulling away without the least sign of fatigue, and we reached Ulva at ten at night, tolerably wet and well disposed for bed.

Even more ready for their beds must have been the men who had done the actual rowing, covering more than thirty miles that day. We might wish that Scott had said more about the playing of the iorram on the pipes, apparently during the voyage.

He does give us an interesting account of the laird himself, about whose character he had his doubts:

Our friend Staffa is himself an excellent specimen of Highland chieftainship; he is a cadet of Clan Ranald, and Lord of a cluster of isles on the western side of Mull and a large estate (in extent at least) on that island. By dint of minute attention to this property and particularly to the management of his kelp-shore, he has at once trebled his income and doubled his population, while emigration is going on all around him. But he is very attentive to his people who are distractedly fond of him . . . and he keeps a sort of rude state and hospitality in which they can take much pride . . . This mode of life has, however, its evils, and

I can see them in this excellent and enthusiastic young man. The habit of solitary power is dangerous even to the best regulated minds, and this ardent and enthusiastic young man has not escaped the prejudices incident to his situation. He beards the Duke of Argyll, the Lord Lieutenant, and hates with a perfect hatred the wicked MacLeans on the other side of Mull who fought with his ancestors two hundred years ago . . .

He finishes the letter: 'The piper is sounding for breakfast, so no more.'

Donald MacKenzie has pointed out that the young laird's care to build up the population of Ulva did the islanders no good in the long run. As soon as the menace of Napoleon Bonaparte was removed in 1815, the bottom fell out of the Hebridean kelp industry as potash became available from foreign sources, and there was no longer a living to support the islanders. Staffa's own prosperity faltered, and he had to sell Ulva to his father-in-law. Massive emigration followed, and Staffa's Hebridean paradise had vanished.

This was the background of Archibald MacArthur's employment as piper to the laird. He must have experienced the same slump from prosperity to poverty, and was lucky to remain in Ulva after he had lost his position as Staffa's piper.

In 1810, John Kay made an etching, a full-length portrait of Archibald MacArthur, which was published in his volume of *Original Portraits* in 1838. It appeared in volume II, and the accompanying text said:

No. CCLXXI. Archibald McArthur, piper to the late Sir Reginald MacDonald Stewart Seton of Touch and Staffa, Bart.

McArthur was a native of Mull and was allowed [considered] to be well skilled in bagpipe music, having been taught by an excellent preceptor, Macrimmon [sic] of Skye. In 1810 he exhibited at the annual competition of pipers in Edinburgh, but failing to carry off the first prize, he refused to accept the second, thereby debarring himself from again appearing before the Highland Society on any similar occasion.

When the King visited Edinburgh in 1822, McArthur, as a matter of course, followed in the train of his Chief, from whom he held a cottage with a small portion of land, in lieu of his services as piper. That part of the Staffa estate upon which his possession was situated having been sold some years since, McArthur, though no longer employed in his former capacity, was allowed to remain by the new proprietor. He died, we believe, in 1834.

Note that Kay believed Archibald to have been a native of Mull, which would have included Ulva. 'Macrimmon of Skye' was Donald Ruadh

MacCrimmon who had returned from America, and lived in Skye between 1792 and 1811, then moved to Glenelg (see below). It was not in 1810 that Archibald entered the Edinburgh competitions, having declined second place in 1806.

Archibald cannot have died in 1834, as he is listed in the 1841 Census, living with his wife and family at Ormaig, in Ulva, at the age of sixty-eight. He is described as 'Crofter and kelper'. His wife Janet was seventy, his son John twenty-nine, daughter Margaret twenty-three and grandchildren Bell eleven and Janet four. Bell was the illegitimate daughter of their son Ranald, and Janet the child of their dead son Robert. Neither Archibald nor Janet appear in the 1851 Census, so probably both died in the 1840s.

Although it is clear that both Archibald and John were Staffa's pipers, only Archibald was designated 'Piper' in the register, living in Ulva. John Kay and Alexander Carmichael named only Archibald, and made no mention of any other piper. Scott referred only to 'the piper in constant attendance', giving no name. But Archibald the son of John the Professor in Edinburgh had a brother called John, who was piper to Staffa in 1804. Did he perhaps give up the position, or did he not remain in Ulva for long? Or did he die young? Or did he emigrate?

Alexander Campbell

An unpublished manuscript in the Library of Edinburgh University (No. 325 of Sir A. Mitchell's *List of Travels in Scotland*) was written by Alexander Campbell, who called it *A Slight Sketch of a Journey Made Through Part of the Highlands and Hebrides*; he said it was undertaken to collect materials for *Albyn's Anthology*. In it he described a visit he made to Staffa on 3 August 1815. There he heard Archibald MacArthur (whom he named) play *The Lament for the Slain on the Fatal Field of Culloden,* in Fingal's Cave, 'with pathos'.

Campbell added a note about Archibald MacArthur, telling us: 'He is a pupil of Lieut. Donald MacCrimmon the celebrated professor, who (it is but just to say) when I saw him at his farm in Glenelg, on my way homeward, spoke warmly of the pupil alluded to as one on whom he had bestowed great affection'.

Without this reference we might not have known who Archibald's teacher was (John Kay was probably following Campbell here) – but, as usual, more questions are raised: did Archibald go to Glenelg for his lessons, or were they earlier, in Skye? How often did he go? How did he get there? At whose expense? And why did Campbell write 'it is but just to say'? These glimpses, while illuminating, always leave us hungry for more.

And what work was the *Lament for the Slain on the Fatal Field of Culloden*? Is it the composition which Simon Fraser called *The Battle of Culloden by John MacCrimmon, 1794*, adding that it had been taught to his father, Hugh Archibald Fraser, by John (Iain Dubh) MacCrimmon himself, in 1816. The claim cannot be proven or disproven. The tune he gave this name was the one we now call *The Desperate Battle of the Birds*, often attributed to Angus MacKay, Gairloch, who died around 1780.

There is evidence that the *Lament for the Children* was also known as the *Lament for the Clans*, the Gaelic for both of these titles being the same, *Cumha na Cloinne*. It is clear from references in the Preface to Angus MacKay's Collection that the two titles, *Lament for the Children* and *Lament for the Clans*, were used side by side in the 1790s, by English speakers, both titles referring to the same work.

If, as is generally accepted, the lament was composed by Patrick Mor MacCrimmon, the title *Lament for the Clans* refers not to Culloden but to the Battle of Worcester, fought in 1651, in Patrick's own lifetime. Patrick may have been present at the battle, in which more than 700 MacLeod clansmen were lost, and other Highland clans had devastating losses. But in later times, particularly when the bitter memories of Culloden were beginning to take on a romantic tinge, the work was associated with the later battle, probably erroneously. It is possible that what Campbell heard in Fingal's Cave was the tune we would today call the *Lament for the Children*.

John Kay published his *Original Portraits* in 1838, the same year that Angus MacKay's Collection came out. Kay states that Archibald MacArthur was born in Mull (which would include Ulva), and this is borne out by the records, but conflicts with the evidence of Willie Gray and Keith Sanger. The local tradition in Mull and Ulva was that the family of the Ulva pipers were MacArthurs who had crossed direct from Islay, as did the Skye MacArthurs around the same time. In both cases, the farm of Proaig is mentioned as their Islay home (see above, Islay).

Until Keith Sanger published his evidence, the theory was that Archibald, with or without John, his brother or cousin, left Ulva where he had been born and brought up, and went to Edinburgh as a young man, seeking his fortune, in the late 18th century. If his (great?) grandfather had been a brother of the MacArthur who went to Skye, he would naturally seek out his (very distant) cousins in the city, and probably people would assume he was a cousin or nephew of Charles, especially if his own father or grandfather was called Charles. He was then presumably offered the position of piper to Boisdale (or his son Staffa, but Ranald was only eleven or twelve when Archibald returned), and moved back to Ulva, bringing his bride Janet Weir with him. This was around 1801. The tradition that Colin of Boisdale appointed Archibald, his piper from Ulva, is supported by the records, and when Colin gifted Ulva and Staffa to Ranald, Archibald the Piper was part of the package. Keith Sanger's evidence appears to counter this theory – see above.

James MacAnna and John MacCormick

In a most interesting booklet, *The Ulva Families of Shotts* (1991), James MacAnna quotes an anonymous traveller of 1806 who wrote in his diary about a visit to Ulva:

> Our arrival was greeted by a number of people on the beach, who were attracted by our piper's music. For as soon as he got within hearing of the island he had struck up a pibroch with all his vigour and continued his music till we landed. He then ranged us behind him and we were marched single file through the village to the tune of some favourite highland air, apparently to the great delight of the natives.

Was this player Archibald MacArthur? It seems likely, as the laird used to send a boat with his piper to meet visitors at the head of Loch na Keal.

James MacAnna also quotes extensively from the book by John MacCormick, *The Island of Mull*, published in 1923 but written about 1870. It is worth repeating a passage, as an example of the rubbish put out about the MacCrimmons and other piping families, in the Victorian age. See how many errors you can find in the following, where MacCormick was writing of Archibald MacArthur:

> At the tender age of nine or ten years, young MacArthur was placed, at the Marquis of Staffa's expense, in the MacCrimmon College at Dunvegan, where he was maintained and instructed in the difficult grips and movements characteristic of pipe music. In those days no student was admitted to the Piper's College above the age of ten; and the course of instruction, even in the case of the brightest pupil, extended to fourteen years. It is little wonder, then, that ancient performers excelled in an art which they cultivated with so much care and with such close application. MacArthur, it appears, was a prodigy at picking up and fingering on the chanter the most difficult tunes and

'crunluth', by which different parts of the piobaireachd are known to the exponents of pipe music.*

He goes on:

So clever was he in surmounting the difficulties which confront beginners that MacCrimmon foresaw in him a formidable rival in his favourite art. He therefore began to be more lax in his instructions to his young pupil; and whenever he desired to play one of his masterpieces he was never at a loss to send the boy MacArthur on some errand.

One day a gentleman came to MacCrimmon's house, and desired the famous musician to play one of his favourite tunes. MacCrimmon consented; and in order to get MacArthur out of the way while entertaining his friend, he sent him on a message to a neighbouring township some miles away. But MacArthur readily construed his tutor's pretexts, and having as much perspicacity in deciphering what his physiognomy indexed for some time regarding himself as he had ability in mastering the quavers and semiquavers, he resolved to circumvent his plans.

He accordingly affected the utmost willingness to obey his master; but, on quitting the house, he ensconced himself at the back door, and waited developments. When MacCrimmon thought him far enough away, he shouldered his pipes and discoursed some of the most excellent piobaireachds known, and in such a way as only MacCrimmon could.

After MacCrimmon had finished, MacArthur galloped off with his message, affecting the utmost concern at having fully confirmed his conviction that his instructor had been shirking his duties as instructor. But his youthful mind had been charmed with the captivating evolutions of the quavers, semiquavers, demisemiquavers, and all the other notes in that tune which he had then heard for the first time. He resolved to practise those beautiful bars in some secluded spot where his tutor could not discover him, and also at home, when the old piper was taking his walk.

---

* In that paragraph, the errors include:
  1. Archibald was not nine or ten when he went to MacCrimmon;
  2. MacCrimmon was in America when Archibald was nine or ten;
  3. Staffa was not a Marquis;
  4. the MacCrimmon college was closed by then;
  5. the MacCrimmon college was not at Dunvegan anyway;
  6. it was not a children's school, and there was no limit of ten years old;
  7. the course was not fourteen years;
  8. crunluth is not the name of different parts of a piobaireachd.

Eight errors in ten lines, I make it.

It was on one of these occasions that young MacArthur was practising the piobaireachd alluded to, when MacCrimmon returned suddenly from his noon-day walk, and, his ears having caught some bars of the tune, which he thought no one but himself could play, he angrily approached his pupil and said, 'You young rascal, where did you pick up that piece of music?' 'I picked it up in the backdoor that day you entertained your friend to it', said MacArthur, assuming the most impassable indifference, 'And', continued he, 'I shall lose no more time in telling the Marquis of Staffa, that you are not giving me the full benefit of your talents, for which you are amply paid by my benefactor.'

Old MacCrimmon felt somewhat alarmed at the stern rigidity and cool indifference with which his pupil addressed him, and, knowing the consequences that would result from the matter being made known to such an influential person as the Marquis of Staffa, he very discreetly confessed his guilt, and promised his clever pupil better attention in future.

Pupil and teacher seem to have got on very well after this incident, and when, in the course of a year or two, MacArthur quitted the MacCrimmon's College [what about the fourteen-year course?], he was ranked among the foremost pipers of his day. Students from various parts of Mull attended his college at Ulva, and most of them were known to be players of high repute. The writer of these sketches, when a boy, remembers having seen an old piper who had received his tuition in the Piper's College at Ulva. The race of pipers who for many years conducted this seminary long ago emigrated from their little island home; but memories of them are still green among the old natives of Mull.

[I have taken the liberty, for the sake of the reader, of splitting Mac-Cormick's vast unbroken paragraph into smaller units. The reader has enough to contend with without struggling through the density of that block.]

Seldom can such nonsense have been expressed in a more execrable style, but we have to accept this account as the fairy-story it is. What is alarming, though, is that this seems to be the earliest mention of a piping school in Ulva. Other references are later, and probably based on this. Neil Rankin Morrison, born and brought up in west Mull, and steeped in the piping lore of the area, said he knew nothing of such a school until he read MacCormick's words. It is clear that he thought not too much credence should be given to them.

Our trust in MacCormick is further strained when we read that the MacArthur college at Ormaig was a croft house divided into four apartments, one for family use, one for receiving strangers, one for cattle and one for the use of students while practising. This has an ominously familiar ring (see above). Thomas Pennant in the 1770s began it when he described the perfectly ordinary house of the MacArthur pipers at Hunglader, in Skye, making no reference whatsoever to rooms for piping students. This was taken up and developed by the Rev. Dr Norman MacLeod, who fancifully added rooms for lesson and practice to his description of the MacCrimmon college at Boreraig. It is a fiction which spread into most subsequent accounts of a piping school, whether in Skye, Ulva, Kilbride or elsewhere; it had become a literary cliché, trotted out whenever a piping college was mentioned.

Among the many ruins of houses at Ormaig, not one has four rooms, not even the house of the MacQuarrie clan chief's family. It is more than likely that the MacArthur 'school' of piping amounted to no more than Archibald MacArthur taking a pupil or two, in his own house, just as Calum Piobaire took pupils at his home at Catlodge, and the MacArthurs at their house in Hunglader. Taking a pupil or apprentice was enough to make a college, that is, a place for learning (but we have to wonder about the Rankin school which closed when the pupil numbers fell to seventeen: where did they teach them? Surely it must have been in small groups, spread over the year).

John MacCulloch

James MacAnna also quotes John MacCulloch, who visited Ulva in 1819. He wrote:

> It is remarkable how very little music is to be heard in the country. Were it not for the indisputable antiquity of this art (music) among them, we might now even imagine that it had never been known to them. I can scarcely remember that, excepting the boat song which the Ulva men sing to their cockneys who visit Staffa, I ever heard five songs throughout all the country during the whole of my acquaintance with it. Once or twice I may have heard a young cow-herd, and as often a milk-maid, chanting some 'snatches of old tunes' through the nose; once I have heard the fulling song [= waulking song], and once the grinding strains . . . but even the bagpipe is become extremely rare. The exceptions, as to instruments, will be found among the pipers still maintained by their chiefs; and, as might be anticipated, on the borders of the Lowlands. [I do not understand this last comment.]

This was the John MacCulloch who was so rude about the music he heard in St Kilda; he had a poor opinion of piobaireachd anyway, describing it as 'very irregular in character, without time or accent, and often scarcely embracing a determined melody, with a train of complicated and tasteless variations, merely adding confusion to the original air'. It does not seem to have occurred to him that he might be missing something.

We are reminded of a certain Dr Mainser who in 1880 gave a lecture, I think in Oban, about the bagpipe. He described it as 'this uncouth instrument, low as is its standard among the more perfect and more civilised mass of communicating sound . . . limited in its mechanism, poor in its expression' (*Oban Times*, 18 September 1880). We can only feel sorry for these blinkered critics, unable to hear beauty.

John MacDonald

In 1836, the *Glasgow Herald*, quoted by James MacAnna, carried a report of the anniversary dinner of the Ossianic Society, attended as guest of honour by Staffa himself. He made a speech 'replete with patriotic feeling, full of the kindliest sentiments, and expressed in the purest dialect of the mountain tongue'. Does this mean that Staffa spoke in Gaelic, or was he merely quoting? The evening's entertainment, to accompany the serious drinking, was music from the Ossianic Society's piper, unnamed, and from the unnamed piper of Colonel MacNeill of Barra, as well as from 'a youth of extraordinary musical talents in the services of Staffa'. This last was young JOHN MACDONALD, a grandson of Donald MacDonald the Edinburgh pipemaker who had published his collection of piobaireachd in the 1820s. Staffa and Archibald MacArthur had parted company, probably when Staffa had to sell Ulva to his father-in-law, and he later took on young John as a replacement. John competed at the age of fourteen in the Edinburgh competitions of 1837, so he was only thirteen on the night of the Ossianic dinner.

MacArthur Families in Ulva

The Old Parish Register for the parish of Kilninian and Kilmore, in Mull, starts around 1766, and shows at least one generation of MacArthurs living in Ulva before Archibald married Janet Weir in 1801. No other pipers are mentioned, but that does not necessarily mean these MacArthurs did not play: Archibald is designated 'Piper' because that was his full-time profession and he was piper to the laird. Clearly someone had taught him, perhaps his MacArthur relatives in Edinburgh, before he went to Donald Ruadh MacCrimmon.

There was an earlier Archibald MacArthur who married Mary Lamont in 1769. He had a brother John who lived at Ormaig and married Catherine MacQuarie, an Ulva girl. John's recorded (baptised) children were Charles, born in Ulva in 1767, Mairon, born Ulva 1770, and Archibald, born Ulva 1773. It was probably the names Charles and John which caused the confusion with the Skye pipers, then living in Edinburgh – but both names go back to the Proaig family of MacArthurs in the late 17th century.

The earlier Archibald MacArthur lived at Soriby, Ulva, and was probably born about 1740. His children were John, born Soriby 1775, Mary, born Cuilinish, Ulva, 1778, and Christian, who in 1782 was born on Staffa, one of the very few who could claim that distinction. Her mother must have been a woman of some fortitude, Staffa being an exposed and isolated island, difficult of access. At that time Staffa belonged to Colin MacDonald of Boisdale, and presumably Archibald senior was working for him. It seems unlikely he was Boisdale's piper, more probably a shepherd: there would be no point in having your piper isolated out on Staffa. Even if he was a shepherd, he could have been a player, of course, but not Boisdale's official piper.

The three families, MacArthurs, MacQuaries and Lamonts, seem to have intermarried freely, and from the MacQuaries the MacArthurs took the name Lachlan, from the Lamonts the name Archibald.

John, son of Archibald senior and possibly related to Archibald the Piper, born at Soriby in 1775, had a son, also John, born in 1819 at Ormaig, who married Peggy MacKinnon from Fanmore, Mull, in 1842. Peggy may have been related to the grandmother of Willie Gray, Jessie MacKinnon who lived at Uisken in the Ross of Mull. John 1819 had four brothers, three of whom were pipers who emigrated together to Australia in the 1840s. There is confusion about the link with Willie Gray, who spoke of a John MacArthur, a boatbuilder who lived in Uisken and had four piping sons who emigrated; but this John does not seem to be the one who married Peggy MacKinnon.

There were many other MacArthurs in Ulva, of the same generation as Archibald senior and John in Ormaig: Duncan, Alexander and Niel, and the girls Mary, Flora, Margaret, Catherine, Christian and Janet. They all married in Ulva or Mull, and had large families. Many of them married MacQuaries or Lamonts. But the 1841 Census has a special note commenting on the emigration of 300 islanders during the 1830s, and it is known that more left in the 1840s.

John MacArthur from Ayr, writing in 1930, left this account of the family history (I am indebted to Jeannie Campbell for sending me this, published in *Piper and Dancing*, November 1940). Referring to Archibald the Piper and his sons Charles and Robert, both of whom died young, he said:

> Charles was young and single, but Robert had married a woman named MacKinnon and left a family of two daughters named Catherine and Janet. Catherine died young, and Janet was taken by my grandfather [her uncle, Ranald MacArthur] and reared in the lowlands. He was the fourth son of Archibald, and was called Ranald MacDonald [as his Christian names] after the Chief who was an intimate friend of the family as well as being the Chief, and it was at the special request of MacDonald that the child was so named.

Ranald seems in fact to have been the third son of Archibald (see above) and his eldest brother Robert married Sally MacArthur, not 'a woman named MacKinnon'. Robert and Sally had a daughter Janet whose baptism was registered at Ormaig in 1836. Janet appears as a four-year-old living with her grandparents, Archibald and Janet at Ormaig, in the 1841 Census. Probably Robert died between 1836 and 1841, and Janet's sister Catherine, too, possibly before she could be baptised.

Ranald MacArthur was not christened Ranald MacDonald, but simply Ranald, which must have been after the laird, as stated, but this was very common practice, to name a child for the laird (or his factor) in the hope of future benefits. The account of the 'intimate' friendship seems fanciful, in view of the laird's marriage in 1812, into the grandeur of his wife's family.

John MacArthur, Ayr, went on: 'Ranald was brought up along with the Chief's son, received the same education, and they were inseparable companions. At the age of eighteen he came to the lowlands and finally settled at Mossend (Glasgow).'

This is most unlikely, with its implication that the laird brought up his children on Ulva. He had married in 1812, and his eldest son Henry James was at least four years younger than Ranald MacArthur; Ranald's brother John was closer to the laird's son in age. It is inconceivable that the laird's sons were educated in Ulva or Mull, and it is far more likely that the boys were 'inseparable companions' only when the laird and his family were up on holiday; perhaps Ranald MacArthur was put in charge of the younger boy for the summer.

John MacArthur, Ayr, continued, about Ranald MacArthur:

> After he had married and settled down (at Mossend), his only remaining brother, John, came south to him, but died of smallpox during an

epidemic and is buried in Old Bothwell churchyard. My father was Ranald's eldest son, and was named John after his uncle who had just died, although it had been intended to name him Archibald after his grandfather. Although a younger son of my grandfather (?) got the family pipes, as he was also a piper as well as being called for the MacDonald and he in turn left them to my eldest brother Ranald MacDonald MacArthur who was named after him. [This seems a little confused.]

Simon Fraser quoted a letter from the same John MacArthur, giving the address 163 Prestwick Road, Ayr, and the date 5 April 1930. Addressed to A.K. Cameron, Montana, it said:

> I am a great-grandson of Archibald MacArthur who died at Salen, Mull. Archibald MacArthur was a son or grandson of Charles MacArthur. He was aware that many MacArthurs (and related MacQuaries) went to Australia at the time of great distress and oppression in the Highlands. Captain John MacArthur who imported the first sheep to Australia and also the Australian's greatest curse, the rabbit, was related to our house of MacArthur. So likewise was General MacQuarrie, the first Governor of Australia and who belonged to Ulva – he lived in Ormaig.

Dr Barrie MacLaughlan Orme, the editor of Simon Fraser's Collection, added a note: 'John MacArthur's uncle had four to five hundred Piobaireachd Tunes which he lent to J. MacDougall Gillies', and he quotes a reference, *Letters of John MacArthur 1930*, NLS 9618.

When this letter says Archibald was 'a son or grandson of Charles MacArthur', which Charles does he mean? The great Charles (I) of Skye and Edinburgh? Charles (II) piper to the Earl of Eglinton? Or was the grandfather of Archibald MacArthur in Ulva also called Charles? His ancestor in Proaig was Charles, and the eldest son of John MacArthur, Ormaig, was christened Charles in 1767, which does suggest that John's father was called Charles. He would have been born in the late 17th century, that is, he would have been a contemporary of Angus MacArthur in Skye, the one who played at Sheriffmuir in 1715. It is possible that Angus MacArthur in Skye was a brother of Charles in Ulva, both leaving Proaig in Islay in the late 1600s. We do know for certain that a Charles MacArthur was living at Proaig in the 1680s and 1690s, and died there in 1696; the two MacArthur brothers (or cousins) left for Skye and Ulva shortly afterwards (see above, Islay).

Those who want to claim a family link between the Skye pipers and those of Ulva are aided by the similarity of the names in both families. This also creates a smokescreen which is difficult to penetrate. Claims such as 'he was a son or grandson of Charles' could mean anything, and prove nothing. Note that the name Angus, which recurs in the Skye family, is not found among the Ulva MacArthurs, and the name Archibald which runs through the Ulva branch is not present in the Skye family. Patterns of this kind would be expected, of course: a name might come in through a wife, and it is likely that Archibald, a Lamont name, was introduced into the Ulva MacArthurs by this route.

John MacDonald (Iain Domhnallach an Dall)

A piper and bard called John MacDonald was born at Lochdonhead in Mull around 1812, and died in Oban in 1884. His parents and grandparents were Mull crofters, his grandfather Alexander and his father Duncan both working as blacksmiths in Lochdonhead. Alexander, known as An Gobhainn Mor, 'the Big Smith', belonged to Glengarry; he was an imposing figure, tall and strong, and always wore his kilt, even in the smithy. He eloped with a girl from Athol called Betsy Stewart, believed to have been one of the piping Stewarts, and as they fled over to Morvern, she became very tired. Alexander picked her up, wrapped her in his plaid and carried her for nine miles on his back.

They lived a while with a blacksmith friend in Morvern, who taught Alexander his trade, before the couple moved to Lochdonhead. Their three sons were all blacksmiths, and most of their male descendants were pipers. The grandson, Iain Dall, was so-called because at the age of fifty-six he lost the sight of an eye through an accident in a wood while gathering nuts, and the other eye deteriorated over five years until he became completely blind.

Iain Dall made himself a set of pipes which he played 'with great glee', according to Dr K.N. MacDonald. One of Iain's brothers was a wood-turner by trade, and 'earned some fame as a maker of bagpipes in Skye'. Iain married a Catherine MacQuarrie from Bunessan, Mull, and they spent their latter years in Oban, where he was a fisherman.

Duncan Campbell

Donald W. MacKenzie, son of the last minister in Ulva, published a book in 2000, called *As It Was, Sin Mar A Bha, An Ulva Boyhood*. He included a most interesting chapter on 'Piping and Pipers', as part of his fascinating account of the history of Ulva, with old photographs and maps. Parts are reproduced here, by kind permission of the author. He lived in Ulva as a boy, from 1918 to 1929.

Mr MacKenzie gives an interesting description of a player he heard in the 1920s:

One of the pipers I remember coming to our house to play for us was DUNCAN CAMPBELL, the ploughman at Oskamull. He was nicknamed 'the Duke', for no better reason, as far as I knew, than that he was a Campbell. Like the great pipers of old, he gave a name to his pipes – he called her Lucy. Lucy was a temperamental creature that demanded much attention before each performance. The hemp on the drone slides had to be dampened, the reeds and blowpipe valve had to be chewed, the bag had to be softened and made air-tight by the application of various concoctions ranging from sugar and water to white of egg and treacle. At length, when Lucy's demands were satisfied, the Duke would begin to play, marching up and down the cement kitchen floor, *The Drunken Piper, Bonnie Ann, The Duke of Roxburgh's Farewell to the Blackmount Forest.* I was enthralled. Not that he always succeeded in completing the tunes, Lucy's tantrums intervening. Then the Duke, modest, not to say self-deprecatory to a fault, would say, '*Chan eil agam ach criomagan*' ('I have only fragments'). He never blamed Lucy; he blamed his calling as a ploughman for any failure in execution. Grasping the iron plough handles tightly in cold weather stiffened the fingers and produced hacks (*gagan*). Joiners and stone-masons who held their chisels and hammers firmly but with a more relaxed grip, he believed, made ideal pipers with their strong but supple fingers.

Unlike Lucy, the Duke's demands were very modest – frequent and copious cups of strong, sweet tea. From time to time throughout the course of an afternoon, he would indicate his need of refreshment with a set phrase – '*Tha pathadh searbh orm*' ('There is a bitter thirst on me'). Tea, long stewed with milk and sugar, was the essential accompaniment of all the social gatherings in the home, where stories were told, songs sung and pipes and fiddles played. To provide it was to pay a very modest price for the pleasure the performance gave us.

Sources

Piper and Dancing, November 1940
Piping Times, 25/11, August 1973
Old Parish Registers, Kilninian and Kilmore
William Gray
A. and A. MacDonald, *The Clan Donald*
Donald MacKenzie, *Sin Mar a Bha*
John Prebble, *The King's Jaunt*
Walter Scott, *Familiar Letters*
Alexander Campbell

Keith Sanger
John Kay, *A Series of Original Portraits*
Jeannie Campbell, *Highland Bagpipe Makers*
John MacArthur, Ayr
James MacAnna, *The Ulva Families of Shotts*
John MacCulloch, *A Description of the Western Isles*
John MacCormick, *The Island of Mull*
Jo Currie, *Mull*

William Gray

Pipe Major William Gray is usually associated with Glasgow, but his paternal grandparents were from Dornoch, Sutherland, and his maternal grandparents belonged to Uisken, in the Ross of Mull. He used to spend his holidays in Mull when he could. He later had a holiday house in Port Ellen, Islay, which he and his first wife, who was a MacTaggart from Islay, used to visit regularly.

As a young man he had been in Mull one summer, and was returning to Glasgow by steamer from Tobermory. In those days the steamers called in at different places to pick up or land passengers or goods, as required, and this one paused at Uisken. On impulse, Willie Gray went ashore and re-joined his grandparents. He stayed there with them for a year, during which he learned to speak fluent Gaelic. His mother was greatly vexed at his wasting the price of a ticket to Glasgow.

Donald MacKenzie wrote of the excitement he felt as a boy, when William Gray came to stay with relatives on the west coast of Mull, just across from Ulva.

> Another piper who visited us in summer was Pipe Major William Gray
> of the City of Glasgow Police Band, one of the most distinguished
> pipers of the 1920s and 1930s. He and Pipe Major William Ross, from
> Edinburgh, dominated the Piping Competitions at the major Highland
> gatherings. Both were inspirational teachers as well as performers, and
> each of them compiled a tutor and collections of pipe tunes. William
> Gray used to spend his summer holiday at Oskamull farm with the
> MacFadyens – Mrs MacFadyen, Katie MacGregor before marriage, was,
> I believe, related to him. We could hear him play of an evening outside
> the farm, the music carrying clearly and sweetly across Loch-a-Tuath.
> He would spend an afternoon with us at the manse – a well set-up man,
> dressed in a tweed plus-four suit, with a genial, affable manner, playing
> his magnificent, full silver-mounted bagpipes that appeared to perform
> perfectly without the need of any cosseting.

At the end of one such visit he presented us with a practice chanter and a copy of his tutor which incorporated a drumming manual by Drum Major John Seton. I determined to master the mysteries of fingering so graphically illustrated in the book, and each evening I sat beside the dying kitchen fire struggling on my own to translate the notation into the appropriate sounds on the chanter. I assumed that the first tune in the collection would be the easiest to learn. It was a tune I had never heard played, although now it must be about the best-known pipe tune there is – *Scotland the Brave*. Laboriously and at length I was able to pick out the notes from the score.

Unfortunately no-one was at hand to point out to me that the small notes were grace-notes, and so I played them as full notes, thereby rendering the melody unrecognizable. The good pipe major, had he heard my rendering of *Scotland the Brave*, would, doubtless, applaud my diligence in perseverance, while his keen musical ear would have been offended by my dismal attempt.

William Gray's brother, Robert, who was an ear, nose and throat specialist in Glasgow, made his home in the Ross of Mull on his retirement. A sister, Lily, also lived there, near Fionnphort, and Lexie MacCallum, who is a niece of Willie Gray, lives at Ardfenaig, between Fionnphort and Bunessan.

Simon Fraser in Australia claimed that his mother was a MacArthur related to the Skye piping family, and it is possible that she was the daughter of a Mary MacArthur, born to Charles MacArthur in Mull in 1810. Charles was of a piping family in Uisken, related to that of Willie Gray.

Sources
Jeannie Campbell, *Highland Bagpipe Makers*
Lexie MacCallum, Mull
Donald MacKenzie, *Sin Mar a Bha*
Margaret Gray, Islay
Simon Fraser, *The Piobaireachd of Simon Fraser*

The MacFadyens

The piping family of MacFadyens came from Mull, and although they lived for years in Glasgow, they are regarded as being Mull people. Their home was at Ardtun (pronounced Ard-TUN, not Ard-toon). It is not far from Bunessan, in the Ross of Mull, the south-western headland of the island.

Hector MacFadyen

Hector was a cousin of the three piping MacFadyen brothers, John, Duncan and Iain. Hector's family lived at Tolls, in the west of Pennyghael, a few miles to the east of Ardtun. The houses at Tolls are now ruins beside the Bunessan road, near to a beach marked on the OS map as Traigh nam Beach. A little to the east of this beach, and on the south side of the road, are two prominent fir trees, and the ruins of Tolls are close by.

The following account of the career of Hector MacFadyen is based on an article by Angus J. MacLellan, published in the *Piping Times* in January 1998, and used here by kind permission of the author.

Hector MacFadyen was born in Pennyghael district in 1923. His first piping teacher was Duncan Lamont, to whom he went at eight years of age. These lessons continued for ten years, until at eighteen Hector was called up for military service. He also had tuition from Willie Ross when he visited Mull, and from Willie MacLean of Kilcreggan, who had a summer cottage at Tiroran, across Loch Scridain from Pennyghael. [These times do not quite add up, and there is a discrepancy with an *Oban Times* report which says he was fourteen in 1939.]

Hector spent the war years with the 49th Division, serving in France, Belgium, Holland and Germany. He was in the army until 1947, and had little chance to play the pipes. He tried to transfer to the Argylls, but was refused on the grounds that none of his family had ever served with the regiment (many of his family had been in the navy).

After the war, Hector began to compete at the games, but confined himself to the light music. Having become a strapping lad, he had success in the heavy events at the games, and there was a danger that this might overtake his interest in piping. Fortunately, however, Donald MacLean of Lewis ('Big Donald', as he was known, to distinguish him from 'Wee Donald' MacLean of Oban) took an interest in Hector's playing, and became his piobaireachd tutor. This lasted until Donald died in 1964, and undoubtedly was the making of Hector as a piper.

The performances of Hector at the games in the 1950s and 1960s 'will linger so long as memory lasts', as Angus J. MacLellan put it. In 1963 he won every first prize for professional piping at Cowal, including the Best Dressed. In 1964 he won both the Gold Medals, at Oban and Inverness. He was the first winner of the Silver Chanter at Dunvegan in 1967. 'But it was not so much his winning as his style of winning. His playing was clean, accurate and vigorous, a model for those with the physical strength to follow.' To this day, a tape recording of Hector's pipe causes great interest among pipers.

At the conference of the Piobaireachd Society in 1990, John Mac-Lellan said that when Ronnie Lawrie and Hector MacFadyen were entering the competitive piping world in the 1960s, Ronnie had pipes with Lawrie drones, and Hector's had Henderson drones. Both had what John MacLellan described as 'fairly full-sounding drones', but then they got some small brass tubes and a special tool, and they inserted the tubes into their drones. The result was amazing: 'how they mellowed was fantastic'. A great deal of scepticism has since been expressed about this, but it is undeniable that Hector's pipe produced a sound which makes pipers' heads turn, and there are recordings to prove it. What may be in doubt is which came first, the fantastic sound or the story of the wee brass tubes.

Angus J. continues:

As a companion at the games he was one who gave of his best, and – win or lose – was able to celebrate afterwards. We admired his courage in his illness as we rejoiced in his support of the oppressed . . . We envied him his bravery, for entering for the Open at Oban one year knowing only one of the set tunes, and getting it to play. (But we were surprised that he tried it again at Inverness two weeks later in the hope that fortune would favour him again – which it didn't).

His fame has, of course, reached all parts of the piping world. In 1966 he was invited to British Columbia and spent a month entertaining the west coast pipers with his piping, his singing and his wonderful stories of life with the pipers – told with a fluency and a wealth of original expression which we could admire but never emulate. It was a visit that Hector and British Columbia enjoyed tremendously.

He was one of the brightest jewels in the professional crown, one of a group who have been called by some of the younger players 'the aristocracy of piping'. Others may achieve admission to the group, but nobody will ever take his place.

In 2000, the *Piping Times*, under the heading '35 Years Ago', published a report:

An enthusiastic response was evoked by the more informal contributions of Hector MacFadyen, John MacFadyen and Seumas MacNeill, who emerged to an amazed Glasgow audience as singers instead of their usual role. Two well-known judges remarked afterwards that Hector MacFadyen and Seumas MacNeill are better singers than they are pipers, which we anxiously assume is a compliment. Only we can't decide whether they meant to infer that John MacFadyen is a great piper or a dreadful singer.

The MacFadyen Brothers

The three MacFadyen brothers, John, Duncan and Iain, as well as their cousin Hector, who was a little older, were all outstanding players; all four of them taught in the College of Piping in Glasgow. Their sister Freena was also an excellent piper, though heard less often. The driving force behind the brothers seems to have been as much their mother as their father, and Iain tells how she made him practise and go for piping lessons when he would rather have been playing football. The only way he could get to the football was to put his boots in his pipe-case and smuggle them out of the house.

Their father was Duncan MacFadyen, who married Effie Beaton from Ardtun, near Bunessan, in the south-west of Mull. Duncan's father was from Tiree, and he had moved to settle in Ardtun as an adult. There were many MacFadyen families in Tiree, especially at the eastern end of the island; Duncan's father came from Ardess, in the township of Caolis. The croft is still in the family.

Duncan and Effie moved to Glasgow, and all the ten children, including twins, were born there. Five of the ten became pipers, initially taught by their father. Duncan was one of the Clyde harbourmasters, a position of considerable responsibility requiring a high degree of skill in seamanship. He had a Master Mariner's certificate and many years of experience at sea.

Effie Beaton, a cousin of Allan C. Beaton, Tobermory (see below), was said by Donald MacLeod – but not by her sons – to have been 'a direct relative of the MacKays of Gairloch', though the connection is not clear. Her family, the Beatons in Ardtun, can be traced back to the 1790s, and her great-grandfather, Donald Beaton, appears in the Old Parish Register for Mull from 1825 to 1844.

At the time of his marriage to Cirsty McGilvra from Bunessan, Donald Beaton, born in 1795, was described as being from Saorphein, beside Loch Assapol, to the south of Ardtun. It is clear that he later had no place of his own, as in 1830 he was a cottar in Tirghoil, that is, he had a cottage on someone else's land. He may have been evicted from his family's land at Saorphein to make way for the creation of a big farm.

The two youngest of Donald's family of eight were born in Ardtun, where the family settled as cottars in 1840, the start of the decade of

Blind Archie MacNeill, when he was in Canada.
Courtesy of the College of Piping

Seumas MacNeill, a brilliant lecturer, in typical pose.
Courtesy of the College of Piping

Above. Islay House, in Bridgend, Islay, where Angus MacKay compiled his manuscript of pipe music, some of which was published in 1838. This is merely the front of the house which extends back some distance. It belonged to the Campbells of Shawfield and Islay, and latterly to Lord Margadale (a Morrison). Pipe Major Willie Ross gave piping lessons here in the 1920s.

Left. Islay House in the 18th century. It is now surrounded by tall trees.

The crag where the MacEacherns had their forge was at Creag Uinsinn, in the rocky cliff behind the house in this picture. Before becoming renowned pipers, they were makers of the famous Islay swords, six-foot blades used in the 15th century.

Looking up the hill towards Conisby, Islay, home of the MacEachern, Johnston and MacIntyre pipers in the 19th and early 20th centuries. The MacEachern house is on the far right.

Left. Neil MacEachern from Islay, playing at Aboyne in 1961. He won the Gold Medal at Oban four years later. *Photograph kindly lent by Andrew MacEachern*

Below. Some Islay pipers at a Gathering in Glasgow (?) in the 1920s. Left to right, back row: MacNiven, Conisby; MacDougall, Bowmore; Robert MacEachern, Corrary; front row: John Johnston; Currie, Port Ellen; John MacEachern, Carrabus; J. Johnston junior. *Photograph kindly lent by Mrs Catherine Campbell, Fort William*

Above. Looking north to Proaig, Islay (on the bay, below a clump of whins), and to MacArthur's Head (on the right, the headland across the bay). This photograph was taken from the track over to Proaig from Ardtalla, on a wet and windy day.

Right. A sketch of Proaig in modern times. *By kind permission of David Caldwell*

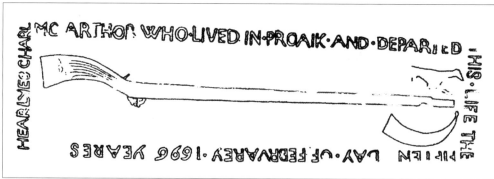

Sketch made in 1895 of the carving on the gravestone of Charles MacArthur in Kildalton Church, Islay. Charles died in 1696. He was probably the father of the MacArthur pipers who went to Skye and Ulva. It is possible that this sketch is an interpretation of the carving, and that others might have seen it as a representation of a single-drone bagpipe. Today the carved image is too worn for any certainty.

The instructors at the College of Piping in 1968. Left to right, back row: John C.Johnston, Iain MacLellan, Donald MacPherson, Bob Swift, Andrew Wright, Duncan MacFadyen, Dugald MacNeill; front row: Bill Summers, Joe Wright, Thomas Pearston, Iain MacFadyen, Kenneth MacLean, Angus J. MacLellan. *Courtesy of the College of Piping*

SPA Competition in Glasgow in 1936. Left to right: D.MacMurchie, unknown, Robert Reid, Hector MacLean, William MacLean, unknown, Duncan MacIntyre, Peter MacLeod junior, Archie MacNab, John Allan MacGee, Philip Melville, Hamish MacColl, J.MacGregor Murray. *Courtesy of the College of Piping*

Lily MacDougall, in her home at Caol Ila, Islay, in 2002. She was 87 when this was taken, and still playing the chanter.

The Islay Pipe Band, Grade 3 Champions 2011 at Cowal Games. *Photograph kindly lent by Siobhan MacLean*

Novel Competition
for the Caledonian Games

NEILL LINDSAY

NEIL LINDSAY INSPIRED THE LADS AND LASSIES WI' THE BONNIE AIRS O' SCOTLAND

PIPERS TO PLAY
FOR GOLD MEDAL

Left. A page from Neil Lindsay's scrap-book, assembled in San Francisco in the 1890s. *By kind permission of Peter Youngson*

Below. Neil Lindsay's house at Caigenhouse, Jura, which he re-built and called Frisco (on left, with porch).

Above. Kiloran Bay, Colonsay, for which Archie MacMillan named his march.

Right. What is left of the stone known as Carragh Mhic a'Phi, MacPhie's Standing Stone, Colonsay, where the last MacPhie chief was shot in 1623.

Andrew and Flora MacNeill on Oronsay. *Courtesy of the College of Piping*

Oronsay House, on the tidal island of Oronsay, off Colonsay. This was the home of Andrew and Flora MacNeill for many years.

Left. The carved gravestone traditionally believed to be that of Allan nan Sop is among the graves in Iona of prominent mediaeval highland chiefs, even though he was base-born. Clansmen of warlike character might succeed to chieftainship through tanist succession, regardless of low birth, and no-one could deny Allan's aggressive qualities.

Below. Duart Castle, in the south-east of Mull. It was held by the MacLeans until 1692, when it fell to the Campbells of Argyll. The Rankins were the MacLean chief's pipers.

Kilbrennan, on the west coast of Mull. Here the Rankins had their piping school in the 17th and 18th centuries. This house probably replaced a long low building, part of which (now modernised) remains beside the main house. The earlier building would have been thatched, possibly with heather.

Cnoc nan Piobairean, a hillock at Kilbrennan, Mull, where the Rankin pipers and their pupils used to practise. Piping competitions were held here, too.

Archibald MacArthur, piper to MacDonald of Staffa. This portrait appeared in John Kay's book *A Series of Original Portraits and Caricature Etchings* in 1838.

Robert Beck in 1965, in the uniform of the Tiree Band. *Kindly lent by Robert Beck*

Right. Pipe Major John MacDonald of the 72nd Regiment (c.1824–1894). He was born in Tiree, and retired there after his army career.

Tiree Pipe Band in 1967. *Photograph kindly lent by Robert Beck*

The castle of Breacacha, Coll, recently restored, in the south end of Coll. Here Hector MacLean was executed without trial in 1578. The old castle was built around 1450. John Garve MacLean of Coll probably lived here.

The burial place of Ronald MacDonald of Morar, in the old Clanranald tomb within Kildonan Church, Eigg, now ruined.

Above. The Piper's cairn in the south of Eigg. Here the bearers of Donald MacQuarrie's coffin rested as they bore it from Grulin to Kildonan for burial. From here the coffin-bearers saw Ronald MacDonald's boat coming over from Morar for the funeral.

Right. The memorial to John Johnston at Arinagour, Coll.

The caves of Eigg, seen from the sea. The big opening is the Cathedral Cave, the Massacre Cave (OS ref. NM 476834) lying along the coast to the right.

Hector MacFadyen, born in Mull, was a cousin of the piping MacFadyen brothers. *Courtesy of the College of Piping*

Duncan MacFadyen, father of the MacFadyen brothers, was a Mull man, himself a piper, who became harbour-master of the Glasgow docks. *Courtesy of the College of Piping*

Duncan MacFadyen junior, one of the piping MacFadyen brothers. He was less competitive than John and Iain, but was a very fine player, with a delicate touch. *Courtesy of the College of Piping*

Traigh Gruinard, the shore at the head of Loch Gruinard where the MacDonalds fought the MacLeans in 1592 for possession of the Rinns of Islay. In the battle Sir Lachlan MacLean was killed. It is possible that the *MacLeans' March* and the *MacNeills' March* are linked with the reprisals which followed. An old Quickstep, *Batail Traigh Ghruineairt*, is still played in Islay.

All that remains of Dunyveg Castle on the south coast of Islay, the scene of the incident which gave rise to *The Piper's Warning to his Master*. Alex Mackenzie in foreground.

Ferry House, sometimes called Achnaha, on the island of Gigha, where Archie MacNeill lived as a boy.

the terrible potato famines. Donald was probably related to Hugh and Angus Beaton, already living there and also born in the 1790s. This may suggest that their father was from Ardtun, but the records do not go back far enough to confirm this.

Two of Donald's sons were called John, known in the records as John senior and John junior. This family tradition was repeated when the 20th-century MacFadyens named two of their sons John and Iain (two forms of the same name). These two earlier Johns had families, born and brought up in Ardtun.

John senior married a girl from Tiree called Julian, and had three children before Julian died in the mid-1860s. He left Ardtun then, but returned when his parents died, and in 1881 was living there with his daughter and family.

His younger brother John junior was born in 1844, and remained in Ardtun until the 1870s, left for a time but was back by 1891. His wife was called Catherine, and they had six children, Mary 1877, Catherine 1879, Donald 1881, Hector 1885, Christina 1887 and John 1890. John junior was the grandfather of both Effie Beaton and Allan C. Beaton, Tobermory.

The three MacFadyen boys, their sister and their cousin Hector all showed early promise as pipers. Taught intitially by their father Duncan in Glasgow, the brothers were sent to leading players for further instruction. Freena attended classes in the College of Piping, Otago Street. All four boys were competing widely from a young age. A report in the *Oban Times* on the Oban and Lorne Mod of 1939 said that only two young pipers had entered the junior competition, and only one of them, Hector MacFadyen of Pennyghael, had turned up. 'The lack of numbers in this item was however more than balanced by the fine playing and attractive deportment of this young piper of fourteen who has already won many honours.'

Later in 1939 the *Oban Times* carried a report of a concert put on by the SPA, and added a note by their correspondent, unnamed: 'At tea I met a very young friend who has hopes of being some day a great piper, Master John MacFadyen, whose father, a Mull man, is one of the Clyde harbour masters. I liked two things about that boy, his ability to talk without shyness, and his piping enthusiasm. He has entered for the April amateur competition of the Association, and hopes to follow in the footsteps of his cousin Hector MacFadyen, who is already a winner.'

The *Piping Times'* comment was 'Young John seems to have been a forceful character with a clear idea of his future, and certainly this report gives us a prophetic glimpse of the man in the making.' At the time of that concert, Duncan MacFadyen senior was secretary of the SPA.

In his biography of Seton Gordon, Raymond Eagle mentions that the young MacFadyens were sometimes 'special guests' at Viewfield House Hotel in Portree, the home of Colonel Jock MacDonald. In his later years, Colonel Jock actively encouraged young pipers and clarsach players by running a day of junior competitions in his hotel at the end of the visitor season. The MacFadyens were competitive by nature, especially John, and relished the atmosphere of rivalry, not to mention the pleasures of winning.

John MacFadyen

John was born in Glasgow in 1926, the second child in a family of ten, and the eldest boy. He was taught by his father, and then went to Roddy MacDonald (Roddy Roidean from South Uist) who as a piper in the City of Glasgow Pipe Band had taken up residence in Glasgow. Another of his teachers was Willie Gray, and John used to travel weekly to Dumbarton for lessons with him.

John won the Gold Medal at Oban in 1960, the Senior Open Piobaireachd three times, the Gold at Inverness in 1966 and the Clasp three times. He, with his brothers, followed the example of their father, to become much involved with the SPA, of which John was the President from 1963 to 1972. He was also secretary of the College of Piping, and of the Piobaireachd Society. He helped to set up the Silver Chanter competition at Dunvegan, and the Piobaireachd Society conferences, as well as the SPA Knockout competition.

In 1973 John was teaching out in Kenya, a career as a schoolmaster which took him eventually to the heights of HM Inspectorate of Schools. He became Primary Schools Advisor in Renfrewshire, a post he held for many years.

In 1952, Grainger and Campbell took over Duncan MacRae's pipe-making business in Argyle Street, Glasgow, and John MacFadyen and Iain Dewar became partners in the company.

John and his brother Iain were much in demand as judges when their competing days were over. John's acerbic comments to young pipers on their appearance and deportment were not always well received, and in more than one case led to the youngster giving up piping altogether; but his opinions on the music and his vast knowledge were always respected. Like Seumas MacNeill, his friend and rival, he was inclined to hone his wit on those not in a position to answer back, though onlookers enjoyed the humour.

John was, however, a kind man, and Dugald MacNeill commented that John was always ready to 'fix and tune anyone's pipes, from Seton Gordon to the shyest beginner', adding 'although I doubt if even he could fix and tune Seton Gordon's pipes'.

It is said that as a young man he fell out with John MacDonald, Inverness, after a short (very short) period of instruction. The story is that he arrived at the door of 3 Perceval Street, Inverness, the home of John MacDonald, and asked to be given instruction. At that time would-be pupils had to pass a rigorous proficiency test administered by the Piobaireachd Society, as so many aspiring pipers wanted to be taught by the master. John MacFadyen had by-passed this, but John MacDonald said he could join the class then in session.

When it came to John's turn to play the tune they were studying, the teacher did not like his interpretation. He showed him how he thought it should be played, and told him to go away and work on it, and come back next week to see if he had it right. The following week, John MacFadyen turned up and played the tune – exactly the way he had played it at the previous lesson. He had made no alterations at all. John MacDonald, understandably incensed, told him to leave and not bother coming back. This story may be apocryphal, or at least exaggerated, but certainly John MacFadyen often spoke acidly of John MacDonald and lost no opportunity of running down his playing.

John was often to the fore at Dunvegan, and was a favourite with Dame Flora MacLeod. It was he who made a recording of Angus MacPherson's composition *Salute to the Cairn at Boreraig*, when the tune won the piobaireachd section of the BBC's composing competition in 1966. And John, with Seumas MacNeill, played at Dunvegan before Dame Flora's funeral.

John published in 1966 a collection of light music, entitled simply *Bagpipe Music*. It was reprinted in 1999. He followed it up with a second collection in 1974. He presented papers to the Piobaireachd Society conferences: in 1975, 'Aspects of Piobaireachd Playing', and in 1977, a joint paper with Archie Kenneth and David Murray, 'The Emendation of Piobaireachd'. He also made several recordings of his playing.

It was not only as competing pipers that the MacFadyens made their mark. As seen above, John was a brilliant organiser, with a finger in many pies. As the Hon. Secretary of the Piobaireachd Society he ran it with a blend of wit and efficiency, particularly effective at the society's conferences. One of his innovations at Middleton Hall was that the starter course of the first dinner of the conference was always Pea Broth, John's little joke.

His friendship with Seumas MacNeill (which some took for enmity) gave endless entertainment as they struck sparks off each other, each sharpening his wit on the other's, like fencers flashing their rapiers.

John retired in 1978, planning to build and run a small teaching centre in Skye, where he and his wife Sheena had a house, near Borve. This plan came to nothing, as John died the following year.

He died on 21 January 1979. He had long been a heavy drinker, though never seen the worse for drink. His steady intake of alcohol made him dependent on it, and eventually it destroyed his liver. When he went into hospital suffering from jaundice, a note in the *Piping Times*, presumably written by his friend Seumas MacNeill, said: 'We wish him a speedy recovery. Meanwhile Ward 15 of the Victoria Infirmary is doing as well as can be expected . . .'

John is buried in Portree, and on his gravestone is carved a snatch of the piobaireachd *Beloved Scotland,* with which he had won his first Clasp. It is a curiosity that there is a tradition about the setting of the tune: that tiny passage from *Beloved Scotland,* it is said, is not the one that John himself played, and not only that, but the carver of the stone is said to have made a note-error – not at all characteristic of John MacFadyen's playing. After his death, his friends and admirers created the John MacFadyen Memorial Trust, which works to support different aspects of piping. It was launched in January 1980 with a public appeal for funds. Alasdair Milne, then Managing Director of BBC Television, became Chairman of the Trustees, a post he held for twenty years, retiring in 2002.

The Trust inaugurated the annual Lecture/Recital at Stirling Castle; it ran an annual concert in Inverness; it held a learned Seminar in Skye; it sponsored a Research Student; and it took over the running of the Silver Chanter competition at Dunvegan as well as the Donald Mac-Donald Quaich recital/competition at Armadale, Skye. Today it has had to modify its activities, through diminishment of funds.

The first Lecture/Recital was in March 1980, in the Chapel Royal at Stirling Castle. Seumas MacNeill spoke of his friendship with John, and a recording of John playing the *Lament for Donald Ban MacCrimmon* brought back many memories to the audience. The two pipers who played that night were John's brothers, Duncan and Iain, and Gaelic singing was included in the programme.

Duncan MacFadyen Junior

Duncan, a very fine player, known for delicacy and finesse, was possibly the least competitive and least known of the three brothers. He was of a more retiring disposition than either of the other two, and did not seem to enjoy being in the public eye, although his recitals were excellent and always memorable. He won the Gold Medal at Inverness in 1962, and at Oban in 1966, and became an instructor at the College of Piping, where he taught an evening class which was fondly remembered by his pupils.

Duncan married Janet Faulds, a granddaughter of Hector MacLean, piper to the Clan MacLean (see above). Duncan's health was not the most robust, and he died of lung cancer in 1987. He is buried at Ardtun, close to the Mull home of his parents, where his brother Archie also lies.

Iain MacFadyen

Iain MacFadyen was born in Glasgow, the youngest son and seventh child in the family of ten: he had a younger sister Mary, who was his twin.

Iain, like his brother John, was a pupil of Roddy MacDonald (Roidean) from South Uist, who was in the City of Glasgow Police Pipe Band. He also had lessons from Peter Bain. When Iain was doing his National Service, he opted to serve in the Queen's Own Cameron Highlanders, from 1957 to 1959, after he had won the Gold Medal at Inverness in 1957. While in the army he had tuition from Donald MacLeod. He made his mark on the regiment, as both piper and footballer, and composed a 6/8 march, *Pipe Major Andrew Venters*.

In 1973, Iain had, by mid-season, already won eight major prizes, typical of his glittering career as a competition piper. The list of the MacFadyen awards is not merely impressive, it is breath-taking.

All four of them won the Gold Medal at both Oban and Inverness, Hector winning both in the one year (1964), Iain in consecutive years (1957 and 1958), and John winning the Gold and the Clasp on consecutive days at Inverness in 1966. In 1968 John won the Senior Open at Oban, his second Clasp at Inverness, the Silver Chanter in Skye, and the Bratach Gorm in London. His third Clasp followed in 1969. He held the Bratach Gorm a record number of times, and Iain won the Glenfiddich championship at Blair Castle four times, also a record (since broken by Willie MacCallum).

Mere lists of triumphs do not do justice to the quality of their playing, however. Hector was renowned for the sound of his pipe, which he tuned to a richness of tone that has been long remembered. Each of the four MacFadyens had a distinctive sound and his own style of playing.

After a career in football in Glasgow, Iain took up a position in 1973 as a schools piping instructor for South-West Ross and Lochcarron, based at Kyle of Lochalsh. His successful career as a teacher culminated in 2003 with the award of an Honorary Fellowship of the Educational Institute of Scotland, the highest award the Institute can bestow. He retired in 2000 after thirty years of school instructing, but continues as a private tutor to many young players, and teaches at the School of Excellence based in Plockton. He was awarded the MBE in 2007.

In 1975, he gave a talk to the Piobaireachd Society conference, entitled 'Teaching Piping in the Highlands'. The talk itself took up three pages in the printed Proceedings, but stimulated discussion covering sixteen.

Pipe Music composed for the MacFadyens includes:

Cameron MacFadyen, by Duncan Johnston 6/8 M 4
Ian MacFadyen, by James Haugh 6/8 M 4
Iain MacFadyen Junior, by Evan MacRae 6/8 J 4
Lament for Duncan MacFadyen, by Donald MacLeod P 5
Miss Freena MacFadyen, by Allan C. Beaton 2/4 M 4
Mrs Duncan MacFadyen, by Donald MacLeod 2/4 M 4

and MacFadyen compositions include:

Hector's Jig, by Hector MacFadyen 6/8 J 4
Jessie from Coulags, by Iain MacFadyen R 4
Mary MacPherson of Kyle, by Iain MacFadyen 6/8 M 4
Pipe Major Andrew Venters, by Iain MacFadyen 6/8 M 4

Iain played *Jessie from Coulags* and *Mary MacPherson of Kyle* as two of his tunes on the tape he made for Lismor Recordings in 1989, Volume Seven of the series The World's Greatest Pipers.

John MacFadyen published many arrangements of tunes, many of them traditional Gaelic airs, in his collection of pipe music. They include:

The Barmaid R 2
The Black Cock's Dance R 2
The Bonnie Isle of Jura, by M. Darroch, arr. MacFadyen 6/8 GA 2
Chi Mi 'n Toman 6/8 SA 2

De'il Tak' the Breeks R 2
Fair Jean (Sine Bhan) 4/4 GA 2
Father O'Flynn 6/8 J 6
Heather Island (Eilean a'Fhraoich) 4/4 GA 2
Hi-Ri, Ho-Ro, Mo Nighneag 6/8 GA 2
Iain Ruaidh's Lament GA 2
If I'd Get A Dram I'd Take It R 2
MacKenzie's Farewell SA 2
Mairi Nighean Alasdair 6/8 GA 2
The Miller's Fair Daughter R 2
Not A Swan On The Lake 6/9 GA 2
Portland Castle 2/4 M 4
Raven's Rock R 2
Rhu Vaternish R 2
Thug Mi Gaol 4/4 GA 2
A Traditional Reel R 2

The above lists make no claim to be complete, and any additions will be welcomed.

Sources

Piping Times
College of Piping
Proceedings of the Piobaireachd Society Conferences
Raymond Eagle, *Seton Gordon*
Jo Currie, *Mull*
Iain MacFadyen

Other Piping Links to Mull

Besides the three families of outstanding pipers, the Rankins, the MacArthurs and the MacFadyens, Mull has produced a host of other excellent players who are perhaps less well known.

Allan MacLaine

The laird of Scallasdale, ALLAN MACLAINE, seems to have been both piper and fiddler. He had a bard, Alasdair Mac Mhuirich (Alasdair MacKenzie of Achilty), who died in 1632, after he had become fourth chief of Achilty. In the early years of the 17th century, Alasdair made a song, *Oran Fear Sgalasdail (Song of the Laird of Scallasdale)* which he put into the first person as if it were Allan himself speaking. His song makes it clear that although Allan had been in love with another girl, he had married one he did not want, when he was too drunk to know what was happening. The song expresses his deep unhappiness about the marriage. He says his heart is now so heavy that he cannot play any music:

Ciamar sheinneas mi fidheall?	How can I play the fiddle?
Tha mo chridhe ro-bhronach,	My heart is too heavy,
Na piob uallach nam feadan –	Nor the noble pipe with its chanter –
'S tric a spreig mi i'm sheomar	I have often blown it in my room
. . .	. . .

He goes on to describe his feelings on seeing his lost sweetheart with her new husband. The whole poem is a self-mocking lament.

The song is unusual in many ways: in that the bard was putting the laird's feelings into the poem as if the laird himself was speaking; in that the bard himself was a laird, or soon to become one; and in that it is rare to find a laird himself as a piper. If he played only in his own house, perhaps he was not a very good one (the word *seomar* probably refers to the main living room of his house). This, too, is unusual: it is unexpected to find a reference to the playing of a pipe indoors as early as this, especially in a private house and not in a great chief's hall.

JOHN RUADH OG MACKINLAY was the name of a piper who was outlawed on 24 June 1628, with several other men from Mull, when they failed to appear to answer a charge of seizing and plundering a ship belonging to a Dumbarton merchant, which had called at the island of Mull laden with goods. It is not known whether the culprits were caught and punished, but it seems unlikely.

Mary MacLeod

Mairi nighean Alasdair Ruaidh, known to the piping world as MARY MACLEOD, was born around 1615, probably in Rodel, Harris – though neither date nor place is certain. She belonged to the line of the MacLeods of Bernera, Harris, and she died around 1705, possibly in her nineties. (For details of her life, see William Matheson, *TGSI* vol. 41, 1951.)

When Mary was expelled from Dunvegan around 1660 or a little later, the tradition is that she was sent first to Mull to live in exile: but her verses still reached Skye from there, and she was banished to more remote parts.

William Matheson said that there were three poems or songs which were probably her work and composed when she was in Mull, but they are not usually included in lists of her compositions. All three have links with Mull, and refer to the MacLeans of Duart, who held much of Mull at that time.

One is *A Song made to Hector MacLean, Laird of Duart, who was killed at Inverkeithing*, that is, Red Hector, 15th Chief, killed in 1651. Another is called *An Cronan Muileach, The Mull Song*, about a MacLean killed in the 17th century, probably the same Hector MacLean as in the previous work; this was made by a female MacLeod poet, almost certainly Mary. The third was a song noted down from the singing of a Mull man called John MacFadyen, and it seems to date from before 1693; it was used as a rowing song, and a version of it was found in South Uist. William Matheson gives his reasons for believing that all three of these poems were made by Mary, presumably during her exile in Mull.

Mull Pipers

Two pipers are named in a Mull rental dated 1679 (see above): PATRICK MCDONALD living at Feirgeyll, near Duart, and JOHN MCEAN VIC EWN VIC ALLAN, piper to MacLean of Brolass; John lived at Gualachaolais, Loch Spelve.

MURDOCH MACDONALD is named in the Notices of Pipers as a famous piper in Mull, 'the last of a long line of pipers in the locality'. He died in 1734 – but to which part of Mull did he belong? The Old Parish Registers, unfortunately, do not go back as far as that for the Mull parishes.

MacNeill Pipers in Mull

The Notices of Pipers state that a family of MacNeills were pipers to the MacLeans of Duart before the Rankins, but there seems to be little evidence to support this claim, and it does not appear to be remembered in oral tradition.

At Lochbuie, however, there is a record of a PATRICK who may have been a MACNEILL. His son was listed as a Mull tenant in 1716: 'Hugh MacPhail alias McFadrich phiobair', which probably means he was Hugh MacPhail, son of Patrick MacPhail, the piper. While Frans Buisman linked this Patrick to a Patrick McNeill roy (ruadh), found in a list of the inhabitants of Mull in 1675, we cannot be certain whether this means Red-haired Patrick MacNeill, or Patrick son of Red-haired Neil. Perhaps it does suggest a family of red MacNeills who had a piping tradition, and possibly came from the Lochbuie district of Mull, but possibly it is more likely they were MacPhails.

HECTOR MACLEAN in 1760 was piper to MacLaine of Lochbuie (the Lochbuie branch always used the spelling MacLaine). Hector was reckoned to be one of the best players of his day, and may have been the composer of *MacLaine of Lochbuie's Lament* (see above).

The *Scots Magazine*, in May 1759, gave a report of a case heard in the Court of Justiciary, Edinburgh, when two MacLeans sued 'John MacLaine of Lochbuy, his servant, his piper's son and two tenants named Macphaden' for seizing the two MacLeans and imprisoning them for two days in the Castle of Moy, Loch Buie. All were found guilty and received seventeen days in prison, plus payment of damages. Presumably the piper's son was Hector MacLean's boy.

James Robertson, Tobermory

DONALD MACINNES, Piper, is mentioned in a diary kept by James Robertson, a lawyer based in Tobermory in the 1840s. He gives no details of Donald, simply saying he had been writing a letter on 3 November 1845 to 'D. Nairne of Aros Edinburgh about the sale of Drumkilbo; Donald MacInnes Piper'. This might mean that D. Nairne of Aros (in Mull) was in Edinburgh, and for some reason Donald MacInnes, Piper, was involved – but how? Perhaps Donald was the tenant living at Drumkilbo – or was he piper to D. Nairne? We assume he was a Mull piper.

Elsewhere in his diary, James Robertson wrote of a sail he made to Lismore, in 1846, and he added 'MacInnes Piper' to his entry. Was this the Donald MacInnes of the earlier entry? There were MacInnes pipers in Appin in the late 18th and early 19th centuries, competing in Edinburgh. Donald may have been one of that family.

James also names a piper who was in Tobermory in 1844: DONALD MACKINNON, described as 'the Barra piper'. He had been assaulted in Tobermory by a local man, Duncan MacLachlan, who was fined five shillings with the option of three days in prison.

James gave us an interesting account of two emigrant ships which in 1843 were lying in Tobermory Bay, waiting for parties from Coll, Knoydart, Arisaig and Eigg. One of them, the *Catherine*, as we know from other sources, had been in Islay before sailing for Mull, and she lay for three weeks at Tobermory, waiting for more passengers to arrive. James was filled with pity for the 'poor wretches' on board, who did not want to leave their homes but had been put out by their MacDonald landlord in Knoydart and Arisaig. The diary says that one ship was for the Protestant emigrants, who seem to have been quiet, sober and grimly miserable; the other was for the Roman Catholics, who were noisy, drunken and bewailed their lot continually. The Catholics had three pipers on board, and the agent, trying to control his passengers, encouraged the pipers to play for dancing and ceilidhs on board. One man from Arisaig, however, drank himself to death before the vessels even sailed, and the lawyer gives the impression that he believed this death was deliberate.

From Nova Scotian records, we know that the ship *Catherine* took 300 people bound for Canada and the *Nith* (or *Neith*) took 200, both going to Cape Breton. When the two ships did set sail, the *Catherine* had been at sea for five days when she had to turn back and put her passengers ashore at Belfast, to be taken on by another vessel. It is not clear if she was unseaworthy or had been damaged in rough weather. She seems to have arrived eventually in Cape Breton, so perhaps she was repaired in Belfast. We can only feel for those poor suffering passengers.

James Robertson made a fleeting reference to Lachlan MacNeill Campbell of Kintarbert, which tells us that he had been ailing for some years before his death in 1852. James wrote in January 1844 'Captain Beatson says the drunken minister of Campbeltown is dead, and L. MacNeill Drumdrissaig is better'. This was the designation used for Lachlan before he inherited his Campbell estates and took his grandfather's name of Campbell – that was in 1838, so James was still using the old form.

MacLean Pipers

ALLAN MACLEAN, believed to have been a Mull man, competed at Edinburgh in 1806 as 'Piper to Alexander MacLean, Esq. of Ardgower'. A good player, he was placed third in the list, but when Archibald MacArthur of Ulva angrily refused to accept second place and was disqualified, Allan was awarded his second. Four years later, Allan won the Prize Pipe, described in 1810 simply as 'from Mull'. The Notices of Pipers say that Allan was the son of NEIL MACLEAN, who won the Prize Pipe in 1783, amid accusations that the result was rigged. Neil was piper to Campbell of Airds.

Recent (2010) correspondence in the *Piping Times*, about 19th-century prints and engravings of pictures of pipers, makes reference to 'Allon, the Piper of Mull', who might possibly have been Allan MacLean, at the height of his fame in 1810. Iain Bain's letter quotes from a poem by Bernard Barton, written probably around 1830:

> For Allon, – in the Vestibule –
> Whose fame through Mull is known –
> His bagpipes has in order set
> And waked their proudest tone.

MURDO(CH) MACLEAN was probably a brother of Allan. He, too, was piper to MacLean of Ardgour, presumably replacing Allan, but by 1814 he was in Glasgow where he became a pipe maker. After 1820, Murdo(ch) was in Inverness. He began competing at Edinburgh in 1807, and came fourth in 1815, then second in 1815. He never achieved first place, although he continued to compete until 1829.

Murdo is best remembered for his skills in reading canntaireachd and writing out piobaireachd in staff notation. In 1816, when Sir John MacGregor-Murray acquired two volumes of the Campbell Canntair-eachd manuscript, the 'authorities' in Edinburgh were totally unable to decipher or transliterate it. The 'code' presented no problem to Murdo MacLean, then in Glasgow, and he offered to interpret it for them, but they declined his offer, presumably not wanting to have their own igno-rance advertised. In 1814 and 1918, Murdo received payment from the Highland Society of London for writing out pipe music on the stave. It is not clear how he learned this skill, or from whom, but presumably someone taught him in Glasgow.

Jeannie Campbell gives a fuller account of Murdo MacLean* in her book *Highland Bagpipe Makers* (2001, 2nd edition 2011).

A possible descendant of these Ardgour pipers was another MUR-DOCH MACLEAN, described in the Notices of Pipers as 'a good player from Mull'. He was Pipe Corporal in the 92nd Gordon Highlanders in 1881, when the 75th and the 92nd were combined as the 1st and 2nd Gordon Highlanders. Murdoch was appointed Pipe Major of the 1st

---

* An interesting sidelight on Murdo MacLean is to be found in the legal records of Inverness: in 1819 he sued Alexander MacKenzie of Millbank and John Ban MacKenzie for payment of tuition fees which he had incurred when he took John Ban as a pupil. Apparently Millbank, an enthusiastic patron of aspiring young pipers, had promised to foot the bill when he sent the young John Ban to Murdo, but he had failed to fulfil his promise. Millbank was a wealthy man living in Dingwall, but he frittered away his fortune, and it seems that Murdo MacLean became of victim of Millbank's extravagant ways.

Battalion (formerly the 75th), taking with him some pipers from the 92nd, as the 75th had ceased to have its own pipers in 1809–10.

WILLIAM MACLEAN who was brought up in Raasay, and was sometimes known as Willie Creagorry, was a pupil of Calum Piobaire, who also had Raasay connections. Willie was born in Tobermory, but does not seem to have counted himself a Mull man. His setting of *Lochaber No More* was played at his funeral by Pipe Major Hector MacLean, piper to the Clan MacLean.

SIR FITZROY DONALD MACLEAN, 26th Chief of MacLean and 10th Baronet of Morvern, was born in 1835. He was described in the clan history (not an unbiassed source) as a soldier, sportsman, horseman, linguist and traveller, and was a patron of piping. An affectionate family man, he is also called 'a model husband and father', with the additional Englishman's accolade in describing a true Scot: 'He loves Scotland so much that he visits it every summer.' Can patriotism be taken further? (It was King George V who said no gentleman visits Scotland in January; I wonder why not.)

A piper reported in the *Oban Times* as 'MR A. GRAHAM' from Bunessan, Mull, led the shinty teams to the field for a New Year match in 1880. He 'discoursed several springs on the bagpipes', which appears to mean he played tunes.

BRIGADIER GENERAL CHARLES MACLEAN OF PENNYCROSS is commemorated in the well known 2/4 march *MacLean of Pennycross*, by A. Ferguson. Charles MacLean came of an old Mull family and was not one of the 'white settlers' in Mull in the mid-20th century, when a number of military gentlemen bought land and tried to farm it, not very successfully, earning the name 'The Officers' Mess' for south-east Mull.

Charles MacLean was appointed to the Argyll and Sutherland Highlanders in 1895, and served on the staff of the 52nd (Lowland) Division in the Gallipoli Campaign in 1915–16. 'On the evacuation of that peninsula he was instrumental in forming the remnants of the pipers of that division into one divisional pipe band, which afterwards did good service in lightening the long marches through Egypt and Palestine. So heavy had been the casualties among the pipers of the 52nd in Gallipoli that on the eve of evacuation scarcely any pipers could be found among the different regiments, and men not enlisted as pipers had to be called upon to complete the band' (Notices of Pipers).

The general was himself an excellent player, we are told, and was keenly interested in piping. He composed a pipe air, *The Lads We Left In Gallipoli*.

He died in Exmouth in September 1947.

Christina Morrison remembers that ALISTAIR MACLEAN OF PENNY-
CROSS was known as 'Scruff' MacLean in the Camerons. He was the
Director of the first Edinburgh Tattoo, in the 1950s, and it is said he did
his best to prevent the pipers in the Tattoo being forced to re-tune to the
equal-tempered scale of other instruments. He often acted as a piping
judge at Highland Games in the 1930s, sitting with Angus MacPherson
and Seton Gordon.

There are two old Quicksteps, *MacLean of Pennycross's Welcome to
the 93rd*, and *Miss MacLean of Pennycross*.

Pennycross is on the south coast of Mull, just west of Loch Buie, near
Carsaig Bay.

KENNETH J. MACLEAN is a descendant of Hector MacLean, and
was for many years piper to the Clan MacLean Association, as well as
being personal piper to the clan chief, Sir Lachlan MacLean of Duart
and Morvern, with whom he travels on trips to America and Canada.

A pupil of Thomas Pearston from an early age, he won the Gold
Medal at Oban in 1974, and from 1956 he taught in the College of
Piping in Glasgow, as one of its leading instructors. He has served on
the committee of the College for many years. Living in Kilmarnock he
is one of a growing number of good pipers who are developing piping
in Ayrshire.

Iain MacPherson composed a 2/4 march in his honour, and named
it *Kenneth J. MacLean*.

A First World War Piper

ARCHIBALD MACPHERSON, from Bunessan, was a piper in the 2nd
Battalion Scots Guards in the First World War; he was one of those
who left an interesting account of the unofficial cease-fire between the
Guards and the Germans at Ypres, celebrating Christmas together, in
1914. Archibald was wounded the following year, but survived the war.

Brigadier General Ronald Cheape of Tiroran

Brigadier General Ronald Cheape was the laird who employed Duncan
Lamont as his piper (see below). He had a most distiguished military
career, serving in the 1st Battalion Dragoon Guards in the First World
War. He was awarded the CMG, the DSO and bar, the MC and the
Croix de Guerre, and was seven times mentioned in despatches. His
homes were Wellfield, in Fife, and Tiroran, Mull. Willie Ross used to
come to teach in Mull, where his host was the Brigadier. The lessons

were held at Tiroran, and Willie honoured the Brigadier with his 2/4 March, *Brigadier General Ronald Cheape of Tiroran.*

The Brigadier's nephew is HUGH CHEAPE, formerly of the National Museum of Scotland, who is an authority on old pipes, as well as being knowlegeable on piping history. He has published *The Book of the Bagpipe* (1999) and many learned articles of interest to pipers. The piping world owes him a debt for his work in acquiring for the nation more than 2,000 items, pipes, pipe-making tools and other interesting objects such as reed staples. Most of these would have been lost if he had not ensured their preservation.

In 2007 he retired afrer thirty-three years with the National Museum, and took up a post in Skye, to lead a research programme at Sabhal Mor Ostaig, the Gaelic college. The memorial of his work in Edinburgh will be a CD, recording all the artefacts he has collected, with sound files, explanations and graphics, so that everyone may study piping culture and share his enthusiasm. In 2008 he published a book, *The Bagpipe.*

Tiroran is in the west of Mull, on the north coast of Loch Scridain, a long sea-loch which separates mid-Mull from the southern peninsula known as the Ross. Tiroran is about three miles west of the head of the loch. It looks out over the loch to Tolls and Ardtun, where the Mac-Fadyen piping families used to live. Willie MacLean, Creagorry, had a holiday home at Tiroran, and visited it every summer.

Pipe Major John Maclean

Col. David Murray wrote of Pipe Major John MacLean, who came from Dervaig, Mull, and had transferred from the Scots Guards to the Cameron Highlanders:

> He was nicknamed 'The Bochd' for some unknown reason [it means 'the Poor Thing']. On one occasion a piper who had incurred the Pipe Major's wrath in some respect was heard to mutter 'that Highland bastard!' He was immediately put on a charge. The officer hearing the case, doing his best to be fair to both sides, asked the Pipe Major if he was sure the piper had been referring to him. The Pipe Major retorted 'I was the only Highland bastard there!'

John MacLean was killed in May 1940 during the fighting in Belgium, but, as Col Murray observed, that anecdote ensured his permanent place in regimental folklore.

Duncan Lamont

A well-known Mull piper was DUNCAN LAMONT, who was the teacher of Hector MacFadyen, both of them belonging to Pennyghael, in the Ross of Mull. He was gardener and piper to Brigadier Cheape at Tiroran, and in the First World War went with him to France as his piper and orderly.

Between the wars, Duncan was a respected competitor, and in 1939 he joined the Argyll and Sutherland Highlanders. The *Cabar Feidh Collection* of pipe music published by the Queen's Own Highlanders has a note to the strathspey *Duncan Lamont*:

> In 1942 he and Donald MacLeod were on Willie Ross's course at the Castle. To Donald's amusement, Duncan at one point said to Willie Ross 'That's not the way you used to play *Bonnie Anne* twenty years ago', thus proving himself a brave man. Donald made the strathspey that night, and called it after Duncan. Next day, Willie was asking for tunes for his latest collection, and Donald offered him the new one. Willie accepted it, but said 'Could you not find a better name for it?'

Later in the war, Duncan, who must have been one of the few who served in both World Wars, was taken prisoner in France, and had to abandon his beloved pipes. When he was taken away to Germany, another Mull man, Roddy Beaton from Uisken, found the pipes, and recognised them. He took them safely home to Mull, and when Duncan returned after the war, he was surprised to find his pipes were waiting for him in his house. In the year 2000, Duncan's nephew was playing those same pipes for Sheila and Ronnie Campbell in Uisken.

Duncan was pictured playing among the competing pipers at Oban, as they marched to the games field, some time in the 1950s. The photograph was published in the *Piping Times* in December 2008 and February 2009.

Bobby Macleod, Tobermory

BOBBY MACLEOD of the Mishnish Hotel in Tobermory is said to have had in his ancestry four MacLeod sisters, 'of striking appearance', according to tradition in Sutherland. They crossed to the mainland, probably in the 17th or early 18th century, to travel with the cattle-drovers ('making them cups of tea and that'). All four of these sisters from Mull married in Sutherland, and among their descendants are some of the best-known Sutherland piping families: the MacKays of Halladale, the MacKays of Kildonan and the Murrays of Rogart.

This tradition of the sisters being related to Bobby MacLeod may not be correct, as Robert MacLeod, son of Bobby, says that Bobby's father came to Mull from Wester Ross, where he lived at Mellon Udrigle. It was there that the young Bobby learned his piping, taught by his father and by Willie Ross who had summer schools in the district when visiting his relatives in Glen Torridon. Bobby's father later taught Allan Beaton, Tobermory, who was a cousin of Effie Beaton, wife of Duncan MacFadyen senior.

The family of MacLeods at Mellon Udrigle was related by marriage to the piping MacLennans of Mellon Charles, not far away. William MacRobbie has made a study of these families, and his findings are published in his book *Achgarve* (1999). These MacLennans at Mellon Charles were the forebears of G.S. MacLennan. It is possible that the MacLeods went to Udrigle from Mull in the first place, and there are vague suggestions of a link between the MacLennans and Mull, 'way back', but there is no strong evidence other than that oral tradition in Sutherland which consistently maintains that the four sisters came from Mull in the time of the drovers.

Bobby MacLeod of the Mishnish was well known and popular in the mid-1900s, as a piper, accordionist, band-leader, composer, entertainer and all-round character, what is known as a 'worthy'. He was particularly noted for his musical playing of pipe-tunes on the accordion, with all the pipers' embellishments accurately reproduced. He was a kenspeckle figure at his hotel on the front at Tobermory, where he used to play his squeeze-box with verve and 'lift', sitting at the front door on summer evenings. He made many recordings of his musical accordion playing, but none (as far as I know) of his pipe music. His son Robert has now taken over the Mishnish Hotel.

One of the players in Bobby's band was Alexander 'Pibroch' MacKenzie, from Muir of Ord, who moved to Mull to be part of it. He was an excellent fiddle player. He died in 1974, and was immortalised by J.R. Riddell of Kirkhill, in his retreat march *Pibroch MacKenzie's Farewell*.

Bobby MacLeod was playing in the pipe band of the College of Piping in 1953, as pictured in the *Piping Times* in February 2009. The band was on tour in Brittany, and included two of the MacFadyen brothers, Iain and Duncan, as well as Kenneth MacLean – and Finlay MacNeill who was Pipe Segeant but also sometimes doubled as the bass drum player. They had thirty-three pipers and three drummers on their books, with Seumas MacNeill in over-all charge. Jeannie Campbell's account in the *Piping Times* gives the full history of this band.

The *Piping Times* for June 1991 reported an appeal for funds to build a boat-house on Tobermory for the new lifeboat, which had been installed there mainly by the efforts of Bobby MacLeod. The notice says: 'The Lifeboat Station was the dream of Bobby MacLeod of the Mishnish Hotel, and it was largely due to his strenuous campaigning over a number of years that the station was eventually established . . . The requirement now is a suitable boat house, and it has been decided that this will be called the 'Bobby MacLeod Building'.

Tunes made for Bobby MacLeod include *MacLeod of Mull*, a 6/8 march in four parts, by Donald MacLeod. Bobby himself made, among other tunes mainly composed for the accordion, a 6/8 march in four parts called *Seumas MacNeill,* and the well-known 6/8 march *Murdo MacKenzie of Torridon.*

Allan C. Beaton

ALLAN C. BEATON is given his name in that form to distinguish him from the other Allan Beaton, his younger piping contemporary, who lives in Skye. Allan C., born in 1906, died at Salen, Mull, on 12 February 1996, just after his ninetieth birthday. He had lived for many years in Oban, before he retired to Tobermory.

His birthplace was Glengorm, near Dervaig, Mull, and he went to school in Tobermory, a walk of about six miles each way, which he did every day. On leaving school, he began his working life on the family farm, but later served his time as a joiner, and worked in several of the Western Isles. Late in the 1930s he went south to the Govan ship-yards in Glasgow, and then became a teacher of technical subjects at a Glasgow school.

After the Second World War he returned to Oban, where he was employed by the Department of Agriculture and Fisheries, latterly becoming their Clerk of Works. But his eyesight was failing, and at the end of his working life he retired to his native island of Mull, and lived for some years in Tobermory. His eyes deteriorated, and he became completely blind.

He was taught his piping by the father of Bobby MacLeod, known always as 'Mr MacLeod of the Mishnish Hotel', who gave him an enthusiasm for piping and pipe music which lasted all his life. He was not a competitor, being one of the vast army of workers who had to work a six-day week, but in later life he attended faithfully the big competitions at Oban, Inverness and London, as well as being a regular attender at the Piobaireachd Society Conferences. A cousin of the

MacFadyens, he took great delight in the brothers' success, following every detail of their careers.

He composed several good 2/4 and 6/8 marches, including *The Sweet Maid of Mull*, which he made for a girl called Jean Campbell; he was sitting on the platform of the Aros Hall, Tobermory, when he saw Jean, who was then seventeen, dancing in the hall, and was inspired to compose this 6/8 march for her.

Allan had a delightful, gentle personality, full of kindliness, which made him a favourite wherever he went. He attended the conferences of the Piobaireachd Society regularly, and was eventually elected a Life Member. He was also a lifetime supporter of the College of Piping in Glasgow, and sent many letters of advice and historical information to the *Piping Times*.

He never married, and his main interests were piping and the church. He became an Elder of St Columba's Church in Glasgow in 1942, and in his later years was an Elder of Tobermory Parish Church; for much of his life he was a lay preacher and a Sunday School teacher.

When his eyesight was failing, he continued to make his way about, independently, for some years. One day on the main street of Oban he met Ronald Lawrie, a very large man. 'How are you today, Ronnie?' 'How did you know it was me?' 'Suddenly it became very dark.'

Peter MacLeod senior composed a march which he gave, written out in pencil, to Hugh Kennedy, who passed it to Robert Beck in Tiree. Peter gave it no name, but it was later called *Allan Beaton (Tobermory)*. The manuscript went to the College of Piping, Glasgow, along with another nameless march and a nameless jig.

Allan was buried in the graveyard at Tobermory. His funeral was attended by a large crowd, which included many members of the Mac-Fadyen family.

Martyn Bennett

MARTYN BENNETT was born in Newfoundland, son of the folk-lore expert Margaret Bennett. Brought up in Mull, Badenoch and Edinburgh, he later returned to live with his wife in Mull.

He was a pupil of Captain John A. MacLellan in Edinburgh, and studied music at the Royal Scottish Academy of Music and Drama, so that he had a good grounding in both classical and folk music. As is the modern way, he played many instruments as well as the pipes, and his band 'Cuillin' played 'an extraordinary blend of traditional Scottish and modern dance music', touring Europe and North America.

He was an experimenter, described as 'one of the most exciting and radical figures in folk music', and his obituary quotes a critic who heard him at the 2000 Cambridge Folk Festival: 'No-one has ever sounded like this before. Half the audience fled in fear of their lives.'

This is the type of piping which traditional purists abhor, but Martyn Bennett opened many eyes (and ears) to the potential of the bagpipes, and in his hands, however extreme the sound, the instrument was well played and musical – which cannot be said of many of the youngsters today bashing out their 'Morse Code' music, to the enjoyment of nobody but themselves.

Martyn died in January 2005, at the age of thirty-three. He is buried in Mull. He left his own memorial: recordings of his music, and his compositions.

Sources

William Matheson, *TGSI* XLI 1951
Notices of Pipers
Frans Buisman, *The MacArthur–MacGregor Manuscript*
Scots Magazine 1759
James Robertson, Tobermory
Jeannie Campbell, *Highland Bagpipe Makers*
J.P. MacLean, *History of the Clan MacLean*
Oban Times
Christina Morrison
Hugh Cheape, *The Book of the Bagpipe*
Cabar Feidh Collection (Queen's Own Highlanders)
Sheila and Ronnie Campbell, Mull
William MacRobbie, Achgarve
Robert MacLeod, Bunessan

Iona

Access to Iona – see above, Mull.

The island's piping history has largely been lost in that of the Ross of Mull, Staffa and Ulva. It was different from these islands in that it belonged to the Dukes of Argyll, until in the late 20th century they donated it to the Scottish nation. It was the burial ground for Scottish kings and important chiefs, and the restoration of the Abbey has made it a tourist Mecca.

Iona is known for two compositions, a setting of the traditional *Iona Boat Song* as a 6/8 Slow Air in two parts (published in the Gordon Highlanders Pipe Music Collection, vol. 1); and the modern (20th-century) piobaireachd work *Salute to the Isle of Iona*, by the American piper John Goodenow from Ohio. This is an evocative piece with seven variations. As with most modern piobaireachd works, it is not often heard – but pipers like it for its melodic flow and its re-creation of the peaceful atmosphere of Iona. It was selected as one of the set tunes for the Clasp at the Northern Meetings in 2008.

It is possible that John Goodenow's *Salute to the Isle of Iona* was the first piobaireachd work composed in the New World. Since then, John Partenen has made several during the late 1990s; one of them is a *Lament for Princess Diana*.

Some say that *MacKenzie of Gairloch's Lament* was made in memory of Sir Hector MacKenzie of Gairloch, who died in 1826, and that it was composed by his former piper, John Roy (Iain Ruadh) MacKay, who had emigrated to Nova Scotia in 1805. If this is so, then that lament would be the first piobaireachd work known to have been composed in the New World, but it seems unlikely. For one thing, John Roy had no great feeling of loyalty or affection for his late laird, who had put the family out of their Flowerdale home; this had been one reason why he left Gairloch. For another, the work is not mentioned in the *Reminiscences* of his son, 'Squire' John MacKay, and I think the Squire would have made much of it, had it been his father's creation. As the lament was included in Peter Reid's collection, dated 1826, and Sir Hector died late in April of that year, it is unlikely that it was composed in Nova Scotia.

It seems more probable that the lament was made by the MacKenzie family's piper back in Gairloch; this may have been John MacLachlan, who was piper to Sir Hector's son and successor, Sir Francis MacKenzie. It may be that Sir Francis commissioned the lament in memory of his late father; John MacLachlan (sometimes spelled MacLaughlan) is known to have been a good composer of light music, but not to have made any other piobaireachd works.

So, possibly, John Goodenow's Salute may be the first American-made piobaireachd composition. Or are there other claimants?

19th-century Piping in Iona

Mairi MacArthur tells of dancing in Iona, which in the 1890s was organised by Marion MacArthur from Clachanach 'on the flat grassy field above Burnside cottage'. Another lady remembered dancing on the road, not far from the Abbey, around that same time, and the children would dance to the fiddle on the flat machair where the turf was close-cropped.

The children danced to the fiddle, but at the big dances held out of doors on light summer nights, a local piper, DUNCAN MACDONALD, used to play; he was from Ardionra, a croft at the north end of the island. He is described in a report in the *Oban Times* in 1896:

> Iona this year can boast of a musical prodigy in the shape of a boy piper, a bareheaded, barefooted boy performing with wonderful grace on the national instrument . . . Duncan MacDonald, his new set of Highland bagpipes the gift of Lord Archibald Campbell [brother of the Duke of Argyll]. The boy's musical talents have so much attracted the attention of Lord Archibald that he is to be forthwith placed under the tuition of one of the best exponents of pipe music in the country.

To whom was the boy sent? And where? And what became of him?

A year earlier, the Principal of the Athenaeum in Glasgow had presented a set of pipes to the island, and two chanters, one for the east end and one for the west end. 'Neil MacCormick, the fiddler, was made custodian of the pipes, and a committee was formed to deal with applications for loaning out the instruments.' I wonder what happened to those pipes.

Mairi MacArthur said that regular concerts on the island usually included piping, singing and dancing when she was a girl.

Lines Written at a Highland Games

Play was scheduled to start at noon,
The wind blew with many a gust –
Number One came on to begin his tune,
And it rained on *The Unjust*.

Then the midges emerged from the trees,
And the pipers lost their cool –
You just can't stop to scratch your knees
In the middle of *Donald Duaghal*.

Out of the funfair a blaring came,
Round marched the local band,
The loudspeaker tried to live up to its name –
They didn't improve *The King's Hand*.

The runners went off at the starter's gun,
The judges from slumber awoke,
And the piper playing *The Only Son*
Was startled into a choke.

Cold was affecting the players' fingers,
Quite blue their extremities went,
Exactly the shade of the judges' lingo
As the wind blew away their tent.

When the sun came out to clear the air
The shock put us all under strain –
Administrative error somewhere Up There?
Soon rectified – back to the rain.

Tiree

Tiree is reached by a 3–4 hour car-ferry trip from Oban. This goes up the Sound of Mull, passing to the south of Ardnamurchan, and calls at Coll before going on to Tiree. On a fine day the voyage is of great scenic beauty and historic interest. There is an airfield, with links to Glasgow.

Tunes Associated with Tiree

Balachan Ban is a Tiree song often played on the pipes. The words originated in Tiree, set to a tune which some say was also made there, but it is identical with the tune known as *Kenmure's On and Awa', Wullie* (6/8 M in two parts), and Robert Beck points out that this was the 6th Viscount Gordon of Kenmure, near New Galloway in the Stewartry of Kirkcudbright. The Viscount was executed after taking part in the 1715 Rising.

Calum Beag has words and music both composed in Tiree. It has 'umpteen verses of a ribald nature', concerning the adventures of a fictional skipper of a Tiree lugger plying between the island and Glasgow. The poet John MacLean, Balemartine (1827–1895) made the words, and it is thought that Calum Beag was the model for a later hero, Neil Munro's Para Handy. Donald MacLeod made over the music to create his four-part Hornpipe *Calum Beag*, a setting which Robert Beck finds 'unnecessarily complex, losing a lot of the original flavour'. Local people prefer it as a one-part song, and the pipers play it as a hornpipe with two parts at the most.

Captain Lachlan MacPhail of Tiree, by Peter MacFarquhar R 4 (this is sometimes called simply *Lachlan MacPhail of Tiree*). It seems that Peter MacFarquhar said he composed the tune for the Shotts and Dykehead Pipe Band, many of whose pipers were coal-miners; he said it was made specially for miners' fingers (then why name it for a Tiree captain? Not many coal-mines in Tiree). Robert Beck has a manuscript copy of the music, signed 'J. Turnbull', and dated 1978, but this probably indicates merely ownership. Peter MacFarquhar's father was from Skye, but his mother from Tiree.

Dr John Edward MacKinnon of Tiree, by Peter MacLeod senior. Dr John Edward was a G.P. from Tiree who practised in Glasgow, and was a friend of Peter MacLeod.

Helen MacDonald of Tiree, by Malcolm R. MacPherson 2/4 M 4.
Helen became Malcolm's second wife (see below).

Hugh Alexander Low of Tiree, by Hugh Campbell 2/4 M 4. Hugh
Low was an entrepreneur who made a fortune by buying and selling
ex-MoD material after the First World War. He tried to buy Tiree,
but it proved impossible as the Argyll Estate had no title deeds.
Hugh Campbell was a pharmacist in Port Glasgow, Renfrewshire,
whose parents were from Tiree.

Hugh Kennedy, by Peter MacLeod 2/4 M 4 (see below).

Mrs Angus MacDonald of Tiree, by Dr John MacAskill 6/8 J 4. Mrs
MacDonald was the mother of the piper Kenneth MacDonald.

Scarinish Bay, by Hector MacLean 6/8 M 4.

The Smith of Cornaig, by Hugh Campbell 2/4 M 4. The Smith was
Donald MacIntyre (Domhnuill a' Ghobhainn), who was blacksmith,
crofter and boat-builder. His smiddy is still exactly as it was in his
day – the last horse to be shod there was a pony belonging to one of
Robert Beck's sons when he was a wee boy.

The Tiree Love Song (or *Bridal Song*), arr. John MacFadyen 6/8 GA
2. As a one-part song it is a very old tune; Alasdair Sinclair's wife,
or possibly his uncle, put words to it. Robert Beck describes it as 'a
lovely one-parted slow air, and played as such on Tiree – but it was
messed about a bit by John MacFadyen'.

Peter MacLeod senior made three tunes, which he wrote out in pencil
and gave to Hugh Kennedy, who later passed them on to Robert
Beck. One was a march which was later given the name *Allan
Beaton (Tobermory)* (see above); the other two, a march and a jig,
remained nameless. Robert Beck gave the pencilled manuscripts
to the College of Piping in Glasgow, where they are in the care of
Jeannie Campbell.

[I owe a huge debt to Robert Beck who has kindly collected for me,
from his many piping friends in Tiree, valuable information about
piping on the island. He has opened my eyes to the richness of the
heritage there. Without his help I would have had little idea of what
lies behind the present revival. Much of the following is based on lively
correspondence with him. I cannot thank him enough.]

Piper's Cave

Yet another Piper's Cave is found on the west coast of Tiree at Kenavara, with the usual tale of the piper and his dog. The piper, of course,

does not return, but this story differs from the rest in that the dog emerges, hairless, from the same cave through which he and his master entered, not having travelled the statutory four miles underground. We assume this deviation from the norm was because there is no other connecting cave for him to emerge from. Associated with this cave there is, according to Fiona E. MacKinnon, a Tiree saying: 'None but a three-handed piper will ever traverse the Great Cave of Kenavara.' This seems to be an echo of the tradition of a piper entering a cave defiantly playing the tune *Da Laimh 'sa Piob, Laimh 'sa Chlaidheamh (Two Hands on the Pipe, One on the Sword)* (see above, Colonsay). 'Three-handed' seems to have become a phrase with the implication 'courageous'.

Robert Beck says that his son Robin and Angus MacPhail once played their pipes in the cave, 'but nothing happened to them'. Perhaps they forgot to take the dog.

Pre-First World War

Donald MacDonald

In his book on the MacDonald bards (1900), Dr K.N. MacDonald wrote of a Tiree piper, DONALD MACDONALD, who was known as Domhnall MacIain Oig. He was born in Tiree around 1773, living at Crossgaire, now part of the farm of Hough, at the north-west end of the island.

Donald was not only an excellent piper, but a skilled bard, full of humour, who made many comic songs as well as a few serious poems. He was well-known in Tiree as someone gifted with second-sight, and his satirical verses were somewhat feared. He had another gift – for giving people apt by-names which 'clung like a shadow ever afterwards to the person so named, and even to his descendants'.

He was considered 'a bit of an idler who could never bring his mind or body to submit to any yoke', and he was not fond of hard work. 'Being an excellent player on the bagpipes it was his habit each winter to absent himself from home and billet himself on his friends in the township of Balameanach. These visits of his were occasions of great joy to the young people about. Dancing was carried on with great gusto'. Donald was popular at ceilidhs in Tiree, with his music, his songs and his wit.

Dr MacDonald added: 'It is a great pity that such an excellent comic poet should have experienced the pinch of poverty in his old age. He left his native island and went to live in Barra, where he died in very straitened circumstances in 1835'. Local people blamed his poverty on his laziness and dislike of hard work.

John MacDonald, Tiree

One of the best-known pipers from Tiree was JOHN MACDONALD, Pipe Major in the 72nd Regiment of Foot (later to become the Seaforth Highlanders), in the mid-1800s. There is some confusion between him and his immediate regimental predecessor of the same name, who was known as Am Piobaire Frangach, 'the French piper', because he had worked on the French railways before joining the British army. He was a little older, and apparently less able, than his Tiree namesake. He is believed to have come from Sutherland, but not much is known about him, except that he spoke French.

To add to the confusion, a Pipe Major of the 79th Regiment in the 1840s was also called John MacDonald: he was the composer of *The 79th's Farewell to Gibraltar* (said to be the first march ever composed for a pipe band), and possibly also *Dornoch Links*.

John MacDonald, Tiree, whose dates are given in the regimental records as 1824–1894, was a pupil of John Ban MacKenzie. He went into the 72nd (Duke of Albany's Own) Highlanders as a piper in 1843, and by 1856 was their Pipe Major, following his namesake who had held the post for only one year.

It is not certain where exactly in Tiree he was born, but when he retired from the 72nd and returned to the island, he lived at Balemartin, in the west end. It is possible that he took over the holding his father had held, and that he was himself born there, but it could be that as a noted army veteran he was granted a bigger croft on his retirement. It is possible that he was related to Donald MacDonald, the piper living at Crossgaire (see above).

He appears in the Census records for 1881 and 91, where his age is given inconsistently, offering a range of possible birth dates from 1817 to 1824.

Although Tiree was a rich breeding ground for boys called John MacDonald, there were comparatively few born in Balemartin within those seven years. The Old Parish Register has the baptism in 1817 of twins, John and Effy, born in Balemartin to John MacDonald and his wife Ann MacKinnon.

In 1841, the Census listed John MacDonald, a crofter at Balemartin, then aged eighty, whose wife, presumably a second wife, was Catherine, aged sixty. The family was Ann, Euphemia (Effy, aged twenty-five), Annabella and Alexander.

Next door was another John MacDonald, a widower of sixty-six, with his son Malcolm, and two women, one of them Malcolm's wife, and a granddaughter Mary. These two families were probably related, but did the Pipe Major belong to either?

Unfortunately most of the 1851 Census for Tiree is lost, and by 1861, only Malcolm and family were left. He could have been a cousin or even a brother of the Pipe Major.

John MacDonald must have left Tiree in or before 1841. Before enlisting in the 72nd in 1843, he was a pupil of John Ban MacKenzie, presumably going to him when he was living at Weem, near Aberfeldy, as piper to Lord Breadalbane at Taymouth Castle. John MacDonald was evidently a favourite with the MacKenzie family, for on John Ban's death in 1864, his widow Maria gave John a manuscript of piobaireachd music which had belonged to her husband. It is thought that it had been written by John Ban's son Donald, for his father (who was illiterate), or possibly by his nephew Ronald. John MacDonald later passed this volume on to his son Peter, who probably took it to New Zealand.

In 1854, when John was Pipe Corporal in the 72nd, the regiment was in the Crimea, where a competition was held for all the Highland Brigade pipers, at Camp Kamara. John won the first prizes for piobaireachd, marches, strathspeys and reels. His prize was a new pipe, which he later gave to his son.

After the Crimean War, the 72nd returned to Britain, and John became Pipe Major. The regiment was in the Channel Islands, and he was given leave so that he could compete at Inverness, in 1856. He won the piobaireachd competition and was awarded the Prize Pipe.

A year later he was in India, at the time of the Mutiny, and he played his regiment into battle at Kotah. The 72nd remained in India for some years, and John's elder son Peter was born in Bombay in 1862. It is not certain who John's wife was at this time: when he retired to Tiree he was married to Christina, born in Tiree in 1835, but she was probably his second wife. We know of the birth of Peter from the Census for 1881, where there is a confused note, with erasures and additions, which appears to read 'born Bombay in house East India, British subject' (but 'in house' is very indistinct and may be wrong).

John retired on pension in 1865, becoming Pipe Major of the Stirlingshire Militia for five years, before he went to Canada as piper to the Marquess of Lorne [son of the Duke of Argyll and son-in-law of Queen Victoria] when he was Governor-General of Canada. It is said that John became quite high-handed and arrogant, and when in the service of Lord Lorne refused to perform any duties other than piping. Not for him the menial role of butler or house-servant.

In Tiree there is a tradition that John MacDonald was piper to the Duke of Roxburgh, possibly at the time before he went to Canada. It is suggested by Donald MacIntyre, Tiree, that he composed *The Duke of Roxburgh's Farewell to the Blackmount Forest* (see below).

By 1874 he was back in Tiree, where a second son, Donald, was born. In 1881, the elder boy, Peter, now nineteen, was described as a fisherman, his father, aged sixty, as a 'pensioner from 72nd Foot'. His wife Christina was forty-six, and the family was living in a house with six rooms, very large for Tiree, where most households were in three rooms. All the family were Gaelic speakers.

In 1891, John's age was given as seventy-three, and the other details remained the same. Christina was now sixty-one, Peter had left home (he joined his father's regiment as a piper), and Donald was now seventeen. Also present was Jane MacDonald, nineteen, described as an adopted daughter, born in Greenock. It is not known just who she was, possibly a niece – or an illegitimate child of one of the family.

The Notices of Pipers say that John was one of the Highland soldiers photographed after the Crimean War, on the orders of Queen Victoria, and that the picture hung on the wall of the Officers' Mess of the Seaforth Highlanders. The Notices also say that this photograph was reproduced in the *Illustrated London News* for 31 January 1857, but there must be some mistake here: no photographs were printed in that periodical until 1880, and the issue for the date given has no drawing or likeness of the Pipe Major, nor is the picture-library of the magazine able to find any likeness of him, at any date. It is odd that the Notices are so specific about the title and date.

It may have been this John MacDonald who composed *The 72nd's Farewell to Aberdeen*, but we cannot be certain. The only other composition which may have been his was *The Duke of Roxburgh's Farewell to the Blackmount Forest*, said in Tiree to have been made by John when he was piper to the Duke. This work is often attributed, as a competition march in four parts, to Angus MacKay, but it is well known that Angus took a number of older two-part marches or quicksteps, and made them over, to create four-part competition marches. It is thought that *The Abercairney Highlanders* is an example, and *Highland Wedding* another.

The tradition is that these, including *The Duke of Roxburgh's Farewell*, were composed as quicksteps in what was called 'the Scotch measure' (2/4 time), and they usually had only two parts. The suggestion seems to be that John MacDonald made one of these for the Duke, and Angus MacKay later turned it into a competition march. The dating, however, does not tally, as the Tiree John MacDonald was probably quite young when Angus MacKay published the tune, and most of the two-part quicksteps date back to the early 19th or even the late 18th century. Perhaps there has been confusion with another John MacDonald?

John MacDonald died in Tiree in 1894 when he was in his mid-seventies. The Census for 1901 shows no trace of the family at Balemartin, although there were then ten other MacDonald families in the township. The six-room house was occupied by a widow, Margaret MacDonald, sixty-two, with two adult sons (not Donald or Peter) and their families. They may have been related to the Pipe Major, but we have no way of knowing.

John's elder son PETER MACDONALD was also a good piper, taught by his father, and he played the prize pipe won by his father in the Crimea. He also had the manuscript of pipe music given to his father by the widow of John Ban MacKenzie in 1864. Peter followed his father into the 72nd, and when a corporal in 1892, he won the Gold Medal at Inverness, playing the *MacNabs' Salute*.

Not long after this, Peter went to New Zealand as piper to Sir D. MacLean, owner of a big sheep station on North Island, and he remained there for the rest of his life. Presumably he took the John Ban manuscript with him when he emigrated. It is not known exactly what this manuscript was: it may have been written for his father by Donald MacKenzie, who had been sent to Edinburgh to learn how to write music in staff notation, or it may have been one of several manuscripts written by John Ban's nephew and pupil, Ronald MacKenzie, of the Seaforth Highlanders. We do not know if this manuscript was a bound volume or loose pages of manuscript music.

Lady Victoria Campbell (1854–1910)

Lady Victoria was the daughter of George, 6th Duke of Argyll. She had had polio as a child, which left her almost paraplegic, and she spent much of her time on Tiree, especially in her later years. Robert Beck describes her as 'an aristocratic do-gooder (some say busybody)', but she seems to have been mainly a force for the good for the islanders, especially in her encouragement of island piping. She brought an Inveraray piper across to teach youngsters – this was probably her father's piper, Duncan Ross, when the Duke was away. Lady Victoria donated at least two sets of pipes to Tiree players, both made by MacDougall of Aberfeldy, both still in Tiree. One was given to PETER MACKINNON, Lodge Farm, who also received tuition; he was the brother of Iain MacKinnon, the coachman and general servant of Lady Victoria. It is now owned by Donald MacIntyre, Gott (see below). The other pipe is now in the care of Angus MacLean, Scarinish.

Lady Frances Balfour wrote a biography of Lady Victoria, published by Hodder and Stoughton (undated). It has just two references to piping, in excerpts from Lady Victoria's diary:

(1) Cannes, 20 November 1878, 'Ross has been playing the pipes in the garden' (p. 122). This was Duncan Ross, who had taken up his position as the Duke's piper at Inveraray in 1875;

(2) Tiree, 2 February 1901, after the death of Queen Victoria, 'Mr MacDiarmid [factor for the Argyll estate on Tiree] after service in the Kirkapol Church, marched the five pipers up to the gate here and proclaimed the King. Then the pipers played laments in the hall' (p. 311). She does not make it clear if these five pipers were an embryo pipe band of Tiree players, or had been brought in from elsewhere.

Between the Wars

Robert Beck has the names, addresses and genealogies of more than sixty pipers before 1939, but adds 'I do not know much about the standard of competence. I suspect it varied enormously. It does show, though, that there has always been a love of piping here. The population then was c.1200 (now just over 700). The problem has always been access to teachers, certainly not lack of interest. Some Tiree lads learned at sea, mainly from Uist sailors; some in the Army, and some while away for other purposes. From 1924 to 1928, an ex-army piper, Alasdair Henderson, lived and taught piping in Tiree, but not much is known about him.'

In the 1930s, two ships of the Donaldson line, the *Letitia* and the *Athenia*, carried small pipe bands on their voyages to Canada, for the passengers' entertainment. 'Wee Donald' MacLean from Oban, Duncan MacIntyre and Peter MacLeod junior were all employed, and of the other players, two were from South Uist, one from Barra, one from

Lewis and four from Tiree. As weather and other duties permitted, they gave concerts regularly, especially when sailing down the Clyde from Glasgow. Of the general crews of these liners, so many came from Tiree that the Donaldson line was known as 'the Tiree Navy'.

After the Second World War

When Robert Beck arrived in the island in 1959, as the resident vet for Tiree and Coll, there were only three pipers who would play in public:

MALCOLM MACLEAN, Salum, known as Calum Salum (1904–1971), a crofter, general merchant and county councillor for Tiree and Coll:

> He was a terribly popular person, with a heart of gold and a delicious (and sometimes naughty) sense of humour. He often acted as chairman on social occasions. People liked him as a piper, as he had a very fine sense of rhythm and he often played publicly. It is doubtful if he could have played successfully in any band, as his tone was highly individualistic, though his instrument was always in tune to itself, and pleasant to the ear. He was taught by Hugh MacArthur, Balephetrish, who learned while serving with the Gordon Highlanders during the First World War.
>
> Calum never tried to play with the band, partly because he had chronic varicose vein ulcers and therefore could not march, but he was a staunch supporter and a great help.
>
> He used to go down to the beach and play to the grey seals, which seemed very interested, and, according to Calum, could differentiate between different rythms, tell the difference between marches, jigs, etc. This could quite easily be quite correct, seals often approach if they hear music, and some animals, horses particularly, have a great love of music and respond to it.

JOHN MACLEAN, The Brae, Cornaigbeg (Iain Alasdair Iain): 'He was a very competent player of Ceol Beag, including many competition-type tunes. He played in public, but was not interested in bands or band work. He was taught by Hugh Campbell, Port Glasgow (his cousin). John MacLean's mother was a sister of Archibald MacEachern, the blackmith commemorated by Hugh's tune *The Smith of Cornaig* (see above).'

HUGH MACLEAN, Salum (no relation to Calum Salum): 'He was taught by Hugh Kennedy when the latter was on Tiree on school holidays from Glasgow – which was as often as possible. Others started in this way, but, rather understandably, without a resident teacher, fell away. Hugh, however, became a very good player (Ceol Beag only) and was one of the founders of the Tiree Band. Just as the band was really starting to be a going concern, however, he emigrated to Australia, where, until his death in 2006, he had a successful piping career.'

Just before Robert Beck came to Tiree in 1959, HUGH MACARTHUR, Balephetrish, who had taught Calum Salum, had been playing regularly, but he had an accident when his hand was caught between a big wooden cart wheel and a gatepost, and he lost a finger. He never played again.

HUGH KENNEDY from Tiree won the Gold Medal at Oban in 1928. He was a schoolteacher in Glasgow, where he became a well-known headmaster. He was a pupil of Willie Gray, Pipe Major of the Glasgow Police Pipe Band.

In July of 1938, John MacDonald, Inverness, under the auspices of the Piobaireachd Society, who paid his salary, gave a course of lessons in Glasgow, presumably in the evenings, going through the set tunes for the Gold Medal and the Clasp. Hugh Kennedy was one of those who attended; the roll-call reads like a Who's Who of the best pipers in Glasgow at that time. The class included the Roidean brothers, John and Roddy MacDonald from South Uist; Charlie Scott; John Johnstone; Archie MacNab; Hector MacLean; Hugh Kennedy; and Mr MacColl of the Scottish Pipers, Edinburgh (who as an amateur player must have been a little out of his depth in that company).

After a week of intensive tuition, the class asked for, and were given, a further week, and then asked for a third, as they felt they were just beginning to see the light as far as piobaireachd playing was concerned. This seems a curious revelation for players of such experience, most of whom had already won a Gold Medal, if not two. We are reminded of John MacDonald's own tutor, Calum Piobaire MacPherson, who is said to have declined to teach John until after he had won the Gold at Inverness: then Calum took him on, saying to his son Jockan 'You have made him good, now I will make him great'.

Hugh Kennedy was a leading light in the Scottish Pipers' Association, acting as both Secretary and Treasurer for some years. He was a close friend of Hugh Campbell (composer of *The Smith of Cornaig* and *Hugh Alexander Low of Tiree*), and of Peter MacLeod senior.

In 1891 there were twelve Kennedy families in Tiree. At Mannal, half a mile south of Balemartin where Pipe Major John MacDonald was living in his retirement, there was a joiner called Neil Kennedy and his wife Flora. Their children were Catherine, seven, and Hugh, four. Neil, the father, was the only one with any English. This Hugh, born in 1887, was possibly the Gold Medal winner at Oban in 1928, though

1887 does seem a little early. His grandparents may have been Hugh Kennedy and Janet MacDonald, married in 1837, both from Balephuil, about two miles from Mannal, and it is likely that the piper Hugh was distantly related to the Pipe Major.

Peter MacLeod made a 2/4 march in four parts called *Hugh Kennedy MA BSc*.

KENNETH MACDONALD from Tiree was taught first by Peter Mac-Farquhar, before becoming a pupil of Roddy (Roidean) MacDonald in Glasgow. It was Roddy who taught him his Ceol Mor. At the age of twenty in 1959, Kenneth won the Gold Medal at Oban, and followed it up with the Gold at Inverness in 1962. Dr John MacAskill composed a four-part jig in honour of Kenneth's mother, calling it *Mrs Angus Mac-Donald of Tiree*. There is a tradition that Dr John and Kenneth were known as 'The Terrible Twins' and a tune was made for them; but this may be confusion with a 6/8 Jig in four parts composed by Dr John and named for other twins of his acquaintance.

JAMES MACNIVEN, born in Tiree, is described in the Notices of Pipers as a piper in the 8th Argylls in the Fisrt World War. 'Being a finely proportioned and handsome man, he was, in 1918, painted by Raymond Desvarreux, the eminent French painter, for the French Republic. It was desired to record, for France, the portrait of a Scottish Highland military piper who had fought in France during that memorable period.'

DUNCAN MACFADYEN senior, or 'Big Duncan', father of the piping MacFadyen brothers and their sister Freena (see above), was himself a piper, and it is thought that he inherited his talent from his own father, who had come to Mull from Tiree. In the 19th century there were many MacFadyen and MacFaden families in Tiree, especially at the eastern end of the island. The family of Duncan MacFadyen came from Ardess, a large croft in the township of Caolis, at the eastern extremity. The crofter at Ardess today is Lachie MacFaden, whose grandfather Neil was a cousin of Big Duncan.

NORMAN MACLEAN, well known as a brilliant comedian, writer, singer, musician and composer, is also a good piper. He made the modern Gaelic piobaireachd poem *Maol Donn*, which won him the Bardic Crown at the National Mod in Glasgow in 1967. He is of a Tiree family, though born in Glasgow. His father was Neil MacLean from Tiree (Niall Mor mac Iain Eoghain Ruaidh), who married Peggy MacKinnon from Cladach Baleshare, North Uist (Peigi Bheag nighean Thoroid 'ic Ailein).

MALCOLM ROSS MACPHERSON, grandson of Calum Piobaire and son of Angus MacPherson of Inveran, made a 2/4 march which he called

Helen MacDonald of Tiree. She later became his second wife, and mother of his son Euan.

HUGH FERGUSON MACDONALD, Kenovay (Eoghainn Eachann) (1888–1975) is described by Robbie Beck as 'as far as I can gather, the best piper who was both a native of and resident on Tiree'. While a young schoolboy, for family reasons, he was sent by his parents to live with his sister Jean near Spean Bridge, and he attended Kilmonivaig School, where his brother Donald was a teacher. He was taught his first piping by Alexander Rose, Jean's husband, who was a forester based at Spean Bridge. Alex's father was also a piper and assisted in tutoring young Hugh, and taught him Highland dancing, too. Rose senior was a very old man at this time, and had to teach dance steps while holding himself up by his hands on the back of a chair.

After a good start in piping, Hugh joined the 1st Volunteer Battalion, Queen's Own Cameron Highlanders, and was taught at summer camps by Pipe Major John MacDonald, Inverness. On leaving school, he learned his trade as a joiner, wheelwright and general contractor.

When he was living at Spean Bridge, he became friendly with William Lawrie, who was then a slate quarrier at Ballachulish. 'They used to visit each other at weekends, Willie Lawrie teaching six other pupils at Spean Bridge, forbye Hugh MacDonald himself.'

Later, when he was working as a tradesman at Craig Dunain, the big mental hospital in Inverness, he was asked to be the Pipe Major of the hospital pipe band – but in 1913, he decided to emigrate to Patagonia. He was there for eight years, but returned to Tiree in 1921, and lived there as a joiner/contractor, until his death in 1975.

It seems that he never competed but had the name of being a very fine player indeed, of both light music and Ceol Mor. He was not a great teacher, being perhaps too rigid and intolerant, too much of a perfectionist. He did give lessons to Hugh Kennedy, whose main teacher was Willie Gray. Hugh Kennedy had an enormous respect for Hugh MacDonald's playing. Another pupil was William MacLean (Big Willie) whose first and main teacher was Lachlan MacDonald.

By 1959, when Robbie Beck first came to Tiree, Hugh MacDonald was no longer playing, but he had a lasting influence on Tiree piping, especially as setting a high standard to aim at. A copy of an interview he gave to Margaret MacKay is in the School of Scottish Studies, University of Edinburgh.

IAIN C. MACDONALD is a piper and top-class Highland dancer. He became an expert dancer while still a boy, and learned his piping from Peter MacLeod senior, who was living in Partick. Iain served with the

1st Camerons while doing his National Service, along with such pipers as Iain MacFadyen and John MacDougall, when Evan MacRae was Pipe Major. David Murray was his band officer. While in the army, he taught Highland dancing to a group of his fellow pipers – and has stories to tell about that! He judges Highland dancing all over the world, teaches dancing instructors, and plays for the dancing at Cowal, where he is the Director of Pipe Music. Living now in Lenzie, near Glasgow, he is of Tiree stock, and has a house on the island. He played in Robbie Beck's band in the 1960s and 1970s, and now in his retirement plays in the band each summer. He does not play Ceol Mor, but is a great strathspey player, and Robbie says he has been an enormous help to him in his teaching, a man who will do anything for his community.

The Sinclair/Johnston Family

ANN SINCLAIR, now Mrs Tommy Johnston, was the first woman to win the Silver Medal at Inverness, a feat she accomplished in 1980. Of her piping family, who came from Tiree, she writes that her father, ALASDAIR SINCLAIR, was a piper, born in November 1919. He died in November 1996. He was the youngest of a family of seven. His father was also a piper, as were two of his brothers. Alasdair learned to play while serving with the REME during the Second World War, his teacher being a pupil of Robert Reid. Tommy Johnston was leading drummer in a Grade 1 band.

Alasdair was deputy Pipe Major to Robert Beck when the Pipe Band was formed in Tiree. It was his uncle (or his wife?) who put words to the tune of *The Tiree Love Song*.

Ann goes on:

> My father started my piping career in 1965, I was aged 11, and all credit goes to him for my success in all the junior competitions. Hugh Kennedy gave me piobaireachd tuition when he would be home on holiday in the summer. I joined the Tiree band aged 13 and played in the World Championships in Oban in 1967.
>
> I came to Glasgow in 1970. In 1973 I joined the Grade 1 band – British Caledonian Airways (Renfrew), under Pipe Major Robert Stewart (now my brother in law). I left the band in September 1976, to concentrate on my solo playing. From then onwards I went to Ronald Morrison for tuition. Ronnie had a great knowledge of Piobaireachd, which he freely shared in a way which was most understandable, and I had many years of pleasure in studying with him – a true gentleman, with the expertise of a giant in piping terms.

Ann gained many prizes throughout her piping career. These included the Silver at Inverness in 1980, the first time it had been awarded to a female piper; third place in the Gold Medal at Inverness in 1982; fifth in the Scotway Piping Competition (Piobaire Os Cionn Chaich) in 1983, being beaten only by Iain Morrison, Andrew Wright, Iain Mac-Fadyen and Hugh MacCallum – she was in distinguished company. In 1984 she was the over-all winner in a competiton run by Lothian and Borders Police Pipe Band – she was first in the Piobaireachd and in the MSR, second in the Jigs.

She played Henderson pipes which are more than 100 years old, and has now handed them on to her son, young Finlay Johnston who is making his mark as a junior player with a promising future. In return, Finlay has returned to his mother the pipe he played as a youngster, which originally belonged to Ann's Tiree grandfather.

Ann's father taught several pupils, including his son ALASTAIR SIN-CLAIR, ALLAN ROWAN (who became a Pipe Major in the Argylls) and DAVID HUNTER (whose tuition was continued by Robert Beck after the death of Alasdair Sinclair). He also started Finlay on the practice chanter, from the age of seven. After that, Ronnie McShannon, a close family friend, took Finlay on, and made him a promising solo player. Finlay has joined his father Tommy Johnston and Ronnie McShannon in the family firm of piping suppliers, Pipe Dreams, in Argyle Street, Glasgow. They make Easidrone reeds. Tommy is by trade a plastics engineer, and his son Finlay is serving his time as a mechanical engineer. Robert Beck's son ROBIN BECK, another piper with Tiree connections, has a part-time business, making small pipes and the reeds for them, as well as his Beckvalves. He supplies these to Pipe Dreams in Glasgow.

Another promising piper in the family is Ann's nephew GAVIN STEW-ART, taught by his father ROBERT STEWART. In 2005, Gavin won the MacGregor Memorial competition, restricted to players of twenty-two or under, at Oban, a piobaireachd trophy fiercely contested by young pipers from all over the world. Gavin came second in the Duncan Johnstone Memorial piobaireachd in March 2006. He plays in the Strathclyde Police Pipe Band, and is training to be a marine engineer.

Ann's husband Tommy is a drummer, born and brought up in Belfast. He played in the Field Marshall Montgomery band, before moving to Glasgow, where he joined the British Caledonian Airways (Renfrew) band. He then moved to the band which is now Scottish Power, when it was under Alex Duthart. Clearly pipes and drums are a family tradition.

Altitude Piping

In an article in the *Piping Times* in September 1994, about piping at high altitudes, the author, assumed to be Seumas MacNeill, recalled an occasion when Iain MacFadyen and Thomas Pearston were flying across the Atlantic. The captain, 'who happened to be a MacKinnon from Tiree', requested the two pipers on board to play him some tunes. This is believed to be the record for altitude piping.

Modern Piping in Tiree

In the late 20th century and early 21st, piping in Tiree has had a revival. Piper ROBERT BECK made his home on the island when he was the vet for Tiree and Coll, and returned there for his retirement. He began to inject life into local piping by teaching the youngsters, and the emergence of ANGUS MACPHAIL, highly skilled as both a solo and a band player, has brought Tiree to the fore. Angus is an accomplished accordionist, who graduated with an Honours degree in Scottish Traditional Music. The group known as Skinninish was formed after Angus had completed his course at the Royal Scottish Academy of Music and Drama, and it rapidly made an impact on the musical world. Living once more in Tiree, Angus plays the Great Highland pipe, bellows pipe and accordion, and is an inspiration to island youngsters, not only from Tiree. The group has made several successful CDs.

Another group, Skerryvore, was formed by Daniel and Martin Gillespie. Both Skinninish and Skerryvore performed with great success in the National Mod at Fort William in 2007.

GORDON CONNEL is an accordion player and drummer in the band, who came to Tiree from Loch Long side, not far from Dunoon. He was formerly the teacher of Modern Studies at Tiree High School, and on his retirement made his home on the island. He teaches accordion playing, and is a great enthusiast for pipe music: as he starts his pupils at eleven, a year before they come to Robbie Beck, he gives them a love and understanding of traditional music and its idiom before they start on the pipes. Robbie finds this a great help in teaching Ceol Beag, and many of the pupils go on to take both accordion and pipes in their school music exams.

Robert Beck

Robert ('Robbie') Beck is a vet by profession, but also a keen piper who is keeping it going in Tiree. He is reviving interest in piping there, and has many pupils.

He learned his piping while at college, but had difficulty in finding tuition and time to practise when exams were looming. After qualifying as a vet, he had to establish his career and it was not until he was married and had his own house that he was able to take his piping seriously. He took what lessons he could, and attended summer schools. Besides piping he is passionately interested in horses, and was 'heavily involved' in the saving and developing of the Eriskay Pony as a breed. He is the Honorary President of Comunn Each nan Eilean (the Islands' Horse Society).

Having been an assistant vet for eight years in different places, he went in 1959 as the vet for Tiree and Coll, and Hugh Kennedy helped greatly with his piping; he developed a love of piobaireachd which has never left him. In 1974 he moved from Tiree to take up a post as teacher at the Dick Vet College in Edinburgh, and became a university lecturer in vetinerary science. At this stage Tom Speirs was his instructor, for two and a half years, during which he took his Senior and Teacher's Certificates (Institute of Piping). Another of his teachers was Peter MacLeod senior, to whom he went for a quarter's lessons at his house in Essex Drive, Partick. Robbie is modest about his own prowess, saying he has never been a really good player, but he has a substantial knowledge of the music, and boundless enthusiasm.

He gave to the museum of the College of Piping in Glasgow the pencil manuscripts of three compositions by Peter MacLeod senior (see above), as well as a very old gramophone record of Glasgow Police Pipe Band, given to Robbie by the Rev Willie John MacLeod, one time minister on Tiree, later at St David's, Kirkintilloch.

When the Tiree pipe band was formed, with young pipers and drummers, Robbie was proud that nearly all the pipers were his pupils. The piping scene there seems to be healthy and flourishing, certainly as regards the light music. It is Robbie's regret that most of the youngsters are not interested in piobaireachd, although he plays it still himself, and always tries to interest his pupils in it. He has two teenage pupils who enjoy playing Ceol Mor, and another pupil, WILLIAM MACLEAN, Balinoe, has taken it up.

Robbie feels his teaching has been restricted by his knowing too little Ceol Mor himself. He started it quite late in life, learning a lot from Hugh Kennedy and Tom Speirs, from attending summer schools and weekend courses, and having lessons at the College of Piping in Glasgow. He has a sound knowledge of at least ten piobaireachd works which he feels confident to teach.

The music teacher in Tiree High School, Joyce Gillespie, writes:

> Tiree High School has been fortunate in having piping tuition delivered by Mr Robert Beck (retired vet and one of the founder members of Tiree Pipe Band). In his experienced hands many prospective pipers have progressed from the elementary stages to be presented in Standard Grade and Higher Music with great success – an opportunity which would not have been afforded to them if he had not been available and willing to be involved at this level. Indeed, apart from providing a constant stream of recruits for the Tiree Pipe Band, several of his students pursued degrees in music.
>
> I can say, without hesitation, that all his pupils, past and present, benefited greatly from their time with him – finding their tutor to be firm but fair and certainly always entertaining! He demands and expects hard work and commitment – qualities which would stand them in good stead long after leaving school. Above all, respect and appreciation for him was always evident.
>
> Recently, he has expressed his concern for the future of tuition in the school, for although he maintains that the pupils 'keep him young in outlook', he accepts that he cannot go on indefinitely. To this end, he has been exploring various avenues to source funding to ensure our young people can continue to have access to the Great Highland Bagpipe.

[It is a pleasure to find a school music teacher who appreciates the value of pipe music. It has been known for a music teacher to arrive from the south denying that the pipe is a musical instrument at all, and declining to include pipe music in the curriculum. Tiree is fortunate to have one so willing to welcome the tuition given by Robbie Beck. I am grateful to Ms Gillespie for her contribution to this book.]

Robbie Beck is indeed appreciated by the pipers in Tiree. He recalls a time in 1968 when his wife was in Glasgow for the birth of their youngest son, and Robbie went down to bring mother and baby home. As they stepped off the plane, pipes were playing at the airport: the two youngest band members, both aged twelve, Ann Sinclair and Duncan MacLean, were playing *Highland Laddie* and *Balachan Ban*, with Ann's father, Alasdair Sinclair, there to tune their pipes. 'Tears were in the een', adds Robbie, recalling the day.

Another occasion green in his memory was in January 2007.

For the Auld New Year (January 12th), the Tiree Feis Committee organised a special musical evening, mainly devoted to piping, with me (Robbie Beck) as the star guest of honour. They brought Barry Donaldson as the star guest player, and ex-pupils of mine, from the mainland. My senior pupils also played. The weather was, possibly, the worst for years. The mailboat, bringing the guests, *two days running* reached Tiree but had to turn back and return to Oban without taking our pier (Angus MacPhail was on board both days). Eventually the gale abated and most of the pipers managed to arrive by plane from Glasgow, and the belated celebration was a great success, with Gaelic singing and a selection on the accordion. It was well attended in spite of storms up to Force 11 and heavy rain. My son, Robin, from Dunoon, was playing at it, but he is not a pupil of mine – he was taught by the late Alasdair Sinclair, Greenhill (Ann's father) – a case of the cobbler's bairns; I was always too busy with the band, etc. to find time to teach him. It is great to be shown appreciation before you are deid!

If every island had a Robert Beck to collect its traditions, I feel sure that even more valuable material would be uncovered, though it is probably too late for some of them. Robbie has not only preserved so much, but has taken every step he can think of to ensure that piping is kept alive in Tiree after he has gone. His latest achievement has been to raise funding for a piping instructor to visit Tiree regularly: 'Big Donald' MacPhee came out once a month to give tuition, and between visits he taught once a week by video link. This satisfactory arrangement is yet another example of what can be done if a Robert Beck is around to put his heart into local piping. We can only salute him, with admiration and gratitude for his enthusiasm.

Tiree Pipe Band

Robbie Beck writes:

When I first arrived on Tiree, I had not been playing for quite a long time. I discovered others with a similar history, and four of us, Alasdair Sinclair (father of Ann), Hugh MacLean, Salum, William MacLean (Big Willie) and myself decided that we should foregather and play, in each other's houses. This continued for some time, and once we were well started we often met in Hugh MacArthur's house. This, of course, stimulated us all to practise, criticise each other and improve. Others who wanted to learn (some of whom had started and given up) joined us. Our little group became a class, which grew into a band without drums, and as such we played in public. We started raising money locally for such things as uniforms, drums, etc.

We wrote to the Chief Constable of Glasgow, offering a house on Tiree, for a fortnight, for a drumming tutor and his wife. This was rather successful, with Alex Connel, the leading drummer of Glasgow Police Band coming with his wife, and, every evening, teaching our potential drummers.

We also got a great deal of help from Glasgow pipers with strong Tiree connections, such as Kenny MacDonald, Archie MacEachern and Iain MacDonald. These three played with us, whenever possible. Iain MacDonald still plays in the present Tiree Band, and is a great help to me in my teaching. He now lives in Lenzie, and has a house on Tiree.

Apart from functions on Tiree, we played at Coll Show and Tobermory Games. Then, in 1967, we competed in the World's Pipe Band Championship at Oban, and won 2nd in Grade 4. David MacBrayne's laid on a special (ferry) boat to bring us home at night. That was certainly a day to remember. The few people who could not follow us to Oban were on the pier to meet us on return.

I do not know why, but the band faded away at one point, but it has been revived, mainly with youngsters as members. They usually leave the island when they leave school, but most come back to play with the band as often as they can. The pipers in the band nowadays, I am proud to say, are mostly my pupils.

When we had raised enough money for uniforms, we had to decide on a tartan. We held a well-attended public meeting, at which the claymores came out of the thatch. By popular vote we decided on MacLean of Duart tartan.

We have to applaud the spirit, determination and enterprise of the islanders, and wish the band all the best for the future.

LACHLAN CAMPBELL was the son of HECTOR J. CAMPBELL, who played in the old band; his son JOHN CAMPBELL is a piper in the Army. Robbie Beck writes: 'Lachlan was born in 1960. He learned his piping from various pipers on Tiree, but his main teacher was Hugh MacDonald, Kenovay (Eoghain Eachain). The Tiree band had been moribund for some years, and 'Lachie Beag' was the prime mover and force behind its revival. Two years after he started to re-organise the band, he died, suddenly and tragically, at the age of forty-one. He was a very proficient player of Ceol Beag, and was Pipe Major of the newly formed band. 'Lachie's place was taken by DUNCAN MACLEAN, the son of HUGH MACLEAN, Barrapol, who played in the original band. Duncan, as a boy, learned from the rest of us, including myself. He is a very competent player of Ceol Beag and does a very good job as Pipe Major. He does not, however, play Ceol Mor.'

Sources

Census records for Tiree
Old Parish Register for Tiree
Notices of Pipers
Piping Times
Angus A. Fairrie
Lady Frances Balfour
Fiona MacKinnon, *Tiree Tales*
Robert Beck, Tiree

Coll

Coll may be reached by car ferry from Oban, a sailing of some two-and-a-half hours through spectacular scenery.

Tunes Associated with Coll

Piobaireachd works:

> The Laird of Coll's Barge (Galley), or The Battle of the Pass of Crieff
> P 12
> The Lament for John Garve (Iain Garbh) MacLean of Coll P 9 (see
> above, Mull)
> MacLean of Coll Putting His Foot on the Neck of His Enemy P
> MacLean of Coll's Claymore P 7
> MacLean of Coll's Triumph P (?)

Light music compositions include:

> The Bonnie Isle of Coll, sometimes called Bonnie Coll, by Duncan
> Johnstone 3/4 SA 2
> The Doctor of Coll's Reel R 2

Hector Maclean

In 1578, Hector MacLean, who is named in the title *Hector MacLean's Warning*, was taken from imprisonment in Duart Castle, Mull, where he had been held for a year by his cousin, Lachlan Mor MacLean, the clan chief. Hector had been plotting against Lachlan's life for some time, and his cousin's patience had run out. After being held at Duart,

Hector was removed to Coll, where Lachlan had him beheaded, an execution without trial (probably the reason why it was done in Coll, more remote than Duart). The beheading is said to have taken place outside Breacacha Castle, in the south of Coll, probably on the machair at a place known as Hangman's Hill. Beheading was considered to be a more merciful execution than hanging, and so was the privilege of the high-born.

Coll Piper in 1715 Rising

Nicholas MacLean-Bristol (1998) has published, for the Scottish Records Society, lists of those involved in the first Jacobite Rising of 1715. After it was over, an inventory was made of arms held in the highlands and islands, to be handed in to the authorities, along with the names of men of military age and whether they were for or against the 'rebellion'.

In 1716, he records, at Arnabost in Coll (NM 2159) a man called 'Angus roy McDonald the pyper', who 'lost his sword at Dundee & gave in his pistol & Durk, he is to give in his target (shield)'. Angus roy (ruadh 'red-haired') has 'r' for 'in rebellion' beside his name. The following entry says 'Sorle McEachnie has no arms & says that the pyper took his sword from him' and beside Sorle's name is the letter 'n' for 'not in rebellion'. At Breacacha, spelled Breakachie, a harper named Murdoch McMurchie is recorded as having no arms and not being involved in the rebellion.

At this date (1716) the laird of Coll, Donald MacLean, was living at Cliad, with one servant of military age, Hector MacLean. Presumably the castle at Breacacha was already in a ruinous state. Nothing further is known about the piper, Angus roy McDonald, but perhaps we might assume that he was piper to Donald MacLean of Coll, since Arnabost is close to Cliad. McDonald was probably a patronymic, 'son of Donald', rather than a surname.

Neil and Condullie Rankin

Neil Rankin came to Coll around 1770, as piper to the 13th laird, Donald MacLean. Neil was piper at Breacacha House at the time when Dr Johnson and Boswell made their visit in 1773. The big house was built in 1750, replacing the old castle as the laird's residence (the castle has now been restored as a dwelling). Dr Johnson described the new house as 'a mere tradesman's box', which seems unmannerly, for a guest. It was later re-built in a more ornate style.

Neil was followed as piper to Coll by his son Condullie, possibly in 1786, when the 13th laird died and was succeeded by his younger brother Alexander. He was the laird served by three eminent pipers, one after the other, Condullie Rankin, Duncan MacMaster and Hector Johnston, between 1786 and 1819.

Neil had been running the Rankin school of piping at Kilbrennan, in western Mull before he came to Coll. He retired to live at Cliad, in central Coll, the family home of many Rankins. Condullie replaced him, but his future as the laird's piper seemed doubtful, so in 1804 he went to the army, and around 1806 he was posted abroad. In 1817 when his wife died, he returned to Coll, and soon re-married. His father Neil died in Cliad in 1819, and was buried at Cill Clunaig. The following year, Condullie emigrated, settling in Prince Edward Island (see above, Mull).

The Rankins recorded in the Old Parish Register for Coll start in 1776, and end in 1819. It is possible that there were Rankins in Coll before 1770, when Neil came from Mull, but the Register does not go as far back as that. The family is recorded both at Breacacha when the Rankin pipers were there with the laird, and at Cliad, the family home, which was then a small township. It is now a relatively big farm.

See also Mull, above, for further discussion of the Rankins.

Duncan MacMaster

When Condullie Rankin enlisted, around 1804, he was replaced as the laird's piper by DUNCAN MACMASTER, who came from Lochaber, 'somewhere about Fort William district'. In 1805 Duncan was entered by his laird in the Edinburgh competitions, where he won first place, being awarded the Prize Pipe.

Duncan was living in Coll at that time, and there he married Mary Taylor, at Breacacha. There were no Taylor families living in Coll, and Mary may have been a maid at the castle, brought in from the mainland – or she may have been known to Duncan before he came to Coll, and joined him there as his bride. No children of the marriage are recorded in the Coll register. Duncan is said to have remained in Coll until his death in 1824, at the age of eighty-six. If this is correct, he was over sixty-five when he had his win at Edinburgh and when he married. Perhaps his wife was beyond child-bearing age.

Duncan MacMaster is said to have been a friend of Donald Ruadh MacCrimmon, presumably after Donald's return from America in

1790. Duncan may have been his pupil, but the facts are far from certain. The waters were muddied by John Johnston, later in the 19th century, when he said at different times that Duncan was a pupil of John MacKay, Raasay, and that it was Hector Johnston who was a pupil of Donald Ruadh, in Skye. It seems that the somewhat shadowy backgrounds of Duncan and Hector have overlapped in transmission, and it is not easy to discern the truth.

The Notices of Pipers added more mud by stating that Hector Johnston was a pupil of Angus Mor MacKay, piper to Dunvegan, who is vaguely said to have 'been for a time piper to the MacLeods of Dunvegan, after the hereditary MacCrimmon pipers were away, and before others of that name were employed'. Does this mean when Donald Ruadh was in America? Or after the deaths of Donald Ruadh and Iain Dubh? Either seems impossible as a time for Hector to have been a pupil, as he was not born until 1791, and left Coll in 1819.

Hector Johnston

It is not known exactly when HECTOR JOHNSTON became piper to the laird of Coll, but he was probably assistant to the aging Duncan MacMaster, his own teacher, before Duncan finally retired. Hector was born in the 1790s, probably in 1791 (see below). In 1819 Hector emigrated to Canada, when Duncan was still living, so he was not the laird's piper for long. If, as John Johnston liked to imply, it was Hector who taught him his piping, it must have been in Canada, as Hector was gone long before John was born. When John made his visit to relatives in Canada, in the 1860s, Hector had moved from Nova Scotia to Prince Edward Island, and there is no evidence that John, whose visits in Nova Scotia and Ontario are well attested, ever went across to Prince Edward Island, or that he ever met Hector.

When speaking or writing of his own piping, John Johnston would claim to have been taught by his uncle or uncles, whom he did not name. He managed to imply that his uncle was Hector Johnston, but the Hector in Prince Edward Island, the laird's former piper, was not John's uncle – he was John's father's cousin. John did have an uncle Hector, his father's elder brother, who also emigrated to Canada and may also have been a pupil of Duncan MacMaster.

In trying to trace the origins of Hector, the laird's piper, we find in the records (as usual) discrepancies between oral evidence and written, and between family evidence and official.

First, John Johnston's uncles, the elder brothers of his father John, who was born in Cliad in 1805, were:

James born in 1791
Hector 1797
William 1799 – he may have died young
Murdoch 1800
Duncan 1802.

James, Hector, Murdoch and Duncan all emigrated in the 1850s, and their nephew John visited them in Canada about ten years later. Some, possibly all four, were pipers, but probably not of the calibre of their cousin Hector.

Thelma Johnston in Prince Edward Island, a descendant of the Coll family and family historian, said that Hector was a first cousin of John Johnston, but none of the uncles had a recorded son of that name. His great-uncle Donald had a son Hector, born 1791, who was John Johnston's second cousin. There was also a tradition in Canada that Hector Johnston was the only son of a Donald Johnston, a farmer at Arinagour, on the east side of Coll.

Again, there is in the records no Hector who was an only son of Donald, nor is any Donald at Arinagour mentioned in the Register.

What we do have is a record of three Hectors:

1. Hector born 1797 at Arnabost, not far from Cliad, uncle of John Johnston, brother of John 1805 and son of John Johnston 1780s and Isabel MacLean. This is not our man.
2. Hector born 1796 at Grissipol, near Cliad, only son of Duncan Johnston and Flory MacKinnon. The relationship to John Johnston is not clear, but, although he was an only son, he does not seem to be the Hector we are after.
3. Hector born 1791 also at Grissipol, second cousin of John Johnston, son of Donald Johnston and Janet MacPhaiden, and one of four brothers. Donald was a brother of John 1760s, who was John Johnston's grandfather. One of Donald's other sons had a link with Arinagour. This seems to be the laird's piper who went to Prince Edward Island, though we cannot be sure.

John Gibson (1998) tells us more of Hector's life. He emigrated in 1819 on board the ship *Economy*, landing in Nova Scotia. He became a schoolteacher at River John until about 1840, when he moved to Prince Edward Island. He had a farm at Brudenell River on land which had been part of Lord Selkirk's original grant. It is thought that he there took up teaching again, and played an active part in the Baptist Church, becoming a Deacon.

Before leaving Scotland, Hector had been a competitor at Edinburgh, and in 1817, he and John Campbell, son of the compiler of the Campbell Canntaireachd manuscript and evidently a friend of Hector, were each given the sum of £1 18s. od. 'additional for music produced by them, and as coming from a distance'. This was a combination of travel expenses and a fee for writing down pipe music in staff notation. The words 'writes music' were written in the Highland Society's accounts against Hector Johnston's name.

Where and when did Hector learn to do this? As a schoolteacher he was obviously literate, and maybe his instruction from Duncan MacMaster included the writing, or at least the reading, of staff notation. Duncan might have picked this up from the MacCrimmons, but there is evidence that Donald Ruadh MacCrimmon became literate only quite late in life, and it seems unlikely that he was teaching his pupils to read or write music – certainly he never taught his own sons to do this. It is perhaps more probable that Hector learned the skill in Edinburgh, perhaps from John Campbell himself. Or, of course, the reverse might have been the case.

Around 1870, Hector drew up his Will, and left the Brudenell farm, to go to live in Charlottetown. He died not long after. His pipes, said by the family members in Nova Scotia to have been out in the '45, and to have been heirlooms of the MacLean lairds of Coll, disappeared. Hector's widow said they had been lost in a house-fire, but some of the relatives believed she had sold them.

John Johnston

JOHN JOHNSTON (1836–1921), Coll, was the last of his line living on the island. He had a fund of knowledge about piobaireachd and its traditions, and was said by John Gibson to be 'the last person alive to know the special "old turnings" which were close to extinction'. In view of the evidence of the old Bruce style of playing now emerging from Australia, this judgment might be questioned.

John was regarded by some as a mad old fanatic, something of a Hebridean crackpot, as he bombarded the *Oban Times* with passionate letters and articles about piobaireachd, expressing 'strong opinions, some of which are sufficiently controversial and unsubstantiated to cause his ideas to be overlooked and, by some, discounted as 'fevered extravagances', as John Gibson put it. But Gibson added: 'John

Johnston could not be accused of any lack of understanding of classical piping in its traditional form,' and it was through him that some detail of that form was preserved for posterity.

The only point on which Gibson differs from his views is the 'exclusivity' theory: John Johnston declared unequivocally that the old pipers played only piobaireachd (Ceol Mor) and despised the light music as 'The Tinkers' Music' (or, as an old piper in the north always puts it, 'treevia, chust'). John Johnston said the old piobaireachd players never played marches, strathspeys or reels, let alone jigs or hornpipes, on the great Highland pipe. John Gibson has shown that in this opinion he was probably mistaken – or, at least, that he took it to extremes.

Seton Gordon came on John Johnston in 1915 when setting up a wartime coast-watching system in the western isles. Johnston was then nearly eighty, but Seton Gordon recruited him for this war work. As Raymond Eagle remarked, 'Seton Gordon was fascinated by Johnston, and wrote about him in several books and articles', such as *Afoot in the Hebrides* and *Hebridean Memories*. The latter has a chapter devoted to him as 'The Island Piper', although his name is not given there.

He became part of the somewhat spurious Celtic scene created by Seton Gordon for a credulous market – and some of the tales are slanted to reflect credit on Gordon himself. An example is the account of his playing piobaireachd before the old man: 'When I had mastered the playing of one of these ancient tunes, he was delighted. Jumping excitedly from his chair, he would exclaim "That's it, that's it, You have it". Then he would again play, lovingly, the old piece.' That use of 'would' is masterly, and typical of Seton Gordon, managing to give the impression that this happened regularly; respected judges have said that he was a relatively poor piper, and John Johnston must have been flattering his visitor.

Seton Gordon knew John Johnston only for his last six years, and he painted an idyllic picture: 'His croft was on the western shore. Near his door the waves broke on a bay of golden sand. His thoughts were always on Ceol Mor . . . he was taught by an uncle who learned his skill from Donald Ruadh, the last of the great MacCrimmon family. Thus John Johnston's piping deserved to be treated with respect, and I count my hours spent with him as profitable. I sometimes persuaded him to play his practice chanter, and after fanning the peat fire to a glow, he would begin, haltingly at first, as if his fingers fought to express the music that was in him' (from *Afoot in the Hebrides*). This description may be found misleading: the croft is not on the western shore, and from the door no beach can be seen, nor the sea.

John Johnston was born on 21 September 1836, at Arnabost, in the west of Coll, close to the township of Cliad, where the Rankin pipers had lived until some seventeen years earlier. His father was another John, born in Cliad in 1805, when the Rankins were still there; he was described as a cottar when living in Arnabost, that is, he had no holding of land, only a house of some sort on someone else's ground, and he was probably a worker on the farm of Arnabost. John 1805 married Janet MacLean, and John 1836 was their only son. He had an elder sister Ann 1834, and there was a younger sister Julian 1841 who died in infancy. Another daughter was born in 1842, but she too seems to have died young.

John 1805 was the youngest (sixth) son of the eight children of John Johnston and Isabella MacLean. They lived at Arnabost, and were related to Johnstons at Ballyhaugh, a few miles away. John senior, probably born around 1760, was a brother of Angus Johnston, and they were two of the four brothers who were the progenitors of the four main Johnston families in the island. Most of them went to Nova Scotia in the 1850s and 1860s, when the population of Coll was halved by emigration.

In 1841 there were eight Johnston households in Coll. By 1851, the Johnstons were reduced to five families, and ten years later, the only Johnstons left in Coll were John 1805 and Janet MacLean, with their son John 1836.

In 1861 John 1805 was described as a grocer, living at Arnabost with his wife and son, who was now a shoemaker. There were then only three occupied houses left at Cliad, with no Johnstons there at all.

When John 1836 was in his mid-twenties, he 'emigrated', possibly intending to stay in Canada, although he said later that he went on a visit to see his relatives in Nova Scotia and Ontario, in order to learn all the piping lore which they had taken with them when they left Coll. As far as can be made out, he was in Canada for about two years, 1864–65, but Thelma Johnston could find no evidence that he visited Prince Edward Island, where his second-cousin, Hector Johnston, was living. John said he learned his piobaireachd from his uncle (or uncles), with the implication that these included Hector; whoever taught him, it must have been during this Canadian visit. It is difficult to substantiate the claim, as Hector had left Scotland long before John was born. John's evasiveness about the name of his piobaireachd teacher makes us suspicious and must lay the matter open to doubt.

Thelma Johnston said that Hector was the only son of Donald Johnston, farmer at Arinagour (see above). Hector's first cousins, who emigrated with him, were Lachlan, whose dates are given as 1787–1861, and Roderick, brothers who went first to Nova Scotia, where Lachlan settled. Hector and Roderick later moved on, to Prince Edward Island.

Lachlan and Roderick were the sons of Duncan Johnston and Mary MacDonald, Lachlan born at Breacacha in 1784, and Roderick at Gallanach in 1794. Their father Duncan was one of the brothers of John Johnston 1760s, grandfather of John 1836, so Lachlan and Roderick were second cousins of John 1836.

John 1836 was always vague about his teaching. He said that his teacher, unnamed, was a pupil of Duncan MacMaster, and we are left to assume that this was Hector. Sometimes he referred to his teacher as 'my uncle', sometimes 'the uncles who taught me', or 'my uncles in Canada', but he never gave them names. In a letter of 1907, he referred to 'the fact that I was a great performer on the pipes myself – perhaps the best of our name since Hector himself died', but he did not specify Hector as his teacher.

He was adamant on two points: (a) his teachers rejected written piobaireachd music and taught entirely by ear; and (b) they despised and rejected any form of light music (Ceol Beag). Perhaps both these claims may be taken with a pinch of salt. He seems to have had sufficient access to published music to know that it differed from his traditional style.

It was Duncan MacMaster who was said to have enraged his laird by playing marches in secret; he was threatened with dismissal if he was caught playing them again. John Johnston told this story in support of his contention that the old pipers did not, or were not allowed to, play light music.

By the late 1860s, John was back from Canada and living once more in Coll. He married in 1870. His first wife was Ann, the widow of a police constable called MacDonald, who must have died around 1869, leaving two MacDonald sons, Robert, born in Dumbarton in 1867, and John, born in Coll in 1869, possibly a posthumous child. Ann herself was a native of Coll, and returned there when she lost her husband.

In 1881, the two MacDonald stepsons were living with the Johnstons in Ballyhaugh after the death of their mother, and old John Johnston 1805 described them in the Census as his grandsons. John 1836 had meanwhile married again, and his wife Margaret, twenty years his junior, appears first in the 1881 Census, and then in the 1891, when the two boys had left.

In 1871, John was described as a house-carpenter. He, Ann and the two boys were living with John's parents at Cornaig, in the north of the island, with two farm servants, the whole household in a house with two rooms. The acreage of the holding was 'not known', but the size of the house suggests it was a small croft. Both John senior and his wife Janet were now in their sixties, and this was the only Johnston family left in Coll. Cliad had become a farm of 400 acres, let to a farmer from Ayrshire, and Arnabost was reduced to three houses, none of them occupied by Johnstons.

The Johnstons were in Ballyhaugh by 1881, and this was the home of John 1836 for the rest of his life. Although the Census refers to Ballyhaugh (which is pronounced Bally-ho), this name was probably a general term for the cluster of houses now known as Totamore. This is confusing, as there is another Totamore about a mile to the south, on the hill above Totronald, and the term Ballyhaugh may have been used to distinguish the two. The Johnston house was the Totamore on the Cliad road; it is the next house north from Ballyhaugh itself, which is now a training school for volunteer overseas workers. Totamore is named in the OS two-and-a-half-inch map, but not on the one-inch.

Seton Gordon, in his chapter 'The Island Piper', in *Hebridean Memories*, waxed lyrical about Totamore:

> The old piper's croft stood on the western side of the island. Within a stone's throw of the door, the long Atlantic waves broke with a deep, soothing sound upon a strip of golden sand. On the horizon, as often as not, one could see the herring drifters rise and fall upon the swell that is rarely absent from the Coll banks. It was a peaceful spot, and of a clear summer's night the westering sun bathed all the long chain of the Outer Hebrides and shone ruddy on the conical heights of Rhum and of the Skye hills behind them . . .

This was the stuff that Seton Gordon's readers wanted, in exile in grimy cities. Never mind that the crofthouse is about half a mile from the golden beach, so the stone's throw would have been a mighty heave – and the beach cannot be seen from the house. Behind the present house there are the ruins of several older dwellings, and a run-rig system of cultivation. From the top of an eminence behind these, a glimpse of the sea may be obtained, but not of the beach. And although Rum and Skye are visible from the north of Coll, they cannot be seen from Totamore. The description, however, is valid for some of the island, and Seton Gordon was exercising a little artistic licence – after all, he had a living to make. He was careful to avoid using specific names, of people or places on Coll, and he said, not that Rum and Skye in the sunlight were visible from Totamore, but that the sun shone on them. And so it did.

In 1891, John and his father, now widowed, were at Ballyhaugh – his father died in 1906. John was an 'Inspector of Poor, and crofter'; evidently he was embarking on his role as spokesman for the islanders. The house at Totamore had three rooms, and all three of the family spoke both Gaelic and English. John himself was remarkably fluent in English, considering how few opportunities he had to speak it. He was widely read in English, and most articulate in writing in English without apparent effort. Occasionally his idiom is Gaelic in construction (he would write 'I cannot but do something' where an English speaker would say 'I can but . . .' or 'I can only . . .') but this gives a pleasant island flavour to his work. It was once remarked that in his letters to the *Oban Times* you could smell the peat smoke.

In 1901, at the age of sixty-five, he was at Totamore Cottage with his wife Margaret, and his occupation was now 'Sanitary Inspector'. Totamore Cottage was now the official designation of his house. His father lived another five years, but he does not appear in the 1901 Census for Coll. He was 101 when he died, and was presumably living in care somewhere.

William Donaldson tells us that latterly John Johnston was the spokesman for the 500-odd people left in Coll, doubtless because of his fluency in English, and his keen intelligence. He took an active part in island life, serving on the School Board; he was a communicant of the Free Church, and also took a lively interest in politics, supporting the Liberal party and plunging into the controversies of the burning topic of the late 19th century, Land Reform. His was a fierce and frustrated intellect: he had an ardent honesty in all he did, but his mind lacked training and system, and he was apt to damage his own arguments by sweeping excesses.

He complained of a feeling of isolation in Coll, and it is clear that he needed mental stimulus. Seton Gordon said he had 'an unusually fine intellect', and commented: 'I have never met a crofter with so wide a knowledge of West Highland affairs, and his breadth of view and his inexhaustible store of reminiscences would have been noteworthy in any man, whatever his station in life' (*Hebridean Memories*). In a later age, John Johnston would undoubtedly have been a county councillor, or indeed a member of parliament.

He used to go over to the neighbouring island of Tiree to play at the annual Tiree Games, but otherwise his yearly visit to the Argyllshire Gathering in Oban was his sole contact with the top pipers, and with the modern style of playing piobaireachd, branded by him as 'meaning-less'. He was increasingly roused to scorn and fury by the playing he heard at Oban. He became deeply pessimistic about piobaireachd, and wrote despairing letters about its future. This is an affliction of elderly pipers and piping enthusiasts of every generation. I have attacks of it myself.

John Johnston had a style of playing regarded as being all his own, though he denied this, saying it was the way all the old masters had played. Like Joseph MacDonald, he referred to a musical phrase in piobaireachd as a 'finger', and he had a special way of playing cadences. His contention that his way was the old way, once played by all, is borne out by material sent from Australia by Dr Barrie MacLaughlan Orme, who plays piobaireachd as he was taught by Dan MacPherson and Hugh Fraser, whose father was a pupil of the Bruces. Dr Orme has made an interesting video film of himself playing all the old movements, no longer practised, such as reverse grace noting, and illustrating how they were used in different piobaireachd works. This style of playing, so rich in its ornamentation, is sometimes ridiculed by modern authorities, who do not appreciate what they are hearing.

In the late 1890s, John travelled to Glasgow so that David Glen could put on record some old, unpublished tunes that only John still knew. In taking these, David Glen wrote down the unusual cadences played by John. Glen did not adopt them himself, nor did he use them in the tunes he printed, but he put in a note to his version of *MacLean of Coll Placing His Foot on the Neck of his Enemy*, so that we know exactly what it was that John Johnston played. His cadences were 'a tumbling run of even semi-quavers', that is, instead of the cadence notes E-A (known as the hiharin, or ealach), John played a downward run, G-E-D-A in quick succession, not unlike the so-called 'Donald Mor run-down', in, for example, the *MacLeod's Salute*.

Was this, as he claimed, a universal style in former times? A Hebridean style, perhaps? Or a John Johnston style? Where did he get it? Certainly it is one of the movements illustrated by Dr Orme in Australia, who attributed it to the Bruces; they came from Skye and were closely related to the MacPherson pipers. Alexander Bruce had been a pupil of Donald Ruadh MacCrimmon and taught his son Peter, before Peter emigrated to Australia; this link through Donald might suggest that John Johnston's old style was MacCrimmon-based. William Donaldson implies that John Johnston might have got it from Donald MacDonald's book, but it seems unlikely that he took any of his piping from a book; more probably he and Donald and the Bruces were all playing the old style which lingered on in the islands after it had been abandoned on the mainland. The gracings of Charles MacArthur as printed in the performer text of the 2002 edition of the MacGregor-MacArthur manuscript have similar movements; again, these are examples of an island idiom.

John Gibson (2002) names a pupil of John Johnston, who learned from him in Coll. Neil Cameron had emigrated to southern Ontario, where he taught his son Allan and the local minister all he had learned in Coll. Unfortunately this knowledge seems to have been lost.

In 1980, Dr Hector MacLean in Eigg wrote to ask Seton Gordon if John Johnston had played these unusual cadences only in the work where David Glen added his comment, or whether they were characteristic of all of Johnston's playing. Seton Gordon was in no doubt: 'His cadences were quite original. Pipers pour scorn on them, but I did not. There was a strange, primitive and haunting charm in them as he played them, rather fast, on his practice chanter, his eyes tightly closed. ALL the cadences I heard him play were in the same unorthodox form.'

In the same letter, Seton Gordon wrote: 'He was temperamental, and I was one of the few people he liked – he would therefore play the chanter to me but to no-one else.' This, of course, was in John's last years, but presumably he must have played his cadences at, say, Oban. How else would the pipers have poured scorn on them, if they had not heard them? (Is this a naïve question?)

John Johnston was curiously evasive on other topics beside that of the name of his teacher. He firmly believed that piobaireachd had its roots in the 14th century, if not earlier, and he said that *Alister Carrach's March* was the oldest work known to the old pipers. It appears to belong (unprovably) to the 15th century.

John had a port (tune) which he said had been played at the extraordinary 'set piece' battle at the Inches of Perth in 1396. He was, said Seton Gordon, 'very shifty' about passing this on, but he unwittingly allowed Seton to learn it by ear from hearing snatches of it played; Seton then went home and wrote it out, before passing a few copies to selected friends, in an equally furtive way, swearing them to secrecy.

It is not clear exactly why the two men played this game. Possibly both wanted to preserve (or create?) the mystery of immense age about the tune. Certainly Seton Gordon enjoyed feeling he had esoteric information known only to him and one enlightened native. But, to give him more credit, he may have felt he should not publish information he had 'stolen' from the old man, without his knowledge or permission.

Of the tune itself, John Gibson wrote: 'It is short but of variational form, and, inter alia, contains *crunnluadh a mach*, a complex grace-note pattern . . .' According to contemporary accounts, the battle where this work was played in 1396 was a set-piece fought out in the presence of the king, Robert III, and his court, as a kind of joust, with thirty or thirty-five men on each side (the sources differ), drawn from two opposing clans: they were said to be Clan Chattan and 'Clan Kay', believed to be either Davidsons or Camerons. It was like an Old Firm game, but fought to the death – or as a historian put it, 'either an affair of honour or a sporting spectacle between two packs of wild animals'. The hope was that reducing clan warfare to 'civilised' formality might help to stamp out the blood feuds of mediaeval times. It did not, of course.

Each side in this artificial battle had its own piper, but it is not recorded which played this tune, if either. It was known as the *Brosnachadh Catha, Incitement to War,* or *The Stimulus*. Its exact purpose is not entirely clear. To inspire the warriors? To imitate the sound of the blows struck in the fight? To rally men to a certain spot? It does seem less than inspirational, but if played over and over again it might induce the urge to hit someone. On the other hand, the tune we call *War or Peace (Cogadh no Sith)*, which we know inspired men in battle as late as Waterloo, sounds very heavy and pedestrian when modern players churn it out so slowly and carefully, and makes us wonder why soldiers were lifted by it; and then when it is played, as Dr Orme gave it to us, in the old style, full of life and lift, at considerable speed, galloping along, all doubts vanish, and it is easy to understand why it was a great battle tune.

Where and how did John Johnston acquire the *Brosnachadh*? He played 'a few gratuitous renditions' in the presence of Seton Gordon, but always with his back turned (or so Seton Gordon said. He was not averse to a certain amount of romantic fiction himself). The very furtiveness on the part of both men might give rise to the suspicion that they both knew fine they were stretching the truth about its origins.

It is more than likely that John Johnston learned the tune from his uncles in Canada. He said he also heard them playing a *Lament for the Lord of Connaught* (see above, Mull), which is now unknown. His second cousin Hector took with him to Canada the old pipe which had belonged to the MacLeans of Coll. The Canadian Johnstons said it had been played at Culloden, and this could be true. But 'could be' is not the same as 'is', and it seems likely that this 1396 port also falls into the 'could be' category.

Prosnachadh

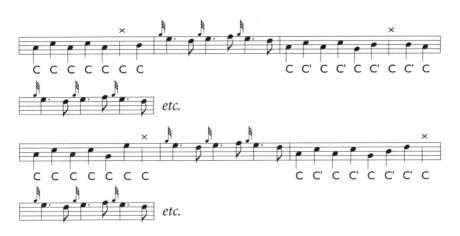

C = ordinary Crunluath;   C' = Crunluath a mach

Music of the Prosnachadh:
this is the version passed on by Archie Kenneth, in his hand.
The idea of the Prosnachadh according to Johnston the Coll piper
(ex Seton Gordon per R.D. Cannon) was that it represented the actual
fighting in a clan battle: the Crunluath beats as the warriors struck
their blows, and the long-sustained E notes as they fell back and
rested, before resuming the battle.

When in 1917 Seton Gordon was transferred from the Hebrides, John Johnston took against his successor running the coastal watch, 'this sprig of a laird', as he called him, ordering him out of the house. John gave up the coastal watch duties, being then eighty-one years of age and unable to thole the new officer. He always greatly disliked being patronised or treated as a subordinate.

In 1920, full of pessimism and fear for the future of piobaireachd, and unable to accept modern developments, he suffered a severe illness, being saved from death from a strangulated hernia by the skill of the island G.P. But the shock and acute pain took their toll, and he never recovered fully, being afflicted by dizzy spells. He died early in 1921, at the age of eighty-five.

He was greatly liked and revered in Coll, and a fine memorial was put up at Arinagour, to commemorate one of the island's most remarkable sons. It is an obelisk above the road, at a house called Craigdarroch. The inscription on it reads:

TO THE MEMORY
OF
JOHN JOHNSTONE
TOTAMORE, COLL
BORN 1836 DIED 1921

A TRUE HIGHLANDER, AN AUTHORITY
ON FOLK-LORE AND PIOBAIREACHD:
AN ENTHUSIASTIC LAND LAW REFORMER
AND AN ARDENT CHAMPION OF THE
RIGHTS OF THE PEOPLE.

FAITHFUL TO AND LOVED BY HIS FRIENDS
RESPECTED BY HIS OPPONENTS
GRATEFULLY REMEMBERED
BY ALL WHO KNEW HIM.

'LAMH THREUNS GACH CAS
CRIDH ARD NACH CEILLEADH'

('A STRONG HAND IN EVERY HARDSHIP,
A NOBLE HEART THAT WOULD HIDE NOTHING')

To give Seton Gordon his due, he immortalised John Johnston in his books. Without his affectionate descriptions, rosy-tinted and romantic though they are, the only picture that posterity would have of the old man would be his persona in the *Oban Times*, fanatical, irascible, intolerant, impatient – though always courteous. Full of knowledge, too, but given to wild theories. Seton Gordon showed us the other side, the sincere Hebridean who genuinely loved piping and was loyal to his ancestry.

It was Seton Gordon who painted this picture of his friend:

It was no easy task to persuade him to play, but of a December's evening when the wind was moaning without and the peat fire burned brightly in the small room, the veteran's interest in the far-off days would be roused by the notes of his chanter. At first he would play haltingly as though his old fingers were finding it no easy task to express the music that ran in his head. But as he warmed to his task, his mind would wander back to the time of his youth, and, with tightly shut eyes, he would play through one piobaireachd after another . . . It was good to see his pleasure, yet it was not easy to follow his playing, for he hurried somewhat, and he had no knowledge of staff notation, was unable to set the notes on paper . . .

Sources

Nicholas MacLean-Bristol
Notices of Pipers
Census records, Coll
Old Parish Register, Coll
Seton Gordon, *Hebridean Memories*
John Gibson, *Traditional Gaelic Bagpiping*
David Glen, *A Collection of Ancient Piobaireachd*
Piping Times
William Donaldson, *The Highland Pipe*

Other Pipers in Coll

NEIL MACDONALD is mentioned in an article by Tommy Pearston, 'Thoughts on Islands' (*Piping Times* February 1995), where Neil is described as a Coll piper 'who was well versed in old Coll tunes and was an expert in making heather ropes. He had a little creel of heather rope to carry his pipes on his back'.

Tommy also referred to the PATTERSONS, a famous piping family in Coll. He said 'They were usually asked to play at the funerals on the island. They were removed from the job when they played strathspeys and reels instead of *Lochaber No More*, on one occasion.' Tommy wondered if there was a connection with Allan Patterson, the Sergeant Piper of the HLI who checked General Thomason's work for him, when he was preparing his collection, *Ceol Mor*, in 1896. Allan's father was in South Uist, but could have had kin in Coll.

The former owner of the Coll Hotel in Arinagour was ALISTAIR OLIPHANT, well known as a professional magician and member of the Magic Circle. He was also an accomplished ice-skater, a graduate engineer, an accordionist and a piper. While at school at Glasgow Academy, he was Pipe Major of the school band, and often used to play at ceilidhs in Coll. He died in 1987, when in his fifties, and his son now has the hotel.

ANGUS KENNEDY was a well-known piper who came from Coll, in more recent times.

Today there are no pipers on the island of Coll.

The Small Isles

Canna

Canna is reached by a ferry for foot passengers and goods which serves the Small Isles from Mallaig, calling at Eigg, Rum, Muck and Canna on different days of the week. Motor vehicles are not transported except with special permission from Highland Council. The crossing from Mallaig to Canna via Eigg, Muck and/or Rum takes about three hours, depending on how many island stops are made, and on the weather. The scenery en route is outstanding.

The name Canna has not been fully explained. It has been said, without much conviction, that it refers to ownership, or tenancy, by a priest or canon, which seems likely enough as the earliest known owner of the island was the church: before 1628, Canna was part of the endowment of the Benedictine monastery at Iona. It may, however, be from Gaelic *canach*, 'bog myrtle', or from an old word *cana*, 'wolf's whelp', or from Gaelic *cana*, 'a small whale or porpoise'. Least likely seems to be Norse *kné-øy* 'knee island', supposedly from its shape; *kné-øy* would not give the form *Canna*.

John MacColl composed *Allan Gilmore Thom of Canna* (2/4 M 4). Thom's father Robert, a Glasgow ship-owner, had bought Canna in 1881, and Allan inherited it in 1911. Both father and son made substantial changes to the island, introducing new buildings and improvements such as a pier and a grain mill, and plantations of trees. Other than this march, little pipe music is now associated with the island. Extensive emigration in the early 19th century robbed it of its foremost players.

John Lorne Campbell, in his book *Canna: The Story of a Hebridean Island* (1984) quotes an interview he recorded with a Canna man, Angus MacLeod, in 1949. Angus was then living in Clydebank, but had been brought up in Canna. He spoke about the smuggling of whisky which went on in the island in the 1870s, and said that when the excise men came over to Canna by boat, they had a piper in the crew. As they came ashore, he would start to play, walking along from the harbour.

This gave warning of his approach, so that the main culprit, Murdo by name, had time to hide the evidence. He then coolly offered the excise man a dram. The whisky was not illicitly distilled in Canna, but came from Tobermory, in Mull. It is clear that piping was something of a novelty in Canna in the 1870s.

Allan MacArthur, Newfoundland

A book by Margaret Bennett (*The Last Stronghold: The Gaelic Traditions of Newfoundland,* 1989) deals with a community in south-west Newfoundland, called the Codroy Valley. A great character there was ALLAN MACARTHUR, who was eighty-five years old in 1969, described as a farmer and piper; he was more than that, however, as he was a fine Gaelic singer, an accordionist, a story-teller, historian and skilled craftsman. His wife Mary was descended from MacDonalds in Glengarry.

Allan himself was the son of Lewis MacArthur, born in Cape Breton, Nova Scotia, and Lewis was the son of Angus MacArthur, who had left Canna at the age of twenty-two, probably in the 1820s. Angus married Sarah MacDonald, of the Glengarry MacDonalds, while in Cape Breton. Their son Lewis married Jenny MacIsaac, of the Moidart family (who are related to the piping MacDonald brothers from Glenuig). In the 1840s, Cape Breton had many families of MacNeills, MacIsaacs and MacLeans.

John Lorne Campbell refers to a Census taken in Canna in 1821, and to a Rental made in 1818. These show a large number of MacArthurs in Canna, but a new laird coming in around 1820 put many of them out of their homes, and they were forced to emigrate. It is thought that quite a few of them were pipers, unable to read music but taught by ear. Allan MacArthur in the Codroy Valley is known to have sung pipe music in canntaireachd.

In 1922, the Newfoundland settlement was visited by Jockan MacPherson (eldest son of Calum Piobaire), piper to a wealthy ship owner, Mr Donaldson, the head of the Anchor-Donaldson Line, who came for the fishing in Newfoundland. Jockan and Allan enjoyed piping evenings together, and it seems that Allan's standard of playing was high enough for them to play on pretty well an equal footing – and Jockan was a very fine player, who taught John MacDonald, Inverness, and Willie M. MacDonald. Allan had some piobaireachd, although his environment usually required music for dancing.

Although many MacArthur families are said to have emigrated to

Cape Breton in the 1820s, the 1841 Census for Canna listed the family of Charles MacArthur, fifty-five, crofter in Canna itself, with his wife and five children. Over on the neighbouring island of Sanda there were still seven MacArthur families, where the heads of households were all in their fifties and sixties. The names are Alexander, John, Donald, Lauchlan, Ronald and Duncan – not Campbell names but MacDonald, suggesting that these families came to Canna from Islay, rather than from mainland Argyll.

Margaret Bennett's book has three photographs of Allan MacArthur with his pipes.

The Jamieson Family

A piping family called Jamieson has been influential in Nova Scotia: LAUGHLIN JAMIESON emigrated from Canna in the early years of the 1800s, believed to have been himself a piper. His son NEIL was certainly a piper, living at Pipers' Glen, Inverness County, N.S., and all of Neil's children played. Some of them moved to industrial Cape Breton, some to the USA, to make their living.

Two of Neil's children were CHARLES and JOHN. Charles married a MacIntyre girl who had four piping brothers; they were descended from the South Uist piping MacIntyres. John (1870–1944) was one of the last pipers living in Piper's Glen.

John Lorne Campbell, OBE, FRSE

In the 20th century the Laird of Canna was JOHN LORNE CAMPBELL (1906–1996), who belonged to the Campbells of Inverneill, a family with many piping connections, especially associated with the Argyllshire Gathering. His great-uncle was Archibald Campbell of Kilberry.

John Lorne Campbell was at Oxford studying agriculture when he attended a class in Gaelic, and was inspired to become a fluent speaker, reader and writer. This sparked a lifelong interest in Gaelic culture, and by 1933 he had produced a major work *Highland Songs of the '45*. He spent some years in Barra, recording songs and stories, and with his friend Compton MacKenzie, also living in Barra, he founded the Sea League, to protect the interests of Hebridean fishermen.

In 1935 he married Margaret Fay Shaw, an American folk-lorist. The ceremony, in Glasgow, was conducted in Gaelic, which the bride did not speak or understand, but with her customary spirit she accepted that, and said her own part was easy, all she had to do was say 'Tha' ('Yes') at the right time. All her life she was remarkable for her ready response to challenges which would have daunted a lesser woman.

Shortly before this, she had met John MacDonald, Inverness, when he was teaching piobaireachd in Lochboisdale, South Uist – she sought him out to discuss the use of modes rather than scales in the composition of piobaireachd. She said he was very kind to her, and sometimes let her sit in at his lessons for local pipers, which at that time were held in a small back smoking-room in the Lochboisdale Hotel. Sometimes John would play his violin and Margaret accompanied him on the piano.

In 1938 John Lorne Campbell bought the island of Canna from Allan Gilmour Thom, and he and his wife built up an extensive collection of songs, stories and photographs, books and recordings, covering the Highlands and Islands. Although neither of them was a piper, both had a deep interest in pipe music and its place in Gaelic cultural life.

The Campbells appointed a working manager on the Canna farm, and he was also the shepherd of their flock of Cheviot sheep. He was 'BIG HECTOR' MACDONALD, a Gaelic-speaking native of Canna, born there in 1901. Hector was a big, imposing man, much respected in the islands for his expertise with sheep and cattle. He was a fine singer of Gaelic songs, and was described as 'an accomplished piper'. He used to go with John Lorne Campbell to the livestock sales on the mainland, and because Hector was always smartly dressed in a tweed suit with plus fours, and John was in his usual scruffy clothes, many assumed that Hector was the laird.

In 1981, the Campbells, anxious to preserve the way of life in Canna, gave the island to the National Trust of Scotland, though they continued to live there. The collection amassed by himself and his wife is housed in Canna, and in handing it to the National Trust John Campbell stipulated that it must remain in Canna. It is at present being catalogued by the Campbells' lifelong friend, Magdalena Sagarzazu, from the Basque region of Spain. The Trust had plans to open a Research Centre for the use of Gaelic scholars, but so far this has proved too expensive. The collection includes sound recordings of Gaelic song and traditional music, including piping. These, made on wax cylinders, wire and reel-to-reel tape, are being transferred to CD. It has been found that the wax and tapes have deteriorated with age, but the wire recordings are as sharp as they were the day they were made.

One of the many treasures of the collection is a handwrtten manuscript book of the Daily Orders of the Western Fencible Regiment, made in 1778. This was a regiment of many Campbells, and Dr Lorne

244 The Piping Traditions of the Inner Isles

Campbell inherited the book from his great-uncle Archibald Campbell. It had been handed down the family, ever since it was written. It is quoted in the Notices of Pipers, which make it clear that Kilberry had studied it in detail, but since then it seemed to have disappeared. It is gratifying that it is safe and sound, and in good hands.

The book consists of the regimental orders of the Western (or Argyll) Fencibles, a regiment raised in July 1778, and disbanded in 1783. In 1782, its 1st Piper was John MacAlister from Campbelltown, but that was after the period covered by the manuscript book, which begins on 8 July and finishes at the end of August of the same year, 1778. Keith Sanger suggests that Colin Campbell of Netherlorn (writer of the Campbell Canntaireachd manuscript) was one of the two regimental pipers, and that possibly he was replaced by Neil MacLean. The book lists the officers in James Campbell's Company (most of them were Campbells), and indicates that it had its own drummer, fifer and two pipers, who are not named. They were to play 'day and day about', taking it in turns.

Much space is devoted to the appearance of the soldiers, with belted plaid, well cleaned shoes, buckles clean and properly put in, hose uniformly tied, clothes brushed – and they had clean shirts on Sundays and Wednesdays. Their hair is frequently mentioned. It had to be 'Club hair behind' with the locks suitably cut and plaited and put up with a comb, all Corporals to carry brushes on parade. No man was to have his hair cut except under the attention of an N.C.O., and on certain occasions, all were required to have their hair 'powdart'. They were to be ready to fall in, and on hearing the Drum beating to Arms 'or the Pypir playing the Gathering', they were instantly to repair to their Alarm Posts. The Gathering was *Cogadh no Sith (War or Peace)*. It is given first in the list of duty tunes, all piobaireachd works, presumably because it was played the most often.

The list given is:

Gathering – Coagive & Shea	(*Cogadh no Sith*: War or Peace)
Revellee – Glaisvair	(*Glas Mheur*: The Finger Lock)
The Troop – Boad acna brigishin	(*Bodachan na Briogais*: Carles Wi' the Breeks, or Lord Breadalbane's March)
Retreat – Gillychristie	(*Cille Chriosd*: Glengarry's March)
Tatoo – Mollach dephit mahary	(*Moladh do ghift Mhairi*: Mary's Praise for her Gift)

Of these tunes, *Cogadh no Sith* has no particular clan associations but was widely used as a battle tune; *The Finger Lock* and *Cill Chriosd* have links with the MacDonalds; *Mary's Praise* has no known clan links, and only *Bodachan na Briogais* is a definite Campbell work. Preserved with the book in the Canna collection is a sheet of paper with Kilberry's notes on the tunes. He dismisses *The Finger Lock* as 'a dull tune'.

Archibald Campbell of Kilberry was John Lorne Campbell's great-uncle, and seems to have given, or bequeathed, the Orders Book to him. He said that it had come to him through his family and had been passed down originally by a family member who was an officer in the Western Fencibles when they were disbanded in 1783. Kilberry communicated the list of tunes and a few details to the compilers of the Notices of Pipers, but the spelling as published there differs slightly from the readings given above; this is probably because the writing in the book is not always very clear. In Col. David Murray's book, *Music of the Scottish Regiments*, the tunes are given in a different order, with Reveille first, as seems more logical. Col. Murray made it clear that he had not then seen the original. Keith Sanger gives a brief history of the short-lived regiment in his article 'Colin Campbell's Canntaireachd – The History of the Netherlorn Family' (*Piping Times*, October 2005).

Col. Murray has shown that this list is similar to one allegedly of the same date, the duty tunes of Lord Seaforth's Regiment, but the latter might be regarded with more suspicion as it is longer and has additional Ceol Beag tunes which may have been added later. It is likely that the duty tune lists of the regiments raised in the late 18th century were based on models from older Highland regiments, such as the Black Watch – but these seem to have been lost.

There can be no doubt at all as to the authenticity of the Western Fencibles Orders Book, which is handwritten throughout and carefully dated. It is interesting that in 1778 all the duty tunes are piobaireachd, with no suggestion of any Ceol Beag. And it is clear that for the routine daily parades, a drummer and a fifer were used, with no mention of the pipers.

This Orders Book from 1778 will remain in Canna, which is appropriate enough for an Argyll Company, since Canna was part of Argyll, even though it then belonged to the Clanranald MacDonalds.

Also in the collection is a CD recording made by Peter Kapp, in California. On it he plays the duty tunes as they might have sounded in 1778 (though I suspect he has a better pipe). This playing in the old style is both interesting and enjoyable.

John Lorne Campbell died in 1996, and his wife in December 2004, having just passed her 101st birthday. She lived in Canna almost to the end, being sent to hospital in Fort William only in her last short illness. Her 100th birthday celebrations on the island were a famous occasion, televised under the title *Among Friends*. She herself played the piano at the ceilidh, and remained mentally alert until her death.

MacKinnon Pipers in Canna

Today (2006) the island belongs to the National Trust for Scotland, and the population dropped to eleven, most of whom are MacKinnons. The MacKinnons on Canna and Sanday are from two lines, one originally from Barra, the other from Skye, and both have piping traditions. Winnie MacKinnon, now living in Canna with her two teenaged daughters, has three pipes which belonged to her family for generations.

One pipe is played by her daughter at school in Mallaig, learning from piper Allan Henderson. This pipe belonged to her great-grandfather, who acquired it in unusual circumstances. A piper was staying in Canna when he had to go to Barra for a short time. He did not want to take his pipe with him, so he put it on the dresser in the MacKinnon house, saying 'Look after these for me – I'll be back to collect them'. But he never came back; his boat was wrecked on the return journey, striking rocks off the eastern point of Canna, and all on board were lost, not even their bodies being recovered. The pipe remained with the MacKinnons, who also have two other very old pipes, not used now as they have no bags. It is not known how long these have been in the family. They both have three drones.

About thirty years ago, there was a piper living on Sanday whose name was MacDonald, but details of him are vague.

Sources

Margaret Bennett, *The Last Stronghold*
Scott Williams, *Pipers of Nova Scotia*
TGSI LIX 1994–96
J.P. MacLean, *History of the Clan MacLean*
Obituary, *The Independent*

Muck

To reach Muck, see above (Canna). The crossing direct from Mallaig takes about an hour and forty minutes. There is also a boat from Arisaig.

The name Muck – which should be pronounced Moochk, with the ch as in loch, but is often called Muck as in English – is derived from the Gaelic Eilean na Muic 'Island of Pigs', or possibly 'Island of Whales or Porpoises' (in Gaelic, both whales and porpoises are known as 'pigs of the sea'). There was an attempt by a Laird of Muck to re-christen the island 'Monk', as he did not like being known by his territorial designation of 'Muck', but it was not accepted, so he called himself 'Isle of Muck'.

He was Hector MacLean 4th of Muck, for whom a long poem was composed, around 1730. Iain Dall MacKay, the Blind Piper of Gairloch, who was also a bard, was visiting his friends the MacLeods at Talisker, in the west of Skye; his host's daughter Isabella was married to Hector MacLean, the young laird of Muck, and to him Iain Dall addressed his *Song to Hector MacLean*.

The wording is obscure at times, and it is not clear whether Hector was present at Talisker when the Song was performed, but the poet does refer specifically to the popularity of the young laird and his generosity to his people in Muck. There is a tradition that Hector paid for all of his islanders to be inoculated against smallpox, and he also paid for regular visits by smiths and tailors, and brought in tutors for the children. This must have been in the 1720s, which was when smallpox inoculations were being tried out in Britain. If the tradition is accurate, it would show Hector to have been well to the forefront of medical fashion, but perhaps it is more likely that Gaelic story-tellers transferred the tale from a later laird, in 1772: Dr Johnson and James Boswell recorded it in their accounts of their Hebridean travels, dated 1773. They said the inoculations had been carried out the previous year, when eighty islanders, mainly children up to eighteen years old, had been treated. Dr Jenner, the father of smallpox control, made his first vaccinations in 1796 – which were safer than inoculations and eventually led to eradication of the disease.

However good to his people, Hector seems to have quarrelled bitterly with his young wife; he left the island and went to her parents in Talisker, where he met the Blind Piper of Gairloch. But Hector died young, leaving no children, and his brother succeeded him. It is thought that the contention with his wife may have been because Hector had contracted syphilis, very common in the 18th century, and his advanced medical knowledge did not save him. The Song does not make any mention of the pipes, though harps were evidently played at Hector's feasts (Hector's forebear, the 7th Laird of Coll, had been a devotee of harp music).

Duncan Rankin and Bess MacCrimmon

Probably the best known piper to play in Muck was DUNCAN RANKIN, one of the famous Rankin pipers of Coll, previously of Kilbrennan, in the west of Mull, where they ran a piping school. Duncan was married to BESS MACCRIMMON, daughter of Donald Donn MacCrimmon who lived at Lourgill, in the west of Duirinish, Skye. Donald was (probably) a son of Patrick Og MacCrimmon, of Boreraig and Galtrigill. Some say he was a nephew.

As is often said of the women in piping families, Bess was herself a player, and better than her husband. The story goes that one evening Duncan was unable to play at his MacLean laird's table, and his wife dressed in his clothes and gave the selection of tunes that Duncan usually played, after which the laird remarked 'Duncan has surpassed himself tonight'. Presumably the light was a few flickering candles, and the claret flowing freely.

This must have been in the mid-1700s, when the Laird was Donald MacLean, the 5th Laird of Muck and brother of the Hector for whom Iain Dall made his *Song*. Duncan and Bess later retired to live in Coll. They died at Grissipoll, Coll, in the 1790s, and are buried in the graveyard at Cill Lunaig (the grave is not marked).

Keill Village

Above the present village at Port Mor, the main landing place in Muck, there are ruins of old houses lying to the south of the road, associated with an old chapel and burial ground. Local people on Muck and Eigg say that this settlement, known as Keill, meaning 'burial ground', was used in the early 19th century to house tenants who had been put out of their homes by their landlord. They were awaiting transport to Nova Scotia. It is said that among them was 'the highest concentration of pipers per head of population in all of Scotland'.

The Mackinnon Family

One of the pipers at Keill was NEIL MACKINNON who emigrated from Muck in the 1820s. He went to East Lake Ainslie, Inverness County, Nova Scotia. His sons included ARCHIBALD 'the Big Bachelor' and DONALD, who had three piping children, ANNIE, 'BIG FARQUHAR' and JOHN. The family was known as 'the MacKinnons of the Music' (Clann Ionghuinn a Ciuil). Barry Shears has good stories about them.

Annie and her brothers were born in the 1830s. Both the boys played the pipes and the fiddle, probably taught by their uncle Archibald. He had been born around 1780, and played both instruments, as well as being an accomplished story-teller. Presumably he, his brother Donald and their father Neil had all left Muck in the 1820s already trained as musicians. Archie was a good teacher, too. He died around 1850, 'having provided for his funeral five gallons of rum; the first dram was to be taken at his nephew Neil Mor MacDonald's, and the last dram was to be taken at the graveside' (we are not told how many attended).

Annie and Big Farquhar sometimes used to play their pipes together, each with a hand on the other's chanter. It is entertaining to see this done, and surprisingly good results can be achieved by skilled players. Niall Matheson and John Don MacKenzie gave several tunes to the Piobaireachd Society Conference in 2005, playing in the bar of the Royal Hotel in Bridge of Allan, taking turns to be the one fingering the music. It is usually Ceol Beag that is played this way, but *The Wee Spree* seems to lend itself to it with good effect.

Big Farquhar, born c.1835, was a very tall man, who became a leading piper in his community. He taught several pupils, mainly his nephews. He was a fine singer who was the Gaelic precentor in the East Ainslie Free Church. He died in 1923.

One of his nephew/pupils was LITTLE FARQUHAR MACKINNON of Cobb Brook, East Ainslie. Like most of his family he was an ear-player and could not read staff notation. He played for dancing in the traditional style, and used to practise every night, out on his porch. One bitterly cold night in February, he stood outside and played for square dancing. Everyone except himself kept warm by dancing. Little Farquhar died in 1941.

HUGH FRED MACKINNON was another most talented nephew of Big Farquhar and brother of Little Farquhar. He was not only a good piper and fiddler, but also an accomplished step-dancer.

Barry W. Shears has a fuller account of this MacKinnon family of pipers, in his book *Dance to the Piper* (2008), which includes a photograph of Archibald MacKinnon's headstone, and pictures of 'Little' Farquhar MacKinnon and Hugh Fred MacKinnon, with their pipes.

At Gallanach, on the west side of the island, a pipe-maker, IAN KETCHIN, has his home. He specialises in making Northumbrian pipes.

Today (2004), the children of Muck who are interested in piping travel across to Eigg on Saturdays, for lessons from Donna MacCulloch (see below).

A lady born on the island of Muck who had piping connections and a considerable knowledge of the music was Margaret Stewart, who became the wife of Willie (Benbecula) MacDonald. They lived for some years in Inverness, where Margaret died in 2007.

Sources

Piping Times
Proceedings of the Piobaireachd Society Conferences
J.P. MacLean, *History of the Clan MacLean*
Scott Williams, *Pipers of Nova Scotia*
Local tradition
Professor R.A. Shooter, Edward Jenner Trust

Eigg

To reach Eigg, see above (Canna). The crossing direct from Mallaig to Eigg takes about an hour and a quarter.

Eigg is pronounced 'egg', 'aig' or 'aik'. It seems to be derived from Norse *egg*, meaning 'edge, ridge', with reference to the prominent ridge known as the Sgurr, which makes the island instantly recognisable.

Tunes Associated with Eigg

William M. MacDonald made a 12/8 March in four parts, called *The Island of Eigg*, which he published in Book 2 of his *Glencoe Collection of Bagpipe Music*. He commented: 'This March is made for the long-suffering and devoted people of Eigg, who fought their way through many difficulties to, at last, taking complete possession of their own homeland. We salute you and wish you all lasting peace and happiness.' This was written in 1999. The island gained its independence in 1997, and a memorial was put up near the pier to commemorate the event.

The Massacre Cave

In 1577, or thereabouts, an atrocity seems to have been committed on Eigg by the MacLeods of Dunvegan. The stories about this vary, but the gist is that a MacLeod galley had put in at Eigg, perhaps for fresh water, and the MacLeods were attacked by the Clanranald inhabitants of the island. This was the version put out by the MacLeods, but the Eigg people said they had landed and maltreated some women who were herding cattle. Most of the MacLeods, a galley full of them, any-thing up to fifty men, were killed, and three survivors were set adrift in a boat, which came ashore in Skye. One version of the story says the MacLeod men were caught raping the Eigg women, whose menfolk castrated all the rapists before killing them. This has the ring of story-tellers' embellishment, and there is no evidence for it. On receiving news of the incident, whichever version, the MacLeod chief at once gathered a force and invaded Eigg.

The MacLeods searched the island for three days, but could find nobody, and were about to leave when they found footprints which led to a cave on the shore. There the entire population of nearly 400 was hiding (the number varies, between 200 and 400). The MacLeods lit fires at the mouth of the cave, and all the MacDonalds inside were suffocated, or killed as they tried to escape.

This deed, although recorded in a historical document of the time, was not widely publicised; it seems to have been overshadowed by an attack on the Small Isles in 1588 by Sir Lachlan MacLean of Duart with a troop of Spanish mercenaries. He destroyed every person and house in Eigg (were there many left to destroy?). He was legally indicted for the crime, though never punished. The fact that the MacLeods had not been publicly accused some ten years earlier has been put down to their political influence, but it seems more likely that two traditions have overlapped.

In a letter written in 1973, John Lorne Campbell pointed out that the slaughter in 1588 was mentioned in the contemporary Privy Council records, and he says that a report was written about the cave attack for King James VI earlier than 1595, but this did not appear in print before 1880 (W.F. Skene, *Celtic Scotland*). The report gives 1577 as the date of the massacre, and names Angus John McMudzartsonne as the Capitaine of Eigg, who died along with 395 of his people. He was the eldest son of the Clanranald Chief, who owned the island. The accuracy of this report has been doubted, as the MacLeod chief respon-sible was said to be Alasdair Crotach, and he died in 1547. His eldest son William was said to have been present; he died in 1551, and after the massacre his by-name was Uilleam na h-Uamha, William of the Cave. Obviously these dates do not tally.

John Lorne Campbell suggested that the date might have been 1517 rather than 1577, and that the latter was a copying error. 1517, however, does not tie in with the ensuing Battle of Waternish.

The next reference to the massacre was in 1630, published in *MacFarlane's Geographical Collections* in 1907. It does not give a date for the deed. When a group of Irish Franciscan priests visited Eigg in 1625, they made no reference to the story, and their report said there were 200 people living on the island at that time. Similarly, the Red and Black Books of Clanranald, compiled by the MacMhuirich family, dating from the 17th and 18th centuries, have no mention of the massacre. Martin Martin, visiting Eigg around 1700, made no mention of it, but did describe a large cave which could hold hundreds of people. This would have been the Cathedral Cave, along the coast from the Massacre Cave.

Although there had been the earlier reports, these were not made public, and the first printed description of the massacre seems to have been that of Dr Johnson, repeating the story told to him by young MacLean of Coll, in 1773. Dr Johnson wrote:

> Another story may show the disorderly state of insular neighbourhood.
> The inhabitants of the Isle of Egg, meeting a boat manned by
> MacLeods, tied the crew hand and foot, and set them adrift. MacLeod
> landed upon Egg, and demanded the offenders; but the inhabitants
> refusing to surrender them, retreated to a cavern, into which they
> thought their enemies unlikely to follow them. MacLeod choked them
> with smoke, and left them lying dead by families as they stood. [An odd
> way of putting it.]

This version differs from the traditional, in that the Eigg people refused to hand over the culprits, and were not hiding in the cave. Dr Johnson may have been influenced by his MacLeod friends in the telling of the tale.

Boswell did not repeat the story, merely remarking: 'I have heard nothing curious in it [Eigg] but a cave in which a former generation of the Islanders were smothered by MacLeod.'

In 1807, a Swiss geologist called Necker de Saussure was in Eigg, and in the cave he saw human bones in large quantities, to his great horror. He described how he had to crawl on his belly to get inside, the entrance being merely three feet in diameter, opening into a lofty chamber some thirty feet high.

When Walter Scott visited Eigg, he went to see the cave, and later wrote that he 'brought off a specimen of a skull from among the numerous specimens of mortality which the cave afforded'. This was in 1814. People on Eigg were horrified, and at once set about retrieving the remaining bones for Christian burial – or so it is said. There is no memorial, nor any tradition of where this burial might have taken place. It is hard to believe that the islanders had been unaware of human remains in the cave.

Only one old woman survived the MacLeod attack, they say, and she put a curse on the MacLeods, saying that just as their chief Alasdair Crotach had been a hunchback, so would all his descendants have crooked bones. She does not seem to have been very effective, as the MacLeod family were not noticeably deformed. Seumas MacNell, however, said Alasdair Crotach was reckoned to have had an illegitimate son by a MacCrimmon woman, and the curse was supposed to have revealed itself when her descendants developed 'Piper's Finger' (Dupytron's Contracture, known also as the Curse of the MacCrimmons). It is caused by infection in the soft tissue of the hand, making the fingers curl; it is not contraction of the ligaments or tendons, as many suppose. Nowadays it is treated by surgery to remove the infected tissue, but in former times there was no cure, and it ruined many a piper's career. Any player who develops the condition should recall the plight of the people of Eigg, suffocated in that cave, now called the Massacre Cave, although its original name was Uamh Fhraing, '(St) Francis' Cave', possibly named after a hermit saint who is traditionally said to have lived there.

This incident led to a reprisal raid by the Clanranald MacDonalds when they invaded Waternish, in Skye, the following year, in the absence of the MacLeod chief. It is, of course, possible that the massacre was moved in time from earlier in the 16th century in order to link it to the Battle of Waternish, said to have been fought in 1578. Perhaps we may say that this atrocity in Eigg led to the composition of a fine piobaireachd work, *The Battle of Waternish,* as well as to the start of Piper's Finger.

Ronald MacDonald of Morar

Another piping link with Eigg is RONALD MACDONALD of Morar. In his prime, towards the end of the 17th century, he lived at Cross, in Morar, on the Scottish mainland opposite to Eigg, but when he grew older he moved to another Clanranald property, in Eigg. Some say that this island farm was also called Cross, and that it was near Kildonan Church, but this is probably confusion with the old stone cross at Kildonan. There is no doubt that he lived at Sandavore (Sanda Mhor), a farm on the hill above the anchorage at Galmisdale, overlooking it from the steep hillside. Ronald held Sandavore on lease from his Clanranald chief.

From there, he was able to look across the water to his former home in Morar. The panoramic views are superb.

Ronald, or Raghnall Mac Ailein Oig, born in 1662, was the third son of Allan, IV of Morar, one of an important and influential family on the west coast. In the first half of the 16th century, the family had been granted extensive lands in South Morar as well as estates in Eigg, Uist, Benbecula and Arisaig.

Ronald, a man of exceptional physical strength, was himself a piper, harper and violinist, and an excellent composer of pipe music; to him are attributed *The Vaunting, The Red Speckled Bull* and *The Finger Lock*. Henry Whyte published in the *Celtic Monthly* the Gaelic words of a song associated with the tune of *The Finger Lock*: it appears to be a drinking song.

Many stories were told of Ronald's exploits in ridding the district of various supernatural beings, including a bull which he killed with his bare hands; some of these tales may be symbolic of his efforts to rid the district of old heathen rites and superstitions – for example, pagan bull-worship was widespread in the Highlands, a lingering relic of pre-Christian times. It was said he could stop a whirling mill-wheel, which, as Alec Haddow commented, was a foolhardy risk for the hands of a piper. A manuscript history of the Clanranalds, dated 1700, described him as 'the best player upon the pype now living'.

Allan J. MacKenzie published in his Collection of pipe music (2000) a Slow Air which he called *C'ul Beinn Eadarra*, apparently meaning 'Behind Beinn Edra'. It is described as being an old tune made for Ronald MacDonald of Morar, to mark his chasing of a headless spectre from Morar to Beinn Edra, in Trotternish, North Skye, 'going through the Glen of Shingle and the Pass of Mirth'. Beinn Edra is a peak in the ridge which forms the backbone of Trotternish. Fionn (Henry Whyte) gave the Gaelic words of a song to this tune.

On Ronald's death in 1741, the beautiful *Lament for Ronald MacDonald of Morar* was made, but we do not know who was the composer. It may have been his son, also called Ronald, who was himself a piper, though not known as a composer. His second son, John, is more obscure, and little is known of him.

Ronald's link with Eigg was as a tacksman and representative of the Clanranald MacDonalds, owners of the island; it was the Clanranald chief who granted him the lease on the farm of Sandavore. He lived there in his old age, before he died there, at the age of seventy-nine. He was buried in a Clanranald family tomb already existing, in the (now ruined) church at Kildonan.

The Rev. Charles MacDonald, priest in Moidart, wrote in his book on the Clanranald MacDonalds (1889) that Ronald MacDonald of Morar, when living at Sandavore in his old age, became blind and bedridden, but still retained extraordinary strength in his arms. He had been very kind and generous to his relatives, during his active life, but when he became bedridden he 'had to suffer somewhat from the neglect and ingratitude of his own family. These persons, however, he always tried to reform, in his own way, first by mildly enticing them within reach, and then by soundly punching their heads when they could not escape from his hands'. Presumably this was a tradition preserved in the MacDonald family in Morar.

Donald MacQuarrie

One of the piping pupils of Ronald of Morar was DONALD MACQUARRIE. His grandfather Laughlin, born on the island of Rum, had been hounded out by his landlord, MacLean of Coll, in 1725, because he refused the Laird's Protestant religion. Laughlin felt he should move to Eigg, for his own safety.

Tradition among the MacQuarries in Nova Scotia says that for some time he lived secretly in a cave, Uamh-Chloinn-Diridh, near the north end of the island, keeping himself alive by hunting, but this may have been a MacLeod in similar circumstances, not Laughlin MacQuarrie. The tradition adds that after a while he emerged openly and went to live in Kildonan. The Rev. C.M. Robertson, writing in 1897, said his house was 'near where the present shepherd's house stands, and the site of his stackyard can still be seen, and is named after him "Iodhlann an t-Sealgaire" (The Hunter's Stackyard). The last day he went to hunt in Straidh, he failed to come home, and was found dead, with an otter and a badger lying beside him, at the well now called Tobar nan Ceann (Well of the Head), at which he had stopped to drink.' It is not clear whose head this was, nor the reason for the name.

According to one book on Eigg (M.E.M. Donaldson, *Wanderings in the Western Highlands and Islands*), this man was the one known as Am Piobair Mor, The Big Piper, but Camille Dressler (*Eigg: The Story of an Island*) says that it was his grandson Donald who was the piper, which seems to be correct. Donald lived at Grulin, at the southern end of the island.

In a census made in the early 18th century, the family is referred to as 'The Piping MacQuarries from Rhum'.

In Eigg, Donald came under the tuition of Ronald of Morar, who later sent him to MacCrimmon in Skye – this must have been Patrick Og, or his son Malcolm, and the time around 1730, at a guess. Donald was asked to play *The Finger Lock*, which impressed MacCrimmon so much that he sent him back to Ronald, saying there was nothing he could teach him ('why has Ronald sent you to mock us?').

To pipers, this story is puzzling: for one thing, *The Finger Lock* is said to have been composed by Ronald himself, so the MacCrimmons would expect Donald to play it well; for another, pupils were sent to the MacCrimmons not to learn how to play but to increase their repertoire by learning MacCrimmon works. The story is clearly intended to enhance Donald's reputation in Eigg, but it may have been a cover-up – had he fallen out with his Skye teachers? Had he been sent back for less creditable reasons? He seems to have been a cantankerous character, so maybe he had picked a quarrel at Boreraig. We do not know, but the story as it stands does not really make sense.

Donald returned to Eigg, where he was known as Am Piobaire Mor, 'the Big Piper'. He married a girl called Catriona, whose family lived on Muck, within sight of her new home in the south of Eigg. Missing her own kin, she used to go down to the shore and light a fire as a signal for her brothers to row over and take her across for a visit. But the visits became longer and longer, and Donald was not pleased. He persuaded an old soldier to intervene, to scare her brothers away, and he did it so thoroughly that they never came back to Eigg.

Donald later took to drink, to the dismay of his two sisters. They resolved to give him a fright which might keep him away from the drink. One night when he was out drinking at a local tavern at Kildonan, they dressed up as ghosts in white, and waited for him on the road he would have to take as he came home. One on each side of the road, they loomed up at him in the dark as he was weaving his way along, and as he passed them nervously, they followed him, until he lost his nerve and ran for it. When he fell, exhausted and suffering from shock, his sisters had to carry him home. The experience certainly cured his drinking, in that he never drank again: he died soon after, apparently from shock.

His funeral was an elaborate affair, 'of appropriate importance', as Scott Williams puts it. As his coffin was carried by the men of the community from his home at Grulin, in the south of Eigg, some two or three rough miles to Kildonan, they paused at the boundary between Grulin and Galmisdale, for the customary drams and oatcakes. And as was the custom, too, a cairn was built there, with each man present contributing a stone – and even now, passers-by add a stone to it, in Donald's memory.

When they were waiting there, the coffin-bearers saw the boat bringing Ronald of Morar (or his son, also called Ronald) to his pupil's funeral, and the procession reached the church just as Ronald arrived. One version says that Ronald jumped out of his boat into the water, and waded ashore already playing his pipe as he strode up the long hill to where the body lay.

Another story is that Ronald, son of Donald's piping teacher, was a drinking crony of Donald MacQuarrie's, and he joined another man, the keeper of the inn where they habitually drank, to pipe the mourners clockwise twice round the church and then to the grave. This ritual had its roots in ancient practice, and is an old tradition still carried on in Eigg until recently. It may have been a reminder of the family's religious struggle on Rum.

Some of the stories were told to Angus MacQuarrie when he visited Eigg from Nova Scotia in 1889. Angus was a direct descendant of Donald, and could recite his line with every generation from the Big Piper himself, every one of them a piper. Today, a MacQuarrie descendant living in Eigg is DUNCAN FERGUSON, who plays the button boxie and is an authority on the traditions of Eigg.

It was the Piobaire Mor's grandson DONALD MACQUARRIE and great-grandsons ARCHIE and JOHN, all born in Eigg, who emigrated to Nova Scotia, in 1850/2 (the exact date is uncertain). Archie is said to have left playing *Cha Till MacCruimein, MacCrimmon Will Never Return*. He was a good player, and a good 'heavy' at the Games, too. He never married.

Barry Shears, writing of the Nova Scotia Militia in the 19th century, observes that the regiment's rifle companies usually included a piper. 'The Antigonish Rifles marched to the music of John MacQuarrie, a recent immigrant from the Isle of Eigg.' John had had some success in piping competitions in Nova Scotia, winning a prize sporran in the 1860s. His grandson was ANGUS MACQUARRIE, well-known as a tradition-bearer in Nova Scotia. Piper, fiddler, fisherman and Gaelic speaker, he died in 2002, father of nine, grandfather of nineteen, a family full of music and dance.

The MacQuarries were all piobaireachd players, and there are many MacQuarrie descendants living in Antigonish, including HECTOR, who is eleventh in the direct line. He is a piper, and began composing pipe music at the age of twelve.

Allan J. MacKenzie included a tune by Hector MacQuarrie in his Collection: composed in 1998, it is called *Angus MacQuarrie's Reel*. Another grandson, JONATHAN GRADY, composed a tune called *Farewell to my Beloved Grandfather* soon after Angus' death.

Ranald MacDonald at Laig

The farm of Laig (pronounced 'Lag') on the west side of Eigg, looking out towards Rum, belonged to the MacDonald family in the early 19th century. They were the descendants of Alexander MacDonald, better known as the poet Alasdair mac Mhaighstir Alasdair, who made the piobaireachd poem *In Praise of Morag*. They do not seem to have been related to the MacDonalds of Morar, being from the district of Glen Shiel. Laig is a few miles from Sandavore, where Ronald MacDonald of Morar had lived, and in 1807 another RONALD (RANALD) MACDONALD was in residence as tenant of Laig; the farm was in the hands of himself and his family for several generations.

That year, a Swiss geologist, Necker de Saussure, was in Eigg, and went to visit Ranald. He and his companion were welcomed with great hospitality by Old Ranald, who was then probably in his seventies. He seems to have been a jovial and hospitable host who enjoyed having visitors, and he entertained them with an excellent meal and plenty of whisky.

After the meal, wrote de Saussure, 'he diverted us much by singing plenty of Gaelic songs; and as he passed as knowing bagpipe airs as well as a piper, we begged him to give us some examples of them. He then sang several pibroch tunes with all their passages and their difficulties, imitating with his voice the sound of the bagpipes in the most pleasing manner' (translated from French, and quoted by John Lorne Campbell, *A Very Civil People*, p. 132).

Old Ronald died about two years after this visit. He was the compiler of the first printed collection of Gaelic songs, known as the Eigg Collection (1776), some 106 Gaelic poems, probably drawn from his father's collections of poetry. This collection included Iain Dall MacKay's poem *Corrienessan's Lament*. Some have doubted if the MacDonald who entertained de Saussure at Laig in 1807 could have been Ranald, but suggest it might have been Ranald's son Angus.

Ranald, the son of Alasdair mac Mhaighstir Alasdair, was described by Dr K.N. MacDonald as having been the schoolmaster in Eigg.

The account given by de Saussure is interesting both as a brief description of the singing of piobaireachd in canntaireachd at that time and as a rare, possibly unique, mention of a man who was not himself a piper but could sing piobaireachd in full detail. We have occasional descriptions of this as the role of non-piping women, such as the sister of John MacKay in Raasay, but for a man to have this ability without himself playing the pipes was unusual – or was it? Does it perhaps suggest that intimate knowledge of piobaireachd was more widespread than merely among the pipers themselves? Maybe the knowledge was not unusual but the recording of it on paper was a rarity.

Ranald was brought up in a household where piping must have been familiar, as we know from references in several of his father's works (e.g. *In Praise of Morag*, a piobaireachd poem, and his poem about Donald Ban MacCrimmon). There is some indication in Alasdair's poetry that he knew the intricacies of canntaireachd, and it is likely that Ranald was brought up in the tradition of singing the music.

More Nova Scotian Pipers from Eigg

A player JOHN ANGUS (JACK) MACISAAC lives in New Glasgow, Nova Scotia. He was born in 1939, a direct descendant of MacIsaacs who left Eigg in 1801, on board the *Dove*. This is another Nova Scotia family which is full of piping talent.

Similarly, JOHN MACKINNON of Williams Point, Antigonish, was the son of a settler who came from Eigg. Was he related to the MacKinnon pipers in Muck? He was born around 1808, and was an excellent player who remained a superb piper for dancing even into his old age. He was a politician who was prominent in the government of Nova Scotia, and his younger brother (not a piper) was Bishop Dr Colin F. MacKinnon.

Donald MacLeod

DONALD MACLEOD (1886–1957) was a piper from Eigg who emigrated to Canada. His grandfather Lachlan MacLeod, born in 1806, is listed in the 1841 Census for Eigg, married to Mary MacDonald. Their son James married Christina MacQuarrie, of the piping MacQuarrie family, and they had three children, John, Donald and Mary. They were crofters in Eigg, and part-time fishermen, and James was also a stonemason who helped to build the old pier at Galmisdale. They were all

Gaelic speakers, musical and steeped in their culture of Gaelic song and story – but their strict religious views prevented their musical talents from flourishing, and when Donald wanted to learn to play the pipes, he had no encouragement from his parents.

In 1897, Christy died, aged thirty-nine, and James left Eigg, taking his children to Taynuilt, near Oban, where work was available, probably in the Bonawe quarries. When James died six years later, his teenaged family moved to Oban, looking for work. By 1908, Donald was in Glasgow, working for the Glasgow Tramways Corporation, and soon became a motorman.

He joined the Tramways pipe band, and here his piping talent burgeoned at last, as the Pipe Major was Farquhar MacRae, an excellent piper and teacher, who came from Skye. Farquhar was a fine piobaireachd player who won the Gold Medal at Oban in 1898, and seems to have given Donald a good grounding in the art. In 1916, Farquhar was drowned while walking home through Glasgow at night, in thick fog: he fell into the canal at Monkland Basin, and was not found until next morning.

By that time, however, Donald MacLeod had already left Glasgow. In 1911, he went to Canada, and settled in Winnipeg where he found work as a Customs Inspector; a year later he joined the Winnipeg Fire Department, where he remained until he retired in 1951. He rose to become the District Fire Chief.

In 1913 he married Catherine Urquhart, who came from Banffshire, and they had a son James the following year. When James was only two, Catherine died. Donald later married Christina Merriman, from Orkney, and they had four children. Because of his bereavement and his responsibilities as a single father of a young child, Donald was exempted from military service during the First World War, but in 1921 he joined the pipe band of the 79th Cameron Highlanders (Winnipeg) Non Permanent Active Regiment (equivalent of a militia or TA regiment).

The Pipe Major was Lachlan Collie: he was an uncle of the famous William Ross of Edinburgh Castle. Willie's grandfather, his mother's father, William Collie, for whom he was named, emigrated to Canada soon after 1871, and his son Lachlan, born at Coulin, Ross-shire in 1858, went with him. He seems to have encouraged Donald to enter competitions as a solo player, and taught him more piobaireachd, building on the repertoire he had had from Farquhar MacRae.

Donald loved piobaireachd, his favourite pieces being *The Bells of Perth* and *The Finger Lock*. His closest friends were fellow-enthusiasts

Lachlan Collie and John Hutton, who came from Perth. All three taught local boys and passed on their piobaireachd expertise. At all times Donald was keen to promote Scottish culture, including athletics.

He played a Henderson pipe made in the early 1900s, before the First World War. They were of African blackwood, ivory mounted, and he added silver caps on all the drones, and had silver engraved mountings put on the drone ferrules and pins; his pipe was unusual in that the silver was mounted over the original ivory. The tone of the instrument was said to be excellent.

By 1925 Donald was Pipe Sergeant of the Camerons band, and was competing as a solo player in competitions throughout western Canada, winning many trophies in Manitoba, Saskatchewan, Alberta and British Columbia. In 1929 he won the Canadian Piping Championship open to all pipers in the Scottish units of the Canadian Militia, and in this year he succeeded Lachlan Collie as Pipe Major of the Camerons band in Winnipeg. He gave up his solo competing within two years, in order to concentrate on the band. He received two medals for his military service and for his efficiency, and is listed on the British Columbia Roll Call of Pioneer Pipers.

He remained as Pipe Major of the 1st Battalion of the Camerons in Winnipeg until 1939, and meant to retire then, handing over to his son William, but William was sent overseas to fight in the Second World War. Donald took over the band of the 2nd Battalion for the duration, and William took on the 1st, on his return from overseas duty.

When Donald retired from the Fire Department, he went to live with his daughter and grandchildren in Vancouver, where he was very highly regarded as a piping authority and judge at many competitions. Both of his daughters were Highland dancers, his three sons all pipers.

Donald MacLeod died in Vancouver in 1957.

[The above account is based mainly on a most interesting booklet about Donald MacLeod, written by members of his family to celebrate a family re-union.]

Angus MacKinnon

The MacKinnon pipers in Nova Scotia may be related to Angus MacKinnon, his father Hugh and his sister Peggy, born in Eigg in the 1920s. All three were prominent in the life of Eigg in the second half of the 20th century, all being tradition-bearers and able not only to speak Gaelic but also to read and write it. They were twelfth-generation islanders, whose family croft was at Cleadale, on the west side of Eigg. Their uncle, Angus MacCormick, had also been a great man for the island culture, and it was he who taught them to read and write Gaelic, and instilled in them a love of music, song and story. He probably taught Angus to play the pipes, though no-one is sure who his piping teacher was. Both Hugh and Angus senior were well known on the island for their humour and wit, and both were makers of Gaelic songs.

When the island gained its independence in 1997, Angus said 'Music and song, you must have that in you, or the island will lose its soul.' After the death of Dr Hector MacLean in 1995, Angus was the only piper left on the island; when Donna MacCulloch arrived from Easter Ross, it was Angus who encouraged her to stay on. She felt he had put into her hands responsibility for piping and traditional dance, and for teaching the local youngsters, so that the traditions would not die.

Born in 1927, Angus MacKinnon was brought up at Cleadale, and, clearly a boy of high intelligence, he went to secondary school in Inverness, during the early part of the Second World War – when he remembered to take his travel pass, needed in wartime for moving around the Highlands. He wanted to be a doctor, but in the immediate post-war period there was a two-year wait for entry to medical school, so he opted for engineering instead. He was already a piper, and had celebrated VJ Day by marching up and down the township of Cleadale, playing his pipes.

Late in 1945 Angus joined the Royal Engineering Corps and was sent to the Middle East. He liked the Arabs, with whom he felt a strong affinity, seeking out their company, discussing methods of agriculture and sharing their love of music. He would play his chanter while they played their flutes, and he found it interesting to compare the instruments.

He then developed his engineering career in civilian life, and was away from Eigg for almost thirty years. In the early 1970s he gave up his lucrative engineering work to return to the island. The landlord of Eigg at that time was the Anglyn Trust, led by Bernard Farnham-Smith, who appointed Angus as the estate farm manager. He started full of ideas and hope, but soon found there was no money to support their schemes. He succeeded his father as the Cleadale grazings clerk, while his sister Peggy ran the island shop and post office. Angus started a machinery club among the crofters, and made many improvements to modernise the croft at Cleadale.

He regarded the landlords of the 1950s, the Runciman family, as the best the island had had. They had encouraged the musical life of Eigg, and held great parties (Yehudi Menuhin attended one, 'a handy man for a ceilidh'). There was then a mutual feeling of goodwill, which did not continue with subsequent landlords. Although himself doubtful when the buy-out was first mooted, Angus supported the campaign wholeheartedly, and worked tirelessly for its success, stressing always that the island culture was of prime importance.

When the great day came in June 1997, three hundred guests arrived and were greeted by a piper in full regalia (DUNCAN NICOLSON from Fort William), who 'marched the jubilant crowd to the marquee . . . The island children sang a traditional Gaelic song from Eigg which Angus MacKinnon, whose grandmother had sung it to Marjorie Kennedy Fraser, had taken great pride in teaching them'. An amazing three-day ceilidh followed the ceremony, 'the biggest party ever'.

Angus lived to see the freedom of the island from tyrannical or negligent landlords. He died at the end of May 2000, and is buried at Kildonan Church, Eigg.

It is difficult to put in words the influence of Angus MacKinnon on the life of Eigg. He is remembered with strong affection and a feeling almost of reverence, mingled with nostalgia.

[The above account is based on Camille Dressler's book, *Eigg, the Story of an Island*, material which is used here with her kind permission.]

Today Angus MacKinnon's mantle as a piper has fallen on DONNA MACCULLOCH, who knew him in his last days and is devoted to his memory. She first visited Eigg in the 1990s, and says that it was Angus who encouraged her to stay – she hopes that her efforts to carry on the musical tradition would have pleased him. She holds classes in traditional music and dance, including piping, on Saturdays, and children from both Eigg and Muck take part in them.

Donna is from Knockfarrel, near Strathpeffer in Easter Ross. She attended Dingwall Academy, where her piping tutor was Pipe Major Andy Venters, formerly with the Queen's Own Highlanders. She later had courses at Sabhal Mor Ostaig in Skye, where she came under the tuition of John Burgess and Norman Gillies, and learned some piobaireachd. Donna's first love was for Highland dancing, and she enjoys participating in ceilidhs with folk-groups. She has a mix of traditional and modern folk music and dance which is likely to appeal to the youngsters of today.

Dr Hector MacLean

Dr MacLean was the GP for the Small Isles, a great character and a lifelong piobaireachd devotee. Born in Montrose in 1912, he was of a family that came from the west, but he was brought up in Hamilton and did his medical training at Glasgow University, graduating in 1935. At the outbreak of war in 1939 he joined the Royal Army Medical Corps, and served in both North Africa and Normandy. In 1951 he became the GP for the Small Isles, living in Eigg and travelling by boat to Muck, Canna and Rum. He worked tirelessly to improve the medical services for the islanders, and became a prominent figure in island life. He fitted in well, being down-to-earth and never afraid to express an opinion – and he took island weather and travelling conditions in his stride, without fuss.

An idea of the conditions under which he worked is given by Margaret Fay Shaw, in her book *From the Alleghenies to the Hebrides*, published in 1993. She relates how an American visitor to Canna became seriously ill during the night, at a time when the island telephones did not work after 6 p.m. Margaret ran down to the pier, to ask the crew of a fishing boat if they would radio Mallaig, on the mainland, for a doctor; but the high hills of Rum lay between them and Mallaig, preventing the radio signals from getting through. 'Leave it to us,' said the fishermen, and they managed to raise a boat far out in the Atlantic, who were able to contact Oban by radio. Oban rang Mallaig, and Mallaig roused Dr Hector MacLean, who arrived in Canna in his boat at 5 a.m.

Hector MacLean married Helen Finline, who died in 1978 when in her sixties. They had three sons. Camille Dressler's book on Eigg has a photograph of Dr MacLean playing his pipes for an island wedding in 1986.

Clearly he enjoyed the characters among his patients, especially the cailleachs (old women) on the crofts, of whom he spoke with great affection. He was a founder-member of the Inducement Practitioners Association, started in 1982 to defend the rights of doctors in isolated places. This Association fought to retain a doctor for the Small Isles, backed to the hilt by the islanders, who regarded this as their first victory. Dr MacLean was due to retire at that time, but when he heard that the Highland Health Board had decided to have a Health Centre at Mallaig, and fly a doctor out to the islands by helicopter once a month, he changed his mind, and decided to stay on. 'Better an old doctor than no doctor,' he said. It was 1991 before Dr Tiarks took over, and

Dr MacLean remained in Eigg until his death in December 1995. He was buried at Kildonan.

He did not live to see the island gain its independence, but he supported the cause, having no use for landlords, who had opposed his plans to build a surgery on Eigg. Life under Bernard Farnham-Smith he described as 'living under enemy occupation without the satisfaction of being able to shoot the bugger'.

He became a District Councillor in the 1960s, trying to win changes for Eigg and the neighbouring islands, but his was a voice crying in the wilderness, and he gave it up in frustration. When Lesley Riddoch held her ground-breaking radio debate on land-ownership on BBC Radio Scotland, Dr MacLean spoke for Eigg, the only person with sufficient confidence to do so, not being a tenant at the mercy of the landlord.

He was an enthusiastic piper, who was a serious student of piobaireachd. In 1960, he wrote to Seton Gordon, enquiring about the old finger movements played by John Johnston in Coll; he wanted to know if John played a particular form of the GEDA cadence in all his tunes or in only a few selected works. One of his lifelong interests was the preparation of a corrected and properly edited version of Joseph MacDonald's Treatise of 1762. His work was forestalled by the publication of Roderick Cannon's edition, but many would have liked to see what Dr MacLean made of it.

Seumas MacNeill recalled a visit to Eigg in 1993, when Dr MacLean was over eighty. On arrival the boat was met by this kilted gentleman who seemed to know everyone on it, except Seumas and his friends. But later word went round that the visitors were pipers, whereupon Dr MacLean called at the house where they were staying, and 'a very informal ceilidh' sprang up. 'There were some tales told, one or two songs, one or two drams and a great deal of piping. This was the highlight of our visit'.

Sources

Piping Times
Rev C.M. Robertson, *TGSI* XXII
Scott Williams, *Pipers of Nova Scotia*
Camille Dressler, *Eigg*
Duncan Ferguson
Emily MacDonald
Donna MacCulloch

Rum

Rum is reached by boat from Mallaig or Arisaig (see above, Canna). The crossing direct from Mallaig takes an hour and twenty minutes.

Rum was often spelled Rhum, but the *h* is meaningless and has been dropped in recent times. In Gaelic the name is pronounced 'room', but nowadays it is generally called 'rum', like the drink. Nobody is sure of the origin or meaning of the name. It may be related to Gaelic rumach 'marshy', or it may be a Norse name meaning 'wide, spacious' – or it could be older than either of these.

The history of piping in Rum is incomplete. In 1826, the proprietor of the island, Dr Laughlin MacLean, decided to clear the island completely, and give it over to deer; he said he had the full consent of all the people, who told him they wanted to emigrate, and he helped to pay for their passages to Nova Scotia. The 1841 Census indicates that not all the inhabitants left, and there were still families of MacIsaacs and MacQuarries on the island. Dr Laughlin MacLean was a brother-in-law of the piper John Ban MacKenzie, their wives being sisters.

Long before that, in 1725, religious persecution had driven the Catholic piping MacQuarrie family from Rum, to live in Eigg where they could practise their own religion in peace.

In the 1730s, Iain Dall MacKay, the Blind Piper of Gairloch, composed his *Song for Hector MacLean* (see above, Muck), in which he refers to the young Hector in his sailing boat, passing between Rum and Eigg on his way to Talisker, in the west of Skye. Iain pictured the white-capped mountain Trollaval looking down from Rum at the small craft on its voyage.

John A. Love, in his book on Rum, makes it clear that the proprietor of the island who built the castle, Sir George Bullough, kept several pipers during his time there, in the late 19th and early 20th century. The castle had a room, 'a small tower bedroom directly over the castle's main door. Above that was the piper's room, accessed from the main stair, eventually leading out to the parapet of the main tower itself'.

Downstairs there had been a secret room, but this was later sealed off, 'leaving an alcove off the dining room where the piper would sit with a dram, waiting to give the household a post-prandial recital'.

Two pipers are named. One was NEIL SHAW, around 1900, of whom John Love writes: 'The household was awoken at 8 a.m. by Neil Shaw playing *Johnnie Cope* on his pipes. Shaw was a steward on the *Rhouma* [Bullough's steam yacht, which had a crew of forty when it went out into the open sea], and he rowed ashore every morning to give his recital'.

The other piper named was DUNCAN MACNAUGHTON, a stalker on the Bullough estate. He had come to Rum in 1918, and he took over the piping duties of Neil Shaw. It seems that neither of these pipers was a native of Rum.

The manager of the Rum estate in the 1880s was Colin Livingston from Morvern, whose son HUGH LIVINGSTON was 'an excellent piper'. He became a businessman in London, but used to visit his father in Rum regularly. Colin was a cousin of David Livingstone, the explorer, whose family originated in Ulva.

As the ferry from Canna to Mallaig passes the north-east side of Rum, the ruin of a tiny house may be seen, beside a small sandy bay. This is Kilmory, where a family called MATHESON lived, said to have originated in Lochcarron, Wester Ross. In the mid-19th century, after losing five of their children in an outbreak of diphtheria, the surviving members of the family left for New Zealand, where two of the sons, Matthew and Alexander, farmed at Hartfield until the 1950s. The two bachelors shared a keen interest in Highland dancing and piping, though it is not clear whether either of them played. Matthew died in 1942, aged eighty-five, and Alexander in 1956, aged ninety-three. These two were brought up in Rum before the Bullough era; did their interest in piping stem from their boyhood at Kilmory? May we assume that some piping had survived in Rum after the mass emigration of 1826?

Stuart MacNaughton (1920–2003)

The piper Duncan MacNaughton was one of the staff in Rum in the 20th century, becoming head keeper and stalker. He was the father of STUART GRANT MACNAUGHTON, one of the few of that time who were born in Rum, and it was there that Stuart first learned his piping, from his father.

At not quite fifteen Stuart joined the Cameron Highlanders in 1935, as a boy piper. He served in Palestine, Egypt and India before the outbreak of war, and later in the Western Desert and Eritrea. Taken prisoner at Tobruk, he was shipped across to Italy, en route for Germany, but managed to escape during the journey: he removed the floorboards of the truck he was travelling in, and dropped onto the line below, letting the train pass safely over him. An Italian family took him in for a year, until the British advance reached them.

Stuart became Pipe Major of the 2nd Batt. Queen's Own Cameron Highlanders after the war, once he had completed the Pipe Major's course with Pipe Major Willie Ross at the Castle, a course he shared with Evan MacRae. He remembered Willie Ross introducing a twelve-year-old boy who walked in playing Willie's own great pipe – it was John Burgess.

On leaving the army, Stuart joined the Inland Revenue, living in Carlisle, where he spent the rest of his life. He died in 2003, and at his funeral the coffin was led by four pipers from his Tuesday evening piping group, playing *The Rowan Tree*. As it was borne into the church, they played his favourite piece, *The Fair Maid of Barra*, and during the committal, *Highland Cathedral* was played on Stuart's own pipe, which had once been his father's, in Rum.

His obituary, written by Roy Armstrong-Wilson and published in the *Piping Times* in December 2003, ends with the words: 'My abiding memory of him will be of his generosity, his good manners and his Highland courtesy exemplified by the way he stood on the step, when you left, until you were out of sight'.

Sources

John A. Love, *The Island of Rum*
Celtic Monthly
Piping Times

Raasay

To reach Raasay, go across to Skye and up the east coast of the island, towards Portree. At Sconser, on Loch Sligachan, a small car ferry leaves regularly for Raasay. The crossing takes fifteen minutes. There are not many roads on the island, and parts of it are accessible only on foot or by boat.

The name Raasay, pronounced with the stress on the first syllable, RAAS-ay, is Norse, possibly meaning 'tide-race island' with reference to the unusual tides to the west of the island, between it and Skye. The incoming tide comes in from both north and south, meeting near the middle of the west side of the island, sometimes causing, on the flood, unpleasantly rough conditions for small boats. The Gaelic spelling Ratharsaidh is, however, against this interpretation – but Gaelic speakers seem uncertain of the meaning. Its neighbouring island, Rona, has an undoubtedly Norse name (hraun-oy 'rough rock island') which makes it likely that Raasay is also a Norse name.

Latterly, Raasay has had an unhappy history under a succession of hated landlords, but this has not prevented the musical and poetic life of the people from developing a rich culture. The main piping families were the MacKays, who were pipers to the MacLeod Lairds of Raasay from the mid-18th century to the mid-19th; and the MacLeans, whose talents flowered to the full in the 20th century. We have glimpses of earlier pipers and poets, but these are tantalisingly sparse. It is evident that the late burgeoning was a final culmination of all the talent which had gone before, building on foundations laid by their forefathers.

Raasay was important in the development of modern piping, as John MacKay, Raasay, was the great authority on piobaireachd in the late 18th and early 19th centuries, and his son Angus wrote down and published the music he had learned from John. Angus is regarded as the father of modern playing, of both piobaireachd and light music, and is held as an authority even today. His importance cannot be over-estimated.

Tunes Associated with Raasay

Tunes associated with Raasay include:

The Battle of Arras, by William MacLean
The Battle of Waterloo, by John MacKay P 9
Climbing Duncaan, by William MacLean R 3
Davidson of Tulloch's Salute (or *Duncan Davidson's Salute*), by John MacKay P 9
Farewell to the Laird of Islay, by Angus MacKay P 7
The Island of Raasay, by A.R. MacLeod/B. MacRae 6/8 J 4
Lachlan MacLean's Welcome to Rockcliffe, by William MacLean 2/4 M 4
Lachlan MacNeill Campbell of Kintarbert's Salute, by John MacKay P 9
Lady D'Oyley's Salute, by John MacKay P 7
Lament for Captain Donald MacKenzie, by John MacKay P 7
Lament for Colin Roy MacKenzie P 7 (6 variations by Angus MacKay)
Lament for the Earl of Seafield, by William MacLean P
Lament for John Garve (Iain Garbh) MacLeod of Raasay, by Patrick Mor MacCrimmon P 8

Lament for King George III, by John MacKay P 9
Lt. Col. H.K. Kemble of Knock, by William MacLean 6/8 M 4
MacLeod of Colbecks' Lament, by John MacKay P 9
MacLeod of Raasay's Salute, by Angus MacKay, Gairloch P 6
Melbank's Salute, by John MacKay P 7
Mrs MacLeod of Raasay R 2
The Old Grey Wife of Raasay, possibly by Iain Dall MacKay R 2
Prince Charles' Lament, by Captain Malcolm MacLeod P
Raasay Bay, by Norman MacDonald 2/4 M 4
The Raasay Highlanders, by William MacLean
Raasay House, by A.M. Lee, piper 2/4 M 4
Roderick Dall MacKay's Lament = MacLeod of Colbecks' Lament P 9
Salute to the Highland Society of London P 7

Angus MacKay, Raasay, composed a number of light music tunes, and also 'made over' or arranged several existing tunes, mainly two-part traditional quicksteps, using them as the basis for bigger competition marches.

John Garve MacLeod of Raasay's Lament

This is sometimes called *Iain Garbh's Lament,* but in Gaelic MacLeod of Raasay was known as GilleChaluim or MacGilleChaluim.

John Garve was renowned for his strength and good looks, and for his likable character. He had become the 7th chief of the Raasay MacLeods in 1648, having been reared at Dunvegan, as a child, in the care of Mary MacLeod. He was married to Janet, daughter of Sir Rory Mor MacLeod, and this is the reason for attributing the composition to Patrick Mor MacCrimmon (or possibly to Patrick Og, depending on the date of Patrick Mor's death, which is uncertain, but thought to have been around 1670. From the maturity and finely developed quality of the work, it is more likely, perhaps, to be late Patrick Mor than early Patrick Og). Alexander Nicolson, in his *History of Skye,* wrote that Patrick Mor 'gave expression to his grief in that epic *piobaireachd* that is rightly considered by the masters of our classic music to be at once the loftiest and the most soul-subduing melody of its kind'.

The Rev. James Fraser gave us the account of John Garve's death, preserved in the Wardlaw manuscript:

This April [1671] the Earle of Seaforth duelling [dwelling] in the Lewes [Lewis], a dredful accident happened. His lady being brought to bed there, the Earle sent for John Garve McKleud, Laird of Rarzay, to

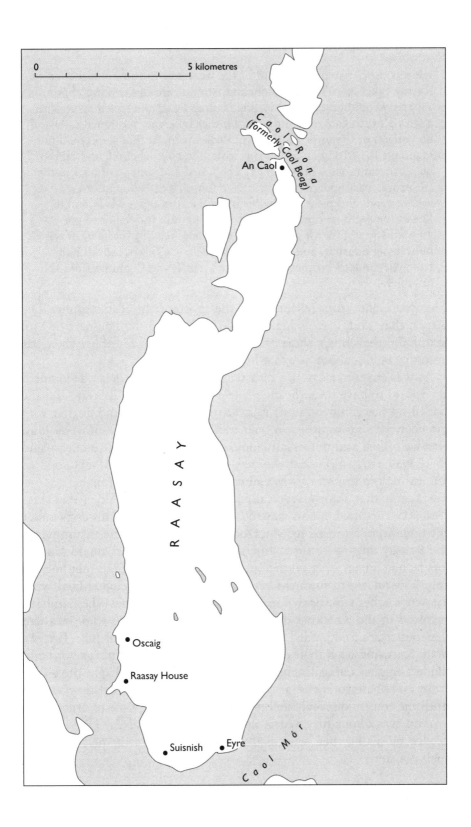

0   5 kilometres

Caol Rona
(formerly Caol Beag)

An Caol •

R A A S A Y

• Oscaig

• Raasay House

• Suisnish   • Eyre

Caol Mòr

> witness the christening; and, after the treat and solemnity of the feast, Rarsay takes leave to goe home, and, after a rant of drinking uppon the shoare, went aboard off his birling [sailing boat] and sailed away with a strong north gale off wind; and whither by giving too much saile and no ballast, or the unskillfullness of the seamen, or that they could not mannage the strong Dutch canvas saile, the boat whelmd, and all the men dround in view of the coast. The Laird and sixteen of his kinsmen, the prime, perished; non of them ever found; a grewhound or two cast ashore dead; and pieces of the birling. One Alexander Mackleod in Lewes the night before had a voice warning him thrice not to goe at all with Rarsey, for all would drown in there return; yet he went with him, being infatuat, and drownd with the rest. This account I had from Alexander's brother the summer after. It was drunkness did the mischiefe.

The poets and story-tellers made the most of this catastrophe. The waves, they said, rose as high as the Cuillin, and the boulders of Mol Stamhain (the shingle shore at Staffin) were hurled far above the cliffs onto dry land – about 300 feet high.

As was customary after a disaster such as this, a witch was blamed: she is said to have been the chief's wet-nurse, living in Raasay, and she boiled up her cauldron until it suddenly boiled over, and at that very moment the ship went down. Her motive is not entirely clear, as John was well-liked and universally mourned, but Somhairle MacLean said there was a tradition that she was bribed to do it by MacDonald of Duntulm, and this story was embroidered with lurid detail.

It seems that John Garve called in at Duntulm, in Skye, the Mac-Donald stronghold, on his way to Lewis. During dinner, his dogs under the table were attacked by MacDonald's dogs, and in the ensuing fight the Raasay dogs were the winners. This annoyed MacDonald (doubt-less he had a heavy bet on the outcome), to such an extent that he paid John's wet-nurse to summon her occult powers in revenge. Many well-known witches were drawn in to help her (the same ones who had been involved in the wrecking of the Spanish Armada), and some of them flew out to sea and landed on the yards and gunwhale of John Garve's boat. Knowing what their presence meant, he drew his great sword and made a mighty cut at the nearest of them, missed, and split the galley from gunwhale to keel – and down she went. (Why had they waited until the return journey? Well, these things do take time to organise.)

John was about fifty years old, but had no children. He was suc-ceeded by his brother, who died within a year, and the heir was then their cousin.

John MacInnes (*TGSI* LVI 1985) said there was a Raasay tradition that some time after the Chief's death, he was seen steering his birlinn between Raasay and Skye and was heard chanting an oar-song (iorram) as he urged on his spectral crew. The refrain of the song was *Buille oirre ho ro an ceann*, where the command *Buille an ceann* ('Aim the head') is divided by the meaningless vocables *oirre ho ro*. Of this song, Bella MacLeod (Beileag an Achaidh) could recall only one couplet:

Ged a reidhinn-sa 'na' Chlachan	Though we make it to the Clachan
Chan aithnicheadh iad co bha ann –	They do not recognise who it is –
Buille oirre, etc	Aim the head, etc

A suitably eerie verse.

Alexander Nicolson tells of a tradition in Raasay that on every Friday for a full year after his death, one of his sisters, named Janet, composed and sang a new lament to his memory. One of these, the *Raasay Lament*, has survived, a song of poignant sorrow. Sorley MacLean quoted it in his paper 'Some Raasay Traditions', and it appears as Appendix 2 in Norma MacLeod's book on Raasay.

It is called in Gaelic *'S mi 'nam Shuidh' air an Fhaoilinn*, ('And I Sitting above the Shore'). The third and fourth lines of each verse are the first and second of the next verse, and the refrain between each verse probably represents sorrowful keening. It goes:

'S mi 'nam shuidh' air an fhaoilinn,	And I sitting above the shore,
'S mi gun fhaoilte, gun fhuran,	And I without cheer, or welcoming joy,
Cha thog mi fonn aotrom	I will not sing a lightsome air
O Dhi-h-aoine mo dhunaidh.	Since the Friday of my woe.
Refrain:	Refrain:

Hi leo:
Hil o ro ho:
Hil o ro bha ho
Hil o ho robhan hil leo

On a chailleadh am bata	Since the boat was lost
Is a bhathadh an curaidh	And the hero was drowned
Siod na fir a bha laidir	Those were the strong men
Ged a sharaich a'mhuir iad	Though the sea overcame them

Gille Chalum a b'oige	Gille Chaluim the youngest
'S Iain Mor, mo sgeol duilich	And Iain Mor, my sad tale
Ann an clachan gun traghadh	In the burial place without ebbing
Tha mo ghradh-sa air uirigh	My beloved is on his couch
Thu gun bhann air do leinidh	You are without a band on your shirt
'S i gun fheum air a cumadh	And it without need for shape
Thu gun shiod air do chluasaig	You are without silk on your pillow
Air lic uaine na tuinne	On the green slabs under the waves
Tha do chlaidheamh 'na dhublan	Your sword is in its scabbard
'S e fo dhrudhadh nan uinneag	Soaked by the leaking windows
Co 's urrainn a ghiulan	Who is able to wield it
No ruisgeas e tuilleadh	Or unsheath it evermore
Tha do mhiol-chion air iallaibh	Your hounds are on leashes
'S iad gun triall thun a' mhunaidh	And they have not gone to the hills
Tha do choinnl' air an smuradh	Your candle is snuffed out
'S tu gun duil ri bhi tilleadh.	With no hope of your return.

One tradition attributes this to John's wet-nurse, repenting of her evil ways, but it is usually ascribed to his sister.

Another poem lamenting John Garve begins:

'Seal a mach an e 'n la e	Look out to see if it is daylight
'S mi ri feitheamh na faire	And me awaiting the dawn
Leis an luasgan th' air m' aigne	With the upheaval on my spirit
Chan euil an cadal 'na thamh dhomh	Sleep is not a rest for me . . .

and it finishes:

Tha a'ghairr-thonn 'gad luasgadh	The turbulent waves are tossing you
Is 'gad bhualadh ri stalla	And knocking you against the rocks
'S tha do ghairdean gun tuairmse	And your arm has no movement
Ge bu chruaidh e na 'n darach.	Though it was harder than oak.

These songs were handed down from generation to generation in the family of Sorley MacLean.

Another poem at one time attributed to Mary MacLeod is now ascribed to Janet, John Garve's sister. It starts:

Och nan och 's mi fo leireadh	O alas for the hero
Mar a dh'eiridh do'n	whom the sea-wave is hiding;
ghaisgeach;	
Chan'eil sealgair na sithne	to the mountain chase now
An diugh am frith nam beann	you will not be riding.
casa.	

And it ends:

Ach b'i an doinean bha iargalt,	But fierce was the gale
Le gaoth a'n iar-thuath 's	and your sail it has tattered;
cruaidh fhrasan;	
Thog i a'mhuir 'na mill	it has roused the black waves
dhubhghorm	
'S smuais i an iubhrach 'na	and your brave boat is
sadan.	shattered.

(This somewhat banal translation is by J. Carmichael Watson.)

Mary MacLeod, his former nurse or governess, made a *Marbhrann* or Elegy for John Garve. It goes:

Mo bheud is mo chradh	It is harm to me, and anguish,
Mar a dh'eiridh da	what has happened to
An fhear ghleusta ghraidh	the skilful well-loved man
Bha treun 'san spairn	who was strong in conflict
Is nach faicear gu brath an	and will not be seen in Raasay
Ratharsaidh.	again.

Bu tu am fear curanta mor	You were a great hero
Bu mhath cumadh is treoir	strongly built
o t'uilinn gu d'dhorn	from your elbow to your fist,
o d'mhullach gu d'bhroig:	from your crown to your shoe:
Mhic Mhuire mo leon	Son of Mary! it hurts me
Thu bhith an innis nan ron	is that you are in the seals' pasture
is nach faighear thu.	and will not be found.

Bu tu sealgair a' gheoidh,	You were a hunter of the wild goose,
Lamh gun dearmad gun leon	your hand unerring and unblemished
Air am bu shuarach an t-or	which was generous in giving gold
Thoirt a bhuannachd a'cheoil,	as a reward for music;
Is gun d'fhuair thu na's leoir	for you have plenty and would spend
is na caitheadh tu.	freely.

Bu tu sealgair an fheidh	You were a hunter of the deer,
Leis an deargta na bein;	by whom hides were reddened;
Bhiodh coin earbsach air eill	trusty hounds were held on the leash
Aig an Albannach threun;	by the mighty man of Alba (Scotland);

Caite am faca mi fein	where have I seen
Aon Duine fo'n grein	any man beneath the sun
A dheanadh riut euchd	who would challenge you in heroic
flathasach?	deeds?

Spealp nach diobradh	A fine fellow, you did not falter
An cath no an stri thu,	in strife or in battle;
Casan direach	your limbs were straight,
Fada finealt:	long and shapely;
Mo creach dhiobhail alas,	the pity of it,
Chaidh tu a dhith oirnn	you are lost to us
Le neart sine,	by the strength of the storm,
Lamh nach diobradh	you whose hand always sailed your
caitheadh oirre.	vessel hard.

Och m'eudail uam	Alas, my treasure taken from me,
Gun sgeul 'sa 'chuan	without trace in the ocean,
Bu ghle mhath snuadh	was very good to look on
Ri grein 's ri fuachd;	in sunshine and in cold;
Is e chlaoidh do shluagh	that is what has pained your people,
Nach d'fheud thu an uair a	that you could not reach them in that
ghabhail orra.	hour.

Is math thig gunna nach diult	A gun that does not fail
Air curaidh mo ruin	would suit my beloved warrior
Ann am mullach a'chuirn	on the summit of the mountain
Is air uilinn nan stuc;	or the corners of the rocks;
Gum biodh fuil ann air tus an	blood would flow at its first shot.
spreadhaidh sin.	

Is e dh'fhag silteach mo shuil	What brings a tear to my eye
Faicinn t'fhearainn gun surd,	is seeing your land without activity,
Is do bhaile gun smuid	now that your dwelling-place has no
	smoke
Fo charraig nan sugh,	under the wave-lashed rock,
Dheagh mhic Chaluim nan tur	excellent son of Calum of the
a Ratharsaidh.	towers, from Raasay.

Mo bheud is mo bhron	It is distress and sorrow to me
Mar a dh'eirich dho,	what has happened to him,
Muir beucach mor	a great roaring sea
Ag leum mu d'bhord,	leaping around your boat;
Thu fein is do sheoid	yourself and your stout crew
An uair reub ur seoil	when your sails ripped,
Nach d'fheud sibh treoir a	you had not the strength to sail her.
chaitheadh orra.	

Is tu b'fhaicillich' ceum	You were the least reckless,
Mu'n taice-sa an de	that time in former days,
De na chunnaic mi fein	of all I saw myself
Air faiche nan ceud	in a field of hundreds,
Air each 's e 'na leum,	mounted on a lively horse;
Is cha bu slacan gun fheum	and no sword was useless when
claidheamh ort.	you were carrying it.
Is math lubadh tu pic	Well could you bend a bow
O chulaibh do chinn	behind your head
An am rusgadh a 'ghill	while making a pledge of valour
Le ionnsaigh nach till	not to retreat in battle;
Is air mo laimh gum bu	and by my hand! your arrow flew
chinnteach saighead uat.	straight.
Is e an sgeul craiteach	This is a sore tale
Do'n mhnaoi a dh'fhag thu	for the wife you have left behind
Is do t'aon bhrathair	and for the only brother
A shuidh 'nad aite:	who has taken your place:
Di-luain Caisge	on Easter Monday
Chaidh tonn-bhaidhte ort	a drowning-wave came on you,
Craobh a b'airde de'n abhall thu.	you, the loftiest tree in the orchard.

Even in translation the quality of Mary's work shines through. It is thought that John Garve as a child had been one of her charges, along with the Chief's children at Dunvegan. It is clear that she felt a strong affection for him, all his life.

Sources

Wardlaw MS
Alexander Nicolson, *History of Skye*
Norma MacLeod, *Raasay*
Sorley MacLean *TGSI* XLIX
J.C. Watson, *The Songs of Mary MacLeod*
John MacInnes *TGSI* LVI 1989

MacLeod of Raasay's Salute

Angus MacKay, himself a Raasay man, said this was a Salute on the birth of James MacLeod of Raasay, in 1761, but Angus seemed uncertain whether the composer was Angus MacKay, Gairloch or his son, John Roy. If it was indeed made in 1761, the composer was Angus MacKay, Gairloch, the son of Iain Dall, the Blind Piper, as John Roy was not then born, or was still an infant. Angus is also said to have composed the *Desperate Battle of the Birds* and *MacKenzie of Applecross' Salute* – and some say he made *Mary's Praise,* but this is doubtful, as the story supporting the claim cannot be true.

If the date of the composition was 1761, that explains why it was made by one of the Gairloch MacKays and not one of the Raasay MacKay pipers: John MacKay, Raasay, was probably born in 1767, and his father Ruairidh may have been a piper but is not known to have been a composer.

James MacLeod of Raasay, born in 1761, was the 12th Chief, and brother-in-law of John MacLeod of Colbecks. He was the eldest of three brothers who had ten beautiful sisters, and his birth must have been both a relief and a cause of rejoicing in the family and on the island: the laird at last had his heir.

He later grew up to become an enthusiastic and somewhat guileless young man, apt to throw himself into grandiose schemes which he could not afford. He became Commanding Officer of the local regiment of Volunteers, formed as a defence against possible invasion by Napoleon, and seems to have enjoyed with great relish this experience of military command, to the amusement of his more sophisticated fellow-officers.

Later, he plunged the estate deep into debt by ambitious schemes for expansion and development in Raasay, and died a comparatively poor man, in or around 1824. He had had John MacKay as his piper until shortly before that, but John had left Raasay, probably in 1823, when the estate became too impoverished to support him.

John MacLeod seems to have been a likeable if unreliable fellow, but his character in later life is irrelevant if the Salute was made to celebrate his birth.

Sources

Angus MacKay, Manuscript
Alexander Nicolson, *History of Skye*
Norma MacLeod, *Raasay*

The Piping Mackays of Raasay

John Mackay, Raasay

There is much confusion about the MacKay pipers of Gairloch and those of Raasay, and this confusion is made worse by the same names appearing in the same sequence in the descent lines (*sloinneaidhean*) of both families.

They have much in common. Both seem to be descended from Mac-Kays in the north of Sutherland who came south, the Gairloch family in the early 17th century, the Raasay ancestor about 150 years later. Both the forebears who came south were called Ruairidh (Rory), and both of these had an only son called Iain or John, and grandsons named Angus and John, so that reverting to a Gaelic patronymic line (Aonghas mac Iain 'ic Ruairidh) gives no clarity. No link between the two families has been traced, but they were probably distantly related.

So, for the sake of clarity, though not consistency, pipers commonly differentiate between the two lines using the following names:

GAIRLOCH

RORY GAIRLOCH, sometimes called *Ruairidh Dall*, Blind Rory, but he was not blind. Came to Gairloch around 1609. A piper.

His only son *IAIN DALL*, the *Blind Piper of Gairloch* (1656–1754)

Had two sons, *JOHN* born c.1731 (went to Canada) and *ANGUS MacKAY GAIRLOCH* (c.1723–c.1775)

Angus' son *JOHN ROY*, born c.1760, went to Nova Scotia in 1805 with all his family.

RAASAY

RUAIRIDH RAASAY(Rory Raasay), rarely mentioned as he does not seem to have been a piper. Came to Raasay around 1750 or a little later. Died youngish.

His only son *JOHN MacKAY Raasay* (c.1767–1848)

Had four piping sons including *JOHN MacKAY junior* (1815–1848) and *ANGUS MacKAY RAASAY* (1813–1859). Both wrote piobaireachd manuscripts.

Angus' nephew was *DONALD MacKAY.*

Using this muddled method, a reference to 'John MacKay junior' should pinpoint the younger brother of the famous Angus MacKay, Raasay, without further explanation, and there should be no problem in distiguishing him from 'John Roy', the grandson of Iain Dall. I am aware that so naming the members of these two families will irritate Gaelic purists, who might not accept the use of Iain and John as forms of the one name within one family; but this is the pipers' practice, and, I repeat, it is for clarity, and it seems to work, even for English speakers, who are easily confused.

Little is known of Ruairidh Raasay, other than that he came from the MacKays of Strathnaver in northern Sutherland, settled in Eyre, in the south of Raasay (we do not know why there, but assume it was because he was employed by MacLeod of Eyre), had two children, a son John and a daughter Christina, before he succumbed to an illness, possibly tuberculosis, when he was in his twenties (it is thought). His wife had died in childbirth, and the two children were left destitute. John was old enough to be employed as a herd-boy by the Laird, Captain MALCOLM MACLEOD of Eyre and Brae, who was himself a piper and taught some of the local boys.

Captain Malcolm had been an officer in the Jacobite army in the '45, and on his return had helped in the escape of the Prince. He was captured and taken to London with Flora MacDonald, but after some months both were released.

In 1773, it was Malcolm who rowed over to Skye to fetch Dr Johnson and Boswell on a visit to the Laird of Raasay at Raasay House. Boswell described him at sixty-two years of age: 'hale and well proportioned, with a manly countenance, tanned by the weather, yet having a ruddiness in his cheeks, over which his beard extended. His eye was quick and lively, yet his look was not fierce, but he appeared at once firm and good humoured. He wore a pair of brogues; tartan knee hose which came up nearly to his knees and left them bare; a purple camblet kilt; a black waistcoat; a short green cloth coat bound with gold cord; a yellowish bushy wig; a large blue bonnet with a good thread button. I never saw a figure that gave a more perfect representation of a Highland gentleman ... I found him frank and polite, in the true sense of the word'. (Camblet was an English word for a type of material made of fine wool, similar to worsted but of a looser weave.)

This clothing was Malcolm's formal wear. It was Malcolm who gave us the only known contemporary comment on Iain Dall, the Blind Piper of Gairloch: of him, Malcolm said he knew of no one who added more to the conviviality of an evening.

Tradition has it that the young herd-boy, John MacKay, Raasay, who could afford neither lessons nor an instrument, used to listen to the other lads learning and practising, and while out on the hill, herding cattle, he made himself a chanter from a hollow stick, with a straw for the reed. On this he played the music he had learnt by ear, and one day his Laird happened to hear him playing, out in the open. He recognised the boy's talent, and took him on as a pupil.

Here tradition falters a little. Once Malcolm had taught the boy all he could, he sent him – to whom? John would have been probably in his teens, around 1780. Both the Blind Piper and his son Angus were dead by then, and Donald Ruadh MacCrimmon was in America. John may have gone to Angus Gairloch's son, John Roy, at Gairloch, or perhaps to Iain Dubh MacCrimmon, Donald Ruadh's brother, in Skye. Iain had returned from an abortive attempt to emigrate: changing his mind when he reached Greenock, he resumed his life in Skye.

John Roy is said to have earlier been sent up to Sutherland to learn to play dance music on the small pipe, but there is no evidence that he passed it on to John MacKay. John Gibson suggests that John MacKay might have gone to Donald Ruadh in Skye in the 1790s, after Donald's return from America; others have thought he went before the college closed and Donald emigrated. The latter theory is based on a handwritten note in Angus MacKay's manuscript: it says that Captain MacLeod sent John 'to the College of the MacCrimmons for three six-months' – but the authenticity of this has been doubted, as Donald left for America in 1770, and it is thought that John MacKay was born around 1767.

Certainly John MacKay is credited with MacCrimmon training, and it is evident that he went to at least one master of piobaireachd. It seems most likely that although the MacCrimmon school was closed, he went to one of Iain Dubh's farms in Skye for tuition, presumably funded by Malcolm of Eyre. The MacLeod connection makes it more likely that he went to Iain than that he looked to the MacArthurs in Trotternish for instruction. In any case, the last MacArthur teacher in Skye seems to have been Donald, who drowned in or soon after 1780.

In the 1970s, Angus MacPherson, son of Calum Piobaire and landlord of the Inveran Hotel in Sutherland, made a tape recording in which he said: 'I know for a fact that my grandfather Angus MacPherson, or the Piobaire Chaim as they called him in Skye, had lessons from John MacCrimmon at Boreraig – he and Angus MacKay who was the son of the great John MacKay of Raasay. They lived beside one another on the island of Raasay and got further lessons from John MacKay, and they played together on the braes of Raasay. My father was born there and naturally he got his piping to begin with from his own father – my grandfather (Angus Cam).' Angus may be mistaken as to Calum's birthplace, but he is pretty definite that both Angus MacKay and Angus Cam went to Iain Dubh MacCrimmon in Skye. This tape, however, recorded when Angus was over ninety, contains a great deal of faulty information, and its evidence should be approached with caution.

Whoever it was that taught John MacKay, Raasay, he had plenty of piobaireachd. John was said to have at least 250 piobaireachd works in his head, and never mixed them up. He was probably illiterate and unable to read music, so all his knowledge was transmitted by ear. Perhaps we should bear in mind that Iain Dubh is said to have passed some 200 works on to Niel MacLeod of Gesto, around this time, and in 1790 or thereabouts, Donald Ruadh returned from the New World. In the 1790s both brothers were living in Skye, with tenancies at different times at Boreraig, Borodale, Trien and Hamara (Glendale).

There is also a story that John MacKay went to Donald MacRa, a piping soldier who came from Applecross, and later retired to Kyleakin. After leaving the army Donald is said to have lived for a time in Raasay. In later years, both Donald MacRa and John MacKay lived in Kyleakin, but overlapped by only a few years, when both were elderly, with their reputations established; John would not have been taking lessons at that stage.

When John returned to Raasay as a trained player, he became piper to the Laird of Raasay, John MacLeod; John had succeeded his father as laird in 1745, and died in 1786, after which his son James took over. John MacKay probably served as piper to both John and James, living at Raasay House when required, but keeping on his house at Eyre, for his family.

John MacKay married a girl called Margaret MacLean, of a Raasay family. When Dr Alasdair MacLean was asked if he was of the same MacLean family, his answer was 'I hope so', but he did not think he was. John and Margaret had a family of four sons and five daughters, and all four sons were excellent players. Dr Alasdair MacLean discussed the family in his lecture at Stirling Castle in 1997 (see below).

The Raasay laird's household included two nieces, Eliza and Isabel Ross; they had been orphaned, and their uncle was bringing them up. Eliza had 'a good knowledge of musical theory' (Norma MacLeod), and was an accomplished pianist. She transcribed a number of piobaireachd works into staff notation, for the piano, apparently basing them on the playing of her uncle's piper, John MacKay. Four of these were written in the manuscript known as the Eliza Ross or Lady D'Oyly MS, now held by the School of Scottish Studies, Edinburgh University. It is dated 1812, the year before Angus MacKay was born.

We might surmise that this contact with Eliza Ross was the inspiration for Angus, John's third son, who was able to write pipe music in staff notation even as a boy. It seems likely that it was Eliza who taught him. Later, Eliza went to India where she married Sir Charles D'Oyley. When she returned to visit Raasay, she brought John MacKay a present, an elaborately carved set of pipes, made in India. In thanks, he composed a piobaireachd work, *Lady D'Oyley's Salute*, to honour her. It would be interesting to know whether these pipes were good to play, or if they were the sort you nail to the wall above the bar, for others to admire.

All his life, John MacKay, Raasay, had this habit of repaying generosity shown to him by naming one of his piobaireachd compositions for a benefactor; his talent for composition was, after all, his form of currency, and he could not hope to match generous gifts or financial payments in any other way. He seems to have had a keen appreciation of monetary reward, probably stemming from his childhood of terrible deprivation.

He made *Davidson of Tulloch's Salute* when Duncan Davidson of Tulloch Castle, near Dingwall, sent him such pupils as the young John Ban MacKenzie. *Melbank's Salute*, which should really be *Millbank's Salute*, was named for Alexander MacKenzie of Millbank, on the outskirts of Dingwall. The name was translated into Gaelic as *Maolbanc*, and back into English distorted into *Melbank*. Alexander MacKenzie was one of the Gairloch MacKenzies, a grandson of the 9th Laird; he had inherited a fortune from his mother, and spent it lavishly on many good causes, including the piping education of young local players of promise, such as John Ban MacKenzie, Donald Cameron and Donald's younger brother Alexander. Millbank spent £20,000 and died destitute, leaving his wife and daughters penniless.

Another of John MacKay Raasay's compositions was *Lachlan Mac-Neill Campbell of Kintarbert's Salute*, made, according to John's son Angus, in 1836. It should not be confused with *Lachlan MacNeill Campbell of Kintarbert's Fancy*, which is an older work, and has no links with John MacKay. The Salute, which is in Angus MacKay's manuscript, has the date 1836 pencilled in by Angus, and that may well be the date that the work was made. That title, however, cannot have been given to it until two years later: before 1838, Lachlan was plain

Lachlan MacNeill of Drumdrishaig, a designation he inherited from his father, but in 1838, the last of his three uncles, his mother's brothers, died childless, and Lachlan inherited his grandfather's estate of Kintarbert. He then added Campbell to his name and joined the Argyll gentry. He was an accomplished piper, a player of piobaireachd taught by the great John MacKay, and he became one of the judges at the national competitions in Edinburgh.

Lachlan probably went to John MacKay for tuition in the 1830s, and must have paid generously, as the Salute was John's acknowledgement. He was presumably also a friend, possibly a pupil, of John's son Angus, since Angus wrote out for him a handsome volume of piobaireachd works, known now as the Kintarbert Manuscript. This was presented to Lachlan, whose brother, on inheriting it, passed it on to Sir Charles Forbes of Newe. It was picked up later by Lt John MacLennan, who left it to his son, G.S. MacLennan. On his death in 1929, the manuscript volume went to his son, George, and it was George's widow, Jessie MacLennan, who generously gave it to the National Library of Scotland, in Edinburgh. (For a description of the manuscript and its contents, see Roderick Cannon, *Piping Times*, vol. 51, issue 10, July 1999.)

Another of John MacKay's works was his *Lament for Captain Donald MacKenzie*. The Captain, who died in 1819, was a MacKenzie of Applecross, the husband of Anne MacLeod (one of the ten daughters of the Laird of Raasay). He had been a Captain in the 100th Regiment of Foot, in the Napoleonic Wars. After his death his daughter Maria was living at Applecross as the ward of her cousin Thomas when she eloped with the piper John Ban MacKenzie, in 1832.

There is a belief (and it appears in the Piobaireachd Society Book 15, which also gives the wrong date for the disaster) that Captain Donald lost his life in the wreck of the steamship *Comet II* in October 1825: the ship was run down in the dark in the Clyde estuary, with the loss of more than eighty lives, including that of John Ban MacKenzie's younger brother, Ronald. The lists of the bodies recovered include a Donald MacKenzie, married to an Anne MacLeod, but a descendant of Captain Donald, Miss Virginia van der Lande, has shown that this was a different Donald, and the Captain had died of natural causes some years earlier.

In 1835, John was commissioned to compose a *Salute to the Highland Society of London*, who ran the Edinburgh competitions. Some consider it is rather a 'pot-boiler', lacking inspiration, though it is a pleasant enough work.

All of the surviving compositions of John MacKay, Raasay, seem to have been made in the 19th century, after his return from the army. In the 1790s, under threat from the French and from potential rebellion in Ireland, several companies of Highlanders were raised, for national defence. John MacLeod 2nd of Colbecks raised one such, mainly from Raasay men, and in 1799 it was sent to Ireland. It is thought to have been the last Highland Volunteer company to be sent out of Scotland on military service. It was commanded by MacLeod of Colbecks, and the regimental piper was John MacKay. The company seems to have been raised around 1796 or 1797, and it was disbanded in 1802.

Rebecca MacKay has a story of Christina, the sister of John Mac-Kay, back at home in Raasay, hearing the sound of pipes as someone played while walking up from the ferry. She said 'If I didn't know that my brother was away with the army in foreign parts, I would say that was his playing' – and it was, he was home, so the date must have been 1802. His sister had a keen appreciation of his playing and knew it intimately, as she took part in his teaching (see below).

John MacInnes had a story current in Raasay about John MacKay, told by Malcolm MacKay (Calum Ruairi) in Fearns, one of the same family. He said that am Piobaire ('the Piper', not named, but it was John) was challenged by a rival, to a competition in which each would play his own composition. This was to be held away from Raasay, perhaps even away from Skye. On the journey to the competition, John was in a boat with a number of others going to hear the piping. He sat on a thwart, fingering his tune on a stick, and unknown to him, his rival, whom he had never met, was in the boat, watching him intently. He studied every movement of John's fingers until he himself had mastered John's tune.

At the competition, the rival played first – and he played John's composition, passing it off as his own, and won the day. I have to say I find this unlikely. How did he know, for example, that what John was fingering was the tune he planned to play? Ah well, it is only a story.

For the next twenty years, John remained in Raasay, living at Eyre and as piper to the Laird in Raasay House; by now, this was James 9th Laird of Raasay. Dr Alasdair told a Raasay story, probably apocryphal, of an occasion when John MacKay was playing his pipe in front of Raasay House, while another employee was trying to rake the gravel of the drive, 'no doubt to their mutual annoyance'. The raker remarked 'There you are, John, with the Devil's black sticks', to which John replied 'And there you are, with Satan's great rake.' Honours even.

At Eyre there are the ruins of a house on the site of John's former home, but this was not the house in which he had lived. His house was pulled down in a clearance of tenants, after he had left in 1823 or thereabouts. Incoming tenants in the mid-19th century, known as the Raiders, rebuilt on the same spot; the house may have been erected on the foundations of the previous building. The estate prosecuted, and some of the Raiders served prison sentences. Their houses were pulled down or had their roofs removed. The remaining walls now stand about five feet high, the dwelling roofless and forlorn. The site is magnificent with views over Skye and Scalpay and the sea. It must be very exposed in winter.

Was it at the Eyre house or at Raasay House that John composed most of his works? In 1815 he made the magnificent *Battle of Waterloo*. As an army man he would have been fully aware of the danger of invasion by Napoleon Bonaparte – indeed, all of Britain was in fear – and this work expresses the general feeling of relief and exultation when the threat was finally lifted. But his *Lament for King George III* (1820) is more puzzling. Did John MacKay really feel much sorrow for the loss of the King, so far away, so alien to his own way of life? Was this work commissioned, perhaps by his Laird or some bigwig in Skye? It has phrases reminiscent of his masterpiece, *MacLeod of Colbecks' Lament*, which was composed some three years later. This might suggest that *Colbecks'* was a final flowering of music which had been simmering in his mind.

MacLeod of Colbecks' Lament, or as it is often called now, *Lament for MacLeod of Colbeck*, was composed probably in 1823, when Colbecks died. The older title preserves the final *s* of the designation used in his own time, indicating that there was more than one estate called Colbeck belonging to MacLeod, as indeed we know there was. One was in Raasay, the other in Jamaica, a sugar plantation which gave the family its prosperity.

The location of Colbeck in Raasay has been disputed, but it is likely that it was the place in North Raasay now known as Kyle Rona, marked on the Ordnance Survey map as An Caol. The house is named after the narrow channel of water between the islands of Raasay and Rona, the strait now called Kyle (or Caol) Rona, but once known as Caol Beag 'little strait', as opposed to the channel to the south of Raasay, which is Caol Mor 'big strait'. The Gaelic Caol Beag gives us the anglicised spelling Colbeck.

The MacLeod family who had Colbeck, apparently in Raasay, started the sugar plantation in Jamaica, and named it after their home, so that they had two holdings of the same name. This was not uncommon in the 18th century, and when it happened, a plural form was created by adding a final -s. So MacLeod became 'of Colbecks', and this is in the old spellings of the name of John MacKay's Lament. It was sometimes spelled Colbex. After the family line died out, the name of the house, farm or estate of Colbeck seems to have been changed to Caol Rona or simply Caol, and this explains why no other trace of Colbeck has been found. Caol (Rona) is at the northern end of the island.

The 1st Laird of Colbecks, John MacLeod, father of the subject of the Lament, was married to Janet MacLeod, daughter of Malcolm, 8th Laird of Raasay. She was a sister of the Laird with the ten daughters. John 1st of Colbecks acquired land in Jamaica, and the plantation made him his fortune. The ruins of it, still called Colbeck, are said to be still there, though the plantation ceased production long ago.

In 1762 (possibly 1783 – Alexander Mackenzie said this was Col John, not his father), John registered his arms, giving his lineage as John of Colbecks, son of Donald MacLeod of Lewis, son of John, son of Torcall, son of John 'only brother germane' of Roderick the last Baron of Lewis (Ruairidh Chaluim). This genealogy may be fanciful in part, but because of it, the MacLeods of Colbecks claimed to be male heirs of the MacLeods of Lewis.

John's son, also John MacLeod, is thought to have served in the Dutch Brigade, where he reached the rank of Colonel. But in the 1790s, he raised a company of Highland Volunteers (see above), and it may be that he acquired his rank from this. He was away with the regiment from 1799 until 1802. On his return he lived as a wealthy 'nabob' in Edinburgh, and does not appear to have returned to Raasay.

He married Jean, seventh of the Laird's ten daughters, who was his first cousin. They had several children, but his only surviving son, Barlow, died of a fever in London, in 1808. There were five daughters, only one of whom, Susan, married. She had two sons, but they did not inherit the designation of Colbecks.

Colonel John of Colbecks himself died in 1823, leaving a wife and daughters, but no male heir to the Colbeck line. When John MacKay made this lovely Lament, which many regard as the last 'real' piobaireachd work (as modern compositions seem to lack the former quality of the genre), he was lamenting not only the loss of his colonel, a prominent local figure, but also the end of the line of the MacLeods of Colbecks.

John MacKay was in Raasay until about 1823, living at Eyre. Here he taught a succession of pupils, sent to him by prominent landowners for their training. John Ban MacKenzie, the two Cameron boys, Donald and Alexander, Archibald Munro (who later taught Calum Piobaire

MacPherson) and Calum's father, Angus Cam MacPherson, Duncan MacMaster (who became piper to MacLean of Coll), and of course his own four sons: all of these pupils became distinguished players and testimony to the quality of John MacKay's teaching.

A description of his teaching has come down to us, but it is third-hand at best, and may have become distorted through time. It was written by J.F. Campbell and published in his (useless) pamphlet called *Canntaireachd*, in 1880; it says that Duncan Ross, piper to the Duke of Argyll, had been told as a boy by 'old John MacKenzie' – whom everyone assumes to have been John Ban – about lessons with John MacKay. We have to be cautious in accepting this account because Duncan Ross adds comments about his informant which cannot be true if it was John Ban (e.g. he says 'old John MacKenzie' was fully four score years old when he knew him, and we know that John Ban died at sixty-seven).

According to this account, John MacKay taught a class of several pupils, in the living-room of his house at Eyre. His sister (Christina) would be sitting beside the fire. John would play a line of the work they were learning, and he always turned his back on the pupils and faced the wall as he played. Presumably he did this to make sure that the pupils learned by ear, and not 'off the fingers'. His sister would then sing exactly what John had played – we assume this was in canntaireachd – and each pupil in turn had to sing it back to her until he had it right. Then they played it on the chanter. And so they proceeded to the next line, until they had mastered the whole work.

This description may have been subjected to a certain amount of Victorian romanticism which relished anything old and 'quaint', but it has a ring of truth about it. It is perhaps of interest that it was John's sister who sang; the singing of piobaireachd songs was traditionally a woman's role, but their singing of piobaireachd itself in accurate canntaireachd is rare, or at least rarely mentioned. She may have used a form of the MacCrimmon canntaireachd, as exemplified in Gesto's Collection and developed in Australia by Simon Fraser.

It was in the house at Eyre that all John's children were born, the third son being Angus in 1813. He was ten years old when his father made the decision to leave Raasay. As early as 1821, the Secretary of the Celtic Society was writing to the Secretary of the Highland Society of Scotland about John MacKay's financial difficulties as Raasay's piper, saying that John felt his abilities were unnoticed and his allowance 'so reduced that he could barely exist'. He was talking of emigration as a last resort.

Some say he left Raasay in 1822, when the laird's huge debts made it impossible for the estate to maintain a piper any longer. Others say he quit when the laird died in 1823, as he disliked the successor. Norma MacLeod has pointed out that if the next Laird succeeded in 1823 or 1824, he would have been still a minor, and when he came of age he had become an officer in the 78th Highlanders, and did not live in Raasay. The dates here are uncertain, and it is not known exactly when James 10th Laird died and his son succeeded. Whenever it was, John MacKay must have looked into the future and seen nothing for himself in Raasay, so he took the chance of employment elsewhere. But did he compose his *Lament for MacLeod of Colbecks* before he left? Or was it made at Drummond?

Another employee at Drummond left us a word picture of the arrival of the MacKay family, walking barefoot, with all their belongings packed into panniers on the backs of two ponies. It is a journey of well over a hundred miles, as the crow flies – as they, of course, did not. The youngest boy was then eight years old.

James MacLeod says it was only the three youngest sons who went with their parents: Donald was already piper to Clan Ranald, and the girls were all married, except for Cursty and Kitty Ogg, who remained at Eyre until 1830.

Dr Alasdair MacLean, in his lecture at Stirling Castle in 1997, told us about John MacKay's family. In 1793 he married Margaret MacLean, whose sister Christina was married to Peter MacKenzie, of another Raasay piping family, probably related to John Ban. Dr Alasdair said the claims of a link between his own line and Margaret's were derived from a family tree which had been fabricated for an American market, which involved a fictitious 'charter' for a croft at Fearns. It is only too easy to divert the course of history.

Angus MacKay left us a list of the children of John MacKay:

1. Katherine Mhor, 1790s, who died in infancy;
2. Donald, 1790s, who married Caroline Kenstain, and died in London, leaving three orphan children;
3. Mary, who married John MacKenzie, Castle Raasay, and died in Raasay;
4. Margaret, who married William Robertson in Badenoch, and died there;
5. Cursty (Christina), who married her cousin Alexander MacLean; they emigrated to Prince Edward Island in Canada;
6. Katherine Ogg, or Kitty Ogg, who married John Munro and went to live in Kyleakin, Isle of Skye;

7. Roderick, who married Elisa Gillis, Raasay; he died in Edinburgh in 1854, leaving four children;
8. Angus, 1813, who married Mary Johnstone Russell, and left four children;
9. John, 1815, who died unmarried, in London.

There is confusion about the two Katherines, of whom one died in infancy, because there was another Katherine Mhor who married Norman MacKenzie and went out to Prince Edward Island, Canada, where they had a large family. Dr Alasdair was of the opinion that the eldest-born of John MacKay was a Katherine who died in infancy, and that her name was then given to the next child, as was often the custom. It is not unusual to have two or more children with the same name in one family, as they were named after different relatives of their parents, on both sides.

Dr Alasdair said that Kitty Ogg married John Munro, who must have died in 1841. She was living, newly widowed, in Kyleakin, in the household of her brother Roderick, with their parents, John MacKay, then aged seventy-five, and Margaret, seventy. The surprise here is that the head of the house was not John, but his son Roderick, thirty, described in the Census as a Merchant, with his wife Elizabeth, twenty, and that John is said to have been Independent, i.e. had a private income. Does that refer to the fees he earned as a teacher? Or did he have a pension of some sort? Another in the family at Kyleakin was Margaret MacKay, fifteen, the only member of the household who was not born locally. Who was she?

Katherine (Kitty Ogg) is also said to have been Independent, and her two children were Duncan Munro, five, and Margaret, one month. Also in the house was Christina Munro, fifteen, a weaver's apprentice – was she Kitty's daughter, or John Munro's sister? The 1841 Census does not tell us the relationships.

Ten years later Kitty's widowed mother Margaret was still there, with Kitty and her two children, as well as the two orphaned sons of Margaret's son Donald. It is thought that John MacKay died there, in the house at Kyleakin, in 1848. Margaret was now Head of Household, and her daughter Kitty was a Hand-Loom Weaver of wool.

Margaret MacLean, John's wife, was a daughter of Angus MacLean and Chirsty MacLeod, in Raasay, and Margaret died in 1855, the first year of compulsory registration of births, marriages and deaths. As luck would have it, this was the only year in which a death certificate had to list the children of the deceased. So her daughter Kitty Ogg gave the list of offspring, and it tallies with the list given by Angus. From this death certificate we know that Angus was named after his maternal grandfather, his elder brother Roderick after their paternal grandfather, and the younger brother John after their father. Many Highland families would not use a father or grandfather's name during his lifetime, as it was considered unlucky.

Dr Alasdair told a gruesome story, current in his family, about Katherine Mhor, as a girl in Raasay: she was known as Ceit (Kate), and she used to listen to her father teaching and playing, and picked up both knowledge and skill. Her father did not approve of girls being pipers, and decided she was becoming too knowledgeable. To stop her from playing, and to make sure she did not put her brothers in the shade, John 'one day asked her to hold a piece of wood he was chopping, and deliberately lopped off her finger at the end joint'. I hope this story is not true.

As Dr Alasdair put it, she survived that as well as death in infancy. She married and had nine children before emigrating, and had four more in Prince Edward Island, Canada, before 1841, By 1930, there were at least 198 descendants from Katherine Mhor. She died in 1883, aged ninety. Her sister, Kitty Ogg Munro, had died two years earlier, aged seventy-five.

John MacKay was at Drummond for only seven years. His employer was Lord Willoughby d'Eresby. Alistair Campsie makes much of Angus MacKay signing the notice of his forthcoming collection with his name and the address 'Drummond Castle', giving this as an example of his delusions of grandeur long before he was certified as insane, but this seems unreasonable criticism. Drummond Castle, after all, was his home at the time, and he had every right to use it as his address. Pipe Major Willie Ross regularly used 'Edinburgh Castle' as his address in his correspondence, and nobody regarded him as insane. In any case, it is likely that this notice was written for Angus by someone, possibly James Logan, representing the Highland Society of London.

We do not know much about John's years at Drummond. Was he composing? Teaching? Was he happy there? Did he give satisfaction to his employer? All we know is that in 1830, he handed over to his son Angus, and left Drummond. He was then sixty-three, and may have wanted to retire. But he had nowhere to go, having given up his home in Raasay.

Piping tradition has it that finding himself homeless, he felt he had no alternative but to emigrate, perhaps to join his daughters in Canada; this is borne out by correspondence between the Secretaries of the Highland Society of Scotland (Reginald MacDonald of Staffa) and of the Celtic Society (William MacKenzie) in 1821, showing that John had let his plight be known to those in high places. MacKenzie wrote: 'the fame of this man is too well known to require any praise from me ... To let this man leave the Highlands will bring deserved obloquy on these institutions who have it in their power to relieve one so capable of preserving in purity the strains of our beloved ancestors, and, in the event of his quitting his native land we lose a treasure, as he will leave none behind him worthy of being his successor ...'

A pension of some £40–£50 was suggested, to be supplemented by his teaching, and it is said that when Lord MacDonald heard of his plight, he thought it disgraceful that Scotland's leading piper should have to leave his native land through poverty, so he offered John a house in Kyleakin, Skye, to be his for the rest of his life. It is not clear, however, whether the tenant was their son Roderick, since he was head of house in 1841, or whether it was let to John Munro, Kitty Og's husband. Certainly Kitty continued to live there after her father's death in 1848. Perhaps Roderick was there in 1841 because of the recent death of Kitty's husband, and he may have been the temporary head of the house. Her brother Donald's two sons lived there for some of the time, and Kitty's son Duncan. Kitty's mother was Head of House in 1851, so it seems likely that if it was indeed Lord MacDonald's house, the tenancy was now in her name.

It is thought that it was to Kyleakin that Lachlan MacNeill of Drumdrissaig came for his lessons, and John had other pupils there. He was visited by his son Angus (John Ban MacKenzie's nephew Ronald later wrote of Angus 'He belonged to Kyleakin, Isle of Skye'), and it is said that there Angus composed a set of variations to *Colin Roy MacKenzie's Lament*, which until then had had variations 'borrowed' from *Craigellachie*, which did not really fit. When, at his father's request, Angus made a new set of variations based on the Ground of *Colin Roy's Lament*, he said that John 'highly approved' of them. This was in 1840.

Another piper possibly living in Kyleakin for at least part of the time that John MacKay was there was Donald Ruadh MacRa, from Kintail and Applecross, who is said by some to have been one of John MacKay's teachers, many years earlier. Donald, who had two army piper sons, was a career soldier who lived to be nearly a hundred, and died in 1855. After leaving the army because of failing eyesight in 1802, he went to live possibly in Raasay, and then in Inverness, before moving to Kyleakin. He was about twelve years older than John, and outlived him by seven years.

Donald, when in his nineties, used to dress in his regimental coat on quarterly Pension Day, and walk the seven miles to Broadford, to collect his pension and meet up with old army cronies, before walking seven miles back. It would be nice to picture John and Donald getting together to play piobaireachd and reminisce about the old days, but if they were in Kyleakin together, it can have been only for a few years at most, if at all, as John died in 1848, and Donald Ruadh's youngest child Janet was born in Inverness in 1844. It is not known exactly when the MacRa family came to Kyleakin, but they were there by 1851, when Donald was described as a 'Chelsea Pensioner, Blind'. He had three children by his second marriage, the eldest born when he was eighty-nine. Some of his MacRa(e) descendants are living in Kyleakin today.

Both John MacKay and Donald MacRa had been leading competitors at the national competitions in Edinburgh. John MacKay won the Prize Pipe in 1792, the year after Donald won it. Forty-four years later, Donald competed for the Gold Medal for Former Winners (now called the Gold Clasp), at the age of eighty, winning a special Silver Medal, probably on account of his age. He also competed at the first Northern Meeting in 1841, when he was eighty-six, but did not appear in the prize list.

John MacKay died at the Kyleakin house in 1848, at the age of eighty-one. He lived long enough to see the publication of his son Angus' *Collection of Ancient Piobaireachd,* and to witness the beginning of the enormous influence that Angus had on piping. His fourth son, John, also made a manuscript collection of the piobaireachd he had learned from his famous father, John MacKay. Until about 1860, after John's death, the term 'the famous MacKay' was used not of Angus but of his father; nowadays the phrase would mean Angus, who dominates the piping scene.

John MacKay is buried in the old chapel near Raasay House. For many years his grave was unmarked, but in the 1960s the College of Piping put up a plaque in his memory, within the walls of the ruined chapel.

The importance of John MacKay, Raasay, has not been exaggerated. He was a vital link with the old world of piobaireachd, the world of the MacCrimmons and the MacArthurs, soon to be replaced by the modern piping brought in by his son Angus, with emphasis on light music, and especially the Competition March. Angus, however, knew the importance of his father, and saw to it that the old piobaireachd was still revered, recorded on paper, and handed on. He was not the only collector preserving the old music: the first half of the 19th century saw Donald MacDonald, Peter Reid, Angus MacArthur and others doing valuable work in this field, but it is to Angus MacKay, and to a lesser extent, to his brother, John junior, that we owe most of our knowledge of John MacKay's music, so that it can be played today in the form in which (we presume) he taught it.

John himself was probably illiterate, and if he could write at all, he was not able to write down his music, nor did he use written music as an aid to his teaching. Had Angus and John junior not preserved his knowledge by writing down what he had taught them, a vast collection of piobaireachd music might well have been lost – not only John's own, but that of his MacCrimmon teachers. John's memory, and its contents captured on paper by his sons, makes up much of what we know about the Great Music today.

MacKay Family Links

The mother of John Ban MacKenzie was Mary MacKay, and local tradition in Strathconon says that she came from Raasay. Her father's name is said to have been Thomas, and he moved to Achilty, in the parish of Contin, around 1790. I am unable to trace his family in Raasay, nor to find out if he was related to John MacKay. Raasay tradition links John Ban to the island through his MacKenzie blood – but the link has not been confirmed, other than through his marriage to Maria MacKenzie of Applecross, whose mother was a MacLeod of Raasay.

Sources

Norma MacLeod, *Raasay*
Seumas MacNeill
Virginia van der Lande (private correspondence)
Roderick Cannon, *The Highland Bagpipe and its Music*
Peter Cook, *Proceedings of the Piobaireachd Society Conference*
John A. MacLellan, 1986
Rebecca MacKay, Raasay
James MacLeod *Piping Times* Jun/Jul 1997
J.F. Campbell, *Canntaireachd*, 1880
John MacLean *TGSI* XLI
Dr Alasdair MacLean

MacKay Sons and their Lives

Family and local traditions agree that John MacKay was a small man, and not particularly good-looking, but all his sons were over six feet tall, and handsome, too.

Donald MacKay

All four sons were pipers, taught in Raasay and at Drummond Castle by their father. The name of the eldest son, Donald, is a puzzle, as is that of his elder (and younger) sister Katherine. We would expect the first two children to be named for their grandparents, that is, the eldest boy would be Roderick or Ruairidh for his father's father, and the first daughter for one of her grandmothers: and maybe she was, as we do not know the name of Ruairidh Raasay's wife. She may have been Catriona or Katherine. Was Donald the name of the father of Angus MacLean, the maternal grandfather? Or was Ruairidh Raasay's father called Donald? Even though in some families the tradition was that a son was not given his grandfather's name until the old man was dead, this cannot have applied here, since Ruairidh was gone long before Donald was born. His name, for some reason, went to the second son, and the maternal grandfather's to the third – and the fourth was given his living father's name.

Donald took over in 1820 as piper to MacLeod of Raasay – or possibly as second piper, assisting his father. He was twenty-seven. Two years later he won the Prize Pipe at Edinburgh, as 'Piper to Clanranald', an appointment which he held for twelve years. In 1834, he went to Queen Victoria's uncle, the Duke of Sussex, where he remained until his death in 1850. He was a pipe-maker who may have made the Prize Pipes for 1841 and 1844, but this is not certain.

A pipe formerly in the possession of John Morrison, Assynt House, Stornoway, has recently come to light, with letters authenticating it, written by John Morrison, Ronald MacKenzie and Colin Cameron, the eldest son of Donald Cameron, Maryburgh. These pipes had belonged to John Morrison's grandfather, Thomas MacKay, piper to Sir James Matheson in Lewis, and evidently John had written to Colin Cameron about their provenance.

Colin's letter, dated 1.2.06 [=1906], is in his own handwriting and says:

Seaforth Cottage, Maryburgh Dingwall.
Dear John, I have recd yr letter and delighted to hear from you. Yr

Grandfather's pipes were made by Donald MacKay, Piper to the Duke of Sussex & a Brother of Angus McKay who was Piper to Queen Victoria. The Chanter with Ivory sole was made by John McKenzie Piper to the Marquis of Breadalbane, he was the best maker of Pipes and Chanters in the World. Take great care of the Chanter as money cant bye them now, their was one sold the other day for £10 [underlined]. I hope yr Mother and Father are quite well also Mrs Gressiman Hughina and your other Aunt with Lord Penryn. Yr Grandfather and my Father were like two Brothers. Please remember me kindly to Duncan Graham & tell him he will have to give me some fishing ere long & how is Campbell my friend of the Landing Peir office & please ask him about the Pibrochs I played for him. I suppose you play well yourself. Should you happen to see Willie Ross Soval, I hope he is very well. We are having it very stormy here at present with Cold winds & rain. I shall be so pleased to hear from you at any time & to know how you are getting on with the Piob Mor. Meantime with most kind Regards to all and a happy New Year,

Yrs very Sincerely, Colin Cameron.

[I am grateful to Neil Campbell McGougan, Dingwall, the owner of this letter, for permission to quote it here.]

The hallmark of the silver mounts dates this pipe to around 1843, when Donald MacKay was in London, in the service of the Duke of Sussex.

Donald's wife Caroline, whose surname appears to have been Kenstain, died young, probably in 1849, giving birth to her third child, Sarah. Her husband soon followed her to the grave, dying of blood-poisoning, after twenty-five years in the household of the Duke of Sussex. The family lived at Kensington Palace, where all three children were born, Donald junior in 1845, John in 1847, Sarah 1849.

On their father's death the two boys were sent to their grandmother in Kyleakin, and four years later Donald, and possibly John as well, were back in London, as pupils in the Royal Caledonian Asylum in Holloway, a boarding school which was partly an orphanage, intended for the children of servicemen who had died in action, or were stationed abroad. This school always had good piping instruction. John died young, at twenty-two, from consumption (tuberculosis), at Kyleakin. Sarah married a Matheson, and lived in Kyleakin.

Donald junior was the only one of John MacKay's grandchildren to become a piper. His father started him at six, and he continued his tuition at school. Later he was a piper in the 78th Regiment (Seaforth Highlanders), and went to John Ban MacKenzie and to Donald

Cameron for tuition. Although he won the Prize Pipe at Inverness in 1863, as 'Donald MacKay, Kyleakin', and the Gold for Former Winners in 1872, when piper to Sir George MacPherson-Grant of Ballindalloch, he was not well regarded as a player, and many thought he won these honours on the reputation of his father, uncle and grandfather. It is said that Donald Cameron, who took very few pupils and disliked teaching, accepted Donald junior only because of his family's old friendship with the Camerons, and because Donald had himself been a pupil of John MacKay.

When he won the Inverness Gold, Donald junior was piper at Ballindalloch, near Craigellachie, and the following year he was appointed piper to the Prince of Wales (later King Edward VII), so he was at the top of the piping tree, good player or no. He helped General Thomason with his book *Ceol Mor*, but it is said that he had a poor memory for the technical points taught to him by Donald Cameron, and there was a general feeling that his understanding of piobaireachd was superficial.

Donald MacKay junior was piper to the Highland Society of London, and honorary piper to the Gaelic Society. An unkind comment was made, that he was very highly esteemed – by those who did not have much knowledge of piping, such as the Royal Family and the societies of the 'jolly boys'. His best pupil was John Cameron from Cromdale, who won the Gold Medal at Inverness in 1892, when piper to the 2nd Battalion The Queen's Own Cameron Highlanders.

Donald junior died in 1884, and his funeral at Kensal Green was an imposing occasion, attended by a large crowd. The cortege was met at the cemetery gates by eight pipers of the 1st Battalion Royal Scots Fusiliers, who escorted the coffin to the grave, playing *Flowers o' the Forest*. Two ministers presided, and beautiful flowers were sent by the Royal Family, including a wreath from the Prince and Princess of Wales 'by whom MacKay's loss is much regretted'. The household of the Duke of Sussex attended the ceremony, and the Prince of Wales 'was represented'.

Roderick MacKay

Roderick, the second son of John MacKay and elder brother of Angus, was named after his paternal grandfather, Roderick being the anglicised form of Gaelic Ruairidh, He was a good piper who won the Prize Pipe in Edinburgh in 1832. He was, first, piper to Colin MacKay of Bighouse, Sutherland, a very distant kinsman, and then to James Murray of Abercairney, a descendant of the man honoured in *Abercairney's*

Salute. Dr Alasdair MacLean said that the piper's house at Abercairney was the only one in Scotland built specially for a piper, and it had a thirty-yard corridor for the piper to march along as he played. It is no longer in existence, unfortunately.

Roderick died in Edinburgh in 1854, aged forty-three, leaving three sons, none of them pipers. There is some doubt about Roderick having perhaps been a merchant in Kyleakin; he is described as a Merchant in the 1841 Kyleakin Census, but this does not necessarily mean he was a merchant in Kyleakin, if he was there only temporarily.

There is a possibility that Roderick, like his brother Angus, was insane at the time of his death, but this is not certain (see below).

John MacKay Junior

The youngest son, John MacKay junior, may have been named after his father as an indication that he would be the last child of the family. This was a common custom (and as a form of birth control it did not always work). This son was a piper, as were his brothers, and he was also an accomplished Highland dancer. He was employed by Sir Robert Gordon, and then by Mr Leslie of Glengarry, apparently following his brother Angus as piper there – but Angus' employer was Lord Ward, who had bought up the bankrupt Glengarry estates in 1840. He lured Angus from Campbell of Islay, after the appearance of Angus' book, but Angus was not there for long. When Angus left to go into Royal service in 1843, his brother John seems to have replaced him, but before long Lord Ward sold up, and John went with the Glengarry estates to Mr Leslie.

John, too, was at Glengarry for only a short time, before he was enticed away by an offer from John MacDougall, 24th Chief of the MacDougalls of Dunollie, Oban. The MacDougall correspondence, published by a descendant, Jean MacDougall, in her book *Highland Postbag* (1984), tells how John MacDougall, (who was the younger brother of Captain MacDougall, commemorated in the *Lament for Captain MacDougall*) had been in the Royal Navy until the death of his brother Sandy in Spain obliged him to come home in 1812, to take up his position as clan chief. In 1845, John electrified his family by deciding to go back to sea – he ended up as an Admiral – and he announced that he wanted to take a piper with him. After consultation with John Ban MacKenzie, then piper at Taymouth Castle, he offered the position to John MacKay junior. The chief's brother Allan made the arrangements, and wrote home:

McKenzie says John is an excellent pibroch and reel player, he was lately Lord Ward's piper, who occasionally lives at Glengarry. McKay asks and McKenzie says a Gentleman's best plan is to give the piper a sum of money as pay and for clothes and that he will dress himself well in plain clothes to act as your body servant [valet] and in the McDougall Tartan for pipe playing, if you will give him £50 and his mess per annum. I see there are no pipers at all the thing out of places [unemployed], so I suspect if you want to give your sailors a reel to the Bagpipes you must give John McKay his own terms. McKenzie says McKay is a *Pretty* man, and a first rate reel dancer as well as playing. ['Pretty' meant 'handsome, well turned out, fine-looking'. It does not imply any effeminacy.]

The reply from the chief was:

I will give him £50 annually, that is to make his pay up to that sum, he being rated my Servant, on the following conditions: he is always to be well dressed in the Highland dress when required to play Pibroch and Reels, or when desired. Engage him, and send him with a good dress of the McD. Tartan. He will mess with my Steward. [Some of these 19th-century terms manage to imply a certain kinkiness to the 21st-century reader. This is certainly not intended by the writers of the letters. To 'mess with' someone meant to take meals with him.]

As John was the official piper to the General Assembly of the Church of Scotland, held annually in Edinburgh, he was granted a delay of two days before reporting to his ship in Portsmouth. His first voyage was to Hong Kong, where, Dr Alasdair told us, he won a silver plaid-brooch engraved with Chinese characters. It is now in the possession of his mother's family in Raasay. The story is that he won it by dancing on a table top loaded with glasses full of drink, without spilling a drop.

John MacKay's naval career was short, as he died in 1848 or 1849, aged thirty-four. There is a hint that he, like his elder brother Angus, may have become insane. The journal written by Angus in his dementia seems to imply that John had delusions similar to his own, and Alistair Campsie quotes the hospital record made when Angus was admitted to Bedlam: 'in the section of the admission sheet under "Relatives similarly afflicted" is entered "Yes". In the section "And degrees of relationship" is entered "Brother". No indication is given which brother was concerned,' but we know that Donald died of blood-poisoning; Roderick died in Edinburgh in 1854, only months after Angus' admission, cause unknown, and it may have been he who was mad.

Angus wrote in his journal in 1854: 'I well remember how my brother John would say he had a large ship and that it went round the world and he was engaged in mason work, and he pretended that

C.M.D. murdered him as he was coming head on, that he was desirous of getting the stones for himself . . .' These words seem to indicate the derangement of poor Angus' mind, rather than that of John, who had indeed had a job on a large ship which went round the world. The rest could be an anecdote once told to Angus by John, and seems incoherent only because we do not know the background.

John MacKay's main significance to the later piping world was not so much his playing as his collection of piobaireachd works which he had learned from his father. This is a useful supplement to his brother Angus' work, and some of the settings he gives seem to be more consistent and pleasing than those of Angus (see below).

Angus MacKay

The life of Angus MacKay, third son of John MacKay, Raasay, is well-trodden ground. He was named for his mother's father, Angus MacLean, a Raasay man, and it is clear that he could read and write from an early age – unlike his father. As a young teenager, he was able to transcribe pipe music into staff notation, probably taught by Eliza Ross in Raasay, before 1823. It is obvious that he was a highly intelligent young man.

He was born in the family home at Eyre, in the south of Raasay, in 1813. His birth certificate, sent from Australia, is now a prized possession of the College of Piping in Glasgow. By 1825, two or three years after his family had moved to Drummond Castle (see above), he was in Edinburgh, where at the age of thirteen he was awarded a cash prize by the Highland Society of London for transcribing pipe music, thus 'presaging his future life's work', as Dr Alasdair put it. Already he had broken away from the traditional teaching of his father, who never used written material and was almost certainly illiterate.

The following year, as a fourteen-year-old competing with the adults, Angus was placed fourth in the Prize Pipe competition in Edinburgh. In 1835 – the competitions were by this time held only once every three years – he won the Prize Pipe. His brother Donald had won it in 1822, and their father John in 1792. Angus was competing as 'piper to Lord Willoughby d'Eresby, Drummond Castle', a post he had taken on when his father left Drummond around 1830.

On winning the top honour, Angus seems to have become piper to Duncan Davidson of Tulloch, Dingwall, a wealthy man for whom only the best would do. Angus would have been following in the footsteps of John Ban MacKenzie, who had been the Tulloch piper until he eloped with the girl his employer was courting. John Ban went to Taymouth, but did Angus go in person to Tulloch? There is a problem with the dating, as the prospectus announcement of August 1835 appeared over the name 'Angus MacKay, Drummond Castle', and he won the Prize Pipe as the Drummond piper even later that year, whereas the Tulloch records indicate that Angus was piper to Duncan Davidson from about 1833. A possible explanation might be that Angus was on the books of Duncan Davidson, perhaps paid a retainer, but was not in residence at Tulloch, being Davidson's piper only in name. Davidson was certainly the sort of lavish spender who would pay handsomely for the prestige of being known as the employer of the foremost piper in the country, even if Angus was not in residence. There is no precedent for this, however, and it does not seem likely that Angus was being paid by two lairds at once – unless by mutual agreement?

The oral traditions of Dingwall do not remember the presence of Angus MacKay at Tulloch, although they do recall both John Ban Mac-Kenzie and J.J. Conan. This, of course, is not conclusive, but might be suggestive. An otherwise unknown piper named George Murchison was competing as the Tulloch piper in 1832; he won 5th prize at Edinburgh.

Probably in 1837, Angus went to the island of Islay as piper to Walter F. Campbell of Shawfield and Islay, and was living at Islay House in Bridgend when he completed his work. It is said that Campbell of Islay took him there to give him the necessary peace and quiet for concentrating on his transcriptions. The Collection, when it finally appeared in 1838, had an enormous and lasting impact, and is undoubtedly the most important piping book ever published. Even today it is regarded as the Piper's Bible, and it is a brave man who questions its authority. He was in Islay for only a year or two, leaving to take up the post of piper to Lord Ward, who had bought the bankrupt Glengarry estates, but neither Angus nor Lord Ward was long there. In 1841, Angus was in Edinburgh for his marriage to Mary Russell, who came from Crawford, Lanarkshire.

Angus left manuscripts of transcriptions of 179 piobaireachd works and innumerable pieces of light music; these manuscripts are now in the National Library of Scotland, in Edinburgh, catalogued as MSS 3753–4. He was only twenty-six when his *Collection of Ancient Piobaireachd* came out, and he clearly drew extensively on the teachings and knowledge of his father. He and his father seem to have been close, and one of Angus' reasons for his publication must have been to preserve his father's life-work for posterity. Similarly inspired was his younger brother John, who also wrote a manuscript (see below).

Angus and John succeeded in preserving for us the old style of the music, handed to their father by the MacCrimmons – preserving it in aspic, some might say, thinking that recording it on paper prevented it from developing as a living entity. Angus MacPherson's phrase, killing it 'by putting it behind bars', represents this viewpoint, and there is undoubtedly something in it. After Angus MacKay's time, no real piobaireachd has been composed, and the secret is lost. But Angus' work shows us what the real thing was like, or at least a semblance of it, and we have always to bear in mind what happened to harp music, which had no Angus MacKay (or Colin Campbell, Donald MacDonald, Angus MacArthur, Peter Reid, etc.) to write it down: it continued as an oral tradition, for a while, but today the form of Ceol Mor once played on the harp has been completely lost, and only the occasional reference tells us that it ever existed in previous times. We owe Angus MacKay and his predecessors a huge debt, for all the pleasure we still enjoy from playing and listening to the Great Music.

The respect accorded to Angus as an authority extends to the Preface to his book, which was for a long time taken to be straight from the horse's mouth, written in Angus' own words. In recent years, it has been shown that this is not so, and the Preface was probably written by James Logan, acting for the Highland Society of London, who published the book (see William Donaldson, *The Highland Pipe and Scottish Society*, pp. 149–61). Similarly, the title, *A Collection of Ancient Piobaireachd*, is almost certainly not Angus' own choice, and it cannot be used as evidence that Angus used the word piobaireachd in this sense. Even the phrase 'Ancient Piobaireachds or Pipe Tunes' in the 1835 prospectus was probably not his, but written by someone else, presumably James Logan.

Angus later used the phrase 'ancient piobaireachd' in a note he wrote on his brother's manuscript. He would have taken it from the title of his own collection.

In the early 1840s, Queen Victoria and Prince Albert visited Taymouth, and the young Queen was captivated by the romance of Highland life, and particularly by the piping. Wanting her own piper, she tried to poach her host's piper, John Ban MacKenzie, but he declined the honour, and also refused to allow his son Donald to accept the position. He recommended Angus MacKay to her, and as Angus passed the test, for excellence of playing as well as outstanding good looks (the Queen liked a clean-cut knee), he moved down to Windsor in 1843.

It is not clear exactly when Angus began to show the symptoms of the violent mental illness which afflicted him in the 1840s. Alistair Campsie's book has an interesting analysis of this illness, and there is no doubt that the cause was the effect of syphilis on Angus' brain. In 1854 he became completely demented and had to be removed to the mental hospital known as Bedlam (Bethlehem), in London. His doctors at one stage described him as the most violent patient in the country. Although his mania seems to have been intermittent, and he was able to continue his work of writing down pipe music – he produced five more volumes of transcriptions – he was not fit to be released from constraint again. He was transferred to Scotland, to spend the rest of his life in Crichton Royal, a big mental hospital in Dumfriess-shire.

In 1859 he escaped from confinement, and is believed to have drowned while trying to cross the River Nith, which was in spate. He was only forty-six years of age. He was seen attempting the crossing, but his body was never recovered, and of course this led to reports that he had been seen in various places in the Borders, busking for a living. His mental state makes this extremely unlikely, and we have to accept that this fine man came to an unhappy end. There is no grave, and until recently, no memorial, other than his musical work. In 2010, however, an appeal was made to collect money for a memorial to Angus MacKay, and a cairn was erected beside the River Nith, with a suitable inscription.

John MacKay's Manuscript

[This account is based largely on the paper given by Captain John A. MacLellan to the Piobaireachd Society Conference in 1986.]

John MacKay was the youngest of the four sons of John MacKay, and was born in 1815. He died in 1848, the same year as his father. The manuscript known by his name was for some years regarded as the work of his father, also John MacKay, and his brother Angus seems to have had a hand in it, too. Angus found it when he was going through his brother's effects and he wrote on it a note: '21st May 1849. The following collection of ancient piobaireachd was found in the portman- teau of my late brother John after his decease, October 1848 – Being a collection of my father's tunes', and he signed his own name.

The manuscript itself (now in the National Library of Scotland, NLS Acc. 9231) has been seriously tampered with, and a suggestion was made that the collection had been compiled by John senior, and that it was Angus who made the alterations. Study by Captain John A. MacLellan, Archibald Campbell of Kilberry and Roderick Cannon has put us right: Angus completed the short Preface, made an index of the contents, and wrote in the titles to the tunes, but only in pencil. His handwriting is familiar enough to the experts for them to recognise it without difficulty. This was the extent of his interference.

As for its being a collection made by John MacKay senior, Captain John pointed out that if that was so, Angus would have written 'being my father's collection of tunes' rather than 'being a collection of my father's tunes'.

Roderick Cannon made the point that none of the works in the John MacKay manuscript appears in Angus' published book (1838). But all are in Angus' own main manuscript, and so it seems likely that it was written between 1838 and 1848.

It is doubtful if John MacKay senior was literate, or that he ever wrote down any pipe music. If he had, surely Angus, the assiduous collector, would have kept examples of his father's writing. John senior taught by ear and stored his piobaireachd in his head: he had no need for written music, which was alien to his generation of pipers.

Captain John quotes Angus' note to the Seaforth manuscript, which he wrote in 1854: 'From original manuscripts in his [Angus's] possession as noted down by him from the canntaireachd of John MacKay his father, from the year 1826 to 1840.'

Probably John junior followed the same procedure, so that his work may be considered in parallel to that of Angus. But John MacKay's manuscript is unsatisfactory for two reasons: it appears to be incomplete, and it has been tampered with – and Kilberry described the intervention of Dr Charles Bannatyne in the 20th century as 'vandalism'.

It seems that John wrote down each work in crotchet beats all the way through, with just some of the gracenotes added in the grounds, but not in the variations. He wrote sixty-two compositions out in this way, and did not give titles to any of them. Angus made a list of the tunes, written in ink, with thirty-eight names in Gaelic, the rest in English. And he put a title to each work, in pencil.

Most of John's settings are the same as those in Angus's MS, with just the odd variation that is different, and Captain John was led to the conclusion that John copied out some of the tunes from Angus' main manuscript, 'although it's not possible to be quite certain about John Junior's source'.

Captain John then gave a brief account of what happened to the manuscripts. After Angus' death in 1859, his widow 'disposed of' all his music to Michael MacCarfrae, a favourite pupil who was piper to the Duke of Hamilton, and MacCarfrae bequeathed most of it to the Duke. In 1904, Dr Charles Bannatyne bought two manuscripts from MacCarfrae's daughter, and these were the MacArthur manuscript and the John MacKay manuscript; they remained in his possession until 1926, when the Piobaireachd Society bought them both, for £20.'

While he had them in his possession, Dr Bannatyne felt free to write on them and make alterations at will. In 1910, Kilberry borrowed the John MacKay manuscript, and copied it for the Society. He found at least two different hands making changes in the manuscript, and of one, he said the alterations were by Bannatyne, and were 'the work of an ignoramus'. The vandalism was always perpetrated in ink, and he wrote boldly over Angus MacKay's pencilled titles, adding tie lines, dots and grace notes, so that the timing of a ground was often completely changed.

Sources

Piping Times
Dr Alasdair MacLean
Alistair Campsie, *The MacCrimmon Legend*
Proceedings of the Piobaireachd Society Conferences
Norma MacLeod, *Raasay*
Mrs Helen MacRae, Kyleakin
Neil Campbell McGougan (private correspondence)
Jean MacDougall, *The Highland Postbag*
William Donaldson, *The Highland Pipe*
John MacLellan
Evander MacIver, *Memoirs*

The MacLeans of Raasay

The five MacLean brothers from Oscaig, in Raasay, belonged to a remarkable family. Their father, Malcolm, was a piper, not very good, but 'passable' enough to inspire his sons to a lifelong interest in piping, and it is clear that he handed on a great deal of piping history to all of them. The MacLeans had been in Oscaig for at least seven generations – there were MacLeans there in 1630, when four earlier generations were named. Malcolm's great-aunt Kate (Catriona) was well-known as a tradition-bearer. Somhairle MacLean said (*TGSI* XLIX 1974) that he believed the family had originated in South Uist, and possibly had lived on MacLeod land in Skye before moving to Raasay.

William MacLean (1876–1957)

One of Kate's nephews was WILLIE MACLEAN, who though born in Tobermory and later associated with Creagorry, in Benbecula, was of the same Raasay family, at Oscaig. He and Sorley agreed that the family originated in South Uist, before moving to Raasay, but they had been in Raasay for many generations.

Willie was by far the best piper produced by the family, and, after his first lessons from his father, was a pupil of Calum Piobaire MacPherson (whose maternal grandparents were at Suisnish, in Raasay). Willie went to Calum at his home at Catlodge, near Laggan, Newtonmore. It is said that there Willie learned over a hundred piobaireachd works from Calum, and had started winning prizes when still a boy. D.R. MacLennan said that in his opinion, Willie's brother, LACHIE, who had the hotel at Kilmartin, in Argyll, was as good a piper as Willie. Lachie played at D.R.'s wedding, at Dalnahassaig, for which D.R.'s brother, G.S., composed the tune *Dalnahassaig*.

As a young man Willie was piper to Malcolm of Poltalloch, in Mid-Argyll, not far from Kilmartin, winning the 1901 Gold Medal at Inverness; he then gave up competing for the next decade, to concentrate on his business career. In 1912, however, he resumed his piping, and went to Oban, to win the Gold Medal, playing *MacCrimmon's Sweetheart*. The following year, with *The Unjust Incarceration*, he won the Clasp at Inverness.

Willie made tapes for the School of Scottish Studies in Edinburgh, in the 1950s, recording his own playing and reminiscences. These are a valuable source of evidence of the older style of playing and of information, but the latter has to be treated with caution as he makes some claims which can be shown to be untrue. He was known as 'Blowhard', and he and his father, who Robert Reid said was called 'Blowharder', were accepted as being apt to exaggerate. Much of this alleged exaggeration was, of course, merely the art of the Gaelic story-teller, as is clear from the tale quoted by Campsie, told to him by Reid. It is an amusing story, and it is equally amusing to see how seriously Campsie and Reid seem to have taken it, as 'proof' of the unreliability of Willie MacLean.

The tone of Reid's story is sarcastic ('a great and wondrous piper called Pipe Major Willie MacLean', whose father Ian – wrongly spelled the Lowland way – 'owned a hotel out in the Uists where he kept Willie just to play pipes and do other important tasks about the place, suited to a piper of such status'), and we have to wonder if Reid was jealous of Willie's reputation. He told how Willie's father was a crackshot with his .22 rifle, and had it beside him when one day he lay down for a snooze. He woke to hear exquisite music coming from above, and lay listening in delight until he realised it was going higher and higher into the sky. Looking out, he saw with horror that it was Willie, playing his pipes, now eighty feet up and still rising. 'And he realised his boy had been playing so wonderfully well that the angels were taking him up to Heaven.' There was only one thing to do, so Iain 'with the skill of a MacCrimmon', put a bullet through the bag, 'letting the wind sooch softly out, and Willie drifted slowly back to earth, playing all the while'. Iain said: 'We needed the boy back. We never had the peats in yet.'

It seems that Willie himself told Reid this story, purely, I would imagine, for entertainment. Surely nobody would imagine it was meant to be taken seriously. But of course neither Robert Reid nor Alistair Campsie came from that tradition of Gaelic story-tellers, and they seem to have regarded it as a typical instance of the inaccuracy of Willie MacLean. Willie gave many stories and traditions to the School of Scottish Studies, and many of them have a core of truth which gives us valuable information about former times. We have to give this serious consideration.

Willie said he was 'not by nature a competitor', but in 1898 he began a successful competing career by winning the Argyllshire Star at Oban, for his light music. In 1901, playing as 'William MacLean, Creagorry Hotel, Benbecula', where his father was the landlord, he won the Gold Medal at Inverness, and in 1912 the Gold at Oban. In 1913, as 'William MacLean, Glasgow' he won the Inverness Gold Clasp. After this, having won nearly all the honours, he retired from competition playing, this time for good.

Recordings of his playing, even in old age in the 1950s, show what an excellent piper he was. Disparaging remarks were made by Robert Reid, and quoted by Alistair Campsie ('No one ever heard of him winning many of the really big prizes in piping' said Reid, and Campsie added: 'Pipe Major MacLean was not known to have won more than a couple of major piping prizes' – only both the Gold Medals, the Inverness Clasp and the Argyllshire Star, which seems to me more than a couple).

Reid believed that piobaireachd reached its peak in late 19th-century Glasgow; anyone who thinks that would be bound to discount the old style of Willie MacLean's generation, but the tapes are lasting testimony to his beautiful playing. He made these lengthy tapes when he was in his late seventies, and they are an interesting contrast to the playing of John MacDonald, Inverness, his contemporary and fellow-pupil of Calum Piobaire. John had to adapt his playing to the 'new' style as laid down in the Piobaireachd Society's publications, but Willie retained the old style. He uses old embellishments which greatly enrich his playing. His account of his lessons with Calum Piobaire in the 1890s is most interesting, and an indication of Willie's intelligence and quickness to learn.

David Ross was a pupil of Willie MacLean, and described how he travelled up from London to Glasgow, arriving around 5 p.m. on the Friday night. After having his tea, he was required to play all that evening and all day Saturday and Sunday – over twenty hours' practice in a weekend – and that was just the first lesson.

Extracts from the School of Scottish Studies tapes were published as an audio cassette in 1976, as No. 10 in the Scottish Tradition series. The recordings were made by Francis Collinson and Calum MacLean in 1953–54, and the notes were by Peter Cooke and H. MacDonald. It became a Greentrax release in 1995. While they are interesting, the published recordings represent only a fraction of the total recorded by Willie, which are still in the School of Scottish Studies.

At the outbreak of the First World War he was Pipe Major of the 3rd/4th Battalion, reserve unit of the Camerons, but then became P/M of the 5th (Lochiel's) Battalion. His pipers led the battalion into Germany in 1918, playing the *Pibroch of Donald Dubh*. They were the first battalion into Germany at the end of the war.

After the war he worked as a sales rep for Youngers' Breweries, as did John MacDonald, Inverness.

Willie MacLean was not a prolific composer, but he made a few tunes. He made a setting of an old Gaelic milking song, casting *Colin's Cattle* as a 3/4 Slow Air in two parts. He used to play a very old setting of *Lochaber No More,* not the one played as a funeral lament today. This old setting was played at his funeral when he died in 1957, at the age of eighty. The pipers at the graveside were P/M Hector MacLean and 'Big Donald' MacLean, from Lewis.

Willie MacLean composed a 6/8 March in four parts, *Lt. Col. H.W. Kemble of Knock* (who commanded the 3rd/4th Battalion Camerons), and a piobaireachd work, the *Lament for the Earl of Seafield.* The 11th Earl died of his wounds in 1915 while in temporary command of the 5th Battalion Queen's Own Cameron Highlanders, at Ypres. At that time, the Earl was Willie MacLean's Commanding Officer. Other compositions by Willie MacLean were *The Battle of Arras,* and *The Raasay Highlanders.*

He also compiled, in 1910, a complete transliteration of the Canntair-eachd of Gesto; this is now in the School of Scottish Studies. As would be expected in a version of the playing of 1828, recorded in Canntair-eachd in Gesto's Collection, the music has the so-called 'redundant A' in its gracings, and when in the 1920s the great and heated debate over the playing of this racked the piping world, Willie MacLean held himself aloof from it, and took no part in the argument. He played the redundant A himself only in the recordings based on Gesto and on Donald MacDonald's music

Of Willie MacLean, John D. Burgess said: 'He was a tremendous dandy, always looked absolutely marvellous in daydress, and pho-tographs show him resplendent in evening dress.' He had two eagle feathers in his Glengarry – to which, it seems, he was entitled as an ex-Pipe Major – and he had some fantastic pistols. He wore a sword, but only for photographs, as it proved unwieldy when he was moving about.

Sources

Proceedings of the Piobaireachd Society Conferences
School of Scottish Studies, University of Edinburgh
Cabar Feidh Collection (Queen's Own Highlanders)

The Five MacLean Brothers

John, Alasdair, Sorley, Calum and Norman MacLean were the five MacLean brothers who had an important role in the development and preservation of Highland tradition, including piping, in the 20th century. They lived at Oscaig, a croft in Raasay, and went to school in Potree, and all five left their mark in the Gaelic world.

Their father, MALCOLM MACLEAN, Oscaig, married Christy Nicol-son, who came from Braes, in Skye, just across the Sound from Raasay. Her family also had piping genes, and her grandfather's grandfather was known as SOMHAIRLE NA PIOBA (Sorley of the Pipe); he was a regimental piper in the Peninsular Wars in the early 19th century. He had to leave the army after his fingers were badly frost-bitten during the retreat from Corunna in 1808. He was commemorated in a Skye song, a Port-a-beul (rhythmic song sung unaccompanied, for dancing, when no instrument was available). It is called *Somhairle na pioba, an gille grian a bha 'Holm* ('Sorley of the Pipe, the lad with bristly hair who was at Holm' – Holm is on the east coast of Skye, north of Portree). Another name for him is, in a neatly rhymed phrase, Som-hairle gun Chomhairle, which seems to mean 'Ill-advised Sorley', or

'Foolish Sorley', presumably because he volunteered for the army. His grandfather, Eoghan, had been put out of a good holding of land near Portree, reputedly for helping in the escape of Prince Charles Edward after Culloden.

This family history was published by his descendant, the poet Sorley (Somhairle) MacLean, in the *Transactions of the Gaelic Society of Inverness*, volume XLIX, 1974–76. Sorley was the best known of the five brothers, as a poet of international repute, writing in both Gaelic and English; but all five were exceptional, clever, intelligent men, all passionate and deeply learned about their Highland heritage, and all successful in their chosen fields, whether as teachers, doctors or collectors of traditional material. All became doctors in one sense or another, a fine achievement for five sons from a Raasay croft.

All were piping enthusiasts, though the youngest, Dr Norman, was the only serious piper. The MacLean family group was a familiar sight at all the major piping events, some of the wives knitting as they listened intently to the piobaireachd. All five collected piping lore, books, manuscripts, oral traditions, and all encouraged young players. All five were members of the Piobaireachd Society.

The eldest brother, DR JOHN MACLEAN, was a teacher, for many years well-known as Rector of Oban High School, where he was influential in bringing Highland traditions to his pupils, and encouraging them to play and sing their traditional music. He himself was a piper, who played only Ceol Mor, having no interest in the light music, but his brothers, whose standards were high, thought little of his abilities – as brothers will.

He wrote many articles and letters about piping, most noteworthy being a paper on Iain Dall MacKay, the Blind Piper of Gairloch, given to the Gaelic Society of Inverness in 1952, and printed in their *Transactions*, volume XLI. He had a vast knowledge of the background to piobaireachd, and the conferences of the Piobaireachd Society benefited from long and informed discussions with him, mainly at Middleton Hall.

DR ALASDAIR MACLEAN (1918–1999) went from Portree High School to St Andrews University, graduating with a medical degree in 1941. He served with the RAMC as an army doctor in India and Burma until 1945. After several short spells as a doctor in different parts of Scotland, he went in 1949 to South Uist, and practised as a GP there for the next thirty-two years. There he met many pipers and piping enthusiasts, named in the obituary written for him (*Piping Times* December 1999) by his friend Dr John MacAskill: he knew Angus

Campbell, Archie MacDonald, Archie's son Neil and daughter Rona, Willie Walker, Adam Scott, Neil MacLennan and Finlay MacKenzie. Dr MacAskill wrote: 'It was certainly during his years in South Uist that his love for the music and its history developed.'

In 1993 Dr Alasdair completed his revision and enlargement of Alexander Nicolson's *History of Skye*, first published in 1930, and long out of print (Alexander Nicolson was Dr Alasdair's uncle). The revised edition was issued by the MacLean Press at Aird Bhearnasdail, near Skeabost, Skye, run by Dr Alasdair's own son, Cailean. The new edition is highly recommended as a rich source of information on island history and island piping, a valuable contribution to Gaelic learning which preserves traditions not found elsewhere.

As were all five of the brothers, Dr Alasdair was a most interesting, lively and informative conversationalist, always ready for a good meaty talk about piping. Dr MacAskill wrote of him: 'Although not himself a player, he knew a good tune played on a good bagpipe when he heard it, and his knowledge of piobaireachd for a non-player was quite uncanny.'

For many, the highlight of Dr Alasdair's retirement was his memorable lecture for the John MacFadyen Memorial Trust, at Stirling Castle, in the spring of 1997. The text was published later in the *Piping Times*. His subject was 'The MacKays of Raasay', and his talk was every bit as good as anticipated – erudite, amusing, informative, pithy and accurate. A great treat, and a memorable occasion, as well as a rich source of new information. Listening in the audience, we knew this was the horse's mouth, and were impressed.

Dr MacAskill summed up his friend with the words: 'He was never boring, always interesting, always joking, and despite his immense knowledge and high intelligence, he was a man of great humility.' To this I would add he was not only interesting but interested, and ready to open his mind to other people's new ideas. Dr MacAskill closed the obituary with a moving account of Dr Alasdair's funeral in Skye, in November 1999. He died at the age of eighty-one.

The brother who died first was CALUM I. MACLEAN (1915–1960), well-known as an eminent folk-lorist with a vast knowledge of Gaelic story, music and song, in both Scotland and Ireland. As a young man, he worked for the Irish Folklore Commission, collecting both Irish and Scottish Gaelic material, recording live oral tradition in both countries. In 1951, he was with the School of Scottish Studies, based in Edinburgh but hardly ever there, as he was usually away somewhere in the islands. In 1959, not long before his untimely death, he published his book, *The Highlands,* described as 'highly individual', and regarded as unorthodox by more conventional scholars. It was re-issued in a revised edition in 1990.

Calum, like his brothers, was an interesting, friendly man, always ready to help the lowliest student or Gaelic-learner, and always very good company. His work in Ireland brought him in contact with the Irish Church, and while living in Clonmel in the 1940s, he converted to Roman Catholicism – a considerable step away from the Raasay family's Free Church tradition of his youth.

He developed cancer as a comparatively young man, and fought bravely to overcome it. Treatment in the 1950s was crude and drastic, and Calum had to have an arm amputated, in a bid to save his life. He surmounted this handicap by simply ignoring it, and pursued his normal life with his customary zest. He made it clear that pity, anyone else's or his own, had no part in it, and sympathy or even admiration for his courage was not required. It was astonishing how his plight could be forgotten in his enthusiasm for his work.

His friend Sean O Suilleabhain told how Calum once had a rough passage across to South Uist, and on the steamer he met another man, very tipsy, who had also lost an arm. As the ship pitched and tossed, the stranger taught Calum how to tie his shoelaces with one hand. 'He was the best teacher I have ever had the good luck to meet,' said Calum.

The cancer, however, was not to be averted, and his other arm had to be removed, too – but all in vain. In 1960, at the age of only forty-five, Calum went into hospital in Daliburgh, South Uist, where he died. His grave is in the burial ground at Hallan, South Uist, which must be one of the most beautiful places in the world. In the spring it is a mass of primroses and daffodils, and the views over the South Uist hills, the sea and the islands of Eriskay and Barra are stunning.

The sorrow felt by his family and friends was similar to that aroused by the death of Willie Lawrie in 1916, or of the young Captain Mac-Dougall in 1812; the sense of loss, the sheer waste of a life so full of promise, is very strong. Calum was a lovely man, a true scholar, and he is still missed, nearly fifty years after his death.

His book is prefaced with a moving tribute by Sean O Suilleabhain, and Gaelic poems by his brothers and friends. These include a poem by his brother John, set to the tune of *Lament for the Children*:

Chaluim, a ghaoil, on do dh'eug thu
's airtnealach trom as do dheidh sinn;

gearr bha do reis, gearr do shaoghal,
buan an creuchd bheum do dhaoine.

'S tusa bha mear eirmseach aotrom
dealasach ceart eibhinn daonda,
fulangach treun gleac ri eucail,
gun fhiamh gun ghealt ri uchd eig thu.

Sgoilear gun mheang tuigseach gleusda
thionail ar fuinn thruis gach sgeulachd;
choisinn thu cliu thall an Eirinn,
's bhos an Albainn mor bha dh'fheum ort.

Blath bha do chridhe fialadh muirneach
Macanta coir coibhneil fiughant,
ach 's fuaraidh an nochd aognaidh udlaidh
leaba na suain as nach duisg thu.

Calum's friend Donald Archie MacDonald translated this into English, not designed to fit the music but conforming to the requirements of bardic metre:

Beloved Calum, since you died
saddened and heavy are we after you:
short was your span, short your life,
long-lasting the wound that smote your kindred.

You were the gay one, witty, light-hearted,
fervid, fair, humorous, human,
enduring, brave, fighting disease
without fear or flinching at the point of death.

Scholar without blemish, judicious, expert,
who collected our tunes, gathered each tale:
you won fame over in Ireland
and here in Scotland there was much need of you.

Warm was your heart, liberal, genial,
gentle, good, kindly, generous,
but cold and damp tonight, cheerless, gloomy
the bed of deep sleep from which you will not wake.

Sorley MacLean wrote his *Cumha Chaluin Iain MhicGil-Eain (Lament for Calum Iain MacLean)*, which he translated himself. It starts:

Tha an saoghal fhathast alainn
ged nach eil thu ann,
is labhar an Uibhist a'Ghaidhlig

ged tha thusa an Cnoc Hallainn
is do bhial gun chainnt.

'S gann as urrainn dhomh smaointinn
gu bheil Gaidheal beo
's nach eil thu 'n aiteigin ri t'fhaotainn
eadar Grimeasaidh 's an Caolas
a'beothachadh na cuimhne aosda
le coibhneas is le spors,

gu bheil thusa an Cnoc Hallainn
's ged tha an comhlan coir –
cho coir 's a gheibhear an aite –
nach cluinnear ann am bristeadh gaire
no gliong air teud an oir . . .

The world is still beautiful
though you are not in it,
Gaelic is eloquent in Uist
though you are in Hallan Hill,
your mouth without speech.

I can hardly think that a Gael lives
and that you are not somewhere to be found
between Grimsay and the Sound,
kindling ancient memory
with kindness and fun,

that you are in Hallan Hill
and although the company is generous –
as generous as is to be found in any place –
that there is not heard the breaking of laughter
or clang on a golden string . . .

Seldom since the death of Iain Garbh can a Raasay man have been so deeply mourned.

The youngest brother was DR NORMAN MACLEAN, who became a medical doctor. He was widely respected as a player of Ceol Beag. In 2002, David Murray wrote of his friend and comrade, Captain Norman MacLean, with whom he had served in the army, 'He was a piper, and a good one at that'; the two of them, with a drummer, Captain Jock MacLeod, were in India in 1945 when the Gurkha Pipe Band was sent to them for a refresher course.

In the *Piping Times* in June 2002, Col. Murray described in his inimitable style how the course went:

The Gurkhas' fingering style was unusual, to say the least . . . and Norman, Jock and I quickly decided that it would be easier to teach the bands a new Retreat set than try to correct the old, so Norman and I took over a deserted cookhouse, each taking half the pipers, while Jock and the drummers set about 'Mammy, Daddy' on three tables in another disused outhouse . . . Norman and I had agreed that *The Heroes of Vittoria* was the simplest 3/4 we knew. Both classes had the first part off by lunchtime (I recall them solemnly marking time as they learned it off my fingers), and the second half in the afternoon. Some days later they returned and played it as a band, and pretty well, too.

Norman and David would set all the chanters at something approaching an acceptable pitch, but when their backs were turned, the young Gurkhas would chew their chanter reeds to get their preferred 'Eastern' tone, or as David put it, 'sounding like bloody snake-charmers again'. In the end he and Norman persuaded the Gurkhas to use all three drones and stronger chanters, and 'even the British officers noticed an improvement'.

Back in civilian life, Dr Norman's medical duties and residence in England put paid to his own piping career, other than playing 'for his own amazement', as he once put it, but he never lost his enthusiasm, especially for piobaireachd.

He and his wife Ailsa, living in Yorkshire, were faithful attenders at all the big piping events, never missing the annual Conference of the Piobaireachd Society. There, he regularly acted as Chairman or host of the piobaireachd ceilidh on the Saturday night, his genial manner being ideal for the occasion. It was only after his death that the Society appreciated how very good at it he had been.

Like his brothers he had a deep knowledge of the background of piping and a real understanding of piobaireachd. He too was willing to share and pass on his knowledge and his recordings and his books, to any fellow-enthusiast.

In 1998, he took ill while travelling to the Glenfiddich championship at Blair Castle, and he died shortly afterwards. It seemed the way he would have liked to go, enjoying his anticipation of a great piping occasion. As his obituary in the *Piping Times* put it, 'his warm and gentle ways will be much missed'. We saw a different side to him at the Conference when as a doctor he acted swiftly and efficiently on being called to a Piobaireachd Society member who had been taken ill in the hotel.

SORLEY MACLEAN (1911–1996) was a great poet whose work is best read, or heard, in the original Gaelic, but retains much of its quality

316 The Piping Traditions of the Inner Isles

in the English translations which he made himself. As Somhairle Mac Gill-Eain, he was born at Oscaig, Raasay, on 26 October 1911, second of the five MacLean brothers. He went from Portree High School to Edinburgh University, graduating in 1933 with First-Class Honours in English. At the same time he also studied Gaelic with Professor W.J. Watson – and played shinty for the university.

A year at Moray House training college gave him his Scottish teaching qualification, and in 1934 he returned to Portree as Assistant English teacher. Three years later he moved to Tobermory, then in 1939 to Boroughmuir, near Edinburgh.

He was called up in 1940, and in December 1941 was sent to Egypt with the Signal Corps. The following year he was wounded three times, once seriously, and discharged on medical grounds in 1943.

He met Renee Cameron from Inverness; they were married in 1946, and had three daughters. By that time he was principal English teacher at Boroughmuir, where he stayed until in 1950 he was appointed headmaster at Plockton, in Wester Ross; he remained there until he retired in 1972. He is said to have had 'a meticulous unfailing sense of duty, and his task as headmaster was made more onerous through his efforts to introduce a Gaelic learner's paper into the Scottish Highers. He took a very active interest in promoting the game of shinty in the school'. (Obituary in the *TGSI* 1997).

He was a kenspeckle figure in Plockton, with his moustache and shock of unruly hair, and was regarded with affection locally, though felt to be too eccentric to be the ideal conventional headmaster.

After retirement from Plockton, Sorley was for two years Creative Writer in Residence at Edinburgh University, a title which amused him; then he had a year as Filidh (accomplished poet) at Sabhal Mor Ostaig, the Gaelic college in Skye.

In 1987 he was made a Freeman of Skye and Lochalsh, an honour he cherished, and he was awarded Honorary Doctorates by the universities of Dundee, Edinburgh, Ireland and Glasgow, as well as receiving innumerable medals and prizes for his poetry. He was also a respected literary critic.

A typical Raasay MacLean, he was a sociable, witty talker with time for everyone, and no airs to him from his growing fame, no conceit about his own achievements. His standing as a poet has been recognised internationally, but he never forgot his roots in the Gaelic world.

For the piping world, Sorley researched the forebears of his own family, and uncovered names of pipers in Skye previously unknown. He had a wide curiosity about pipers and piping, and once sent me, a total stranger, a friendly message asking what I could tell him about the life of John Ban MacKenzie. This led to a lively correspondence about John Ban, Donald Cameron and other piping worthies of the 19th century. Sorley was an erudite man, never afraid to admit ignorance and always eager to enlarge his knowledge. It was a privilege to know him – and each of his four remarkable brothers.

Today Dr Alasdair's son CAILEAN MACLEAN works for the Gaelic department of the BBC, and gives the occasional welcome Gaelic touch to the piping programme 'Pipeline', when he interviews pipers in the north. He appears often in Gaelic television programmes on BBC2 and Alba.

As well as his involvement in television and radio, he has become a publisher of books and CDs, dealing mainly with works of Gaelic or Highland interest.

Recently he has replaced Andy Anderson as Convener of the Skye Games, a position that few would envy him.

Sources

TGSI XLI 1952 and LXIX 1974
Norma MacLeod, *Raasay*
Calum I. MacLean, *The Highlands*
Piping Times
Dr John MacAskill

Calum Piobaire MacPherson

John MacLean (*TGSI* volume XLI) said his brother Sorley had been told by their cousin, Willie MacLean, that Calum Piobaire MacPherson or Bruce (the two surnames were interchangeable) was born in Raasay. One of his parents – it was his mother, Effie MacLeod – had 'some relationship' with the MacLeod tacksman at Suisnish in Raasay, and this MacLeod was called Iain Mac Sheoc' (Iain son of Jock). Effie was his daughter. The phrasing suggests illegitimacy, but this is not borne out by the records. 'Relationship' here must mean a blood connection.

This Iain mac Sheoc had a shop at Suisnish as well as holding the tack (long lease) on the land. A rock below Suisnish is called Sgeir 'ain mhic Sheoc. Eventually he emigrated to Australia. Sorley said there were five MacLeod families in Raasay, none of them connected, at least not on their male (MacLeod) side. Later, John MacLean said he had seen Calum Piobaire's birth certificate, and it showed that he was born at Uigshader, not far from Skeabost, in Skye, in 1833, and not in Raasay at all. But he continued to visit his maternal grandparents at Suisnish, every summer, and maintained the link with Raasay.

This claim that his 'birth certificate' gives Uigshader as Calum's birthplace may be open to question. In 1833, when Calum was born, were there birth certificates as such, in Skye or in Raasay? Was John MacLean referring to the birth entry for Calum in the Old Parish Register for Portree?

This entry itself is puzzling, as it gives the parents' names, Angus MacPherson and Effie MacLeod, and the date of birth is 5 December 1833 – but although the entry is under Portree, the place of residence is given as 'Uigg', and Uig is not in Portree Parish but in Snizort, further north. No other entry in the Portree register lists Uigg as Place of Residence. It does not say that Calum was necessarily born there, just that Uigg was his parents' residence at the time. And he does not seem to have been baptised; at least, there is no entry in the Date of Baptism column. Why, if they lived in Uig, did they register the child in Portree? And why, if he was not baptised, is his name in the baptismal register? Sometimes, if a child was registered in a Parish other than that of his birth, a second entry was made in the Parish to which his parents belonged, but there is no trace of Calum's birth in the Snizort register.

Two years later, another entry lists Angus MacPherson, this time residing at 'Uig shader' (two words), described as a Widow, registering the birth of a son, Norman. Evidently Effie MacLeod had died in childbirth. The snag now is that this entry is under Snizort Parish, and Uigshader is in Portree Parish. A further complication is that although there was no Uigshader in Snizort parish, there were two in Portree parish: one not far out of the town of Portree, between it and Skeabost, and the other well to the west of Bernisdale on the road to Dunvegan. I wonder if perhaps these two Uigshader settlements are irrelevant: could it be that 'Uig shader' in two words does not mean either of the Uigshaders in Portree, but refers to the township of Shader, at Uig, in Snizort? That is, 'Uig shader' really means 'Uig (Shader)'. This would tie in with the reference to 'Uigg' for Calum's birth.

In Trotternish, however, there is a strong tradition that Calum Piobaire was born some five miles north of Uig, to a Bruce family, on a Bruce croft, now a ruin, known as An t-Holman (or Toloman). It lies below Hunglader (where the MacArthur pipers lived), above the shore near Bornaskitaig. In modern times, Bornaskitaig Bay has two concrete jetties, and An t-Holman is near the more northerly of the two.

Trotternish tradition says this was the home of piping Bruces. There is no way it could be described as 'Uigg' or 'Uig shader'. And it is in neither Portree nor Snizort parish, but in Kilmuir. However, in the late 19th century there are often references in the Census to people in other parishes (especially the Bruces in Glendale) having 'Uigg in Kilmuir' as their place of origin, and even 'Kilmuir in Uigg'. Clearly the geography was not exact.

The 1841 Census has an entry for a family at Barn of Monkstot, in Kilmuir, two miles south of Bornaskitaig: Norman MacPherson, thirty-one, is described as a Cottar (i.e. he had no land, just the rented house), with a wife and sister, both called Catherine, and a daughter Marion, nine; he also had in the house a five-year-old child, Malcolm Bruce, who just might have been Calum Piobaire, living with an uncle after the death of his mother. He would have been seven, not five, but if small for his age, he might have looked only five. Ages were often vague in early Census entries, and relationships are not given.

Wherever the birthplace was, the father, Angus, did not remain there after the death of his first wife. He re-married (he had four wives in all, and was widowed three times) and went to live at Laggan, near Newtonmore, as piper to his chief, Cluny MacPherson.

It is sometimes said that Calum's father Angus Bruce (known as Angus Cam because he had a droopy eye which gave his face a lop-sided look) later changed his name to MacPherson when he went to work for Cluny. There is, however, evidence that the two names were used interchangeably in the family long before that, and there are several examples in the Register for Kilmuir of men called either 'MacPherson or Bruce' or 'Bruce, alias MacPherson'. (The term 'alias' simply means 'otherwise', or 'also known as', and has no sinister undertones.) This was as late as the 1830s, and there are earlier (18th century) legal documents which have a man named MacPherson in one paragraph and Bruce in the next, or named as MacPherson in the deed but signing his name Bruce at the bottom of the page. Some of those called Bruce in the Old Parish Register appear as MacPherson in the Census. There is no suggestion that this use of an alternative name was intended to deceive, and it was clearly accepted as legal practice. Possibly it arose from the name Bruce being Norman rather than Gaelic, and a Gaelic name MacPherson would be more familiar to Gaelic speakers. There are other examples of families with alternative surnames, such as the Rankins in Mull who were also called Clan Dullie. As patronymics gave way to set surnames, in the late 18th century, these alternative family names became more common.

This interchanging of the names Bruce and MacPherson seems to have been particularly common in Kilmuir parish and in Glenelg, which might suggest that these Bruces in Trotternish were the same family as those living in Braes, and also at Glenelg.

MacLeod Pipers

Sorley MacLean in his paper on 'Some Raasay Traditions', published in *TGSI* volume XLIX, names Bella MacLeod (Beileag an Achaidh) as a noted Raasay genealogist (whose mantle today seems to have fallen on Rebecca MacKay and Norma MacLeod). Bella was a sister of the Rev. James MacLeod, a Free Presbyterian minister who lived latterly in Greenock. She is reputed to have said the MacLeods were a noted family of pipers, of whom the best known was DOMHNALL MAC SHEUMAIS (Donald son of James). It was said of him that he had the ability to compose both words and tune together, while playing the tune on the pipe, all simultaneously.

The Notices of Pipers list one of the pipers to MacLeod of Raasay in the mid-18th century as ALISDAIR MACLEOD, saying he was with his laird in the Jacobite Wars of 1745. 'His Bagpipe of three drones, made of laburnum, on which he played in the campaign, was sold in Edinburgh for £4, in April 1910.'

Another Raasay MacLeod who was a piper was Pipe Major NORMAN MACLEOD (1821–1886). He learned his piping in Raasay, and in 1844 competed in Edinburgh as being 'from Raasay', before going to Dunollie in Oban as piper to the MacDougall chief. He composed a tune *Dunolly Castle* before he left Oban to join the Ross-shire Buffs (78th Regiment). He was their Pipe Major during the Indian Mutiny, playing on the historic march to Lucknow (Notices of Pipers). He composed a march *The 78th's March to Lucknow*, and remained Pipe Major from 1849 to 1860, before retiring to the Argyll and Bute Militia. When he finally left the army for good, he went to live in Campbeltown, where he died.

Sources

John MacLean, *TGSI* XLI
Census records for Portree, Uig, Kilmuir and Glendale
Seumas Archie MacDonald
Local tradition in Trotternish
Phosa MacPherson

Angus MacRae

Angus MacRae, from Harris, was piper to the Raasay laird, E.H. Wood, from 1879 until Mr Wood died in 1886. Angus competed at Inverness and Oban as Mr Wood's piper, and won both Gold Medals. He figured prominently in the prize lists of the Games in the 1880s, and was particularly successful in the newly formed Skye Gathering. After Mr Wood's death, Angus went to live in Callander.

Two Raasay Place-names

There are two curious place-names to the east of North Arnish, in the north of Raasay: Sgeir an Fheadain Ghairbh 'Rock of the Rough Chanter', clearly named from Am Feadan Garbh, 'the Rough Chanter', and in contrast there is Am Feadan Min, 'the Fine Chanter'. In each case the Feadan is a long narrow steep-sided gorge. Presumably the wind whistles through them. Feadan was quite a common word for a narrow ravine.

Alasdair Gillies (1963–2011)

[When the *Piping Traditions of the North of Scotland* was published in 1998, I persuaded Alasdair to accept a complimentary copy. He asked if he was in it, and I told him he was mentioned but only briefly, as I did not discuss pipers currently competing. He said that was a pity as he would have liked fine to be in a book. I promised that, as soon as his competing career was over, I would put him in a book, and he laughed, and said 'warts and all'. I have kept that promise, in circumstances that could not then have been foreseen. This account probably differs from other tributes to Alasdair, which mainly stress his military career: this is based on personal knowledge of a great piper and a good friend.]

The piping Gillies family of Ullapool, NORMAN and his son ALASDAIR, belonged to Raasay before Norman moved to Glasgow. Norman said he thought they had originated in Uist 'way back', but regarded themselves as a Raasay family, and still had relatives on the island. In the 19th century, Roderick MacKay, brother of Angus MacKay, Raasay, married a Raasay girl, Elisa Gillis, of the same family.

Alasdair was born in Glasgow, but when he was a boy, his father was appointed Schools Piping Instructor for part of Wester Ross, and the family moved to Ullapool.

Norman Gillies was a good piper – a competent piobaireachd player, but an excellent player of the small music. Perhaps his greatest achievement was his training of his son Alasdair, who became one of the greatest pipers of all time. From him Alasdair inherited not only his piping ability but also his aggressive manner, under which he concealed low self-esteem.

Taught to a high standard by his father, Alasdair later had army training, but long before that, he was competing and winning prizes as a junior player. The obituary in the *Times* newspaper told how the young Alasdair once beat his father in a competition for all ages, and on the way home, he said to Norrie 'I hope this doesn't affect your job'. Doubt has been cast on this, as Alasdair once said his father was most strict with him about his triumphs – as a boy, he was not allowed to mention his wins at all on the way home from competitions, permitted only to tell his mother the results when they reached home.

Another discipline imposed on him by his father – and as a youngster he resented much of his father's strictness – was the Blue Fingers training. Norrie used to drive him up into the hills above Ullapool in the depths of winter, and make him stand, out in the wind and snow, playing all his tunes, to teach him how to cope with harsh conditions – while Norrie sat in the warmth of the car. Alasdair said later that his friendship with his father did not really begin until he himself started to win important prizes and to appreciate how much he owed to the rigorous training of his youth.

Living in Ullapool, his secondary schooling was at Dingwall Academy, where he stayed in a hostel with other west coasters. He was not a success at school: he was made to feel stupid and incompetent, and the experience left him with a feeling of inferiority. In a maths examination he once scored 0%, itself an achievement, and one of his school reports said that he had nothing in his head except piping and seemed to think that was all he needed to make a career . . . This pleased his father, but did nothing for Alasdair's confidence.

He left school as soon as he could and at fifteen joined the Queen's Own Highlanders (QOH), his father's old regiment, as a Boy Soldier, his first Pipe Major being Andy Venters. When he moved on to the adult regiment, he came under the instruction of Pipe Major Iain Morrison. He later went on to take his Pipe Major's Certificate under Captain Andrew Pitkeathly, and in 1986, passed with distinction.

At twenty-eight he became Pipe Major of the Queen's Own, and served seventeen years with the regiment (1980–1997). He was its last Pipe Major before the amalgamation with the Gordons, and the first of the new regiment, the Highlanders. He served in several campaigns including Northern Ireland – though for part of the regiment's tour there, Alasdair was kept back in Scotland, too valuable to risk on the streets of Belfast, his commanding officer being a fan of his.

He later joined his men in Ulster, a tour he hated because the cramped conditions and security restrictions made piping impossible, so nobody could even tune a pipe. With all the players out of practice, they were annoyed to be sent to perform in the Edinburgh Tattoo, an event they disliked anyway – because they were required to re-tune their pipes to the piano scale, an insult to any piper. Alasdair found himself playing a solo part in the 'Ode to Joy', quite surprised to be playing Beethoven on the pipe. Made a nice wee change, he said – but he never mentioned the Tattoo without a swearword in front.

He was in the Gulf in 1991, and it is widely believed that the painful attacks of gout which began to afflict him dated back to this period, when the troops were given injections to which some had adverse reactions.

His famous tour of duty was in the Falklands campaign, when he was photographed playing his pipes to the penguins in South Georgia, a picture which went round the world.

Most of the time during his army career he was competing in solo competitions, with enormous success. He won the Gold Medal at Oban in 1989, which he followed in later years by winning the Senior Piobaireachd. When he won that first Gold, he emerged from the hall to find Captain John MacLellan, the Director of the Army School of Piping and himself a QOH man, waiting to shake his hand: 'Number 47, I believe', he said, Alasdair being the 47th Gold Medallist for the regiment. Alasdair said it was the proudest moment of his life.

The Gold at Inverness eluded him for some years, after he achieved the dubious distinction of being the only player ever sent off the platform for tuning too long. This was mainly the result of an outburst of temper on the part of the judge, David Murray, driven beyond endurance by the heat, the long list and even longer tuning of too many players – but Alasdair's admirers felt that he had been treated shabbily, singled out and humiliated without justification, and that he behaved admirably in accepting the verdict, saying 'I brought it on myself'. He later admitted that whenever he was on the stage tuning to play for the Gold after that, the memory came rushing back to unnerve him. He finally won the Gold at Inverness in 2004, by which time he was playing as 'Alasdair Gillies, USA'.

He had won the Clasp at Inverness in 1992, and the Senior Open at Oban a few years later. But his greatest triumph was, of course, in the

March Strathspey and Reel competition for Former Winners. Playing for the Silver Star, he was supreme, winning it eleven times, a record unlikely to be beaten.

Crowds flocked to hear him play wherever he went, in the big competitions or the smallest Games. One of his favourites was Helmsdale, on the east coast of Sutherland, where the small Games ground has a special Highland atmosphere in which he felt at home. He also enjoyed an advantage there as it is exposed to cold winds off the sea, with which he could cope when many could not.

At the Skye Gathering the entrance fee for the audience for the Light Music was '£4 until Alasdair Gillies has played, thereafter £2'. He became hugely popular, especially in the Highlands. Taking round posters for his recitals was an experience: shop girls would say 'Sorry, we don't put up posters – oh, Alasdair Gillies, did you say? That's different, we'll do that for you'.

Another of his gifts was for organising, both pipe band parades and solo recitals of a small group from the QOH Pipes and Drums. It was a revelation to watch him prepare for a joint parade of his men, very professional, and a small and inexperienced local band, rather nervous and in awe of him. He had the knack of breaking down their reserve by his friendliness, explaining the procedures in clear detail to give them confidence, tuning their pipes and asking what tunes they were happy to attempt – without being patronising about it. By the end of the practice session they were his devoted slaves.

Organising a recital under the regimental auspices, he was a pleasure to work with. If he said he would ring on Thursday, he rang on Thursday; he answered letters promptly; he made helpful suggestions; he turned up in good time – and then he played like the Angel Gabriel, as one fan put it. Anyone who has run recitals will know how rare the likes of Alasdair are, and all the more appreciated for that.

In 1997, his devotees assumed the 'Castle job' as Director of the Army School would be his – one of his men said: 'Alasdair will go to Edinburgh Castle, and within two years its name will be changed to Castle Gillies' – and it was thought that this would be the crown of his career, but he was turned down on health grounds. Suddenly cast adrift from the army after seventeen years, he was offered a job as Director of Piping at Carnegie Mellon University in Pittsburgh, Pennsylvania. To the dismay of his thousands of fans in Scotland, he accepted it, and departed for the USA.

He returned each year to compete, but lacking sufficient competition in the States, his standards began slowly to slip. Rumours of heavy drinking were filtering through, and it was clear he was losing his edge – but still he was winning the MSR at Inverness, although, as one of his admirers admitted, 'he was hanging on by his reputation, latterly'.

Alasdair said that he was always conscious of the fragile nature of his talent. If for any reason he became unable to play, through bad health or injury, or merely the gift leaving him, he would have nothing, he said, and would be nothing. Nobody could convince him how much he would still have to offer, how truly gifted he was, and as he gradually lost his supremacy, he must have looked into the future and seen blackness. This would be the perfect breeding ground for an addiction, and gradually he was overwhelmed by alcohol. The death of his father when he was away did not help.

In 2009 he returned to Scotland, having lost his American job through his excessive drinking. He had always been a heavy drinker, encouraged into it by his father, but as his health deteriorated and his music with it, his addiction seemed to get a hold on him which he could not loosen. When he was younger, he and his father made an agreement that they would give up the drink for three months every year, leading up to the Meetings (at Oban and Inverness). In those days, Alasdair stuck to it better than Norrie did – but those days were past. By the time he left America, he was in the grip of a serious addiction, refusing all assistance, medical or psychological, and nobody could reach him. The Regimental Association offered rehab, but he would not countenance it, let alone admit he needed help.

A low point was reached when he went missing in Inverness. The police were alerted and a police message was put out, in the papers and on the radio, seeking the whereabouts of 'Alexander Gillies aged 47' with a recognizable physical description but mercifully no mention of piping, so that many people did not realise it meant Alasdair. He was picked up on the streets of Inverness next day, in a bewildered state. After this he went to Ullapool, where his family were living, but continued on his downward path, until on 27 August 2011, after suffering a series of seizures but still refusing all medical attention, he died.

What a terrible waste of a wonderful talent was the universal reaction to the news. The Northern Meeting was about to start in Inverness, and a moving tribute was paid to him at the start of that MSR Competition which he had made his own.

The day after the Meetings finished, in dull drizzly weather, pipers flocked to Ullapool to give Alasdair a fitting send-off. Every Scottish piper of any note was there, all the big stars turned up in full dress, and piping notables from all corners. The funeral arrangements were made by the Queen's Own Highlanders Association, and it was an unforgettable occasion.

The church was packed, the minister speaking with affection of Alasdair, whom he had known from a boy. With so many pipers and soldiers, the singing was impressive, and the well-known Gaelic singer Kristine Kennedy sang a Gaelic psalm, unaccompanied, to the tune 'Loch Broom', hauntingly beautiful and delivered with great feeling. The eulogy was given by Rona Lightfoot, a lifelong family friend, who wisely kept it light and anecdotal, in an atmosphere heavy with emotion. After the service, men of the former Queen's Own shouldered the coffin and bore it through the streets of Ullapool, led by a piper. When they paused to change the bearers, two pipers were waiting to take up the music until the new bearers were in position. The folk from the town lined the route, and the congregation walked behind the coffin.

At the cemetery, it was piped to the graveside by Michael Gray, playing lovely Gaelic airs. Then the names of the cord- and tape-holders were read out: beside three family members, fifteen Pipe Majors came forward to lower Alasdair into his grave. These were all Pipe Majors with links to the Queen's Own; Pipe Majors from other piping regiments were also present. The bugler, under some emotion, played the Last Post, and then Niall Matheson, who was not only a distant relative but had been a QOH piper in Alasdair's day, played Donald MacLeod's piobaireachd, *Cabar Feidh Gu Brath*, a suberb and moving performance.

No-one who was there that day will ever forget it. The piping world gave Alasdair a really good send-off, expressing the universal feeling of grief and regret at his sad passing.

His son NORMAN ('Young Norrie') has taken up the baton: taught by his father, he is competing with increasing success in Junior piping competitions.

Sources

Alasdair Gillies
Norman Gillies
Niall Matheson
Regimental Records
The Ross-shire Journal

Skye

Although the Isle of Skye belongs to the Inner Isles, it is omitted here for reasons of space. There is so much material about Skye that it has had to be published separately, in a fourth volume of *Piping Traditions*.

Bibliography

[*TGSI* = *Transactions of the Gaelic Society of Inverness*]

ARRAN HIGH SCHOOL PROJECT 2002

BANKS, Noel 1977: *Six Inner Hebrides*

BENNETT, Margaret 1989: *The Last Stronghold: The Gaelic Traditions of Newfoundland*

BOSWELL, James 1785: *The Journal of a Tour to the Hebrides with Samuel Johnson*

BRISTOL, Nicholas MacLean 1982: *Hebridean Decade, Mull, Coll and Tiree 1761–1771*

BRISTOL, Nicholas MacLean 1995: *Warriors and Priests: The History of the Clan MacLean*

BRISTOL, Nicholas MacLean 1998: *Inhabitants of the Inner Isles, Morvern and Ardnamurchan 1716*

BRISTOL, Nicholas MacLean 1999: *Murder Under Trust, The Crimes and Death of Sir Lachlan Mor MacLean of Duart*

BROTCHIE, T.C.F. 1911: *Rambles in Arran*

BUDGE, Donald 1960: *Jura, an Island of Argyll*

BUIE, T.R. and Scott 1983: *The Family Buie: Scotland to North America* (published Texas, USA)

BUISMAN, Frans and WRIGHT, Andrew 2001: *The MacArthur–MacGregor Manuscript of Piobaireachd (1820)*

BYRNE, Kevin 1997: *Colkitto! A Celebration of Clan Donald of Colonsay (1570–1647)*

CALDWELL, David 2001: *Islay, Jura and Colonsay, A Historic Guide*

CALDWELL, David 2008: *Islay, The Land of the Lordship*

CAMPBELL, Alexander 1802: *A Journey from Edinburgh Through Parts of North Britain*

CAMPBELL, Alexander 1816–18: *Albyn's Anthology* (2 volumes)

CAMPBELL, A. 1926: 'The manuscript history of Craignish', *Miscellany* iv, Scottish History Society.

CAMPBELL, Lord Archibald 1885: *Records of Argyll*

CAMPBELL, Jeannie 2001 (2nd edition 2011): *Highland Bagpipe Makers*

CAMPBELL, John Lorne 1984: *Canna, the Story of a Hebridean Island*

CAMPBELL, John Lorne 2000: *A Very Civil People, Hebridean Folk, History and Tradition*

CAMPBELL-GRAHAM, David 1978: *A Portrait of Argyll and the Southern Hebrides*

CAMPEY, Lucille H. 2004: *After the Hector: The Scottish Pioneers of Nova Scotia and Cape Breton 1773–1852*

CAMPSIE, Alistair 1980: *The MacCrimmon Legend: the Madness of Angus MacKay*

CANNON, Roderick 1988: *The Highland Bagpipe and its Music*

CANNON, Roderick (ed.) 1994: Joseph MacDonald's *Compleat Theory of the Scots Highland Bagpipe.*

CHEAPE, Hugh 1999: *The Book of the Bagpipe*

COLLIE, William 1908, reprint 1992: *Memoirs of William Collie, a 19th Century Deerstalker*

CURRIE, Jo 2000: *Mull, The Island and its People*

DICKSON, Joshua 2009 (ed.): *The Highland Bagpipe, Music, History, Tradition*

DONALDSON, M.E.M. 1938: *Wanderings in the Highlands and Islands*

DONALDSON, William 2000: *The Highland Pipe and Scottish Society 1750–1950*

DRESSLER, Camille 2007: *Eigg, the Story of an Island*

EAGLE, Raymond 1991: *Seton Gordon, The Life and Times of a Highland Gentleman*

ECHSTEIN, Eve 1992: *Historical Visitors to Mull, Iona and Staffa*

EXCHEQUER ROLLS OF SCOTLAND ed. 1878, J. Stuart et al.

FAUJAS, Bartholemy de Saint Fond 1907: *A Journey through England and Scotland to the Hebrides in 1784* (2 volumes), ed. Archibald Geikie

FOWLER, Malcolm 1955: *They Passed This Way: A Personal Narrative of Harnett County History (North Carolina).* Centennial Edition, published by Harnett County Centennial, Inc

FRASER, Simon, ed. B.J. MacLauchlan Orme 1979 (2nd edition 1985): *The Piobaireachd of Simon Fraser, with Canntaireachd*

GIBSON, John 1998: *Traditional Gaelic Bagpiping*
GIBSON, John 2002: *Old and New World Highland Bagpiping*
GLEN, David 1880–1907: *A Collection of Ancient Piobaireachd*
GLEN, David 1900: *The Music of the Clan MacLean*
GORDON, Seton 1925: *Hebridean Memories* (re-issued 1995)
GORDON, Seton 1950: *Afoot in the Hebrides*
HADDOW, Alec 1982: *The History and Structure of Ceol Mor*
HASWELL-SMITH, Hamish 1996: *The Scottish Islands, a Comprehensive Guide to Every Scottish Island*
HILL, J. Michael 1993: *Fire and Sword, Sorley Boy MacDonnell and the Rise of Clan Ian Mor 1538–90*
HOWARD, J. and JONES, A. 1990: *Isle of Ulva Visitors' Guide*
INNES, C. (ed.) 1859: *The Book of the Thanes of Cawdor, 1236–1732*
JOHNSON, Samuel 1775: *A Journey to the Western Isles of Scotland*
JUPP, Clifford 1994: *The History of Islay*
KAY, John 1837–8: *A Series of Original Portraits and Caricature Etchings* (2 volumes)
KELLY, Douglas F. and Caroline S. 1998: *Carolina Scots, an Historical Genealogical Study of over 100 Years of Emigration*
LOVE, John A. 2001: *Rum, A Landscape Without Figures*
MACANNA, James 1991: *The Ulva Families of Shotts* (booklet)
MACARTHUR, Dugald 1987 (paper): 'Some Emigrant Ships from the West Highlands' in *TGSI* LV 1986–88
MACARTHUR, E. Mairi 1990: *Iona, The Living Memory of a Crofting Community 1750–1914*
MACARTHUR MANUSCRIPT: see BUISMAN, Frans
MACCORMICK, John 1923: *The Island of Mull*
MACCULLOCH, John 1819: *A Description of the Western Isles of Scotland*
MACCULLOCH, John 1824: *The Highlands and Western Isles of Scotland* (4 volumes)
MACDONALD, Alexander 1881: *The MacDonalds of Clanranald*
MACDONALD, the Rev. A., Killearnan, and the Rev. A., Kiltarlity 1900: *The Clan Donald* (2 volumes)
MACDONALD, the Rev. Charles 1889: *Moidart, or Among the Clanranalds* (reprinted 1989)
MACDONALD, D.A. 1974: article 'An Dubh Ghleannach' in *Tocher* 15
MACDONALD, Donald of Castleton 1978: *Clan Donald*
MACDONALD, Dr K.N. 1900: *MacDonald Bards From Mediaeval Times*

MACDOUGALL, Jean 1984: *Highland Postbag, The Correspondence of Four MacDougall Chiefs 1715–1865*

MACINNES, J. 1989: 'Gleanings from Raasay Traditon', in *TGSI* LVI 1989–90

MACIVER, Evander 1905: *Memoirs of a Highland Gentleman*

MACKAY, Angus 1838: *A Collection of Ancient Piobaireachd*

MACKENZIE, Alexander 1884: *A History of the Camerons*

MACKENZIE, Allan J. 2000: *Co-Chruinneachadh MhicChoinnich, Pipe Music from Cape Breton and Away* (Volume I)

MACKENZIE, Ann 2002: *Island Voices, Traditions of North Mull*

MACKENZIE, Donald W. 2000: *Sin Mar A Bha, As It Was: An Ulva Boyhood*

MACKINNON, Fiona E. 1992: *Tiree Tales*

MACLEAN, Calum I. 1960: *The Highlands*

MACLEAN, John 1952: 'Am Piobaire Dall', article on Iain Dall MacKay, in *TGSI* XLI 1952–4

MACLEAN, J.P. 1889: *History of the Clan MacLean*

MACLEAN-BRISTOL, Nicholas 1995: *Warriors and Priests: The Clan Maclean 1300–1570*

MACLEAN SINCLAIR, the Rev. A. 1903: 'Clann Duiligh' in *MacTalla* 2, No.2

MACLEAN, Sorley 1975: 'Some Raasay Traditions', in *TGSI* XLIX 1975–76

MACLELLAN, John 1986: article on John MacKay junior, *Proceedings of the Piobaireachd Society Conference*

MACLEOD, Norma 2002: *Raasay, the Island and its People*

MACPHAIL, J.R.N. (ed.) 1914: *Highland Papers,* volume I, second series 5, 1337–1680 (Scottish Historical Society)

MACPHEE, John 1970: *The Crofter and the Laird, Life on a Hebridean Island*

MACROBBIE, William 1999: *Achgarve*

MALCOLM, A.D. 1945: *The Argyll and Sutherland Highlanders: the 8th (Argyllshire) Battalion, 1939–45*

MARTIN, Martin 1716: *A Description of the Western Isles of Scotland* (2nd edition)

MATHESON, William 1938: *The Songs of John MacCodrum*

MATHESON, William 1951: 'Notes on Mary MacLeod' (1) Her Family Connections; (2) Her Forgotten Songs, in *TGSI* XLI 1952–4

MATHESON, William 1970: *The Blind Harper*

MITCHELL, Joseph 1883–4: *Reminiscences of My Life in the Highlands* (2 volumes)

MORRISON, Alick 1974: *The MacLeods, The Genealogy of a Clan*, Section 4

MORRISON, Neil Rankin 1934: paper 'Clann Duiligh, piobairean Chloinn Ghill-eathan' (Clan Dooley, Pipers of the MacLeans) in *TGSI* XXXVII 1932–4

MUNRO, Neil 1931: *Para Handy* (omnibus edition of the Para Handy stories)

MURRAY, David J.S. 1994: *Music of the Scottish Regiments*

MURRAY, W.H. 1966: *The Hebrides*

NEWTON, Norman 1990: *Colonsay and Oransay*

NEWTON, Norman 1995: *Islay*

NICOLSON, Alexander 1930 (3rd edition 2012): *History of Skye*

NOTICES OF PIPERS in successive issues of the *Piping Times* throughout 1968. Originally compiled by Captain John MacLennan, later supplemented by Archibald Campbell, Ian MacKay-Scobie, D.R. MacLennan and others.

OLDHAM, Tony 1975: *The Caves of Scotland*

PENNANT, Thomas 1774–6: *A Tour in Scotland and Voyage to the Hebrides 1772*

PERMAN, Ray 2010: *The Man Who Gave Away His Island: A Life of John Lorne Campbell of Canna*

PREBBLE, John 1988: *The King's Jaunt*

RAMSAY, Freda (ed.) 1991: *The Day Book of Daniel Campbell of Shawfield 1767, with relevant papers concerning the Estate of Islay*

RIDDELL, Carol 1996: *Tireragan, A Township in the Ross of Mull*

ROBERTSON, the Rev. C. 1898: 'The Topography and Traditions of Eigg', in *TGSI* XXII 1897–98

ROBERTSON, James 2001: *The Mull Diaries of James Robertson 1842–6*, transcribed by J.B. Loudon

SANGER, Keith 1992: 'MacCrimmon's Prentise – a Post Graduate Student Perhaps', in the *Piping Times* 44/6, March 1992

SANGER, Keith 2007: 'From the Family of the MacArthurs to P/M Willie Gray, Glasgow Police', in the *Piping Times* 49/6 March 2007

SANGER, Keith 2009: 'Newspaper Report Sheds New Light on "The Piper's Warning"', in the *Piping Times* 61/5, February 2009

SCOTT, Walter 1810: *Familiar Letters*, vol. 185 of the Complete Works

SHAW, Margaret Fay 1993: *From the Alleghenies to the Hebrides*

SHEARS, Barry W. 1995: *The Cape Breton Collection of Bagpipe Music* (publ. Halifax, Nova Scotia)

SHEARS, Barry W. 2008: *Dance to the Piper: The Highland Bagpipe in Nova Scotia*

SKENE, W.F. 1880: *Celtic Scotland*

SMITH, G. Gregory 1895: *The Book of Islay*

STEVENSON, David 1980: *Highland Warrior, Alasdair MacColla and the Civil Wars*

URQUHART, Judy and ELLINGTON, Eric 1987: *Eigg*

WALKER, the Rev. Dr John (ed. Margaret M. MacKay) 1980: *Report on the Hebrides of 1764 and 1771*

WATSON, J.C. 1934: *The Gaelic Songs of Mary MacLeod*

WATSON, W.J. 1926: *History of the Celtic Place-names of Scotland*

WATSON, W.J. 1937: *Scottish Verse from the Book of the Dean of Lismore*

WEBSTER, David 1973: *Scottish Highland Games*

WEDGWOOD, C.V. 1952: *Montrose*

WHYTE, Henry 1904: prize essay on the Rankins in Mull (Tobermory Museum)

WILLIAMS, Ronald 1984: *The Lords of the Isles*

WILLIAMS, Scott 2000: *Pipers of Nova Scotia, Biographical Sketches 1773 to 2000*

WILSON, Barbara Kerr 1954: *The Piper of Keil*

WITHALL, Mary 2001: *Easdale, Belnahua, Luing and Seil – the Islands that Roofed the World*

YOUNGSON, Peter (ed.) 1888: *Rev. Charles Robertson's Collection of Ancient Hebridean Tales of Jura*

YOUNGSON, Peter (ed.) 2001: *Jura, Island of Deer*

Index of People

In this Index, Christian names take precedence over titles, ranks or designations, so that (e.g.) *MacLean, Brigadier General Charles of Pennycross* is treated as *MacLean, Charles* and comes between *MacLean, Catherine* and *MacLean, Christina*. Mac, Mc and M' are all treated as Mac.

Abbreviations: b. = born, br. = brother, d. = daughter, f. = father, gf. = grandfather, gs. = grandson, jr = junior, m. = mother, mar. = married, NS = Nova Scotia, NZ = New Zealand, PEI = Prince Edward Island, P/M = pipe major, s. = son, sis. = sister, sr = senior, w. = wife, WW = World War

Index of Places

Index of Tunes

This Index does not include the alphabetical lists of compositions and tunes associated with particular composers or locations, to be found in the text as follows: